LOVELY, DARK, and DEEP

THE COLLECTORS

LOVELY, DARK, *and* DEEP

SUSANNAH SANDLIN

Montlake
Romance

Text copyright © 2014 Susannah Sandlin
All rights reserved.

Published by Montlake Romance, Seattle

www.apub.com

ISBN-13: 9781477822449
ISBN-10: 1477822445

Cover design by Michelle Taormina

Library of Congress Control Number: 2014905377

Printed in the United States of America

To the real Jagger, Charlie, Harley, Chevy, Cleo, Gretchen, Zena, Duke, Holly, Ricky, Jindal, Huckie, and, of course, Shane and Tank, who have made our hearts and lives richer.

PROLOGUE

Weston Flynn slammed the lid of his laptop and glowered at his office door. A lower-level aide, inherited from the last person to hold this position, had stuck his head inside without waiting for a response to his short, sharp knock. "Sir, I—"

"Never open that door without permission, Lawrence. Never. Do you understand?"

The young man's freckled face flushed the same dull red as his hair. "I'm sorry, sir. I just wanted to remind you of—"

"And when I need a reminder about anything, I'll let you know. Close the door."

"Yes, sir. Sorry, sir."

West waited until the door clicked shut before once again flipping open his laptop. He clicked the "Play" button on the video, wanting to see it once more before making his decision official. The wrong choice would cost him a fortune or worse, ruin his career. Of course, the risk was a big part of the thrill and this new find excited him more than any he'd seen in a while.

On the screen, a young, dark-haired woman sat in a generic, small-town TV studio. She was about to be introduced by a perky reporter for one of those noontime local-news shows that people only watch out of boredom. WGUL, voice of Levy County, Florida, wasn't must-see TV in this or in any other universe.

Which was a good thing, because the fewer viewers who saw this particular show, the better for Weston Flynn. It had aired three days ago, and he'd spent most of his free time since then working quietly with his personal assistant to put his plan in place.

The reporter went through her introductions. "We're talking today to Gillian Campbell, a biologist who works for the state of Florida caring for the animals in the Cedar Key Scrub State . . ." This wasn't the important part, so West advanced the video clip to the halfway point.

The biologist looked to be in her late twenties, with an easy smile, an athletic build, and a lot of self-confidence. Her demeanor during the interview suggested the earnest passion of an obsessive personality, a character trait he could use to his advantage—he simply had to get her obsessed over the right thing.

West knew all about obsessive types because he was one and had never seen it as a fault. He obsessed over his political career. His investment portfolio. His public image.

But the obsession he most enjoyed? Membership in the exclusive C7 club he'd helped found five years earlier. Seven collectors scattered around the world, each competing to obtain some of the world's most valuable treasures before the others got them first. And not another one of them had likely seen this obscure little bit of TV footage or were willing to gamble that they could be the first to claim it.

Gillian Campbell's current obsession appeared to be her side job as a nuisance-alligator trapper, which held no interest for West. What mattered lay in her answer to the question of whether she feared being injured by one of the beasts it was her job to care for, catch, and relocate.

"I probably should be afraid," Campbell said, laughing.

West edged the volume higher.

"My family does fall under the Campbell curse, after all."

"*Oooooh,*" crooned the reporter. "Tell us about the curse."

"It's a family legend." The woman shrugged. "One of my ancestors, Duncan Campbell, supposedly stole a priceless ruby cross from the Knights Templars back in medieval times, and he and all his descendants were cursed by the Templars to die young until the cross is returned to its proper place. Of course that was hundreds of years ago. The Knights Templars no longer exist, and both my thieving ancestor, Duncan, and the cross went down in a shipwreck hundreds of years ago off the coast of Canada."

The reporter leaned forward. "And *do* people in your family die young?"

The biologist had been smiling throughout the interview, but at that question, her face grew still and inscrutable, as if a mask had been dropped over it. "Let's just talk about the gators."

West stopped the video, shut down the browser, and slid the computer into his briefcase. He wanted that goddamned cross worse than any of the treasures the C7 had competed for since he and his German counterpart founded the group. For years, he'd followed rumors of Templar treasure being lost off the Canadian coast, but he'd never heard anything this specific.

Any of the Knights Templars' lost treasure would be worth even more than the billions West had inherited from his oil-tycoon father. His family genealogy, another obsession, had been tracked back to one of the Templars, so it wasn't just about money—the best quests never were.

He wanted the Templars' cross. And he wanted to get to it first. What a legacy to leave to his own sons. They'd given up a lot for him to pursue his political ambitions. Of course, he'd given up a lot to stay married to their witch of a mother. The C7 games kept him sane.

Since discovering the video through one of his regular web searches for stories on the world's great lost treasures, West had sent his two most trusted operatives, guys from Texas he'd known most of his life, to investigate Gillian Campbell and her family.

They'd found nothing to indicate she was anything more than what she claimed. Her people had been in Nova Scotia until the French Acadians were driven to Louisiana in the 1700s, which jibed with the time and place of the shipwreck. Now her parents ran an alligator-rescue farm just west of New Orleans. She'd attended college on an athletics scholarship, then grad school at the University of Florida. She'd been widowed five years ago. Since then, she'd lived in the middle of nowhere, playing with alligators in Levy County.

Gillian Campbell would need a lot of help, but the rules of the C7 were clear. Civilians had to obtain the prize. They could be coerced or assisted or bribed. Beyond the quest itself, they couldn't know why they were being manipulated, or the identities or existence of the C7. And they had a time limit.

After that, the C7 motto was "any means, fair or foul." Although if no one died in the quest, the winner collected an extra bonus from the others. West would forego the bonus if he had to, as long as he ended up with the Templars' cross.

He pulled out his cell phone and punched the number seven on his speed-dial list. Brenton Sullivan's name popped up on the screen; he was the only other American in the C7 and, at thirty, the youngest of the group. Thanks to the dot-com boom and the good sense to sell before the dot-com bust, he also was one of the richest.

"Mr. Flynn, good to hear from you." Brenton sounded cheerful. "I'm bored—hope you're going to jump on that Templar cross."

Damn it, Sullivan obviously did the same Internet searches. "Why haven't you jumped on it yourself?"

"Too complicated," Brenton said. "You not only have to convince the woman to cooperate, but she—or you—would need a salvage diver to locate the ship and the cross, and then smuggle it out under the Canadians' noses. It could be messy."

West smiled as he swiveled his chair around to look out the large window behind his desk. It was the Friday before Labor Day, and even though multiple layers of fencing and landscaping separated him from the view, he knew the traffic along Pennsylvania Avenue would be gridlocked as people left their offices early and streamed out of the capital for the long weekend. He had already found the right salvage diver and the right leverage to force Gillian Campbell to cooperate.

"Your loss, then," he said, watching a leaf drift in zigzag patterns to rest on the immaculate lawn outside the West Wing. "I'm calling dibs on a cross believed to be a part of the lost Knights Templars' treasure, and I'm claiming the full thirty-day option."

West winced at Brenton's shrill whistle; the man sounded as if he were in the next room, not across the country in San Francisco. The whistle was deserved. The thirty-day option wasn't taken lightly by any of the C7. It meant he had a month-long head start to look for the cross before the others could even try. A nice advantage, except for every day until the treasure was in his possession, he had to fork over a million dollars. At the end of the month, or whenever the cross was found, the others would split the money—up to $30 million if the mission hadn't been completed.

He didn't intend to lose that $30 million. "Don't start counting your money just yet, Brent, you greedy bastard. Consider this my formal notice. You'll spread the word to the others?"

"Oh yeah." Brenton laughed. "Let the games begin."

West placed two additional calls, one to his chief operative, who'd already gotten in position, the other to a discreet computer hacker he'd used a few times before, one of those genius kids who cared more about the challenge than the legality of a job.

He'd barely barked out the second set of instructions and ended the call when a timid knock sounded from the office door. He waited a few seconds to see how well the officious Lawrence had learned his lesson. Satisfied that Freckles wasn't going to make an unauthorized entrance, he said, "Come."

Lawrence stuck his head in only far enough for his eyes to peer around the edge of the door. "Mr. Flynn, the president is waiting in the Roosevelt Room."

Weston Flynn straightened his tie, tucked his briefcase in the bottom shelf of the credenza, and locked it before grabbing the sheaf of papers on the edge of his desk. The sheet on top contained two typed words: "North Korea."

"Then we better not keep the president waiting."

I

Gillian tripped on the threshold of the ICU doorway, attracting a small flurry of alarmed nurses. By the time she assured them she was a habitual klutz and not a terrorist or the crazed lunatic family member of a patient, she'd eaten up a considerable chunk of the paltry half hour set aside in the evening for visitors.

Not that Viv knew she was here. Gillian tugged the heavy wooden chair closer to the bed, using her thumb to stuff a tuft of padding back into the ripped mint-green vinyl seat. For the first few seconds, she tried to comprehend the beeping machines and wires and IVs holding her best friend together.

Not just her friend. Vivian Ortiz was her neighbor and mother figure, dispenser of wisdom and light beer and home remedies to get rid of fire ants. She was also the only other woman Gillian knew who was crazy enough to live in a single-wide trailer at the edge of a wildlife reserve in hurricane country.

They'd been separated at birth, only in different generations, Viv always said.

Gillian took her friend's hand, which looked naked and frail minus its normal assortment of oversized rings, most purchased on one of those TV shopping channels Viv was addicted to. Tears pressed heavily against the back of Gillian's eyes. Vivian was warm and full of life, not hot and dry like this husk of skin.

She whispered the question the sheriff's deputy couldn't answer: "What the hell happened?"

Viv couldn't answer, either. She could only lie there, her eyes closed, dark lashes resting on her cheeks, her warm olive skin pale against the sterile white sheets under fluorescent lighting. An automobile accident, the deputy had told Gillian after finding her phone number in Viv's purse and tracking her down. Viv had plowed into a tree not a mile from her trailer, scattering groceries across Highway 24 near the old Rosewood Baptist Church. A one-car accident, the officer said, but a blinding rain had been coming down about the time it happened.

Vivian was the slowest, most cautious driver Gillian had ever met. They laughed about it, about how Viv said if God meant people to go fast, he wouldn't have invented middle-aged women and old men. About how, especially if one of Florida's afternoon storms was in full force, Vivian's car could be outrun by a slow-moving gator.

A bell sounded from somewhere near the two monitors sitting on the desk outside the glassed-off cubicles, announcing the end of the day's last visitation period.

A nurse in green scrubs waved at Gillian and pointed toward the door, ready to spend her evening hovering over the monitors, watching to see if Viv or the person in the other cubicle, so old and wrinkled Gillian couldn't even determine a gender, might need transferring from the county's little hospital here in Williston to Ocala or even Gainesville. Waiting to see which patient's condition descended from stable to critical, or rose from serious to stable. These categories didn't mean much when held up beside a pale face, closed eyes, shallow breathing, and hot, dry hands.

Gillian stopped in the hallway and dug in her pocket for quarters to plug in the soda machine, giving a startled jump at the buzz of her phone vibrating in her jeans pocket. The screen read "Private Caller." Since she was the only licensed nuisance-gator trapper in the county, "on call" was a constant state unless she found another trapper to cover for her. Alligators couldn't care less that Labor Day weekend was imminent or that Viv was hurt.

She sat in one of the three plastic chairs in the waiting area and scrambled in her shoulder bag for a pen and pad in case she needed to write down an address, then hit the "Talk" button. "Campbell."

"Is this the Gillian Campbell who was on the *Noonday Chat* show Tuesday?" The man spoke with a deep baritone and a Southern twang—not a twang from the Deep South or from Louisiana, but maybe Texas or Oklahoma. *Jeez-Louise*, she hoped he wasn't some whacked-out stalker.

"Yes it is. Can I help you?" His answer to that question would determine whether she ended the call or kept listening.

"I want to talk to you about that ruby cross, the one your ancestor lost."

Gillian laughed. "Look, that's just a family legend, and what I said on the show is all I know about it. Sorry, but I can't help you."

"Oh, you'll help me, honey."

Honey? She might be a state employee with a responsibility to be polite to the public, but she didn't have to listen to sexist cowboy stalkers. "I assure you, I can't help. Good night, sir, and please don't call again."

It had to be the damned Campbell curse. As long as she could remember, her grandparents and parents—and now Gillian herself—blamed old Duncan Campbell and his thieving ways for anything that went amiss, from a hangnail to a creepy phone call.

The phone buzzed again before she reached her vehicle, again from "Private Caller." "Forget it," she muttered, unlocking the door of her five-year-old silver pickup and tossing her bag on the passenger seat. Another buzz told her the jerk had left a message. Private Caller needed to get a life.

She stared at the phone a moment, knowing she should just erase it, but curiosity trumped common sense. She jabbed at the screen and turned up the volume. "As I was trying to explain before you cut me off, Ms. Campbell, I represent someone with a keen interest in acquiring the ruby cross you talked about in your little TV interview."

The voice paused so long that Gillian had her finger poised over the "Erase" button when he spoke again. "That car accident your friend Ms. Ortiz had? I hope it got your attention. I'll call back at 10:00 p.m. and, honey, this time I suggest you answer."

Silence weighed heavily as adrenaline raced through Gillian's system. She used her elbow to lock the driver's side door, then leaned across the seats to lock the others. Was he here somewhere, watching?

Her fingers trembled as she retrieved the list of recent calls on the phone, and she stared stupidly at "Private Caller." Surely it was a sick prank. Maybe the guy worked at the hospital. Maybe he'd watched that silly television interview and recognized her when she came in to visit Viv. Maybe he was watching her now, from a window or from the deep shadows the hospital's single outdoor light didn't reach.

The afternoon's storm had moved out quickly, as storms in Florida usually did, but a dense layer of clouds remained to blot out the moon and stars. The parking lot was nearly deserted, and the drive from Williston back to Gillian's trailer halfway to the coast was over dark two-lane roads through dense forest. If experience proved true, there would be no other traffic.

You're being an idiot. All the same, she double-checked the truck's door locks before shoving the key into the ignition and turning it. She'd grab a snack from the convenience store down the street, drive home, and watch the Home Shopping Network or QVC in Viv's honor. She'd not let a crackpot phone call ruin her day. If he called again, she'd contact the county sheriff's office.

At the Stop-n-Go near the high school, she parked in front of the entrance, unable to shake the willies. She shouldn't let a call like that creep her out, but she couldn't quiet the nagging voice that told her to get a hotel room at the Sleep Inn down the street. Spend the night here where there were people around and drive the twenty miles home in the daylight, when people would have their RVs on the roads, heading for a long weekend at the beach.

Two other cars sat in the Stop-n-Go lot. One had a foursome of teenagers hanging around outside it, laughing and drinking beer and flirting. The other was empty and probably belonged to the store clerk. Taking a deep breath, Gillian got out of the truck and waved at the kids as she walked into the store and looked around for the ATM.

"Over in the back corner." The clerk squinted through orange-framed cat's-eye glasses almost the same color as the thinning hair that floated in tufts around her head. "It's been tore up, but we finally got 'er fixed today."

"Thanks." Gillian finally spotted the machine, half-hidden by a display of Pop-Tarts, and swiped her debit card through its reader.

Terrific. "Transaction Declined; Please Contact Financial Institution."

"Damn you and your curse, Duncan Campbell. Give me just one freaking break." She tried again, with the same results.

Obviously, the ATM wasn't fixed after all. She walked down the aisle of junk food and finally settled on a bag of tortilla chips, taking it to the counter along with a jar of her favorite chunky salsa. She'd eat it in Viv's honor while TV shopping for the biggest, most garish ring she could find. Viv would love it.

She paused over the debit card and decided not to use it, just in case the problem was with the card and not the debit machine. Instead, she pulled out a Visa and handed it to the clerk. "I think your ATM might be torn up again."

"It's those dang kids. Can't keep nothing working around here." The woman rang up the chips and salsa, then stared at the register screen, shaking her head. "Sorry, but your card's been declined. You wanna pay cash or put the stuff back? Don't feel bad about it; happens all the time."

The store clerk continued to pop gum while she talked, a skill Gillian figured she'd been honing for years. At least she didn't look judgmentally at the customer with the rumpled T-shirt and jeans, not to mention the droopy ponytail, whose bank had declined her five-dollar purchase of junk food.

The woman might not be judgmental, but the exchange didn't stop Gillian's face from heating with embarrassment. She'd gotten paid yesterday and had used the card to buy gas this morning, so what was up with her bank? She fished her wallet out of her bag and said a prayer of thanks when she found four one-dollar bills and some quarters jammed into the zippered coin compartment.

On the bright side, at least she'd been spared the humiliation of being turned down for a room at the Sleep Inn because of a declined card. If she stayed in Williston tonight the only "sleeping in" she'd be doing would be in her vehicle, which settled that internal debate. She'd be driving home.

Back in the cocoon of the truck, she locked the doors, reached under the seat, and pulled out the gun she took on gator calls. She didn't use it to shoot alligators; she carried the gun in case a poacher or backwoods yahoo decided to hassle her.

She laid it on her thigh within easy reach, and looked at the dashboard clock. It was almost ten, and she had to decide whether to answer the crackpot's call—and she was pretty sure he would call. If nothing else, he sounded like a persistent crackpot.

When the ringtone sounded, right on time, she took a deep breath and relaxed her shoulders before answering. "All right, who are you? What is it you want?" No point in pretending she didn't know it was him.

"Who I work for doesn't matter, lady. What matters is that the individual who employs me is serious and has a lot of reach. He doesn't like to be told no."

Reach?

"Meaning what? He runs innocent women off the road because he wants some ancient relic that probably doesn't exist?"

"Oh, it exists, or you better hope it does." The man paused, and Gillian thought she heard the sound of a radio or television in the background, something with a canned laugh track. It only made the conversation more surreal. "Kinda embarrassing to have your cards turned down, wasn't it?"

The thread of fear that had stretched taut through Gillian since the first phone call finally snapped, and she fought the urge to crawl under the floorboard and hide. Who the hell were these people? Where were they hiding?

Her spine tingled as if a line of ants were marching down it. "What do you want from me?"

She needed to get to the Williston PD. Find out how to trace private numbers. Surely there had to be a way the police could do it.

"We want the Templars' cross. I thought I made that clear," the man said. "You have thirty days to find and deliver it, and then you can have your life back. We might even give you a little something for your trouble."

A laugh escaped her before Gillian could stop it. Tex, as she'd come to think of him, was clearly insane, which didn't make him any less dangerous. "Thirty days. Are you serious?"

"Oh, I'm deadly serious, Ms. Campbell, and you'd do well to remember it."

Gillian's temper finally overrode her fear, not to mention her common sense. She would not be bullied. "Look, Tex. Here's a reality pill for you to swallow. First, that whole story about my ancestor and the Templars' cross? It's a family tall tale I remember hearing as a kid. There's no proof it's true. It's probably been exaggerated and embellished so many times over the generations that any bit of truth in it has been lost.

"Second, even if it were true, Duncan Campbell was lost in a freaking shipwreck in the sixteenth century.

"Third, even if I knew where the ship went down, how the hell would I go about finding something that's been on the bottom of the ocean for four hundred years?"

Her outburst was met with a long silence. Good. She'd made her point.

"That's why you have thirty days," the man finally said. "So I suggest you take a leave of absence from those alligators of yours and get busy."

Yeah, she'd get busy all right, with the police department and the phone company. "Here's what I suggest, both for you and whoever you work for: go fuck yourselves. And you can quote me on that."

"That's what you want me to tell Holly, that sweet little niece of yours?"

Gillian froze, and a layer of gauze fell into the space between her and the world outside. The laughter of the teenagers in the parking lot grew tinny and muffled. Colors faded and dulled. Her own voice came out reedy and two pitches too high. "Wh . . . what?"

"You heard me. Surely after what happened five years ago, you don't want to be responsible for the death of another little kid, do you? Your niece is what, three years old? Sweet little thing, too. One of my associates saw her down in Fort Lauderdale today; sent me a photo, in fact, from the Rainbow Road Preschool. She looks a lot like you."

"You wouldn't touch her." No one could be fanatical enough to hurt a child, especially over something this stupid. She wanted to scream, to rant, to cry out at the heavens, but her mouth had grown so dry she could barely swallow. Only one strained syllable came out. "Please."

"We won't—as long as you cooperate. I'll call in the morning with instructions." Tex's voice became obscenely cheerful. "This phone can't be traced, so don't bother. Talk to the police and you'll find our retribution fast and ugly.

"And if you talk to that little niece of yours, you tell her the pink dress she wore to day care today—the one with the kittens on the front? That was real, real cute."

2

He wasn't sure what woke him, but the first thing Shane Burke saw when he cracked open his eyelids was the bottle of Jack Daniel's, tipped over and resting on its side. He could've sworn he finished it off last night, but there was at least an inch of rich amber liquid still resting inside.

Good. Now he didn't have to wonder what he'd have for breakfast.

The second thing he saw was a great pair of legs. Well, technically, a great pair of ankles above a pair of leather sandals, and then the legs.

Obviously, he was starting his Saturday morning with hallucinations.

Only one good solution for that. He dangled an arm off the side of his bed and almost had his fingers wrapped around the neck of the bottle when one of the leather sandals kicked his buddy Jack Daniel's under the bed, clipping his hand in the process.

"Ow." Hallucinations didn't take his booze and kick him in the knuckles.

Ignoring the throbbing in his hand and the stabs of hangover agony behind his eyeballs, Shane rolled onto his back and squinted at the rest of his nonhallucination.

Shoulder-length hair that fell in a sheen of dark chestnut brown, fair skin, fierce brown eyes, red lips compressed in a tight line, black skirt and white blouse, big briefcase-style purse. Had he picked her up at Harley's last night? If so, he had to cut back on the sauce.

"Sorry," he mumbled. "I forgot your name." Pity, 'cause she was a hot little number, way classier than the regulars at Harley's. It's not like he got laid so often that he could afford to forget it when he did.

"We haven't met." She propped her hands on her hips and muttered something that sounded like, "And you're supposed to help me?"

Help her with what? Wait, maybe she was a charter. Had he chartered *The Evangeline* out to a tour group or fishing party today? Surely he'd remember if there was money coming in.

Color him officially confused. He struggled to a seated position and gave her another look. "What am I supposed to help you with?"

She crossed her arms and raked a ball-shriveling gaze the length of his body. "I came here to offer you a job, but I don't think you're up to it."

He tugged the sheet up in self-defense. "I'm not at my best. Ever consider making an appointment? Not dropping in at the crack of dawn?" He had no idea what time it was, but it couldn't be that late.

"It's past noon. And I didn't figure, given your financial situation, that you'd be so picky about what time of day someone offered you money." She shook her head. "Never mind. This was a mistake."

She banged her head on the low doorway out of the master cabin, which served her right, the sanctimonious shrew.

Shane eased himself to a standing position and waited to see if last night's bourbon was going to make a reappearance or if he might topple over. Neither happened. Today would be a good day.

By the time he'd shuffled into the postage-stamp-sized bathroom, taken a leak, and brushed his teeth, he'd remembered the reason for last night's bender. Not that he needed a reason, but last night he'd had one. First Bank and Savings, said a guy named Ralph (who bore an uncanny resemblance to a bullfrog), had grown tired of waiting for Mr. Burke to get current on his payments on *The Evangeline*. First Bank and Savings, so sorry, would need back payments in full within thirty days or the boat would be foreclosed on and put up for sale.

First Bank and Savings, so sorry, could go screw themselves.

Shane splashed water on his face, studied the dark-blond stubble on his chin, and decided not to shave. The bristle looked good with his bloodshot green eyes. Plus, he needed to get used to looking like a beach bum. If the bank took *The Evangeline*—which wasn't just his boat but was also his home and his meager livelihood—he'd be doing any future shaving on a park bench or in the community bathroom of a shelter.

Shit. How was he going to put his hands on almost a hundred grand in a month?

He jerked open the bathroom door and almost fell over the brunette. "I thought you left." He edged around her. "You're taller than I thought."

"I reconsidered." The edge of her mouth quirked. "You're wearing more chocolate than I thought."

They both looked down at his boxers, black and covered with images of red foil-wrapped Hershey Kisses. "They were a gift," he said. A total lie; he'd found them on eBay. "Think you could wait for me on deck?"

"Good idea." The woman's cough sounded suspiciously like a laugh. He doubted whatever job she had to offer would pay enough to satisfy the bullfrog at First Bank and Savings, but on the off chance that she was an heiress in need of a washed-up trawler captain, he'd dust off his manners and put on pants.

He watched her climb the steps and disappear through the hatch. Nice ass, but kinda wobbly on those sandals, which had silly narrow heels. Either she wasn't used to wearing them or the sight of his man-candy had upset her sense of balance. Stranger things had happened. Probably.

Shane pulled on jeans and a white Way Key Marina T-shirt, waved a comb in the vicinity of his hair, and decided to make it a shoes-optional day. At the end of the passageway, he climbed the short stairway and exited onto the deck.

The woman stood near the stern, looking oddly comfortable despite being overdressed for a weekend on the water. Around *The Evangeline*, the smallest of Cedar Key's three marinas was busy. Tourists bustled on and off the boats as they returned from a morning of fishing and diving or embarked on afternoon cruises around Seahorse Key or to one of the beaches.

Yesterday's storm had left the sky blue and bright and cloudless. Shane closed his eyes to enjoy the warmth of sunlight against his eyelids, then took a deep breath of salt-tanged air to clear his head. Gulls cawed as they trolled the area for food, and the water lapped gently against the sides of the boats.

Damn it, he couldn't lose this, especially when he could blame only himself, his bad attitude, and his inability to forget the past. He might not deserve the peace he'd found here, but he didn't want to throw it away like he'd tossed aside everything else in his life. Running away, trying to emulate dear old dad, had grown tiresome.

"There's nothing like it, is there?" The woman's voice jolted him out of his thoughts. She'd walked to within a few feet of him but still looked out at the water off the stern. "I always feel like I've stepped into a time warp when I come here. I know it's been rebuilt a few times after hurricanes blew in, but they always build it back the same, and I love that. I doubt Cedar Key looked very different fifty years ago."

Shane smiled. "I totally agree." He held out his hand and, when she took it, said, "Shane Burke. But I guess you knew that since you came looking for me. Sorry about . . ." He jerked his head in the vicinity of the door.

"Gillian Campbell." She glanced up at the windows of the pilot-house. "Can we go up there and talk? I don't want anyone to over-hear us."

He hated to break the news to her, but everyone at the marina had places to go and people to talk to. No one gave a crap about his business except his first mate, Jagger, who had to have his hangover behind the tour-booking counter at the marina by 8:00 a.m.

But Shane could play cloak-and-dagger if she wanted. "Sure, after you."

He deliberately didn't look at her ass as he followed her up the steps to the pilothouse, which he thought showed a great deal of professional restraint just in case he did go to work for her. "There's a little office area to the left, and we can talk there. Or we can sit in the captain's chairs if you want to enjoy the view."

The Evangeline pilothouse was high and made for comfort; iron-ically, he'd bought the forty-seven-foot trawler after she'd been fore-closed on down in Tampa. Before that, she'd been foreclosed on in Louisiana, which explained the name. She deserved better than she'd gotten in terms of owners.

"It's a nice ship." Gillian looked around at all the honey-stained birch and sat at one of the two wooden chairs beside a small table laden with charts and maps. He swept them into a sloppy pile, gath-ered an armload, and dumped them on the floor. Then he took the chair opposite her.

Hell, maybe she would hire him despite the way they'd started, assuming it was a job worth doing. "You said you had work for me. Tell me about it."

"I need to hire a diver."

Shane's hopes crashed to the deck. "I occasionally take people on dive tours," he said. "I can give you pointers on good spots to dive, but I don't give lessons and I won't dive with you. Before we went out you'd have to sign a waiver of responsibility." He paused, think-ing about how he might keep the job-prospect door open. "I can do special charter tours, though." For a hundred grand, he could make it really special.

Gillian seemed unsure what to do with her hands, clutching them together on the table in front of her, moving them to her lap, leaving one in her lap and putting the other back on the table. Fidgeting, in other words.

"You don't understand," she finally said. "I need to hire a diver for a special job, not to give me lessons."

Shane leaned back in his chair and studied her. Gillian Campbell looked tired. And nervous. And hadn't made eye contact since they sat down. "You can't walk down G Street without tripping over a scuba diver," he said. "Where'd you get my name, and why would you think I'm the diver you need?"

From her comments about the hurricane rebuilding, she'd been to Cedar Key before, maybe even lived nearby. But she didn't hang in his circles—with the regulars at Harley's, in other words. He'd never seen her. And most of the folks at the bar, including old Harley himself, wouldn't recommend Shane Burke for a dive job. Not without talking to him first.

"You're not telling me everything. If you want me to work for you, I need to hear it all."

She finally looked up at him, and nodded. "I'm a scuba diver myself, but a recreational diver's not what I need. I want to hire a technical diver, someone who can locate a shipwreck that might be sunk in deep water. Once the wreckage is found, I need something from it."

"Oh, well, if that's all, why didn't you say so?" Shane regretted the sarcasm when she winced at his words. "Sorry, but wreck salvage is highly regulated." The fine state of Florida didn't take kindly to people looting things off the floor of the Gulf, nor did any other coastal state, for that matter. "When did this ship go down? I haven't heard of anything around here in the last few years."

She opened the front compartment of the satchel she carried and spread out a map. "It's an old wreck from sometime in the early 1600s that set sail from Spain or Portugal. The ship was called *The Marcus Aurelius*."

She shoved the map toward Shane, but he ignored it. The woman was nuts. "You think anything from a wreck that old is still salvageable?"

At her stricken look, he took a deep breath. "Look, people get big dreams about finding sunken treasure left from pirate ships or old warships, but the vessels back then were built of wood. An iron or fiberglass ship might survive, but a wooden ship would have broken into matchsticks under the force of the waves unless it's in deep water. Even if you knew exactly where this *Marcus Aurelius* sank—which I'm assuming you don't since you mentioned locating it—chances of finding anything from it are . . ." He shook his head. "I think you're on a fool's mission."

Gillian blinked several times and looked down at her leather purse. *Aw shit*, she was going to cry. On a good day, one without a hangover, Shane didn't know what to do with a crying woman.

Her voice came out strong, though, not tearful. "I have to try. Please—you're the only technical diver in this area. I can pay you." She reached inside her bag and pulled out a stack of bills, setting it gently on the table between them. It was a tall stack, and the top bill had a picture of Benjamin Franklin on it.

Holy shit. Shane slowly pushed the money back toward Gillian with his left hand, not trusting himself to be that close to it, and pulled the map toward him with his right. He looked down, expecting to see one of those dive maps of the Gulf of Mexico sold in the tourist shops, but he didn't recognize the coastal area it showed. At least not until he pulled it closer and leaned over.

Okay, now he knew she was crazy. "You're looking for someone to dive the North Atlantic? Why the hell are you looking in Cedar Key, Florida?" He shoved the map back at her and took a last, longing look at Ben Franklin and his friends. "You need to go to New England or, hell, Halifax or Newfoundland. Not Florida."

"I have to find someone who can go quickly, and I live here—well, over in Sumner, near the reserve."

Shane scrubbed his hands over his stubbly face. The pounding of little jackhammers in his temples had grown in intensity. He needed a drink. "I'm not set up for cold-water diving; it takes special equipment." Expensive equipment, and a little retrofitting.

Hell, *he* wasn't retrofitted for that climate; he'd done dives in the North Atlantic before, but not in a long time and not when he was looking for a needle in a sand-filled haystack. He needed that money, but he had to be a realist.

"I'm sorry, but I'm not your guy." At her look of horror, he added, "I'll ask around, though. I'll see if anyone can recommend a diver who's equipped to tackle something like that. It's the best I can do."

Shane pushed his chair back and stood, frowning as Gillian made no move to leave. She'd picked up the stack of bills and had been flipping through them. *Damn*, but Ben had a lot of other friends who looked just like him. She reached in the satchel and put two more stacks on the table.

Shane swallowed hard. How the hell much money *was* that?

"This is to get your equipment and provisions, and to retrofit your boat," she said, looking him in the eye with a hard blue stare. "It's more than you'll need, and you keep the rest. When you find *The Marcus Aurelius* and retrieve my family heirloom, there's another million for you. All cash. All under the table."

Son of a bitch. Shane looked at her, at the money, at the map of the Canadian east coast.

How hard a dive could it be?

3

Gillian walked with a deceptively calm gait until she felt confident that she was out of Shane's field of vision. Then she found an unoccupied bench near the end of the dock, sat down, and wrenched off the blasted heels.

She'd done what Tex had told her to do. She had pretended, without actually saying so, that she was rich. That she had unlimited money to burn on a whim. But she'd never even seen that much money—almost a quarter of a million in three neat stacks. She knew, because she'd counted it.

Acting was not her forte, though, and she wasn't sure how much Shane Burke had bought. She could barely walk on the freaking heels. One didn't trap nuisance gators or patrol wildlife reserves in heels.

The only thing that saved her was recognizing the truth in what Tex had told her about Shane Burke. He was desperate for money and on the verge of losing his boat. Obviously, the man drank, and judging by how well he was functioning on what appeared to be a serious hangover, he drank frequently.

Not the kind of man on whom she wanted to risk Holly's life, but also not a man she wanted to drag into this mess. It would be easier, maybe, if she hadn't liked him. Truth was, she admired Shane on some levels. She hated to think his looks had anything to do with it, although he did remind her of the guys who'd been on her college swimming and diving teams—tall, long-limbed, with powerful shoulders and thighs, and that cocky attitude that seemed to be the domain of men who spent a lot of time in the water.

Mostly, though, it was the fact that he was a tec diver, which meant he could do things she'd never had the nerve to try. She was scuba-certified to thirty meters, but he'd be able to go much deeper. Stay longer. To stay certified, he'd have to prove himself able to think under pressure, stay calm, and handle decompression issues, which scared the hell out of her.

Why he was tucked away in Cedar Key, known more for its shoals and clams than for deepwater diving, she didn't know. Tex probably did, but the less she talked to Tex, the better. The less she came to sympathize with Shane Burke, the better, too. Otherwise, Tex and his evil twin employer might find a way to coerce him to cooperate the way they'd forced her.

Gillian stuffed the heels in her bag and wiggled her toes, trying to restart the circulation. She'd ferreted the shoes out of a back closet early this morning after her phone call from Tex. "Look on your stoop," he'd told her, and she'd found the bag full of cash. "Dress like a rich girl. Wave money in front of Shane Burke's face. He needs it. Don't tell him more than you have to. Go off script and you know what will happen."

Just in case she'd forgotten, at the bottom of the bag of bills was a grainy photo of Holly in her pink dress with the kittens on the front. A dress Gillian had bought her, but surely Tex didn't know that. Then again, he seemed to know an awful lot.

He and his lunatic employer—if he was telling the truth and wasn't behind this whole crazy scheme himself—even seemed to know she wouldn't cross many lines to save herself. The lines she'd cross for a child, however, especially this child, were unlimited.

After massaging her feet, Gillian walked back to her truck parked behind the marina, the hot concrete baking her heels and the undersides of her toes. She dodged families with strollers, kids playing chase, even a couple of canine escapees racing along the dock trailing leashes. The population of sleepy little Cedar Key was already swelling with Labor Day crowds of hippie college kids from Gainesville a couple of hours inland and families from neighboring counties who wanted to enjoy a pristine waterfront without all the commercial trappings of the Panhandle beaches.

And in the middle of all this crowded wholesomeness she walked, a woman who loved alligators and her solitary lifestyle. A woman whose nightmares had come to life, whose fear threatened to paralyze her. She'd lived this fear before, five years ago. But she couldn't think about Ethan, or about Sam. It would be too much; she had to keep her thoughts clear and her mind sharp.

She'd think about Shane Burke instead. She kept his smile, boyish despite the hangover and the stubble, and his sun-lightened blond hair in her mind while she drove to the county seat of Bronson. She parked in front of Coastal Bank, wedged protesting feet back into the heels, and marched inside ready to do battle.

Now that she was cooperating, everything was back to normal. There must have been a computer glitch, the teller said. Gillian withdrew as much as she thought she could spare, glad her monthly bills were set up on bill pay so that she didn't have to worry about those. She still had the stacks of hundreds from Tex, but that would be for Shane Burke to get his boat ready if he decided to help her. As for herself, she wouldn't spend dirty money if she could avoid it.

She next stopped at the tiny office that her wireless company's only local employee shared with a State Farm agent. The phone guy, whose name tag identified him as Tim, was more interested in singing the praises of the newest iPhone than listening to her tale of woe, but when she mentioned the police, he settled down and tried to look older and wiser than he probably was. If she had to guess, she'd say he was a nineteen- or twenty-year-old, working his way through the University of Florida or the community college in Ocala.

He listened, nodded his head vigorously enough to flop a strand of lank black hair in his eyes, and thrummed nervous fingers on his Formica desktop. "Far as I know, we don't have any way of tracing a private caller," he said, then snapped his fingers and jerked out a desk drawer. After rifling through what looked like an even mixture of forms and gum wrappers, he pulled out a manual and slapped it on the desk. "What we can do, though, is set up your phone to block any calls from a private number. I have the instructions right here and can do it for you. That should solve the problem."

Right. That would be the absolute worst thing Gillian could do. She wanted to track Tex down, not block him out, piss him off, and send him straight to her sister's house.

"What about the police?" She snatched her phone off the desk before Tim could reprogram it. "Do you know if they can trace it?"

Tim gave her a blank, gator-in-headlights look. "I don't know. You don't want me to block the calls?"

Gillian made her escape, and drove across town to the county sheriff's department, where she was absurdly happy to see Terry Miles, the young deputy who'd tracked her down in person to tell her about Viv's accident. Make that Viv's nonaccident.

"How's your friend?" He motioned her to a desk in a room off a short hallway, his dark blue uniform blending with the dark blue institutional carpet and the light blue walls. Even the table in the windowless meeting room had been painted blue.

"She's stable this morning. If she does okay today, they're going to move her out of ICU." That news, at least, had gotten the day off to a good start.

All along the drive back from Cedar Key, following the narrow state highway through the densely forested county, Gillian had thought about how to start this conversation. She'd finally decided a bit of honesty—but not too much—might convince the deputy to help her. "I started getting some threatening phone calls last night," she said, explaining about the private caller. "He claimed that he caused Vivian's accident to get my attention. Do you think someone could've tampered with her car?"

This might be a small-town deputy in a very small town, but he didn't laugh, or blow her off, or pretend knowledge he didn't have. "I guess it's possible. Since the rain was coming down so hard we didn't really look for a sign of tampering." He frowned and scribbled a few lines on a clipboard. Gillian tried to read it but beyond her own name, it all looked like gibberish.

"Is there any way to trace the call?" She hated the desperation in her voice.

"Can I see your phone?" Gillian handed it to him reluctantly, wondering how far the reach of Tex's employer really went. Did it extend to knowing what she said or did inside a cinderblock building in Bronson, Florida?

Deputy Miles looked at the list of recent calls and tried to redial one of the private listings.

"I tried that," Gillian said, and he gave her a sheepish smile.

"You'd be surprised how many people don't think of it." He handed the phone back to her. "I assume you don't want to block the calls, right? Want to keep track of what the crazy dude's up to?"

Deputy Miles was no dumb bunny. "Right." Gillian set the phone on the table and stared at it as if it might suddenly spit out some answers. "I'd just like to find out who the guy is. You know, see how seriously to take him."

"You've always gotta take crackpots seriously these days. Exactly what is it he wants from you?" The deputy leaned back in his chair, reached in his pocket for a stick of gum, and proceeded to unwrap it slowly enough that the sweet smell of Juicy Fruit filled the room before he finally got it in his mouth. "Is he asking you to give him money, or to meet him somewhere? If you wanted to set up a meeting with him, we might be able to trap him."

Here's where it got tricky; if she set Tex up that blatantly, whoever was watching Holly—whoever had taken her picture—could hurt her in an instant.

"He found out about a family heirloom and thinks I have it," Gillian said. "He says he wants it. It's just an old piece of jewelry. I told him that I don't have it; I've never even seen it. But if he caused Viv's accident . . . I mean, what else will he do? I've gotta admit; he's creeped me out."

"I can imagine." Deputy Miles leaned forward and propped his elbows on the table, training his hazel eyes on Gillian's. "Here's the problem. We don't have any way of tracing his call without working with your phone service and monitoring all of your calls—we might even need to set something up at your house so we have a fixed position to work from."

And if that happened, no telling what Tex would do. He or someone working with him had delivered that bag of money to her trailer during a night when she'd barely slept, and she hadn't heard a thing. Her dog, Tank, who practically had heart failure at the sight of a squirrel in the yard, hadn't let out a single suspicious bark.

"I don't think that will work, but I'll keep it in mind."

"At this point, he hasn't broken a law that we know of, so there's nothing we can do." The deputy tapped his finger on the clipboard. "Except I will ask the impound guys to tow your friend's car over to Joe-Tom's garage and have him check it out. If a line was cut or something was tampered with, JT can find it."

"Thanks. I appreciate that." Gillian stood up, although her legs felt as if they'd been dipped in concrete, stiff and almost immovable. Without realizing it, she'd let herself hope that someone here could help her. But deep down, she'd known better. Even if they could prove Viv's wreck wasn't an accident, she doubted Tex and his associates had been careless enough to leave a calling card.

Back at the Jeep, she pulled a blue flyer advertising a free car wash from beneath her windshield wiper before unlocking the door and climbing in. She backed out of her parking place and sat at the lot's exit, waiting for traffic to clear enough for her to turn left onto the main road. Only that wasn't really what she was waiting for.

Her real wait was for the phone call, and it came less than thirty seconds later. She didn't bother with a greeting. "I didn't tell them anything."

"Go home, Ms. Campbell. No more running by the phone company. No more trips to the bank. And you sure as hell better not talk to any more law enforcement. Do you understand me, or do I need to send you a reminder?"

Gillian felt hot tears trailing down her cheeks. She wanted to rage and scream. To explode. To kill something. Not to sit here and beg. "Please, no reminders. I'm sorry. I understand."

"Fine. Now tell me about your meeting with Shane Burke. My employer would like an update."

Interesting that they had eyes all over Bronson but apparently not on *The Evangeline*. How sloppy of them, whoever "they" were. "I can tell he wants the money. I'm supposed to meet him back in Cedar Key tomorrow at lunch."

"Good job." Yeah, now the SOB sounded jovial. "Close the deal tomorrow; rent a place there so you can keep an eye on him. You now have twenty-nine days."

Gillian closed her eyes. Like she could forget that deadline. "Can I ask you a question?"

"Well, of course." Tex was all too happy to be helpful now that he was getting his way. But what if she couldn't deliver?

"What if I get Shane to Canada and he can't find the wreck? What if it's just not there anymore—wooden ships get beat up by the waves over the course of four centuries, you know." Not that she'd known that until today. "Or what if we find the wreck but there's no cross?"

Tex paused a long time before answering, and his response surprised Gillian. She'd been expecting a sinister warning about Holly, or Shane, or Viv, or even her sister. Her parents at the gator ranch over in Louisiana.

"If you do your due diligence and can't find the Templars' cross . . . I don't know what will happen to you, or those you care about. That will be my employer's decision. But I can guarantee that if you don't make every attempt to find it—*every* attempt, to our satisfaction—*those* consequences you will not be able to live with."

Somehow, Gillian didn't doubt that.

4

As soon as Gillian had disappeared down the dock, tottering on high heels she clearly wasn't in full control of, Shane climbed to the flybridge deck atop the pilothouse and watched her progress from a higher vantage point. About three-quarters of the way down the dock, she sat on a vacant bench, staring out at the vessels coming in and out of the marina's west end.

He grinned when she took off the sandals. *Gotcha.*

A lot of things didn't add up with Gillian Campbell, including the fact that she threw around so much cash while telling a pile of lies and half-truths. That bothered him more than anything.

He knew this much. She was trying to give him the impression that she was a rich girl on the hunt for some family bauble, yet she handled that money like Ben Franklin himself was going to bite her. And if this priceless treasure had been at the bottom of the North Atlantic for four centuries, why was she in such an all-fired hurry to get at it now? What exactly was this thing she was willing to pay him big bucks to risk his life for? Because this was not a simple dive. Nothing simple about it.

Those were the questions he needed satisfactory answers to when he'd meet her for lunch tomorrow. As hard as it would be, he'd have to turn down the goddamned money if she told him more lies.

"Some girls give me money, some girls buy me clothes . . . and some guys have all the luck."

Shane broke into a grin at the boozy, bluesy sound of his first mate and best buddy Jagger coming from below, butchering yet another Rolling Stones song. He leaned over the flybridge rail. "We need to have a talk, my man."

By the time Shane clambered down to the forward deck, Jag had propelled his wiry frame from the dock to the rail without bothering to use the gangway. He slid over the rail in one smooth move, landing on his ass.

"You're gonna break something with that trick one of these days. Be different if you were better at it." Shane gave him a hand up and glanced down the length of the dock. No sign of Gillian from this angle. "How much of my visitor did you see?"

"Nice ass. Wound a little too tight. Looks like money, though, so my vote is yes."

He had no idea. But if Shane was even considering this half-baked treasure hunt, he'd need his first mate. "Better wait until you hear what you're voting on. Let's take our girl *Evangeline* on a run up the coast and back, have a little chat away from the marina. You game?"

Jagger—or, more properly, Calvin Terrence Mackie Jr., who claimed to be the Number-One Fan of the Rolling Stones—looked at him suspiciously. "I thought you were conserving fuel because you were too broke to buy more."

"Yeah, well, that might be changing. I want to talk out some shit, and I don't want to do it here."

He left Jag humming the tune to "Jumpin' Jack Flash," went down to the engine room, and gave the 480-hp Cummins a quick check. He took care of *The Evangeline* a hell of a lot better than he took care of himself, as Jagger often reminded him after a binge like last night's, so she was ready to roll within minutes.

Back in the pilothouse, he set the course and guided her out of the marina and into open water. "Let's head up toward Preacher Hole," Shane said, settling into the pilot's seat. "Won't be as crowded as the south coast."

"Sounds good. You still got sodas in that cooler?" Jagger went to the back to grab a couple of Cokes, but halted next to the table where Gillian Campbell's map was still spread out.

"Don't tell me the woman wants to charter a Canadian dive. Seriously?" Jagger handed Shane a soda and leaned over to study the map of Nova Scotia. "She came to the right place, I guess. You're the only one around here qualified to go in those waters."

Shane didn't answer, just pointed the boat's bow northward and sailed up the coast toward the mouth of the Suwannee River. He found a quiet inlet past the northern edge of the Cedar Key reserve and dropped anchor. "Let's go on deck."

Shane stretched out on his back with Gillian's map over his face, letting the afternoon sun burn off the last lingering effects of the previous night's binge. He thought about Jagger's comment. He probably *was* the only one around here who'd done any cold-water diving, but it had been a while. He only did enough deep dives now to keep his tec certification current, and it had been at least a decade since he'd done a wreck dive. Around here, the only real technical diving to be done was in underwater caves, and even there the water clarity led to disappointing dives as often as not.

He wanted Jag's input; the guy had grown up with Cal Sr., a commercial fisherman who'd worked most of the North American East Coast waters. "What's your read on diving that area? You've fished the waters up there, right?"

Jagger sat on the deck next to Shane and grabbed the map. He was lean and tan and not an inch over five nine, no matter what he liked to claim. People who met him looked at the shoulder-length black hair and the big smile and the Stones' songs he sang for every occasion, and they invariably underestimated him. The man was smart, and he'd grown up on the water. He could read weather maps and sonar like nobody's business.

"My dad fished in this area a lot when I was about middle-school age." He pointed to the rugged coastline. "We made some runs up around Cape Breton, but mostly stayed down here off Louisbourg. Scatarie Island's a bitch." Jagger looked over at Shane. "You know this area has the largest concentration of shipwrecks anywhere in North America? There's a reason for that. You name a water hazard, man, Nova Scotia's east coast has it."

"Awesome." Shane had been to the area a couple of times, but not since he quit diving with a partner. "What about solo dives?"

Jagger wasn't a diver, but he'd handled plenty of dive vessels. "Do you know how deep?"

He didn't know jack shit. Not yet anyway. "Not a clue. Shipwrecks tend to happen in shallower water, but the deepwater wrecks are better preserved. We don't know what kind of conditions we'll face until we get there and try to locate the ship, unless Gillian has more information than she's shared so far." She'd seemed pretty damn clueless.

"Damn." Jagger looked out at the clouds gathering to their north, and Shane retrieved the map. Jagger was right; that coastline looked brutal.

"I'd say a solo dive is doable, but you'd want to go down with a line," Jagger said. "You know, to haul your ass up when you run out of air. Better yet, break your own rule and dive with a partner, especially if it's deep enough that you'll have decompression stops."

He didn't like diving with a line, especially in a tight space like a cave or a wreck, and a dive partner was out of the question. He dove alone. "We'll work the details out later."

"Hot damn. You're gonna do it. Need a first mate?"

Shane grinned. "Always. Now cast your eye on those clouds and tell me if we make a run for it, or we wait it out."

As if in answer, a heavy bolt of cloud-to-ground lightning streaked from the dark mass and, with a loud crack, struck something just onshore. The first heavy drop of rain nailed Shane square in the eyeball. "Never mind, weather guy. Let's ride it out."

They raced to the door and managed to get inside with a couple of seconds to spare before the deluge began. "This one's gonna take a while to play out." Shane led the way down the interior passage to the salon and galley and rummaged in the cabinets for chips while Jagger stretched out on the gray-and-white-striped cushions that adorned the seats and backs of the benches and booths. Whoever had decorated *The Evangeline* before foreclosure had done a hell of a job. Good thing, because Shane would be lost in an interior design store.

He tossed a bag of popcorn to Jagger, who'd already stuffed in earbuds and was singing a slightly off-key version of "Sweet Virginia."

Shane took his bag of chips, ambled back along the side passage and cut across to the master suite. With a sigh of contentment, he stretched out on his bed and let *The Evangeline* rock him into relaxation. He loved this damned boat. Loved the feel of it moving beneath him like a woman, sighing and heaving gently in the restless waters. He loved the way its heavy hull and tight fittings muffled the sounds of thunder and wind and rain to a soothing level. Nothing could touch him here.

Damn it. If he had to freeze his ass off in a deepwater dive to find the locker of Davy Jones himself, it would be worth it to keep this boat. Funny, a week ago, when he'd first caught wind in the Harley's gossip mill that the bank was tightening up on its past-due accounts, he'd thought up a bunch of stupid options.

He could walk away from *The Evangeline* before they took it from him, and try to pretend the choice had been his.

He could call his uncle Charlie up in North Carolina and beg for a loan, and try to pretend he was just making amends for walking out on the man who'd raised him.

He could shoot his old Marine Corps service weapon one final time and put himself out of his misery. At least with that option, he wouldn't have to tell himself lies because he wouldn't be around to hear them.

Gillian Campbell was a liar, of that much he was sure. Chances also seemed good that whatever she had up her sleeve was illegal. If it involved him taking something from a wreck site in Canadian waters without governmental permission, it sure as hell was illegal and he was implicating himself in God only knew what.

But it beat his other three options. He still might end up dead, but at least he wouldn't be dying a coward. A fool, probably, but not a coward.

The storm played itself out in about an hour, so Shane returned to the pilothouse to take them home, leaving Jagger zoned out in the salon with his earbuds pumping out the Stones loud enough for Shane to recognize the heavy guitar chords of "Hand of Fate."

Once in the pilot's seat, he checked the controls on the navigation panels, glancing out the side window when the sound of an approaching engine reached him, the first he'd heard since they'd arrived at the inlet.

A boat bearing the seal of the Levy County Sheriff's Office marine unit buzzed up alongside *The Evangeline* and idled. *What the hell?*

Shane took the steps leading from the pilothouse two at a time, and emerged on the port deck just as a navy-uniformed deputy approached. "Are you Shane Burke?"

A law enforcement officer knowing your name without an introduction couldn't mean anything good. "I am. What can I do for you?"

"Mind if I come aboard?"

The officer didn't have to ask, and they both knew it. "Sure."

Shane lowered the gangway to the smaller vessel while the deputy stopped in the doorway of the marine-unit cruiser and spoke to someone—another officer, Shane assumed. When the man returned to the gangway, he'd removed his mirrored sunglasses and tucked them halfway into a breast pocket.

Carrying a clipboard, he crossed over to *The Evangeline* with more caution than Shane would've expected from someone accustomed to working on the water. "I'm Deputy Taylor, Levy County Sheriff's Office."

"Guess you already know my name." Shane pasted on his friendliest smile. "Is there a problem?" *The Evangeline* had just gotten her seasonal overhaul a couple of weeks ago, and it had been thorough, as Shane's empty bank account could attest. No way they were citing him for some glaring safety violation.

"Depends." Officer Taylor, a fit-looking late-fortyish guy with dark hair beginning to gray at the temples, flipped through some papers in his clipboard. "Where are you headed today?"

None of his business, that's where, but Shane figured that response probably wouldn't serve him well. "A friend and I decided to get out of Cedar Key for a couple of hours and ran into the storm. He's in the back." He pointed in the direction of the salon. "We were about to head back to Way Key Marina. What's this about?"

"We received a call that you might be planning to leave the country without filing a navigation plan." As he spoke, Deputy Taylor had been scanning the shoreline, but now he looked Shane in the eye. "Maybe trying to move your boat into international waters to avoid foreclosure?"

Humiliation sent a rush of heat over Shane's face, and he knew he'd probably turned the color of a freshly boiled lobster. "I didn't realize my financial situation—and I have twenty-nine more days to bring my loan up to date, by the way—was a legal matter." At least not yet.

"It is if you're headed to Mexico or the Caribbean and haven't filed a navigation plan or port notification." The deputy tucked his clipboard under his arm. "We've been asked to consider you a flight risk and keep an eye on you. We'll follow you back to the marina— just to make sure you get there safely, of course."

Asked by whom? Ralph the bullfrog?

The last sentence had been delivered with an excess of sarcasm, and Shane took a closer look at Deputy Taylor. His navy shirt and pants looked blandly official, but he wasn't wearing a badge. Wasn't that a requirement? His gun looked real enough, though. "Sure, no problem. Follow us if you want."

Shane took a step to the side to get a better look at the smaller boat. The marine-unit decal looked genuine, not that he'd ever seen one this close up. But he didn't see any radios or diving equipment. A big part of marine law enforcement involved water rescues, which in turn involved diving.

If this guy was a real deputy, Shane would give up bourbon for a year.

He took a step closer, wishing like hell his own pistol wasn't tucked beneath the seat in the pilothouse. "Could I see some identification, deputy? Maybe get a badge number?"

Was it his imagination, or had the maybe-not-a-deputy Taylor flinched?

"I don't think that'll be necessary, Mr. Burke." Taylor, or whoever he was, reached down quickly and unholstered his gun. A nice big .45, from the looks of it. Enough to blow a nice big hole in Shane. "Just don't even think about leaving Cedar Key until we're ready for you to go."

"Who the fuck are you?" Shane's shoulders tightened, his hands curling into involuntary fists. Just in case he needed to throw a punch.

Taylor crossed the gangway back to the smaller vessel, then reached down and shoved the wooden boarding ramp back onto *The Evangeline*. His accomplice in the boat's wheelhouse started the motor, and Shane had to strain to hear the words he shouted as the skiff pulled away.

"Talk to you very soon, Mr. Burke."

What the hell just happened?

5

Gillian knocked softly on the door of Vivian's hospital room and entered at the muffled response that might or might not have been "Come in."

Vivian held a napkin to her mouth and discreetly spat out whatever she was chewing. "This stuff is for shit. You bring breakfast?"

After the past twelve hours, it felt good to grin. She held up the Hardee's bag. "Steak biscuits. You're lucky they brought you to Williston instead of Ocala."

Vivian laughed and snatched at the bag, moaning and clutching her rib cage when she bent over too far. "Damn, that hurts. You are a lifesaver. I was about ready to go back in ICU and be fed from a tube so I didn't have to eat that crap."

Gillian smiled again, but the irony didn't escape her that Viv had called her a lifesaver when this whole thing was her fault. She had always told Viv everything; Viv was the only one who knew about Ethan, about how she ended up in a trailer in Levy County. She'd stayed up half the night trying to figure out how much to tell Viv and had finally settled on telling her the truth.

Gillian went to the door and stuck her head out, looking up and down the hall before closing the door to Viv's room. She'd have locked it if she could. Not that Tex was loitering around the hospital corridors and eavesdropping, but then again he might be.

When Gillian pulled the chair up to Viv's bed, her friend quit eating and watched her with a concerned frown that almost broke Gillian's heart.

"What's up with you, chica? I know you were upset about this stupid accident, but I'm gonna be okay—they're even talking about letting me go home tomorrow. It's more than that, so talk to me."

Gillian took a deep breath and glanced over at the door. She kept her voice low. "It wasn't an accident, Viv. Somebody tampered with your car."

"What? Get out of here. You're joking with me, except . . ." Viv's brown eyes probed Gillian's face. "Except you're not joking. Better tell me."

"First, you have to promise to keep quiet about this. I mean tell nobody. Not even Jimmy." Jimmy Ortiz was Viv's ex-husband, current boyfriend, and possibly future husband, all rolled into one. "I know you don't like keeping things from him, but it's safer if he doesn't know."

While Gillian talked, Vivian wrapped up her biscuit and stuck it back in the bag. "Put this in the drawer and hide it. I don't want those bossy nurses throwing it away. I'll eat it later."

Gillian nodded and stashed the bag in the drawer of the bedside table. "You promise not to tell?"

Vivian nodded. "Not Jimmy or anybody else. Now talk to me, Gillie. You're making me nervous."

So she told her all of it, then felt guilty when she felt lighter and saw the burden on Viv grow heavier. But Vivian had been used to control Gillian once already, and she needed to be on her guard or, better, out of sight.

She held up another bag from Hardee's. "This is money, Viv. A lot of it." Almost a third of Shane Burke's bribe money. "You and Jimmy are both retired. Take a vacation. Don't tell anybody where you're going, not even me. I'll call you when this is over and I know you're safe."

The longer Gillian talked, the more Vivian's frown deepened. "Let's all go away for a while. Or get the FBI involved. Somebody."

"You think I haven't considered all of that?" Gillian felt the tears threaten and she swallowed them down in one hard lump. There would be time to cry later. "I mean, this still might turn out to be some mean prank, or these guys might be bluffing. But you did have the accident. And I can't take the chance with Holly. You know why."

Ethan. Sam. And Holly was the only child her sister Gretchen could ever have, not that one child could ever take the place of another anyway.

"I know, baby girl." Vivian patted her hand. "I'll tell Jimmy I inherited the money from a dead aunt back in Cartagena. He's seen so many movies about Colombian drug lords that he's convinced I'm related to one anyway."

She paused, then asked softly, "What do you think are your chances of finding that cross, Gillie? I'm thinking next to none, or worse."

Gillian nodded and thought about Shane Burke, and all that was riding on his broad, bourbon-soaked shoulders. "Probably worse."

She left Vivian with a quick hug and a refusal to cry, at least until she got in the hallway. Once in the pickup, she waited five minutes with her phone in her hand, waiting to see if Tex would call to tell her there would be *ugly repercussions* for telling Vivian the truth. But the phone remained silent. She'd asked his permission to visit Vivian this morning when he'd called with his instructions, and he hadn't objected. Guess he'd overestimated her ability to keep her mouth shut.

He also didn't seem to have the hospital rooms bugged. She couldn't say the same for her trailer with certainty, although she'd gone through everything in the early hours this morning. She'd taken radios apart, looked on the undersides of tables and chairs, felt behind picture frames. Nothing looked or felt out of place.

Tank, her Heinz 57 dog that was part boisterous retriever and part reticent, surly chow chow, had known something was up. He'd clung to her heels like an eighty-pound toddler. And had still been barking at her in protest as she pulled out of the drive to come to the hospital this morning.

Now, as she drove the two-lane back to pick up Tank and head to Cedar Key, she tried to anticipate what she might need to do in order to convince Shane Burke that he wanted this job. Sure, he'd looked tempted by the money yesterday, but his green eyes had also harbored a lot of suspicion and he hadn't tried to keep any of it. Maybe she should tell him the truth, too, except if she did, he might start up *The Evangeline* and sail off to parts unknown, leaving her to her fate. And she wouldn't blame him one bit.

After her wasted trips to Bronson yesterday, she'd gone home and done as she'd been told. She'd arranged a hasty thirty-day leave of absence from the state, claiming a family emergency; it helped that she'd never taken as much as a sick day in five years. All they'd needed was a written request, and she'd been able to submit the paperwork online.

The gator problem was stickier, but she'd finally convinced two licensed trappers in the Gainesville area to split the next month's Levy County calls.

She'd packed up a week's worth of clothes, and all of Tank's gear and food. He was going with her, whatever happened. She needed to know there was at least one trustworthy soul around.

The phone conversation with her mom had been awkward as she fabricated an elaborate spur-of-the-moment cruise vacation for herself and Vivian. No phone contact would be possible, but she'd call as soon as she got back. She wasn't sure her mom bought it. Fortunately, Lila Campbell had always been easily distracted. As soon as Gillian changed the subject to the matter of Duncan Campbell and the family curse, she had been off and running on the new topic.

Unfortunately, the few details Lila had remembered were the same things Gillian already knew. "That's it? We don't have any documentation?"

"You'd need to talk to your dad, although I doubt he could tell you any more because . . . Wait a minute." Gillian had chewed on her nails while her mom carried on a stage-whispered conversation with her father in the background. Finally, Lila had come back to the phone. "Dad says the person you really need to talk to, if you want to learn more about Duncan Campbell, is your great-great-uncle that lives up in Paducah, Kentucky. Zeke Campbell. Your granddad's youngest brother. He's been doing the Campbell genealogy for years."

Gillian had vaguely remembered the name from old family pictures, accent on *old*. "He's still alive?"

After more consultations with her dad, her mom had confirmed that, as far as they knew, old Zeke was still breathing. "He'd be at least ninety, though. Who knows what he can remember."

It beat nothing. Gillian had written down the last address they had for him and figured she could find a phone number later.

Her final task of the night had been renting a cottage on Way Key for the month. She'd finally found a spot on a secluded street that backed onto the short runway of the biggest island's tiny airport.

After a quick stop at the trailer to pick up Tank, she drove toward the cottage, the back of the truck piled high with book boxes and a wooden trunk of old family papers and memorabilia she'd rescued from her grandmother's attic after she died. Lila came from the scorched-earth school of housecleaning, which meant anything of Grandma's that Gillian thought she might need to save from the garbage dump needed to be grabbed fast.

That had been five years ago, before everything had fallen apart in her life. She'd stuck it in the back of the closet when she'd moved to the trailer, and there it had stayed until now.

Tank snored happily from the passenger seat, content now that he knew he would be part of whatever Gillian was up to. She just hoped Shane Burke liked dogs.

With water encroaching close on either side of the highway, she crossed the series of short bridges leading onto Way Key, the "big island" closest to shore. This was "Cedar Key" the village, where about seven hundred residents lived year-round and clamming drove the local economy, as opposed to "Cedar Key" the chain of islands, one of the country's oldest protected-wildlife areas.

Gillian navigated the pickup around the small downtown area until she found the rental office and held her breath until she was sure her credit card would clear. She didn't know when Tex might decide to "get her attention" again.

Once she had the key, she followed the winding, narrow road along the coast, passing massive live oaks weighed down with Spanish moss, sheltered bays with shards of sunlight glinting off the still blue water, and then the Gulf of Mexico beyond.

Tank stood in the passenger seat with his head out the window, his nose turned toward the water. Gillian knew from experience that the retriever part of him liked the water while the chow part wanted to watch it from a distance. How he'd react to being on a boat, she wasn't sure. Taking him along was probably selfish and maybe she'd rethink it, but right now she wanted him with her.

She found the mailbox with "NO. 8114" painted on it and turned onto a drive of sand and shells that led between two oak trees. The moss scraped across the top of the truck like fingers as she passed beneath the trees' bent and gnarled branches, but just past them she saw the cottage and wished it was hers for real.

It was a squat, flat-roofed building fifty feet from the water, painted the color of orange sherbet except for its sage-green window and door trim. The back side of it was all glass and looked out on a private wooden dock into water that made up for its muddiness by its still calm. Beyond the tuft of marshland that enclosed this little cove, Gillian could see the Gulf, bright and blue.

Tank didn't stop to appreciate the serenity—or the privacy. He took off after a critter of some kind and stopped at the water's edge, willing to go no farther.

By the time Gillian had unloaded the truck and spent a few minutes exploring the cottage—essentially one big room partitioned off like an efficiency apartment—it was almost noon and time to meet Shane at a place called Harley's. She'd passed it on C Street on the way through town.

Gillian pulled on a clean pair of jeans and a white button-front sleeveless shirt. Neat, but too geeky to be a tourist.

She pulled out some dog treats and left them on the floor of the kitchenette as a peace offering. "Hold down the fort, Tankmeister."

Tank looked at the treats suspiciously and barked at her when she closed the cottage door behind her. He'd get over it soon enough. With all the glass in back, he had plenty of things to watch. She'd already spotted great white herons on the marshland nearest the end of the dock and frogs splashing around the shallows in front of the house.

The drive to Harley's took less than five minutes, and she found it as unassuming as most of Cedar Key—a raised rectangle of aqua-painted wood with dark shingles and a giant clam on a cedar stump out front. Gillian stopped inside the door and blinked to adjust her vision to the dim interior. The mingled aromas of fried seafood and beer gave it a corner-bar feel, and the folks seated at most of the tables had older, more weather-beaten faces than the ones she'd seen at the marina yesterday.

Locals ate and drank at Harley's, not tourists. Gillian liked that.

"You the one meetin' Shane and Cal for lunch?"

She turned to see a middle-aged man behind the bar, pulling glasses off the polished wood with one hand and wielding a wet dishcloth with the other.

"Yeah, well, Shane anyway. Who's Cal?" Maybe Cal was a dog.

"Calvin Mackie's boy and general ne'er-do-well who likes to call himself Jagger. You find Shane, you find Jagger nearby. Anyway, take that table over in the corner." He opened a Miller Light and slid it across the bar. "On the house."

"Thanks." Gillian took the beer and made her way to the corner, sitting in the seat that gave her the best view of the door.

In all the scenarios she'd imagined of how today's meeting might go, she'd never factored in the possibility that Shane might bring someone with him. This Jagger guy was just one more thing to make Tex nervous. One more person being put in harm's way. One more voice of reason who might try to talk Shane out of taking the job.

The door opened, and at first Gillian thought the man silhouetted in the doorway was Shane, but once the door closed behind him, it was easy to see the guy was too short, his hair too dark. His blue sports coat and neat khakis looked more tourist than local, though, and he took off his mirrored sunglasses and scanned the room, much as she had when she arrived.

When his gaze met hers he paused only an instant, but it was enough to send a chill over Gillian's skin. She reached for the beer bottle without looking, tipped it over, and made a quick mid-air grab to keep it from spilling.

When she looked back at the newcomer, he'd taken a seat at the bar on the far end, ordered a soda, and pulled out a cell phone. When he reached for the phone, his jacket fell open enough for her to spot a shoulder holster tucked under his left arm.

He watched her as he made his call, talked for only a few seconds, and gave her a small, cold smile when he stuck the phone back in his jacket.

Gillian couldn't prove it, but she knew it all the same—he'd been reporting in. Calling Tex.

Or was he Tex? And if she got her hands on his phone, could she find who he worked for?

6

Harley's had the best air-conditioning in town. As soon as he entered the doorway, Shane's stress level dropped just from the sweep of cold air across his skin. In a pathetic stab at being socially acceptable, he'd worn jeans instead of shorts and a polo shirt instead of a tank. He'd even worn shoes. Gillian Campbell should be impressed. It was practically his version of a tuxedo.

"That AC is sweet." Jagger gave a mock salute to Harley, who once upon a time had fished with the Mackies, father and son, before Calvin Sr. died from the big C. "I'll get our sandwiches and beer—the usual?"

Shane spotted Gillian in the corner and waved. She jumped like he'd shot her, then smiled with a faint upturn of her mouth. Very faint. She looked like she hadn't slept in a day or two. "Yeah, and order half a sandwich for our friend over there. And a bowl of chowder. Might calm her down; she looks twitchy."

Jagger leaned around Shane and grinned at Gillian, who did not grin back. In fact, she didn't look amused in the least. "Ouch. She's cold."

"Most women react that way to you, my friend." Shane slapped him on the shoulder and headed toward the back table, glancing at an uptight, buttoned-up guy at the end of the bar who'd obviously wandered onto the wrong end of C Street.

"You weren't supposed to bring anybody." Gillian's voice came out in an unhappy blend of a hiss and a snarl.

"Is that so? Why not?"

Uh-huh, he thought so. She didn't have an answer but just looked pissed off and drank her beer. Because the answer was probably *I don't want you to tell anyone because what I want you to do is illegal, Shane.* Or maybe, *I want to keep this a secret so that people won't realize you took a dangerous and illegal job out of greed, Shane.* Take your pick.

"Look, if I'm going to take this mysterious job of yours, I'll need an experienced person to handle the boat while I do the dive. Someone I trust, and I trust my friend Jagger over there."

She blinked once. Twice. He found himself studying her eyes. They tipped up slightly at the outer edges in a shape that was almost almond. They were dark, warm brown. They were narrowing at him beneath lowered brows.

He cleared his throat and looked at the bar, relieved to see Jagger threading his way through the tables with two beers and a basket of chips. He was in need of both, not to mention a social bailout.

Jagger set the chips in the middle of the table, handed Shane his beer, and slid into one of the two vacant chairs next to Gillian. Shane had to look down to avoid laughing at her not-quite-discreet attempts to move away. The woman was wound tighter than a Timex.

"I'm Cal Mackie." Jagger held out a hand to Gillian, who stared at it a second before shaking it. "Everybody calls me Jagger because I not only move like the master but am the world's foremost expert on the Rolling Stones. Anything you need to know about the world's greatest rock 'n' roll band, I'm the guy to ask."

Gillian gave him a deadpan look. "That skill must be in great demand in Cedar Key, Florida."

After a moment of silence, they all laughed at once, even Gillian, and the tension lifted from the table and dissipated. "Sorry," she said. "I couldn't resist. It's nice to meet you."

She sounded as if she meant it, but Shane saw the evil eye she cast in his direction when Jagger looked away.

For the next few minutes, they talked about the idle things strangers focus on when they don't know what else to talk about: weather, tourists, jobs.

"How many tours do you take out on *The Evangeline*?" Gillian asked. "Will it hurt your business if you take some time off to . . . uh . . ."—she looked at Jagger and faltered—"do a private job?"

Shane smiled. "It's okay. Jag knows about your dive offer so anything you can say to me, you can say in front of him." He pulled a big salt-laden chip from the bottom of the pile and crunched into it. "No, it won't hurt business. I don't run a steady tour service. I just pick up some extras when Harley over there has more than his people can handle." Or when Shane got desperate and needed a quick bailout.

"Did I hear my name?" Harley wound his way toward them, deftly balancing three glasses of water and three paper plates filled with oversized po'boys and coleslaw. He set them on the table and pointed to Gillian's bottle. "You want another?"

"Better not, but thanks." This time, her smile was genuine. Warm, even. What did a guy have to do to earn one of those smiles? Ply her with beer, maybe.

"Harley has never brought our food to the table." Jagger slid the plates around until they each had one in front of them. "Never. Gillian, I think he has a crush on you."

This time, Jagger got the warm smile. Shane was starting to get a complex. He sank his teeth into four inches of fried grouper stuffed between slabs of homemade bread and chewed while he pondered why the woman disliked him and, maybe more importantly, why he cared.

"What do you do for a living, besides hire guys for tough dives?" Jagger asked.

Shane chewed and listened; he'd wondered the same thing but knew that if he'd asked that question, she'd have given him the cold-bitch glare and not the laugh directed toward his friend—that would be the friend she'd been angry about him bringing here a few minutes ago.

"I'm a biologist over at Scrub State," she said. "Mostly, I keep an eye out for new wildlife that might have come into the area to upset the balance of things, make sure visitors don't feed the animals junk food, that kind of thing. And I'm the nuisance-gator trapper for Levy County."

"Seriously?" The word slipped out before Shane could stop it. "You catch them and relocate them?"

She raised an eyebrow at Shane. "Seriously. Don't look so shocked. I was raised on a gator ranch in Louisiana. I've been around them all my life."

"You just didn't mention gainful employment when we met earlier." She'd just thrown around a lot of money.

"It didn't seem important to our discussion. Speaking of which . . ." She took a sip of her beer and looked at Jagger, then Shane. "Will you take the job?"

Finally, down to the negotiations. "There are some things we need to do first, as I told you yesterday. I need to bring Jagger in to handle the dive boat, whether it's *The Evangeline* or something we lease on-site. Right now, I'm thinking it makes more sense for me to use my own equipment and take my own boat. Having Jagger along is nonnegotiable. I'll pay him out of what you're paying me, so don't worry about the money."

Shane didn't think he'd ever said the words "don't worry about the money" in his life. It felt kind of nice.

"Understood." She nodded, but her brows were knit in a worried expression as she turned to Jagger. "This might be a dangerous trip. You realize that, right?"

Jagger nodded. "That's why you need me. I used to fish that area with my dad, so I know it pretty well. And *The Evangeline*'s gonna need some work."

"Right, Shane told me that." She looked back at Shane. "How long will the retrofitting take?"

Shane pushed his plate aside and leaned back in his chair. He'd been thinking about a timeline. "Well, the hull might need to be re-plated to withstand the rough seas, all the mechanical and electrical systems and air locks will need to be checked. Most of that can be done here. We'll need to do a scouting run ahead of time, set up a base in Canada, and get the permits."

Gillian's face had grown pale, and her eyes widened in what looked to Shane like alarm. He continued. "There's more. We'll need to identify someone from the area to help us navigate, not just the water but the local politics. We don't know what the locals are sensitive about, and I'm guessing we want to get in and out without attracting a lot of attention."

She nodded but still had a glazed look on her face. He could see it as clearly as if she'd written "unprepared" across her forehead with a permanent marker. She had no clue what she'd asked of him. Which sort of pissed him off, a million dollars or not. Did she think he'd just sail up the coast, slip on some fins, and go wreck hunting?

"Finally, before any of those things happen, we need to know where we're going," he added. "Canada has more coastline than any other country on earth, and a hell of a lot of it borders the North Atlantic. We have to narrow it down if we have any hope of finding your ship."

Gillian finished off her beer, set the bottle down, then began picking the paper label off in shreds. "I'm sorry; I had no idea how complicated it all was, but it sounds like you know what you're doing.

"About the last part, the location, I might have some answers tonight. I've rented a place here in Cedar Key and brought an old trunk of family papers with me. I have no idea what's in it yet, but I'm hoping it will give us a clue."

Jagger cleared his throat. He'd been uncharacteristically silent while Shane went through his list of preparations. "Is there anybody in your family who might know more? The ship was coming from Spain, right? In the 1600s?"

"Yeah, that's my understanding." Gillian gathered her beer label shreds into a small pyramid. "I'm not sure exactly where the ship was headed, but I do know my family was part of the Grand Derangement."

Shane looked at Jagger, who looked back with a shrug. Good. He wasn't the only stupid guy at the table. "Explain."

She shoved the denuded bottle aside and took a sip of her water, running her fingers through the condensation formed on the sides of the glass. "Well, to make a long story shorter, the British ran the French colonists out of the maritime provinces in the mid-1700s. A lot of them in the so-called Grand Derangement, the Great Expulsion, fled to Louisiana. The French word for them, Acadians, got bastardized down to 'Cajuns' in modern times.

"The point being, though, that at the time of the expulsion, my family was in Nova Scotia, around Louisbourg. The family legend I've always heard is that Duncan Campbell, my ancestor, had a young son with him on the ship, and the boy survived. And here I am, all these years later." She laughed and shrugged. "No idea if that part's true, but obviously old Duncan didn't father babies from the depths of the Atlantic."

Shane grinned. "That would be a whole different kind of story."

Jagger broke into a chorus of the Stones' "2000 Light Years from Home," and Shane's head shaking finally earned him a genuine smile from Gillian. He liked it. Maybe too much.

"Can it, Mick." Shane had another question, a big one he should've asked yesterday. "Assuming we figure out where this ship went down, and assuming we can get the boat retrofitted and successfully anchor it in Canada, and assuming we find the shipwreck . . ." Those were a hell of a lot of assumptions already. "What are we looking for?"

Gillian looked down at her plate and picked at the remains of her sandwich. "It's a cross. Sort of a pendant, like you'd wear around your neck on a chain, except pretty big." She pointed to the smallest of the paper plates on the table. "Probably about that size. Like a priest might wear. It's worth a lot of money."

Shane studied her downcast eyes, fidgety hands, soft voice. This wasn't about money. "Why do you want it, Gillian? Why now? If I'm going to risk my life to find this thing, I at least want to know why I'm doing it."

"It's made of gold and is inset with garnets and rubies, or at least that's what I've read." She looked up at him, brows raised, but Shane shook his head. Not good enough. She could have one of those made for a thousand dollars.

"What about this particular cross makes it so valuable?"

She bit her lip and stared at the bar. Shane followed her gaze to the overdressed tourist guy he'd noticed when they arrived. Whoever he was didn't seem to be paying any attention to them, so she was stalling.

Shane leaned forward and kept his voice low. "Gillian, if you can't answer that question, I can't do the dive. Something doesn't add up, and I need to know the truth. You trap gators and work for the state, so you don't make the kind of money you were throwing around yesterday. What's so fucking special about that cross?"

She flinched but looked him in the eye. "It's believed to have belonged to the Knights Templars—you know, from the Crusades." She lowered her own voice to a whisper. "It's worth billions. And I need it."

Holy shit. Shane had heard of the lost Templar treasure; any diver who'd ever had delusions of finding some strike-it-rich sunken treasure knew about the riches that had never been found. "There was more lost than just one cross; the Templars had a lot of treasure that's unaccounted for."

"Here's an interesting thing," Jagger said. "My dad used to tell me stories when we'd be out on the trawler. Some folks over the years believed that part of the Templar treasure was lost off Nova Scotia on ships following the old Viking trade routes."

"So it could be true!" Gillian leaned back in her chair.

"I've heard those stories too," Shane said. "But the thing that doesn't jibe with Duncan Campbell is that the treasure was lost in the 1300s, not the late 1600s."

She nodded, her face still flush with excitement. "It still works with the family legend in a way. I've read that part of the Templar treasure was sent to the New World, but some of the Knights stashed in other European countries. Our family stories say that old Duncan somehow found the cross and stole it from the Templars, then grabbed his family and hopped the first ship to the New World. Ship sinks and—poof—the cross is gone, and so is Duncan."

Things still didn't add up for Shane; there was more Gillian wasn't telling them.

But what a story. His blood heated at the thought of going after a piece of the Knights Templars' treasure, warming up his muscles and firing off synapses in his diving brain. His thoughts spiraled into what breathing apparatus and mix of gases he'd need, how deep a wreck that old would have settled and how cold the water would have to be for it to have remained intact. Where Duncan Campbell might hide something so small and yet so valuable.

"Uh oh, Shane's thinking." Jagger grinned at him. "And I bet you're thinking this is the coolest damned thing you ever heard."

Shane laughed and finished off his beer. "Pretty much. What I still don't understand is why now? Why do you need to find this thing now when it's been forgotten for so long?"

The light went out of Gillian's eyes, and the circles under her eyes seemed to darken. "I've told you all I can," she said, her voice so soft he had to strain to hear it over the bar chatter. "Let's just say someone's life depends on us finding it. Someone really important to me."

Shane blew out a frustrated breath. He had a feeling that was all the information Gillian was willing to give for now. Maybe he could wear her down enough to trust him with the truth eventually.

In the meantime, he had enough to hook him: a million dollars and the chance to discover something archaeologists and historians had been puzzling over for centuries. He'd be like a fucking underwater Indiana Jones.

"Okay," he finally said. He looked at Jagger, who nodded. "We'll do it."

There—the warm smile again. Give the woman what she wants and she'll reward you. A good thing to remember.

"When do you think you can get started?" Gillian had come back to life, losing the haunted look as she leaned over the table, brown eyes warm and twinkling. "What can I do to help?"

This question Shane had prepared for. "We're going into the winter season now, so I figure we can get *The Evangeline*'s work done here while we research Duncan's story and ship. Then we can sail her up the East Coast, do our business in Louisbourg or wherever we decide's the best place to set up a base . . ."

He counted on his fingers until he reached nine. "We should be able to do our test dive by the end of May, first of June. Then we'll hit prime diving season in July."

Shane had expected Gillian to be excited by that timeline—it was fast, but realistic. Instead, she'd gone all pale again, with eyebrows knit in a worried line. She bit her lip so hard he expected to see blood gushing out.

"That won't work," she said, taking a quick glance at the bar. "We have to be finished by the end of September."

He stared at her. "Tell me you mean September of next year."

Gillian shook her head. "We have twenty-seven days."

7

Gillian's hopes sank with each change of expression on Shane's face.

"Twenty-seven days?" Disbelief.

"Right, you're joking. Funny." Sexy smile.

"Good God, you're serious." Smile replaced by lowered brows and frown.

"Why the hell would you even think that was possible?" Shane finally settled his face into a seabed of confusion. She knew how he felt. When he'd described all the things they needed to do in order to make this dive happen, fingers of panic had begun creeping around her throat and she'd had to pick at the beer label to distract herself so that she wouldn't hyperventilate.

She spoke softly and couldn't bring herself to look at him. "I know this sounds melodramatic, but someone's life really does depend on the dive being done this month."

Shane shoved his plate away and drained his beer, setting the bottle back on the table with a thud. "Whose life? And your story better be convincing."

God, what she wouldn't give for a nice snarling gator to wrangle right now. Alligators were simple and predictable. They'd run from you if they could and fight if they had to. She seemed to be trapped, afraid to either run or fight.

If she told Shane the truth, he might do something to jeopardize Holly. Tell the authorities, maybe, or confront the gun-toting guy at the bar.

If she kept lying to him, or only giving him half-truths, he might walk away. But she'd seen his imagination take hold during the Knights Templars story. His green eyes had lit up like they had a flame behind them, and he practically radiated adrenaline and testosterone.

She had to rely on his financial problems, his ego, and the lure of adventure to keep him committed to the dive. She couldn't risk Holly's safety.

"Well?" Frustration had given way to impatience, and he thrummed long, tapered fingers on the top of the table.

"I can't tell you any more. Please believe me when I say it's important, though. Someone could die if I don't come up with that cross."

Shane leaned forward, his green eyes narrowed and a dangerous curve to his lips. "But you're sure willing for me to die on some half-assed, half-planned treasure hunt, aren't you? Well forget it. I might be broke, but I'm not stupid. You can keep your bag of money. I might lose my boat, but I'll still be alive."

He pushed his chair back, caught Jagger's gaze, and jerked his head toward the door. "Have a nice life, Gillian Campbell."

She sat frozen in place, watching him walk away, the bang of the door slamming behind him audible even over the bar noise. "Will he change his mind?"

Jagger pushed his chair back as well. "Not unless you tell him the truth. Shane's been through some shit and he's still trying to put his life back together. He doesn't trust people easily, especially if he thinks they're using him."

She shook her head. "He needs the money, and I'm offering a lot of it. Why does it have to be any more complicated than that?"

Jagger smiled, and Gillian couldn't help but think how easy it was to underestimate this guy with his laid-back mien and his Rolling

Stones songs. He said Shane didn't trust easily, but this was a person he did trust.

"Shane's not a simple man, so you might want to keep that in mind and not expect simple reactions from him. Yeah, he needs the money. He probably even thinks he's considering the job because of the money. But it's more than that."

Gillian stared at the closed exit door, willing Shane to walk back in, to make things easier. "If he's not doing it for the money, why *is* he considering it?"

Jagger paused before answering. "If you tell him I said this, I'll have to kill you."

Gillian let out a harsh laugh. He'd have to get in line behind Tex and his cohorts. "Fair enough. What?"

"Shane needs this job to remind him how good he is at this kind of thing. Planning. Organizing. Doing complicated dives. He needs to find himself again; he's been lost for a long time." Jagger stood up and threw his napkin on the table. "He'll help you if he can, but not if you don't come clean with him. Your choice."

Gillian didn't know many Rolling Stones songs, but she caught the chorus of "You Can't Always Get What You Want" before Jagger exited Harley's.

What a nightmare. She rubbed her temples and looked up to see Tex, or Son of Tex, or whoever the guy was, watching Jagger leave. He shifted his gaze to her, and suddenly the air-conditioning felt too cold. Chill bumps spread up and down her arms, and her palms grew clammy. Could he have heard what they were saying?

He cocked his head at her and tapped his watch. She got the message: the clock is ticking. Like a bomb.

She put some cash on the table and avoided another look at the gun-toting terrorist on her way out of the restaurant. The midday heat felt good and she leaned against the giant clam to let it soak into her skin and bring her numbed hands and feet back to life.

"Looks like your negotiations went south."

Gillian jumped away from the clam, tripped over the edge of the stump it sat on, and pinwheeled to stay on her feet. "You think?"

Son of Tex didn't smile. His expression was inscrutable, his features bland. Short mud-brown hair. Mud-colored tanned skin. Probably had mud-brown eyes, but Gillian wouldn't know because she hadn't gotten close enough in Harley's to see their color and he again wore his mirrored sunglasses. She only saw a funhouse mirror version of herself.

"Here's what I do think. That you need to go after Mr. Burke and change his mind. If he's no longer useful to us, we'll provide you with another diver to find the object my employer wants. But you've lost valuable time, and you'll have the death of Mr. Burke and his friend on your conscience."

Gillian's mouth went dry. "Why would you kill them? They don't know anything."

"To show you we're serious, Ms. Campbell. Your actions, or in-actions, have consequences."

"Why can't your employer just hire his own diver and leave me alone?"

"It's against the rules."

Gillian frowned. Rules? "Rules for what?"

He didn't answer, but walked down the ramp of Harley's. He turned back when he reached the sidewalk. "We'll be in touch to-night. I suggest you have Mr. Burke convinced by then. Try giving him a blow job. Works for me."

Not even at gunpoint, asshat. Gillian watched him walk toward the head of C Street. As soon as he turned the corner onto First, she jumped in the pickup and drove after him. It wasn't Tex—the accent was slightly different. But he worked with Tex. If she could find out where he was staying, maybe she could convince Deputy Miles to keep an eye on him or find out what he was driving and get a license plate to trace.

By the time she turned, however, he'd been absorbed into the Saturday bustle of the village, and First branched off into a dozen side streets. He could've gone anywhere.

Gillian looped around the downtown blocks a few times but never spotted the guy.

Finally, she turned toward the marina. She had to tell Shane the truth and hope Jagger was right about his willingness to help.

She parked at the edge of the lot and, on impulse, called her sister. Gretchen and her husband had tried for years to have kids before they'd final gone the in vitro route. Even then, it hadn't looked like a baby was in their future. They'd begun researching adoption possibilities when she finally got pregnant.

Holly had arrived seven weeks early, a tiny, shriveled, pale thing who'd grown over three years into a black-haired, vivacious miracle, full of life and energy and sunshine. Because of medical complications, she was the only child Gretchen would ever have.

Gretchen's phone kicked over to voice mail, and Gillian closed her eyes at the singsong lilt of Holly's voice. "We isn't here right now. Leaves a mestige . . . a what, Mommy?" Then a giggle before the beep.

Gillian left a quick "How are you? Just checking in" message and repeated the lie she'd told her parents about going on vacation with Vivian. "If anything happens and you need to talk, call my cell." She couldn't think of anything else to say that wouldn't make Gretchen alarmed or suspicious.

Gillian ended the call, exited the truck, and went into the busy little marina-gift-shop-turned-convenience-store-turned-office. A bottle of bourbon and five minutes later, she stood on the dock next to *The Evangeline*, screwing up her courage.

If she told Shane the truth and he still wanted out—and who would blame him?—what in God's name was she going to do?

"You might as well come aboard."

She looked across the deck from bow to stern, finally spotting Shane on top of the pilothouse. He'd changed into a pair of baggy olive-green shorts that hung a little low on his hips and nothing else that she could see. Not that she hadn't already—all the rest, except what had been wrapped in chocolate-themed boxers.

She held up the bottle. "I brought a peace offering."

His voice dripped cynicism. "That's all you brought? No more bags of cash?"

Gillian took a deep breath and dove in. "The cash, plus some bourbon and the truth, if you'll hear me out."

After a long pause and a skeptical look, he said, "Come on, then."

He disappeared from view and a few seconds later emerged from the door that led both to the pilothouse and to his master suite. It really was a nice boat. Not fancy, but comfortable.

She walked across the gangway and had gotten almost to the deck rail when a bell sounded from the boat moored at the next slip, surprising her. She twisted to see the source of the noise and tripped.

The fall seemed impossibly slow, although Gillian's rational mind told her it happened in a matter of seconds. The bottle of Jack Daniel's sailed toward the bow while the rest of her lurched toward the stern. Then her eyes latched onto a close-up of tanned skin stretched over firm pecs; Shane had caught her.

His hands grasped her waist and she had a shameful urge to rest her cheek against his chest. He smelled like the sun and some kind of citrus-based soap or tanning lotion, and she could feel his heart speed up.

Shane didn't seem any more anxious to let the moment pass than Gillian, but she finally stepped back and broke contact. He looked down at the broken bottle of Jack Daniel's Black Label, glass and amber liquid spreading across the wooden deck like diamond-studded honey.

"That is a pity." He shifted his focus back to her. "You're a danger on two legs, you know that? Anyone ever called you a klutz?"

Gillian smiled. "Thanks for catching me instead of old Jack over there. And everyone knows I'm a klutz. My dad always said it was a miracle I learned to walk at all, for all the falling I did." She leaned over and picked up one of the larger pieces of glass. "Show me where the supplies are and I'll clean this up."

"Later." Shane took her elbow and propelled her past the bourbon puddle and toward the hatch door. "You wanna talk up top or inside?"

Gillian thought about Son of Tex and his gun, running around somewhere on Way Key. "Inside," she said. "You never know who might be listening. Is Jagger here?"

"No." Shane opened the door and motioned her inside. "Take a left down the hallway. We'll talk in the salon."

She followed the narrow hallway to the rear of the boat and was surprised when it opened onto a large room that held booth seats upholstered in gray stripes, built-in tables of the same honey-golden wood she'd seen in the pilothouse, and a well-outfitted kitchen. "*The Evangeline* doesn't look this big from the outside."

Shane pulled a couple of sodas from the small refrigerator tucked beneath a counter. "It's forty-six feet, but whoever planned the interior space was a genius. Every inch is used well." He held up a regular and a diet soda.

"Diet, thanks." Gillian took the can and popped the tab. The carbonation didn't mix well with the acid churning in her stomach. She needed to get this conversation finished. Get things settled.

Shane motioned to the benches and they sat facing each other with one of the small tables between them. She set the leather messenger bag with the money on the table. The seconds ticked by, each a heavier weight than the one before.

"Well?" Shane crossed his arms over his chest. "This is your dime, but my time isn't unlimited."

Gillian nodded. "I'm not sure where to start, but I guess I'll begin with my friend Vivian's car wreck, the one I at first thought was an accident but then learned otherwise."

She went through it all. Every conversation with Tex. The threats. The bank account. The money left on the steps of her trailer. The attempts to track Tex down with the phone company and the sheriff's office.

When she began the story, Shane did a lot of grimacing and eye rolling. She wasn't sure at what point he started believing her, but by the time she got to the part about the guy with the gun sitting at the bar in Harley's, he uncrossed his arms and leaned forward.

"I noticed that guy. Harley's doesn't pick up much tourist trade—basically because it looks like a dive." Shane frowned. "Well, it is a dive. But that guy wasn't even trying to blend in, so he wanted you to know he was there. Has he followed you anywhere else?"

Gillian shook her head. "I don't know. Maybe. But he was there today to make sure you took the dive job. After you and Jagger left . . ." God, she hated to tell him the rest.

Shane reached out and took her hand, and when he spoke, his voice was gentle. "After we left, what? He threatened you?"

"Not me. You and Jagger. He said if you didn't do the dive, he'd find someone else for me to work with and I'd have your deaths on my conscience."

"Did he now." It wasn't a question. Shane had turned into a thundercloud with a face. "He might find he's threatening the wrong guys."

He got up and walked to the kitchen, his movements slow and deliberate. He poured the rest of his soda down the sink. Leaned against the counter with his arms crossed over his chest. Looked down. His face was a mask, carefully composed and revealing nothing.

"Go home, Gillian."

Her heart sank. "Shane, he wasn't making idle threats. I really—"

"I'm not saying no. I just need to think. I need to talk to Jagger because he's been dragged into this too, and he deserves a vote. Leave me your phone number."

A tiny ember of hope sparked to life in Gillian's gut. He hadn't said no. She pulled out one of her Florida Wildlife Commission business cards, jotted her cell number on the back, and pushed it to the center of the table. "I rented a cottage across the key, behind the airport." She paused, not wanting to push but needing to. "You won't wait too long to decide, will you?"

Shane finally looked up at her, his brows in an angry line above fierce green eyes. "I know: twenty-seven days."

8

Only once in his life had Shane felt more helpless, less in control of his destiny. That time, he'd deserved it and more. This time, he hadn't done anything wrong.

Or maybe God was still punishing him for ten years ago, the Almighty's idea of an almighty big joke. *Yeah, see old Shane Burke down there, St. Peter? He thinks he's socked himself away in the middle of nowhere, where he won't be responsible for anyone but himself. So let's throw him a little curveball. Let's make him responsible for not only his best friend's life, but a little kid's and a woman's. And, just for kicks, let's give him the hots for the woman.*

Thanks, and amen. He hoped God was enjoying the joke.

Shane took a curve too fast and skidded his beat-up Jeep off the narrow road, lurching to a stop less than a hand's width from the trunk of a massive live oak. *Fuck!* He beat his fists on the steering wheel and then rested his forehead on it and closed his eyes.

He hadn't sent Gillian home because he needed the time to think; he'd just wanted to get rid of her so that he could have a drink. Except he'd poured the whiskey into the glass, looked at it for a good minute or two, and then poured it down the sink while his taste buds mourned.

Because he had to help her; he'd known from about halfway through her story that bailing wasn't an option. And he had to be sober when he did it or he'd fuck everything up. He might fuck everything up anyway, but at least he'd do it sober.

Maybe it was all a big, sick joke—that's what he'd thought at first. Maybe her friend's accident had been nothing more than an accident. Maybe a simple computer glitch had temporarily frozen her bank account. Maybe "Tex" and his buddy at Harley's and their boss, whoever he or she was, were nothing but sadistic freaks.

But they'd had photos of the kid. Knew what she was wearing, where she lived, where she attended day care.

They'd known about him. About his financial situation, that he had the technical skills to do the dive and that he might be desperate enough to jump at the cash.

Who had access to that kind of information on private citizens, especially private citizens in rural Florida? They'd found Gillian through that local-yokel TV interview, which was bizarre unless someone were doing regular searches for things related to the Knights Templars. Anyone savvy enough to do a search for certified technical divers in this area could probably have come up with his name.

But to get that much intel that quickly after Gillian's interview had broadcast? It took someone with a lot of money, a lot of power, and not many scruples.

Even if Shane had been able to walk away from the threat to the child, he'd unwittingly dragged Jagger into this mess. He didn't give a shit what happened to himself, but he cared a lot about his friend.

They'd been buddies since Shane's Marine Corps days in San Diego. When he'd had free weekends, which wasn't often, he'd leave Camp Pendleton and drive down to La Jolla for the cave diving. Jagger, two years younger, was in college in San Diego and would go to La Jolla on weekends for the surfing.

On the surface, he guessed the Marine and the hippie had made an odd twosome, but they had a lot in common. Both had grown up with commercial fishermen and the whole culture surrounding the industry. They were more comfortable on water than land.

When he'd run into trouble, gotten discharged, and started drinking too much, it was Jagger who'd convinced Shane to come with him to Cedar Key. His dad was fighting cancer and he wanted to be with him in his last days. Shane hadn't known where else to go.

He wasn't going to let this ridiculous game destroy his friend. And the "rules" comment Gillian had shared made him think it was a game to whatever sick fucks were behind this.

After he calmed down, he drove to the little wooden shack—"cottage" was too grand a word—Jagger had inherited from his father. Cal Mackie had built the thing himself after its predecessor had been flattened by a hurricane in the eighties, saying it made no sense to put a lot of money into housing that was just going to get bulldozed by a force of nature every decade or two.

In a nod to the Stones' "Paint It Black," Jagger had coated the house in dark-charcoal exterior latex with a bright-red door. Shane's buddy marched to his own drummer, and it wasn't always Charlie Watts.

Jagger opened the door before Shane reached it. "I had a visit from our friend Gillian," he told him, raising his voice to be heard over the countrified tones of "Sweet Virginia."

Jagger raised his eyebrows. "Did she break down and tell you the truth? And did you believe her?"

"Yeah, and you're gonna need to sit down for this one."

A few minutes' worth of talking later, Jagger poured out his beer and turned off the sound system that had been blaring out "Exile on Main Street." "Even Mick has to shut up sometimes," he said, shrugging as he sat in his dad's old recliner and popped the footrest up. "Man, this is seriously screwed up. It's too damned creepy not to be true."

Shane slumped down on his end of the sofa and propped his feet on the scarred brown coffee table. "I thought so too." He tried to figure out a polite way to say what he wanted to say, but polite had never been one of his skills. He took out a black pouch he'd brought with him from the Jeep. He'd stuffed it full of money from Gillian's stash, which she'd insisted on leaving on *The Evangeline.*

"Look, I want you to take this and get lost for the next thirty days. Cover your tracks and stay out of sight until this is over, one way or another."

Jagger leaned over and snagged the pouch with one hand, unfastened its velcro straps, and looked inside. "Cool. Always did like Ben Franklin." He slowly refastened the straps, then lobbed it at Shane's head hard enough that it hurt when it clocked him in the mouth.

"Ow." Shane touched a finger to his lip and it came back bloody. "What was that for?"

"Go fuck yourself. You can't do this alone. You need me."

"I . . ." Shane closed his eyes. Damn it, he did need Jagger, not just for moral support but to get *The Evangeline* refitted and stocked. "I just don't . . ." He slumped down farther on the sofa. "Whatever."

Jagger laughed. "You are such a caveman. You need to get in touch with your inner warm side so you can express yourself in more than one-syllable words."

"So now you're Martha-fucking-Stewart?"

"Does this house look like Martha's been anywhere near it?"

Every surface except the ones they sat on—and the pristine sound system—supported pyramids of clothes, mountains of take-out boxes, and stacks of books. Shane stuck his tongue to his lip to see if it was still bleeding. "You have a point."

Jagger leaned forward. "Here's the deal, Lucille. You don't want me to get hurt. I know that. You don't want to go through a repeat of when Kevin died, but you've gotta put that shit behind you and realize it's not the same scenario—even if you had done something wrong back then, which you didn't."

"I—"

"Shut up, Shane." Jagger pulled his hair back into a tail and snapped the elastic band on it that he usually wore around his wrist so that he wouldn't lose it. "This isn't up for negotiation. I'm in. Just tell me what's next."

Shit. On some selfish, asshole level, he was relieved. "You got a calendar?"

They spent the next half hour looking at dates. "Everything's going to have to fall perfectly into place for this to happen," Shane finally said, sitting back and rolling his shoulders to loosen up the muscles grown stiff from bending over the coffee table.

"Assuming Gillian's right and the ship went down near Louisbourg, it sure would be helpful to have somebody in place who had everything ready for us by the time we got there." Jagger stretched and propped up the recliner footrest again. "I don't have any of my dad's old contacts, though."

Shane finally entertained a thought that had been trying to nudge its way into his head all afternoon. He'd been ignoring it, but now he had to let it out. "Damn it, I might have to call Charlie."

After his dive partner Kevin died, Shane had gone back to Charlie's retirement spot in North Carolina, south of Wilmington. His head had been too screwed up to accept Charlie's tough love, and Shane had walked out. He hadn't talked to his uncle since.

"Think he'll talk to you? He probably still knows some guys up north."

Yeah, he probably did. Whether he'd talk to his long-lost nephew was another matter. "All I can do is try. In the meantime, start making a list of supplies to buy and what retrofitting you know we'll need besides the stuff we've talked about. Tomorrow, we're going to have to toss around a whole lot of money to get work done fast."

"Will do." Jagger leaned back and flipped the Stones back on, albeit at a lower volume. "One thing that will help is that we're going into the off-season, even for the Gulf. So it might be easier to find workers."

Shane hefted himself off the sofa. "While you work on lists, I'll go and let Gillian know we're in, if not exactly by choice." Except a part of him felt as if it had awakened from a long sleep and was excited to be back in action, which was pathetic. "She said she had a trunk of old family stuff with her; maybe we can get some more clues as to where *The Marcus Aurelius* went down." Jagger didn't answer; he already had his head bent low over a notebook and was writing at a fast clip.

Shane let himself out and drove across the key toward the little airport—a fancy name for a couple of short runways that often had seagulls walking across them, no terminal or control tower, and room for four single-engine planes. Several cottages sat along a narrow strip of land beside the runway, convenient for visitors who wanted to fly in and walk a few hundred feet to their rental accommodations.

He eased his Jeep along a road barely wide enough to accommodate two cars, peering through the twilight gloom until he spotted a silver pickup like the one Gillian had described as hers, sitting next to an orange rectangular house that looked like someone had plopped a crayon box down in the middle of a dense stand of live oaks and palms.

Pulling in behind the truck, Shane sat for a moment looking out at the narrow inlet and the Gulf beyond. The sunset bled vivid reflections of orange and gold and crimson onto the water, and a couple of white herons stood out in stark relief against the marsh vegetation on the little spit of land on the other side of the inlet.

There were no doors on the back side of the house facing the street, so he walked around to the waterfront side—and straight into a hellhound. Big, solid black, with bared white teeth, bristling fur, and . . . good God, the beast had foam coming from his snarling lips.

"Hey, buddy." Jagger needed to add guns to his supply list. Shane's service weapon was too big to carry discreetly, although it would be nice to have now.

Shane and the dog seemed to be at a standoff. If he ran back to his truck, it would not only be unmanly; the dog would chase him. It might be more macho to order the demon dog to cease and desist.

"No," he said firmly. The dog snarled and took a step closer. "Sit. Stay." The black muzzle wrinkled and contracted, showing more teeth.

"Tank, down." Gillian stepped out the back door of the cottage and propped her hands on her hips. "Come."

With a final deep growl, the hellhound turned and walked to Gillian, circled her, and sat beside her. His upper lip curled in a canine Elvis impersonation, except with evil intent.

"Nice dog." A mutt if he'd ever seen one, but she probably thought he was Westminster worthy. "His name is Tank?"

She leaned down and scratched behind the demon's ears and the black fuzzy tail thumped happily. "What did you do to him?"

"Me? I was minding my own business and he attacked me."

"Uh huh." She looked him up and down, but then frowned, and came closer. Tank moved with her. "Did he cut your lip?"

Shane touched his finger to the wound. "Well, no, Jagger did that."

Gillian laughed. "You're certainly popular today."

"Yeah, let's not even talk about the guy who threatened to kill me."

Her smile faded. "Did you make a decision?"

Part of him wanted to make her wait, let her sweat a while longer. But this wasn't her fault. "Yes, I'll help you. Jagger's in, too. At least we're going to do our best."

Oh, hell. She was going to cry.

She threw her arms around his neck in a tight hug. "Thank you. God, I'm sorry you've gotten dragged into this, but thank you."

Shane glanced down to see how the hellhound was reacting to his master's public display of affection, but the damned dog had gone to sleep. Might as well take advantage of the opportunity. He slipped his arms around her and hugged her back.

Shane was six three, so he gauged Gillian to be about five eight, a nice height for hugging. Her dark hair smelled like lemons and he wished more than anything he was here for pleasure, that they could order a pizza and watch the sunset and get to know each other.

She looked up at him, and he felt the moment her heart rate sped up, beating a steady rhythm against his chest. He angled his head and leaned in, touching his lips to hers in a soft exploration, then grazing her cheek below her closed eyes, then her jawline.

He stepped back, and the look she gave him when she opened her eyes was sad and maybe filled with the same regrets he was feeling. "I wish we'd met under different circumstances," she said.

"Me too." But they didn't have time for personal stuff. Not now. Maybe not ever, depending on how this adventure played out. Shane glanced back at the water, which looked black now that the disappearing sun had only a few faint glimmers left. "I thought maybe we could go through your family stuff."

She nodded. "Yeah, I have it on the table inside." She stepped over the now-snoring dog and held open the back door. "Want a sandwich or something?"

"Sounds good." He'd only made it through half his lunch and had been too preoccupied since then to think about food. He'd been too busy avoiding alcohol.

He followed her into the little house, where she opened the hinged lid of the carved wooden box that sat on the table. Musty envelopes covered in ornate writing slid off the top, and Shane glanced at the postmarks. Most were from the 1940s of Louisiana, addressed to various Campbells and Jeffersons and Mitchells.

For the next hour, they ate turkey sandwiches, made small talk, and combed through a lot of old family documents. The only thing useful, or at least Gillian hoped it would be useful, was a letter from her great-uncle Zeke to her grandfather.

"It has a phone number on it," she said. "The letter's more than ten years old, but it's a start, at least. Maybe he still has the same number."

Shane read the letter, which didn't make any mention of the Campbell legend. "What makes you think he'll know anything?"

"My dad said Zeke had done some digging into the family genealogy." She gathered the plates and took them the four steps into the kitchen. "Plus, he's the oldest living Campbell, by far. I just hope he can remember something useful. Of course we have to find him first."

She sat back down at the table and began piling papers back into the box.

Shane laughed and held up a photo he'd set aside. "Care to explain this?"

"Oh jeez, let me see that." Gillian snatched the photo from him and groaned. "Why did my grandmother keep this?"

It showed a teenage Gillian, all long legs, short shorts, and big hair, sitting astride an alligator, her hands placed on its neck.

"Were you riding him? He doesn't look too impressed." Shane grinned. "Nice legs, though. Yours aren't bad, either."

Gillian shook her head. "Her name was Bertha, and she was one of the first gators my parents brought to the farm. She was pretty tame—well, as tame as any gator ever gets. They'll still take an arm off if they get in a mood."

"What gets a gator in a moo—"

Outside the door, Tank sprang to life and barked, but this time he wasn't barking at Shane.

"What's he barking at?" Gillian pushed her chair back, but Shane beat her to the door. He walked onto the patio, looking around. He didn't see anything—until he followed the dog's gaze. Tank seemed to be barking at the sky.

"Look up, over the tree line." Gillian came to stand beside him and pointed in the direction of town. One section of the night sky glowed with a golden, hazy light. "Looks like a fire, coming from the direction of town."

"Maybe we should check it out." Shane pulled his Jeep keys from his jeans pocket while Gillian tugged Tank inside and locked the cottage door.

He was behind the wheel and she'd climbed halfway into the passenger seat when an explosion seemed to rock the very land beneath them, followed by a plume of flame that shot high in the sky from the other side of the island. They'd gotten to the end of the airport runway and curved toward town when the second explosion went off.

This time, more flames were visible, reaching red, angry fingers all the way to heaven.

9

The closer they got to town, bumping along the uneven roads in Shane's old Jeep, the higher the flames in town grew. Gillian hoped God forgave selfish prayers made by frantic women; still she prayed that this fire—these explosions—had nothing to do with her.

"Damn it." Shane jerked the Jeep to a stop when he tried to turn onto C Street and found the road crammed with traffic at a standstill. He managed to back out and continued another block. This time, he got a couple of streets farther before running into a makeshift barricade manned by a young uniformed cop who didn't look a day over eighteen.

"Let's walk from here." Shane pulled the Jeep into an alleyway and tucked it tight next to a building so that another vehicle could get by if necessary.

They got out and walked toward the fire. Its heat warmed Gillian's skin even from two blocks away and by the time they rounded the next corner, it had become downright hot. The air smelled of smoke and charred wood and rotten eggs.

"Gas," Shane said. "Probably what caused the explosions."

At least the night was still, the wind fairly calm for the islands, so maybe it wouldn't spread and burn the whole town down.

Oh, God. "It looks . . ." Gillian didn't want to say it.

Shane said it for her, his tone flat. "It looks like it's coming from Harley's."

They remained silent the rest of the way, and Gillian had to walk fast to keep up with Shane's long strides. Even before they turned the last corner, they saw it. Harley's was engulfed in flames, and Cedar Key's volunteer fire department personnel were out in force with ladder trucks, a fire engine, and rescue vehicles.

A lot of their work seemed focused on hosing down the adjacent structures to keep the fire from spreading. Gillian didn't see how anything in the restaurant itself could be saved.

She spotted Jagger near the far end of the building, leaning over a figure on the sidewalk. "Shane, look."

"Shit." Shane wove through the onlookers, and Gillian trailed in his wake.

Harley sat cross-legged on the ground, the tears that streaked down his cheeks reflecting the red of the flames. Shane knelt beside him and talked for a moment, then he and Jagger walked a few yards down the block, deep in conversation.

Did Harley have family? Did he have a home, or did he live here? Gillian couldn't stand to see him sitting there alone, so she went to stand beside him, leaned over, and gave him a hug.

"It's all I have." His salt-and-pepper hair was wet and plastered to his head, and he had a scar on the side of his head near the hairline that Gillian hadn't noticed at lunch. He still wore the old apron he'd had on in the restaurant earlier, but it was more black than white now.

"Did you live here?" Gillian sat on the sidewalk beside him and, after a short hesitation, took his hand. Harley needed to talk, and listening might be the only way she could help.

"Yeah, I do—I did." The tears had stopped, but he still watched the fire as if in a daze. "Bought this place with Cal Mackie when he came back to Cedar Key for good, about a year before he got sick."

"That's Jagger's dad?"

Harley nodded. "Fine man. Jagger is, too, although he tries like hell to cover it up. He'll find himself eventually; took Cal a while to figure things out, too."

Harley's voice had calmed from a thin, shrill rasp to something deeper, closer to what Gillian remembered from their brief acquaintance. She needed to keep him talking. "What about Jagger's mom?"

Harley smiled. "She thought she was a free spirit, said she didn't mind that her man stayed gone most of the year riding out the summer season in New England and Canada and the winter fishing in the South. But she wandered off and left the boy behind when he wasn't but five or six.

"Fine man, Cal." His gaze followed the line of flames, which had finally begun to lose some height. "Did I tell you I bought this place with Cal when he came back to Cedar Key for good?"

Gillian was no doctor, but state wildlife employees had to be trained in basic emergency treatment. Though she didn't think Harley was hurt, psychological trauma was another matter. They needed to get him someplace where he could dry off and get warm.

She craned her neck to look around the sea of legs surrounding them and finally spotted Shane and Jagger walking toward them. Jagger looked almost as shocked as Harley and also was wet and dirty. Shane's face was set in granite, his jaw clenched, eyes stony and cold. The man was pissed.

Gillian's heart took a dive toward her ankles. That expression had to mean her worst fears were true; this fire was somehow related to her. *Damn it.*

All the stress of the last two days sat on her shoulders, and it felt almost too heavy for her frame to support. She struggled to her feet just before Shane and Jagger reached her.

Jagger nodded toward Harley. "How's he doing?"

Gillian dropped her voice so that Harley wouldn't hear. "I think he's in shock. Is there somewhere we can get him some dry clothes? I guess"—she looked around at the emergency personnel and spotted a couple of Levy County Sheriff's Office sedans—"the deputies will want to talk to him but maybe they can do it later?"

Shane had spotted the cars as well. "I'll talk to them. We've got a short-term solution at least."

"I'm gonna take Harley to *The Evangeline*," Jagger said, looking back at the bar, which continued to burn but at least was well under control. "I'll stay there with him tonight and Shane's staying with you."

Gillian dropped the volume of her voice even further. If Shane thought she needed a big bad protector, that confirmed her suspicions. "Was it the guy we saw at lunch today?"

Jagger nodded, and Gillian realized she'd never seen him so serious. No songs, no grins, no jokes. "It was my fault. I went after him and this is what happened."

Gillian needed to hear that story, but not now. Jagger had his own shock to cope with. "Harley loves you—you know that?"

He looked back at her, a bedraggled stray cat now instead of a swashbuckling rocker. His brown eyes told her he felt the same way about Harley. "He loved my dad," Jagger said. "He worked for him for years, whenever Dad would fish the Gulf. I thought going out on the open water with them was the coolest thing in the world."

"He loved your dad, but he loves you too—a lot." She looked down at Harley, who seemed to have sunk into his own world, a world that had nothing in it but his stunned mind and the smoking ruins of his life. "I think you're probably the only one who can help him through this unless . . . does he have family?"

Jagger smiled at the older man. "No, he's an old bachelor play-boy." He smiled bigger. "Me, I guess. I'm his family." He stuck his hands in his jeans pockets and shivered. "Just so you know, I told Shane we should take Harley with us on the dive. He doesn't know the waters in that area, but he knows *The Evangeline* and he can fix anything with a motor in it."

Damn it, no. Not another person at risk. "I don't want him involved. He needs to—"

"He needs something to keep him occupied and whether we like it or not, he's already involved." Jagger stepped around her and knelt down beside the older man, their foreheads almost touching, Jagger's long dark hair mingling with the short white-tinged brush cut of the old fisherman as they talked.

Harley nodded, and Jagger helped him to his feet. "When Shane gets back, tell him we're headed to the marina. He can tell the cops where to find us."

On impulse, Gillian stretched her arms around Harley's waist and, in a few seconds, she felt him return the hug. "I'm so, so sorry," she whispered. About more than she could ever tell him.

She watched them walk away, Jagger with his arm looped protectively around Harley's shoulders, never mind that the older man had at least two or three inches of height on him.

"Let's go—cops say they can talk to Harley tomorrow."

Gillian flinched at Shane's voice close behind her. She was so damned jumpy, but that seemed normal under the circumstances. Shane's face still wore that stony, cold expression, so she walked alongside him and didn't try to talk.

They remained silent on the drive to *The Evangeline*, until Shane parked in the marina's private lot. "I'm going to spend tonight at your place but need to pick up some clothes. Come on board while I get them."

Gillian bit her lip to keep from telling him to stop being so damned bossy but reminded herself he had every right. She got out of the Jeep and slammed the door. "You going to tell me what happened?"

"No." Shane locked the vehicle and headed toward the slip where *The Evangeline* was docked. Gillian could either trot after him or walk at a more dignified pace.

Hell, she grew up on an alligator farm; she'd never been dignified. She ran to catch up with him. "'No' isn't an acceptable answer. I have a right to know what kind of damage I've caused now."

He wheeled on her, causing her to crash into his chest. And here they were again, with his hands on her waist and her nose pressed into that sexy little dent between his pecs—which she could see because her nose hit at the exact point he'd stopped buttoning his shirt.

They stayed that way for a few heart-racing seconds before Shane released her. "Stop being a martyr. You're a victim here as much as anybody; nobody's blaming you except yourself. And I'll fill you in. Let's just get back to your place first."

"Okay, sorry."

"And stop apologizing."

"Sor . . . Okay."

The tension between them dissipated, and he walked at a more comfortable pace, turning along the maze of piers until they reached the gangplank. Shane stood back and motioned her ahead of him.

"Aren't you being gallant tonight." She walked across the narrow wooden structure and stepped down onto the deck.

"Not really. You're a klutz and I have a better chance of catching you—and not ending up in the water—if I'm behind you."

"Nice." Except, as soon as they walked back to the door into the interior, Gillian remembered why they were here and her lightened mood came crashing back to earth. "Is Harley going to be okay?"

"Yeah, he's tough. He'll reel for a while, but he'll land on his feet." Shane led the way through the door and cut right into the hallway behind the pilothouse, then descended a few steps into the bedroom.

Now that she wasn't distracted by an almost-naked man with a mostly empty bottle of bourbon, Gillian had a chance to look around. She stood in the doorway while Shane went into the bathroom and banged drawers and cabinets. Like the rest of *The Evangeline*, the room was heavy on the honey-colored wood—birch, she thought.

But it was a lot more spacious than she'd have expected on a ship this size. The queen-size bed had enough room on either side to walk; an entertainment system and nightstands had been built into the slightly curved wall that followed the shape of the hull. She'd spotted a small washer and dryer in an alcove across the hall.

Shane came out with a toiletry case and tossed it on the bed, then went to the closet and pulled out a small duffel. Black straps stretched around the sturdy gray-green camouflage sides. Stamped on the outside was "Burke, S."

"You were in the army?"

Shane glanced around at her as he tucked the toiletry case into the duffel and went back to the closet. "Marines. Long time ago."

Wait. "Do the Marines have divers, sort of like SEALs? Is that where you trained?"

He stuffed a few clothes in the duffel and strapped it shut. "I grew up on the water, but I was a combat diver for the Marines, yeah, and a SEAL instructor."

Shane's history had developed a minuscule crack, but he didn't seem inclined to open it further.

"And let me guess," she said. "We'll talk about it later."

"Nope." Shane hefted the duffel on one shoulder and gave her a look she couldn't interpret. "We aren't going to talk about it, period."

Okay. Add that to the list of subjects to explore later. Then again, she probably shouldn't make the mistake of thinking they were friends. They were, as he said, victims, and victimization probably wasn't a good basis for a healthy relationship. Plus, she had her own ghosts whose chains she didn't want rattled.

Gillian waited on deck while Shane checked on Jagger and Harley, then they walked back to the Jeep.

"How's he doing?"

Shane shook his head. "Shocked. Angry. He knows damned well it wasn't a kitchen fire that started it; he's worked in ships' galleys too long and is too careful. What we've got to decide—you and me—is how much we tell him."

Shane drove back across the key toward the west end, taking the curves and ruts a lot slower than he had on the way into town.

"So tell me what happened," Gillian said.

"After I left Jagger's yesterday and had filled him in on everything, he went to Harley's for dinner. He spotted that same guy we saw there at lunch—the one who threatened us."

Damn it. Son of Tex. "Did he see him set the fire?"

"No. He hung around Harley's until the guy left, then followed him back to one of those little B and Bs on Dock Street—only he wasn't very stealthy. The guy knew he was being followed and spewed some shit about Jagger having to toe the line now that he was involved. Said he needed to be taught a lesson."

Jagger had struck Gillian as pretty laid-back. She'd underestimated at first how deep his feelings went, but he still didn't seem the fistfight type. "So Jag just left him there?"

"Oh no. It takes a lot to make Jagger truly anger, but he'd finally had it." Shane laughed a little. "He pushed past him to go inside and talk to the B and B owner, find out who the guy was. The guy didn't follow him in."

Gillian groaned. "No, he went and set Harley's on fire."

"That's the presumption. McCaul, the innkeeper, said the guy paid for the room in cash, for the week." He glanced over at Gillian. "He used your name and address—well, Gill Campbell, with an address on Highway 24."

Damn it. Surely these guys had to slip up eventually. At least now she understood why Jagger wanted Harley out of town, even if it meant on *The Evangeline.* "Jagger told me he wants to take Harley with us."

"Us?" Shane frowned at her for a second, then looked away. "Yeah, he told me. It's not a bad idea, because I think we'd have trouble getting him to take a long vacation like you were able to do with your friend."

Gillian hoped Vivian had taken her advice, told Jimmy a big old lie, and left the country. Not that it guaranteed their safety, but it would be less convenient for their guy with the long reach.

"So we either tell him the truth to make sure he'll be forewarned, or we tell him it's an adventure and we want him to join us?"

"Riiiight . . ." Shane glanced at her again. "Exactly what do you see as your role on this expedition, Gillian?"

What? Oh hell no, I see where this is going. "I see my role as being the one whose ancestor started this whole mess and who's getting the instructions from whoever's really calling the shots. Don't think you're going without me."

"Ships are floating metal boxes. People prone to claustrophobia or"—he gave her a pointed look—"klutziness don't do well on long trips. You get cabin fever or injured, and suddenly our whole schedule is off. Everything has to run like clockwork if we have any hope of meeting that deadline."

Gillian stared out the window as he pulled the Jeep into the driveway of the cottage. Tank began a steady barking before Shane had killed the engine. She wouldn't confront Shane about that belittling comment—at least not yet.

If she'd learned one thing about Shane Burke in the last couple of days, it was that he was stubborn. Forget stubborn. He was downright pigheaded and had an annoying tendency to think he was always right.

But he was dead wrong if he thought *The Evangeline* was heading for Canada without Duncan Campbell's great-great-great-to-the-nth-degree-granddaughter on board.

10

A shard of sunlight stabbed Shane in his right eye, jolting him awake. His lower back hurt like a son of a bitch and his legs seemed to be paralyzed. Or trapped beneath the cover of the foldout futon on which he'd tried to sleep.

Mostly, he'd stared out at the sky, thanks to all the waterfront windows with no curtains or shades, enjoying the most intense thunderstorm he'd seen all summer. With the little house so near the water and so small—he doubted there was a quarter inch of insulation beneath that flat roof—it was almost like being out in the storm, except not as wet.

He'd finally drifted to sleep when the storm died down. At least he'd drifted off after indulging a few stray, irresponsible thoughts about the woman sleeping in an oversized T-shirt only a few feet away. Just his luck the first woman he'd been attracted to in forever had a curse on her head. Not to mention a stupid ancestor. What kind of guy would think he could tiptoe out of Europe with something belonging to one of God's medieval holy warriors? A guy with more imagination than brains.

What the hell is up with my legs? Shane tried to roll onto his back and shift his legs, and they finally budged, followed by a growl. A low, menacing, evil, gonna-eat-your-balls-for-breakfast growl.

He propped up on his elbows and looked at where his feet would be if they hadn't been covered by a light quilt and pinned by Tank the Hellhound and his mouthful of glistening white daggers.

"Uh, Gillian?" He wriggled his feet, hoping to make the beast uncomfortable enough that he'd move; instead, Tank snapped at Shane's foot. If not for the quilt, he'd be minus a big toe.

Damn, but he didn't want to start the day out having to ask for help with a stupid dog, for crying out loud. He was a former Marine, albeit a disgraced one, and besides that, he was doing Satan's master a favor.

"Shoo," he whispered to the dog, which responded with that lip-curling Elvis thing he did so well. "Scram. Get thee behind me."

Tank rose on all fours, and Shane had to admit he was beaten. "Gillian!"

A rustle reached him from behind his head. "*Wha?* Huh?"

"Your dog is trying to eat me for breakfast."

"Oh, that's silly." She yawned—at least he thought it was a yawn. He couldn't turn to see her with his body pinned under a woolly mammoth.

"C'mon Tank, let's go outside." She shuffled toward the door, and Shane was treated to a hundred pounds of canine using his groin as a staging platform from which to dive toward the world outside.

Shane gritted his teeth and curled into a fetal position. He would not cry. He wanted to sob, but he was a better man than that. He forced himself to unbend and prop his hands behind his head. No pain here.

"What's wrong wi—crap!"

The spot recently vacated by the satanic spawn now was treated to Gillian's elbow as she tripped and landed on top of him. God help him, the woman was going to be the death of him before he even had a chance to dive and get himself killed in manly pursuits.

"Sorry." She sat up and blew a strand of hair from in front of her lips. "Are you okay?"

"Sure. I didn't want to have children." And his voice sounded sexy a little more tenor than baritone, or so he told himself.

"Pity." She gave him a wicked little smile. "They'd be really pretty and stubborn as a gator in a mud pit."

"Fighting words." He reached up and flipped her on her back, pinning her with the portion of his lower body that was aching less every second. He propped up on his elbows and was rewarded with that sweet, warm smile he always had such trouble wresting from her, although she gave it so freely to his friends.

Suddenly he was aware of the thin quilt and not much else between them. Heat spread along his nerve endings, and he could tell the moment she became aware of him not as a playmate but as a man who wanted her. Her lips parted. Their hearts beat in rhythm against each other, as if trying to escape their prisons of flesh and bone and muscle.

"This is a really bad idea." He lowered his mouth to hers, sucked gently on her lower lip, and finally kissed her.

"Mmm-hmmm, an awful idea." She ran strong fingers over his scalp, grabbed two handfuls of hair and pulled him back to her.

Gillian slid a hand beneath the quilt. "Damn, now he wears pants."

A buzzing sound from the table interrupted his assault on her earlobe. They both froze for a second, then Shane rolled off her and went to get it.

"Your sister's named Gretchen Bryant, right?" He held up the screen with Caller ID.

"Oh, God. What do I tell her?" Gillian grabbed the phone and took a deep breath. "Hey, Gretch. How are you?"

Shane couldn't deduce a lot from Gillian's side of the conversation, but she'd mentioned calling yesterday and leaving a message about going on a cruise. Sounded as if her sister hadn't believed the story.

Shane paced around the small living area, watching Tank chase a duck across the yard. She needed to say enough to get her sister on alert, to watch what was going on around her, but not enough to send her scurrying to the police.

He looked around and spotted the box of family papers that had proved pretty useless, and took out an envelope. He found a pen on the counter and wrote:

Tell Her U Have Stalker. She Shld B Carful.

"Okay, okay. I'll come clean, but I don't want you to worry." Gillian frowned at his note and mouthed "carful"?

Great. If she wanted an English teacher, she shouldn't have come to the marina. He wrote an "E" above the word and held it up again.

"It's nothing really," she said, smiling, and making Shane wish that phone hadn't rung. Knowing the interruption was for the best and liking it were two different matters.

She continued with the stalker story, assuring Gretchen she was working with the local authorities. "I just want you to keep your eyes open, you know, in case this whacko comes down your way."

Next came some baby talk between "Aunt Gillian" and the little girl, Holly, and Shane grimaced, grabbed his clothes, and went to take a shower. That call was a good reminder of why they were here—not to play tongue tussle and watch the pretty sunsets. A child was in danger. Gillian's friend had been injured. Harley had lost his home. Jagger had been threatened.

He had to focus on getting *The Evangeline* stocked and ready, which started with calling his uncle Charlie. And if that thought didn't kill any remaining libido, he didn't know what it would take.

When he came back out, Gillian had folded the futon back into its makeshift sofa form.

"Thanks for the save," she said. "The stalker story worked, I think."

"No problem. Now I have to go back and make my own difficult phone call."

Gillian set the box of papers in a corner and took one of the seats at the table. "What's the deal between you and, what's his name, Charlie?"

"Mostly me being stupid." Shane closed up his duffel and set it on the floor beside the door.

"Seriously? I find that hard to believe." She gave him that smile again. He could get used to that, well, except that he was getting ready to sail as soon as possible and she wasn't going. Whether she knew it or not.

"You don't know me well enough to agree that quickly." He stared out the window at the soft sunlight, thinking about Harley and how that could have turned out. Harley was like a dad to Jagger now.

And Shane had Charlie, the crotchety old man who'd taught him everything. Except running away. He'd learned that all by himself. If he didn't make it through this fiasco, he didn't want things to end with Charlie the way he'd left them for the past decade. Even if it meant eating a big dish of crow.

"I'll let you know how it goes. Hopefully, he'll still have some contacts in Canada and be willing to share them without me going into too much detail."

Gillian wrapped her arms around Shane's waist and pulled him into a hug. She was warm and generous and affectionate. And sexy. Why was she alone? No cadre of friends around her except the one in the wreck. No mention of coworkers.

There was a story behind Gillian Campbell that had nothing to do with old Duncan, but Shane figured it was no more his business than his Marine Corps experience and problems with Charlie were hers.

He kissed her, memorizing the feel of her lips as they molded themselves to his, the taste of her, the way her hair smelled of lemons and sunshine. In a perfect world, he'd come back with the cross, the bad guys would disappear, and they could see if they had any chemistry in their normal lives. But in a perfect world, there would be no bad guys. In a perfect world, he'd never have met her.

He leaned over and picked up the duffel. "Okay, I'm off."

"What's next? Need me to go along?"

Shane shook his head. "Try to get hold of that octogenarian great-uncle of yours and see if he can remember anything. I'll talk to Charlie and see if . . . well, I'll see if he'll talk back." Charlie wasn't much of a conversationalist, or hadn't been ten years ago. "Jagger's taking Harley to talk to the sheriff, and then they're going to start making lists of the retrofitting we'll need to do, a tally of food and water and fuel supplies, all that fun stuff. I'll call you after I talk to Charlie and see what you've learned from your uncle."

He looked out the window again, knowing what he was about to say would be a lie. "Then maybe you can come over to *The Evangeline* tonight for pizza, and we'll look at schedules and routes."

"Sounds good." She opened the door and walked outside with him. At the edge of the drive, not growling but also not happy, sat Tank. "Give Harley my best. And Jagger."

Shane unlocked the Jeep and got in, hating that he might not see her again unless the trip was successful, but knowing it was safer for everyone if she didn't go along on the dive trip. And it wasn't because she was a klutz or claustrophobic or might get hurt.

No, he wanted Gillian at home because she was a distraction, and it had been a long time since Shane had done a technical dive this complicated. He couldn't afford to be distracted.

When he reached the marina, he didn't see any sign of Jagger's old blue VW Beetle, which was good. He could make this phone call better without witnesses.

Shane boarded *The Evangeline*, went to his bedroom for his old address book—a tattered black thing the size of an index card that he'd hauled around with him since his days in California. He took it back to the galley, poured himself a bourbon and, after a moment's reflection, poured the bourbon down the sink. Pouring out booze was getting to be a bad habit, but necessary. He also needed to pull out his weights and start a running routine—he needed to get back in prime diving condition.

But not this morning. Chili would be a healthy breakfast, right? Right. He pulled a can from the pantry shelf, popped off the top, considered heating it, decided it was too much trouble, and sat down at the salon table with a spoon.

As he punched in Charlie's number, Shane had a moment of panic. What if his uncle had moved on? He wasn't that old—early sixties, Shane guessed. Retired from the hard life of seasonal commercial fishing. He could have moved or gone back to work.

The call rang through, and equal parts of relief and dread washed over Shane at the sound of that deep, gruff voice: "Burke."

Shane had been thinking since last night about what to say, how even to begin this conversation, and hadn't come up with anything clever. Instead, he went the simple route. "Charlie? It's Shane."

Faced with a protracted silence on the other end, Shane was tempted to hang up, call it a wash. But the image of Harley on the sidewalk in tears, his life burning to ash before his eyes, propelled Shane to take a deep breath. "Guess you're surprised to hear from me."

"How are you, son? Been thinking about you lately, and here you are, out of the blue. You must need money."

Shane winced, but it was a fair assumption. For the first six months after leaving the Corps, he'd spent a couple of weeks at a time wallowing in drunken self-pity and whatever woman he could shack up with. Then, when he ran out of money, he'd crawled back to Charlie's.

When his uncle cut off the money and told him to grow up, he'd walked out instead.

"No, I don't need money, believe it or not. I need some advice."

At first the sound coming over the phone sounded like the man was choking, and it took a few seconds for Shane to register his laughter. He smiled himself. "Yeah, that's a change of pace for me, right?"

"I'd say so. But you know I've always got opinions."

Yeah, that was for sure. *Opinionated* and *stubborn* were two words that should have Charlie's photo next to them in the dictionary.

"Spit it out, then."

Part of Shane wanted to say never mind, let's just talk. But he wasn't any better at directly tackling the elephant in the room than his uncle. They'd have to talk in circles until they finally got there. At least this particular circle, the request, was something he'd decided how to handle.

"I've been offered a quick-turnaround job up in Nova Scotia and wanted to see if you still had some contacts up that way to grease the wheels for me."

"What kind of job is it—fishing? Bad time of year for that. You still in Florida?"

Shane was surprised. Last time he'd talked to Charlie, Shane had just left North Carolina and gone back to San Diego. "How'd you know I was in Florida?"

Charlie harrumphed. "Harley Dugan gives me a call now and again."

That old buzzard. Of course, Shane knew these fishing guys were like a big club. It's why he'd called Charlie in the first place, to tap into that network.

"Then you'll probably be interested to hear that Harley's bar burned down last night."

"Damn. What are you mixed up in, boy?" Charlie paused. "On second thought, don't tell me on the phone. Get up here and tell me in person. It's been too long."

And Shane realized he wanted to go. Needed to, even if Charlie gave him hell. Which he probably would. He'd been awfully quick to assume the fire at Harley's had something to do with Shane. "I'd like that. I'm glad you asked."

Charlie cleared his throat. Twice. Shane's had a pretty big lump in it too.

"So, tell me about this job, and what kind of wheels need greasing."

Thank God. They had skated awfully close to the edge of Talking About Feelings; time to skate around another circle.

"It's a salvage job, trying to locate an old shipwreck and recover something from it."

Charlie was all business now. "You looking at next summer?"

"This month. By the end of September."

Another long pause, and Shane waited for it.

"That's the goddamned most idiotic, damn-fool thing I've ever heard. You know how cold and rough that water is this time of year?"

Yep, exactly the response he expected. "I agree, but it's complicated. I'm retrofitting my boat—it's a forty-seven-foot live-in trawler." He held out a carrot. "Maybe I could stop in Wilmington on my way up."

Charlie huffed a snorting noise into the phone. "That's a cheap bribe, Shane. How senile do you think I am?"

He was right. "Sorry. I need your help, though. I thought you might still know someone up in Nova Scotia who could help us with the local authorities."

"Help you, like, with permits? And who is 'us'?"

Here was the big carrot. "Cal Mackie's son, and I think Harley's coming."

"Did Cal Jr. ever cut his hair and admit those Rolling Stones had nothing on the Beatles?"

Shane laughed. "That would be a 'no' on both counts."

"Okay then. I know some folks outside Louisbourg, in Main-à-Dieu, but a salvage permit, especially for an American crew, is gonna take a while. Not going to work in your short time frame. You know how federal agencies work here, and they're the same in Canada."

Shane took a deep breath and plunged. "Well, we kind of want to avoid the feds, both ours and the Canadians."

Okay, this pause was epic, but Shane knew his uncle had to think it through. If he was still the same Charlie, he'd figure it out pretty quickly.

"Sounds like this is an under-the-table job. Any chance you're going to get yourself arrested or dead?"

Dead was more likely, either at the hand of the sick freak whose game they were playing or beneath the waves of the North Atlantic. "There's a chance, yeah."

"I got some people who can probably help you, but I have a price."

Money? Knowing Charlie, probably not. "What is it?"

"I ain't giving it to you over the phone. You come here and get it. When you get here, you tell the truth about what you're up to, and I'll decide whether or not to help. And while you're here, we'll get your boat up to snuff."

Shane closed his eyes with a relief so profound it made him dizzy. "Agreed. We'll be there in three days, four tops." Which took them down to a deadline of just over three weeks to retrofit, scout, and dive. "Make it three days. We'll leave tonight and provision when we get there."

After ending the call, Shane considered calling Gillian but decided to wait until she had a chance to talk to her great-uncle.

Then he and Jagger and Harley would slip out of town, and he'd call her from Charlie's. She'd just have to get over it.

11

"I don't trust that man as far as I can throw him." Gillian tossed clothes into her small red rolling suitcase without refolding them. "Seriously, Tank. You should've bitten him this morning. He thinks I'm not going with him to do this job? I was an alternate on Team USA in swimming five years ago, for God's sake. I'm a certified scuba diver. Who does he think he's dealing with? Arrogant oaf."

Good kisser, but an arrogant oaf nonetheless.

Tank sat between Gillian and the door—his way of telling her she wasn't going anywhere without the dog. Every time she even looked at a suitcase, he went on door patrol.

"Don't worry, you're going. He's not leaving me behind, and I'm not leaving you. So you'll probably still get a chance to bite his ass." She'd never had Tank on a long boat trip, but he'd do okay; it wasn't like they'd be spending days on the open ocean.

First thing she had to do, though, was try to call Zeke Campbell.

She tried the number from the letter she'd found among her grandmother's things, but got another person who said they'd had the number for several years.

On a whim, she used her smartphone to do a WhitePages search for Zeke Campbell in Paducah, Kentucky, but came up with only an obituary. *Damn it.* She clicked on the obit link and said a prayer of thanks that this Zeke Campbell was a forty-year-old. Then she prayed an apology for being thankful that anyone was dead. Except Tex and Son of Tex and their employer who was too chickenshit to do his own dirty work. She didn't apologize for hoping all three of them, and whoever else was involved, keeled over where they stood.

Zeke was probably short for Ezekiel, so she typed in "Ezekiel Campbell" and widened the search to a hundred-mile radius of Paducah. Bingo! The age looked right for an Ezekiel across the river in Metropolis, so she jotted down the number, said another prayer, and called.

A man answered on the second ring. A very old man who Gillian suspected was hard of hearing because he shouted so loud into the phone she had to put him on speaker. It hurt her ear to hold the phone close.

A few attempted explanations later, Zeke said, "Let me get my hearing aid," and the call ended.

Gillian opened the door for Tank. "This could take a while. Go and chase something. If you see Shane, bite him."

She waited a few minutes and then called Zeke again.

This time, he answered on the first ring. "Where'd you go?"

Gillian decided to let it pass. "Can you hear me better now?"

"Clear as a bell. Tell me who you are again?"

"I'm your great-niece." She went through the connections again, now that he could hear her. "We've never met, but my dad told me you might be able to tell me more about Duncan Campbell."

"The thief! I been looking for information on that rascal for almost sixty years. Always wished I could get my hands on that cross."

Gillian considered telling him the cross was her ultimate goal but decided against it. Instead, she claimed to be a budding genealogist, trying to track information on their notorious ancestor.

"'Course we don't know the story of the cross was true," Zeke said after rambling through the places he'd gone to do research—including several spots in Europe. "We only have his son's word for it, passed down from generation to generation."

Gillian paused in her note taking. "I thought his son was a baby when the ship sank, and one of the ship's crew saved him."

"Not a baby. He was eight or nine years old, according to the ship manifest—found that over in France. We thought for years it had sailed from Spain or Portugal, but we finally tracked it to France, and let me tell you that took some sniffing out. So my guess is, and it's just a guess, that the little boy knew what his daddy had done and went on to tell his children and so on. Was it true, or did he make it up, or did he misunderstand? We'll never know."

What if this whole thing—all the threats, all the hurt, all the fear—was based on something that never even happened? She'd warned Tex about that from the beginning and, if she had it to do over, would never, ever mention the Campbell curse to anyone, ever.

"I wrote all this up, if you've got one of those computers." Zeke paused for a phlegmy cough that echoed through the phone.

Gillian leaned forward in her chair; this was the first thing Zeke had said that excited her, except maybe that she had to extend her search to France for ship records. "It's online?"

"My son put it up on one of those genealogy sites. Figured your daddy knew about that. Hold on, I got it written down somewhere."

And the call ended. Gillian beat herself in the head with her own phone. Zeke needed a few lessons about the difference between "hang on" and "hang up." She gave him a few seconds, and hit the "Redial" button.

"Where'd you go?" Zeke either had Caller ID or just assumed it was her. Or he didn't get that many calls.

"Did you find the genealogy information?"

He slowly read off a web address for a popular genealogy site, and Gillian felt like beating herself in the head for not checking those places herself.

They talked a while longer, and Gillian wished she had time to fly up to Kentucky and meet him in person. Families got scattered and fell out of touch and lost track these days, not that she'd made much attempt at maintaining ties. After Sam and Ethan died, she'd thrown herself into her work, bought herself a trailer in the woods, and become a self-imposed hermit. Or as much a hermit as one could be with Vivian Ortiz living next door.

Gillian vacillated a few moments. Though she wanted to search out the website, she also had a feeling Shane was going to bolt. He'd gotten way too closed off the two times she'd mentioned the dive trip, and there was nothing to prevent him from moving *The Evangeline* somewhere else to do his retrofits.

She'd play the game first and call him. Tell him what she'd learned from Zeke. Make him think she planned to spend the afternoon using the Internet at Cedar Key's little public library. See if he let anything slip.

"Hey there." He answered just as the call was about to be forwarded to voice mail. In the background, loud clanking noises were almost as jarring to her ear as Zeke had been, pre-hearing aid. She put him on speaker as well.

"What's that racket?" A wrench banging against a metal drum, maybe. Or a really bad marching-band percussion section.

"Harley's doing some work on the plumbing system. Wait." The knocking and clanging grew muffled. "Is that better? I went up to the pilothouse."

"Yeah, much better. How's Harley doing?"

"Jagger was right about him keeping busy." Shane lowered his voice, and Gillian took him off speaker so that she could hear him better. "As soon as we told him about the dive and asked him to come along, it was like he had been dead and suddenly came back to life. He needs this now."

Sounded like he'd be a handy guy to have along anyway. "How much did you tell him?" Gillian worried about spreading it too far. She'd told Viv, and now Jagger was in the middle of it. She wasn't sure if it was safer for Harley to know everything or know virtually nothing.

"I thought about telling him everything, but right now I think it would put him in more danger," Shane said. "If we were leaving him behind, I'd tell him. But I think he's less vulnerable if he's with us."

Gillian bit her lip hard enough to draw blood. What a hypocrite. Wasn't she also less vulnerable—all of them, really—if they were together? Maybe she'd misjudged him. Maybe he had no intention of leaving her behind. Or maybe he was going to find the cross and take off with it, make his own deal for more money. She didn't think so, but either way, she didn't plan to risk it. She was going. And just in case he decided to be heavy-handed, she didn't plan to ask his opinion.

"Did you get in touch with your uncle?"

He paused. "Yeah, it was good to talk to him, and I think he has a lead on someone who can help us get the cruise permits for Canada, do some of the bigger retrofitting jobs, and maybe help us when we get to wherever we're going. Where *are* we going?"

Maybe she should withhold that information—Zeke had said the area offshore from Louisbourg wasn't thought to be where *The Marcus Aurelius* foundered, but farther east, near the village of Main-à-Dieu and offshore Scatarie Island. "There's even a cove just north of there called Campbell's Cove," Zeke had said. "Don't know the connection, but there's gotta be one. You're young; maybe you can find it."

"I don't know where we're going yet." Accent on the *we*. "I'm off to the library to do some Internet work, follow up on some solid leads I got from Zeke."

"Why don't you tell me what they are? I have a computer with wireless Internet here on the boat; we can both look."

She wanted to trust him; she really did. But she didn't trust him. There was too much at risk. "I'll stop by tonight and let you know what I find. Dinner about seven? I can bring the pizza."

His very long pause told her what she needed to know. He was over there at the marina, getting *The Evangeline* ready to sail—probably to where his uncle lived in North Carolina. Maybe Charlie had promised his nephew they could get the retrofitting done faster there than in Florida, which was probably true. They would have to take the boat farther south, to Tampa, or north, into the Panhandle, to get it done nearby—*if* they could find anyone who knew how to prepare a boat for rough Atlantic seas.

Finally, he said, "Yeah, seven's good. Don't bring dinner, though. We'll order here."

In other words, don't waste your money on food for four because the three of us menfolk are going to be long gone.

Okay, maybe she was putting words in his mouth. She'd have to see.

She optimistically didn't take everything with her—just clothes and toiletries she'd need. She stuffed every available nook and dead space in her rolling bag with Tank's stuff. Food, treats, his favorite stuffed frog, and a stack of plastic lined pads for onboard bathroom emergencies. Tank was much better equipped than she by the time the packing was finished.

She lugged everything to the truck and didn't have to call Tank. He'd been trailing every step she took, especially when he saw his stuff going into the bag. When she opened the passenger door, he leapt into the front seat and assumed the riding position, hanging his head out the window as soon as she lowered it.

She was halfway out of the driveway when the phone rang, and she answered it without looking at the screen. Maybe Shane had had a change of heart and realized they were better on this trip with her going along.

"Checking on your progress, Ms. Campbell." The dulcet tones of Tex made her skin crawl. "I trust Mr. Mackie understands where we're all coming from on this mission?"

Anger that she'd transferred to Shane most of the morning rushed to the surface like lava, and this particular volcano was set to blow. "I don't think any of us has any doubt where we're coming

11111111111111

from. Do you have no morals? This is all a game to you, but look how many innocent lives you're trying to destroy." Already have destroyed, in Harley's case. "And for what? I can't even confirm that Duncan Campbell ever had that cross."

"I'll be sure to let my employer know that you don't feel you can complete the job." Tex's voice was cold and passionless. "Whether he feels further incentives are needed . . . well, we'll see, won't we? By the way, your friend Vivian Ortiz and her ex-husband arrived in Honolulu this morning. I thought you might want to know where they'd decided to go. I'll check in with you t—"

"Wait." Gillian would never forget the sight of Viv lying in that hospital bed. She'd been lucky—not going very fast and wearing her seat belt. She'd rebounded quickly. But a little faster, a little more rain, a different place to lose control, and the outcome could have been a lot different. And Tex, or his employer, had been willing for Viv to die. There was no reason to think they couldn't get to Viv and Jimmy in Hawaii.

"We don't need more reminders. Believe me, we are taking you seriously. In fact, we've already begun the retrofits on *The Evangeline* to take her to Canada, and I am tracking down leads on where the ship went down."

Tex laughed, and that made Gillian madder than ever, but she had to hold it in. This gator was too dangerous to poke. "Good answer, Ms. Campbell. I'll be in touch."

Gillian sat in the pickup for a couple of minutes, willing her hands to stop shaking so that she could drive without ending up wrapped around a tree herself. Tank whined and put an oversized black paw on her arm.

She gave him a hug, burying her face in the ruff of his thick, soft fur. "I'm okay, buddy. Let's go for a ride."

He went back to hanging out the window before she cleared the block, and the five-minute drive gave her the chance to plan a strategy. She hoped she could get to *The Evangeline* in time to stow away.

Once the boat got under way, Shane Burke couldn't do a thing about it.

12

"No way she's going."

Shane took the bolt from Jagger and replaced one in the bottom of the watertight door. This door could seal off the aft end of the area amidships. Three sections of the boat would then exist independently in case of emergency, each with its own self-contained air supply. The first rule for retrofitting was getting everything as solid and tight as possible in the most basic areas: nuts and bolts and screws.

He and Jagger had been arguing for the past hour about Gillian and whether she should go with them to North Carolina. It was already 3:00 p.m., and he wanted to be away from Way Key by 5:00 p.m. Yes, he was an absolute asshole. He knew Gillian would be standing on the dock two hours later, realizing he'd lied to her deliberately. She'd probably think that he was blowing her off because she wasn't one of the boys.

He wouldn't admit a big part of his reluctance stemmed from his attraction to her.

"She has a right to go. Hell, if anybody has a right to go, it's Gillian." Jagger handed him the wrench and looked at the next bolt. "Damn it, half these are stripped. I might have to go back to the hardware store."

"We'll get them in Wilmington." Shane tightened the new bolt, giving it a few extra vicious turns. "I know she has a right to go, and I know she's going to hate us." Hate him. She'd know it was his decision.

Jagger was silent for a while, and Shane wished he'd go back to singing his tune for the day, "Beast of Burden." Because when Jagger was silent, Jagger was thinking. And when he thought this hard, something Shane didn't want to hear was usually forthcoming.

"You're afraid we won't be able to find the wreck or find the Templars' cross," Jagger finally said. "And you don't want her to see you fail. You don't want to let her down, at least not where she can watch it happen."

Shane sat up without clearing the edge of the hatch and cracked his head on the steel door. "Shit." He opened his mouth to argue with Jagger, then closed it. No point in arguing with the truth. He hadn't thought about it in those terms, and he'd like to think he was man enough to feel comfortable failing in front of a woman whose opinion he cared about, but that wasn't the way he rolled. Sue him.

He snatched the next bolt from Jagger's outstretched hand and hit his head on the other side of the heavy door on his way back to his supine position.

"Oh ho, not even going to argue?" Jagger laughed and dug in the box for yet another heavy bolt. "Then might I add that one of the reasons you don't want Gillian to see you as a failure is because you have the hots for her."

"Fuck you." Shane refused to sit up again before he finished this bottom row of nuts and bolts; if he cracked his head too many times and ended up with a concussion, a successful dive wouldn't be possible. "You forgot the part about how many years it's been since I did a dive as complex as this one has the potential to be."

"Yeah, there's that, too. But she still has a right to be here."

Shane didn't answer. He'd said all he cared to on the discussion of the trip and Gillian's absence from it. Jagger had even argued that they take her at least to Wilmington, but Shane didn't want Charlie telling tales Gillian didn't need to hear. His uncle had always possessed the manners of a timber wolf, and Shane had no idea what kind of past history the man would dredge up when they arrived.

Jagger wasn't giving up. "Besides that, you two look good together. Once this is all over, who knows? She might be the one. Not many women would put up with your lack of social skills."

Shane finished up the bolts and gave his friend a sour look as he climbed to his feet. "My social skills are fine." Unlike his uncle's. "Now you're not only Martha Stewart, you're also handling advice for the lovelorn? Look in the mirror, hippie boy. I haven't seen you finding *the one* despite your self-proclaimed social skills."

"I'm like my man Mick. I like to spread it around."

"Yeah, you're spreading around something, all right." They walked back to the salon and settled on either side of the table, where Shane had placed a couple of rolled maps. "When's Harley getting back?"

"Should be soon. Hope it's okay—I gave him about five hundred dollars from the safe in the master suite. The man didn't even have underwear. My clothes are too little for him, and yours are too big, you ox."

"That's Mr. Ox to you, and of course it's all right. Whatever he needs." Shane unrolled the set of maps depicting the US East Coast. "Our cruise permit's good for anywhere in the US, right?"

Jagger went to the fridge and came back with two beers. He handed one to Shane, who looked at it longingly and handed it back. "I'm on the wagon."

Swapping the beer for a soda, Jagger returned to the table and leaned over the map. "Yeah, since we're not on a commercial run, we should be good. I think we just need to check in at Wilmington when we get there, or at the nearest port of entry if we stop along the way. I'm not sure about Canada. We're not on a commercial venture, at least as far as the Canadian government is concerned, so it shouldn't be complicated."

They spent the next hour going over their routes, looking at the pros and cons of cutting through the river routes of central Florida to reach the Atlantic instead of traveling all the way to the Florida Keys. Every decision had to be made with Tex's ticking clock in mind.

Speaking of deadlines, they really needed a solid destination if they were going to make this whole scheme work. Shane rerolled the map and snapped the rubber band back around it. "You think it's possible Gillian's holding out on us about the location? I kind of got the feeling her great-uncle told her more than she let on."

Jagger finished off his beer and let out an echoing belch. "What a novelty that would be. One of you hiding something from the other. Could that possibly be true?"

"Asshat."

"Fucktard."

"I might be better off living in the ashes of my house than stuck on a boat with two grown men who act like thirteen-year-olds half the time." Harley dropped a pile of bags on the salon floor and turned back to the passageway. "Don't mind me, by the way, I'm only sixty. I don't mind bringing all this shit in from the deck by myself."

Shane groaned and stood up, twisting to stretch his back. He was still sore from sleeping on that damned futon. "I dunno, Jag. I think he's gonna be grouchy."

Jagger followed Harley down the hall. "Yeah, and I can already tell he's going to play the old-man card whenever the heavy lifting starts."

On deck, they found boxes and bags scattered over both sides of the gangplank entrance. Most of the bags were unmarked white plastic; a lot held clothes. "Where'd you get all this?" Shane hadn't shopped in a while, but this was a ton of stuff for only five hundred bucks.

"Let's get this stuff below and then I'll tell you about it. Take it to the salon and we can sort it there." Harley's voice sounded gruffer than usual, so Shane let it go. He and Jagger carried armloads of bags back to the salon, which he'd always thought of as a combination dining room-meeting room-game room. There was a DVD player and screen tucked behind a wooden panel on the back side of the galley cabinets.

"We can sort the clothes and put them in the smaller bedroom; Jagger and I will share the master," Shane said. He and Jag looked at each other with a tacit understanding: *I will not sleep with you. One of us will sleep on the floor.* After age twelve or so, there were places friends didn't need to go, and the possibility of accidentally waking up in a spooning position was one of them.

About half of the bags contained food and household goods. Nonperishables, sodas, and snacks. Detergent and soap and toilet paper. Shane held up a box of tampons and raised his eyebrows at Harley. "Is there something you haven't told us about yourself?" Before the man could respond, Shane turned to Jagger. "And don't you dare sing 'Let It Bleed.'"

Jagger grinned. "I wish I'd thought of it."

"Please don't sing at all. I've had a hard-enough day." Harley slumped on one of the upholstered benches. "Sit down; I want to talk something through with you."

Jagger took the bench opposite Harley, so Shane sat on the floor with his back propped against the lower galley cabinets.

Harley looked hard at Jagger, then at Shane. "First, today was a humbling day." He looked down, his Adam's apple bobbing as he swallowed hard. *Damn it, the man was going to cry.* The only thing worse than a crying woman was tears from a man he respected the way he respected Harley.

"What happened?" Shane crossed his legs, yoga-style, and propped his elbows on his knees.

"I went to Tierney's to pick up some clothes—nothing fancy for me, you know. T-shirts and underwear and pants. Simple stuff."

Shane dropped his gaze to the floor and picked at a loose thread on the sturdy red and brown rug. Damn it, the whole idea made Shane want to barf, or shoot someone. This man had worked too hard to have to start over. He or Jagger should at least have done the shopping for him.

"Something happen at Tierney's?" Jagger asked.

Harley nodded. "I put all the stuff in my cart, took it up to the front to pay, you know? People stopped me in the store, told me they were sorry about the bar. Not just my regulars, either. Folks I didn't know. So I go to check out, and the clerk bagged it up and said it was on the house. Wouldn't take the money. Told me to go on up to the Baptist church and there were more things there people had been dropping by since last night."

He looked away from them, pretending to watch something outside the small side windows, but Shane had seen the tears on his cheeks. His own eyes had filled, and he fought back the urge to give in to it.

Jagger wasn't even pretending not to cry. "All this stuff was there?"

"This is a damn fine place, Cedar Key." Harley nodded. "Which is why I want to go with you to do this thing you're doing. But you have to be straight with me. I'm not stupid. It has something to do with that woman, Gillian. And something to do with that guy you chased after, when he left the bar last night, Cal." He rarely called Jagger by his nickname and probably never would make it a habit.

He looked down at Shane. "And you're up to your neck in it, Shane Burke. The fact you called Charlie tells me it's serious. And if it's the thing that caused my bar to be burned down, I deserve to know what it is."

Shane banged his head against the wooden cabinet he was leaning against. "Yeah, you do. I went back and forth as to how much to tell you, what would put you in the least amount of danger."

Harley leaned forward, every year of a hardworking life etched into the lines on his face, and the stress of the last twenty-four hours darkening the skin below his blue eyes. "I figure I'm already in it, whether you want me to be or not. I know neither of you visited this on me, so don't think I'm casting judgment. It's just that I've got some experience behind me, and I might be able to help. It's my fight now, too."

So Shane told him. Once he started talking, he found it helped to unload. He began his story with the visit from the First Bank and Savings bullfrog, because even though he didn't like to admit it, the money was the first lure for him. "The thing was, Gillian knew I was in big trouble and desperate for money so I wouldn't lose *The Evangeline*. She knew that because the guys putting the screws to her knew it. They researched the person who might be stupid enough and desperate enough to do a suicide dive for the money."

And damn it, he hated—*hated*—being that person.

"And they knew Jagger was your friend, just like that Vivian woman was Gillian's friend," Harley said. He was staring into space, his dark brows gathered. "They knew the two of you had a connection to me. They knew about Gillian's little niece down in Fort Lauderdale." He shook his head. "If this whole Templars' cross thing wasn't known to them before Gillian's TV interview, that means these people had less than three days to pull together all that information. Not just anybody can get that much detail on somebody, not that fast."

Shane had been thinking the same thing. "It's somebody rich as God, but we already knew that. Gillian had almost a quarter million in cash with her that first day, and she offered me another million for the dive." Of course she'd pretended it was her money, her project, but her acting skills weren't that good. She was basically an honest person and all this subterfuge didn't fit her well.

"Not just rich," Jagger said. "It's also gotta be somebody with a lot of connections, with . . . I don't know the word."

"Reach," Shane said. "That's what this Tex guy told Gillian. That his employer has a lot of reach."

"Then at the risk of sounding like one of those loony, paranoid conspiracy theorists, gentlemen, I'm guessing we're dealing with a military guy—intelligence, maybe."

"Or a politician," Shane said. "Maybe a dirty one. Somebody who deals in favors and secrecy."

They sat in silence for a few minutes before Harley got up. "I'm going to fire up the engine, let it warm up, make sure everything sounds like *The Evangeline*'s ready to go. Shane, you mind if I pilot her out?"

"Don't mind at all, Harley—go for it." Besides, he wanted to think about this military or political connection some more. He'd been thinking maybe it was someone in law enforcement, someone familiar with surveillance equipment, but it also had to be somebody with that infamous "reach," which local law enforcement wouldn't have.

So maybe it was someone on the national level with both reach and a big financial reserve. He needed to do some Internet research of his own. There couldn't be that many people who met all the criteria. Unless they could get to the guy in charge, Tex and his arsonist buddy wouldn't be touchable.

Which reminded him of Gillian. She was smart, and the research end of things was where she could really help them. She was off doing research at the public library right now—and she was going to be seriously pissed when he called her. The thing that would piss her off the most was that she couldn't withhold that information on Duncan Campbell for long without jeopardizing all of them.

While Shane had been thinking and Jagger had been puttering around the galley, putting away food, Harley had started up *The Evangeline*'s big engines. The rumble from underneath was a sensation Shane loved. It meant open water and blue skies and salt-tanged wind was coming. In a half hour, just before five, the grind of the anchor being raised drove Shane's adrenaline level skyward, and he and Jagger exchanged knowing smiles. Yeah, it was dangerous, but this is what they were made for.

A few minutes later, they were under way. Jagger took a sidestep into the galley and grabbed the edge of the counter. "Gonna take a day or two to get our sea legs. It's been too long with nothing but short coastal runs."

"Way too long." Shane blinked and looked toward the ship's bow. "Did you hear something?"

"No, I—" Jagger frowned as another loud thump sounded from near the pilothouse. "I'll see if Harley's okay."

He walked out of the galley and stopped, staring down the passageway, hands on his hips and a big shit-eating grin on his face. He broke into a chorus of "Play with Fire."

"What is it?"

Shane had climbed halfway to his feet when something hard barreled into him, knocking him flat.

He looked up at the foaming lips and white teeth of the world's most evil dog.

Tank.

13

"Do I know how to make an entrance, or what?" Gillian followed Jagger down the narrow side passage and turned left toward the master suite. He pulled her red rolling case, and Tank trotted behind them.

"That was classic." Jagger had grinned continuously since Tank had charged Shane, knocked him flat, and dripped foamy drool on his chin.

Shane hadn't come within a fathom of grinning. He'd climbed to his feet, given her a fierce look with eyes burning like green flames, and pushed past her on his way to the pilothouse. His only words: "That hellhound better not piss on my boat."

The pilothouse door was, thankfully, closed. "Think he'll cool off, or throw me off at the first port?"

Jagger switched her bag to his right hand and with his left, opened the door to Shane's room. Tank sat in the hallway, not entering the room that smelled like his archenemy Shane, but at least not growling. Gillian said a silent prayer of thanks that—so far—her dog was giving Jagger the treatment he gave most strangers: ignoring him.

"Shane'll get over it; he never stays mad for very long." Jagger deposited her bag at the foot of the bed. "We'll figure out who's bunking where later. I'm just gonna set this in here for now. Might want to take a shower. You're kinda bloody." He looked pointedly at the reddened scrapes on both knees, one with a trickle of blood that had trailed all the way to her running shoes and dyed the built-in white lining a shade of pink. "You fall down a lot?"

Too much, and she had scar tissue beneath the scratches on both knees to prove it. Her parents had hoped she'd outgrow it, but when her teenage clumsy phase extended into a college clumsy phase, they'd given up. "Any shower rules for living on board?"

"Keep it short. We didn't have time to fill the extra tanks."

Yeah, they didn't have time because Shane was in such a freaking hurry to leave without her. "Look, I know you guys don't want me aboard, but let's make the best of it. I can sleep in a corner somewhere."

Jagger showed her where the built-in linen closet was located, tucked above the tiny washer and dryer halfway down the starboard passageway. He handed her a towel. "For what it's worth, I told him you should be here. So did Harley."

Yeah, but the big old bully had prevailed, and Gillian was tired of being bullied. "Even though you outnumber him, Shane still got his way."

Jagger shrugged. "It's his boat, plus he's the diver, not me or Harley. However this dance ends, its outcome sits on his shoulders, and he feels the pressure even if he doesn't show it." He paused and lowered his voice. "Look, if you tell him this, I'll throw you overboard myself. He didn't leave you behind because he didn't think you had a right to be here. He won't admit it, but it's because he hasn't done this kind of dive in a while and he's nervous about it. He's afraid you'll distract him."

A flush of fury spread through her quick as a brushfire after a long drought. "Distract him? So he thinks I'll be sitting on deck, perfecting my tan and buffing my nails? Treating this like a party boat?"

That did it. Forget the shower. She and Shane Burke were going to clear up a few things, beginning now. Gillian edged past Jagger and stuffed the towel back in his hands. "You can let that spoiled brat have his way if you want, but I'm going to show him what a real distraction looks like. His days of bullying me are over."

"Whoa, hold on." Jagger wrapped his fingers around her wrist and stopped her forward motion. "I didn't mean that. I meant . . ." He winced as if the words he was about to say might rip out a few teeth as they passed his lips. "He's . . . into you. That's all. He's not afraid you'll distract him; he's afraid he'll let himself get distracted whether you intend it or not."

Gillian jerked her wrist free, but she'd lost the burning desire to duct-tape Shane to the navigation seat and kick him senseless. Sure, they shared a mutual attraction, but they'd agreed this wasn't the time or place for it to go anywhere, even if they wanted it to.

And Gillian didn't. She wasn't looking for a relationship. Not a loner by nature, she'd worked hard at becoming one over the past five years. She'd let Vivian in because the woman didn't understand the concept of "leave me alone," but no one else. Her heart wasn't ready for anyone new; her mind sure wasn't ready. It might never be, and she was at peace with that.

Jagger pointed her toward the master suite's tiny bathroom. "Use the shower, and then come back to the salon. Luckily, Harley will cook after we hit open water, but tonight, it's you and me. I'm a sandwich-making ninja." He stepped aside to make way for Tank, who'd observed the exchange from the passageway and finally decided to come inside the suite.

"Don't let him piss on Shane's bed," Jagger said with a grin, then closed the door behind him, leaving her alone with her dog and her tangle of thoughts.

Gillian sat on the bed, inspecting her knees for splinters. "We'll just have to figure out a way to make this work, Tank." She pulled out a sliver of wood. "And you. Make an effort, please. You are not helping my case by mauling the man who seems to be making all the rules."

Tank jumped on the bed, sniffed it from end to end, and turned three times before slumping on the pillows. He was snoring within seconds. Gillian picked up a half-full bottle of Jack Daniel's from the top of one of the built-in nightstands and considered pouring it out. Instead, she unscrewed the top and took a sip. A sweet, smoky heat filled her mouth and burned its way down her throat.

As long as she was plundering, she might as well do it properly.

She paused to listen for any signs of life outside the door—or at least any that were audible above Tank's vigorous snores—but heard nothing. She peeked inside a cedar-lined closet that smelled of tangy wood and housed neat stacks of clothes, heavy on denim. Most of the hanging clothes were shirts. A couple of pairs of running shoes lay on the floor, alongside a pile of fins and diving masks.

Well, that wasn't very illuminating. All she learned was that Shane Burke was neat, and she could've guessed that from the state of *The Evangeline* in general. Except for the messy pile of maps she'd seen in the pilothouse on her first visit, nothing seemed to be out of place.

Tugging open the deep nightstand drawer, she expected to see the rat's nest of stuff people always collect in such hideaways. Instead, the drawer revealed a deep, dark secret. Shane Burke, Mr. Bossy Diver, was a chocoholic. A serious one. At least thirty or forty bars of all varieties filled the drawer, stacked with obsessive neatness. Big gourmet squares piped full of salted caramel or mint or raspberry or orange. A lidless cigar box stuffed with foil-wrapped Hershey's Kisses. Bars of exotic darks and creamy whites. Milk chocolate with various assortments of nuts. And those were just the ones she could see without disturbing his meticulous drawer packing.

No wonder his kisses had a hint of sweetness. His veins were pumping half blood, half cocoa.

The thought of those kisses sapped her amusement and reminded her that his talented mouth had kissed her one minute and lied to her the next about the fact that his dive-trip plans didn't include her.

She picked a small chocolate bite from the drawer, unwrapped it, and let it melt on her tongue, savoring the sweetness even as she indulged in a moment of sour thoughts about Shane, aka Old Cocoa Breath. Oh well, she could at least wash off the blood before she saw him again. Maybe by then she'd decide whether she wanted to play nice or fight dirty.

What the shower lacked in space or water pressure, it made up for in heat. The hot water relaxed her tense muscles, and she inhaled the aroma of the shower gel and the shampoo sitting next to it on the little shelf. It was the scent she'd unconsciously come to associate with Shane—citrus, with an overlay of ginger. Thinking about him in this shower, those broad shoulders coming within a nanoparticle of brushing the sides of the stall, water streaming down his chest . . . and fury erupting from his eyes.

Get a grip. The man was a Neanderthal who had somehow made this whole venture about himself. If he thought he could shut her out again once they reached Wilmington, he had a lesson to learn. She didn't care how *into her* he might be.

She poured a dollop of shampoo into her palm, spread it through her hair, and dug her fingers in, working up a vigorous lather. The more she thought, the harder she scrubbed. Now that she couldn't see his charming, boyish grin, Jagger's tall tale struck her as a desperate attempt at peacemaking. He'd concocted that whole distraction theory because he didn't want Gillian to storm into the pilothouse, berate his buddy Shane, and create drama. Jagger hadn't wanted Shane to overhear what he told Gillian because his little distraction story was a complete fabrication.

She closed her eyes and stepped underneath the hot spray to rinse her hair, letting the warm streams of water heat her body—at least until her heart rate stutter-stepped in shock. The water had suddenly turned ice cold. By the time she fully registered the temperature change, the showerhead was dry as the Sahara. *What the hell?*

Suds ran into her eyes when she opened them, burning her corneas and sending tears down her cheeks. The showerhead went in and out of focus as if she were looking through a pair of cheap binoculars. She reached up and adjusted the settings. Turned the faucet off and back on. Thumped on the nozzle. Nothing.

Awesome. She not only had globs of shampoo in her hair, but she'd broken Shane's shower. This was likely to cause a distraction.

Gillian opened the frosted glass door, tripped over the toilet, and caught herself on the sink. One good thing about showers made for hobbits: one couldn't actually fall unimpeded.

There also wasn't room to bend over and rinse out her hair in the shallow sink, at least not comfortably, but she tried. By the time she finished getting the biggest soapy mounds of shampoo from her hair with the faucet's grudging trickle of cool water, she was shivering and wondering why she hadn't brought clothes into the bathroom. Not that there was room to dress.

Turning around, she cracked her elbow on the shower stall door. The world stopped for a second while the frosted glass rattled in its metal frame. If she'd destroyed the door as well as the shower, Shane wouldn't have to toss her off the boat. She'd jump and save him the trouble.

It stopped rattling and settled back into place. Relieved, Gillian squeezed as much water from her hair as she could, then wrapped the damp towel around her goose-pimpled body. She couldn't wait to get topside and let the warm sea air chase away the chill.

She opened the door only to see Tank sitting upright in the middle of the bed, his body tense, his upper lip curled to expose big white teeth.

Uh-oh.

Gillian poked her head out the door and followed Tank's laser-beam vision to Shane, who stood next to the bed, stuffing the last of a miniature Snickers bar in his mouth and glaring back at the dog.

"Hi." *Brilliant, Campbell. You can sound more intelligent than that.* "I broke your shower."

He flicked his gaze to the bathroom door, slid it to her face, then let it take a leisurely wander down to her bare feet and back up again. She stifled the urge to feel the bottom of the towel and make sure the vital bits were covered.

He didn't comment on the shower; he didn't comment on anything. He chewed his candy bar and looked at her with enough heat in his eyes to erase any residual chill she might be feeling. In fact, the room was awfully warm. Who needed sea air?

They both jumped at the thump of Tank hitting the floor as he hopped off the bed and padded over to sit between them. Thank God, a distraction. Shane had it all wrong. Distractions were good.

"What happened to the shower?" Shane walked around her and peered in the bathroom door. "I heard a crash. Did you fall? Oh, wait. Let me rephrase that. Did you fall—again?"

She'd almost given herself a concussion on the edge of the sink. "Not technically. There's not enough room to actually hit the floor."

He coughed to cover what sounded suspiciously like a laugh. "True enough. Talk to me about the shower; did it suddenly stop working?"

Ah, maybe it was a recurring problem and not her fault at all. "It did. Turned ice cold for a few seconds and then just *pffft*—nothing."

"You were in there too long; it's set to shut off after ten minutes to conserve the water supply." He sidled around Tank. "Shipboard life, rule one: short showers."

If he was giving her rules, maybe he'd accepted that she was here for the duration. She could afford to be generous. She did need him, and Jagger had been right. The success or failure of the dive, and thus her ability to keep Holly safe, rested with him.

"Look, I'm sorry for sneaking on board. It's just that I feel so damned helpless." The fear and anger and sadness of the past few days tangled into a big knot of pressure behind her eyes. If she ever began to cry, she didn't think she could stop, so she mentally compacted the pressure and stuffed it down. "Being here makes me feel as if I'm doing something, even though I'm not."

Shane took a step closer and rested a hand on her shoulder. It was big and warm and strong. Gillian wanted nothing more than to take the implied invitation, move toward him, accept comfort.

But Tank, who'd been sitting sandwiched between their legs, barked and jumped up, forcing them each to step backward.

"Couldn't you have boarded him or found a dog sitter?" Shane bared his teeth at Tank, who gave him teeth in return.

"He just needs to settle down." She didn't want to make the pathetic confession that, other than Vivian, Tank had never been forced to share her attention with anyone else. "And I'll work hard. Just tell me what to do and I'll do it." As long as he didn't try to bully her again, or lie to her.

"There is something you can do, but . . ." Shane's face flushed beneath his tan. "I think it would be easier if you were wearing clothes. You're kind of . . ."

"Ahhh, yeah." Maybe Jagger had been telling the truth. Gillian didn't plan to ask.

"Meet me in the salon, back by the galley?"

She smiled. "Sure. And don't worry—I'm not planning to take over your bedroom. I can sleep anywhere."

"We'll figure it out." Shane walked to the door and looked back with raised brows. "Just stay out of my chocolate drawer."

What? How could he—? As soon as the door closed and she'd had a chance to stand next to the drawer where Shane had been eating his Snickers bar, Gillian spotted the wadded-up foil of the Kiss she'd stolen. Busted.

She dressed quickly, tugging on her favorite worn jeans and a long-sleeved red T-shirt. *The Evangeline*'s air-conditioning system worked well and kept things cooler than she was used to, working outside in the heat most of each day at the reserve.

"Okay, mister." Gillian sat on the edge of the bed and gave Tank a stern look. He gave her a stubborn, serious look in return. "You can stay here by yourself." Bad idea; he might pee on Shane's bed to make a statement, the way he always dowsed the door at the vet's. "Or you can go with me and learn how to socialize. It's okay if I have friends."

Friends. Ironic that she'd consider these guys her friends, but she did. Or at least she could pretend they were friends until reality slapped her upside the head again. She'd been slapped enough in the past few years to know it was inevitable.

She was headed along the portside passage toward the galley, when the boat shuddered and jerked. Gillian caught herself on the wall and listened. The steady hum of the motor and soft whir of the air-conditioning system sounded normal, so she continued on. Shane sat in one of the salon chairs, looking at a map of Canada's eastern provinces. She'd studied that coastline enough in the past couple of days to recognize it from across the room.

She peered into the galley. "Where's Jagger?"

Sandwich-making stuff and bags of chips sat on the short counter, alongside simple blue plates and mismatched silverware.

Shane looked up from his map. "He went topside to see why we stopped. It's probably nothing."

Gillian sat in the upholstered booth across from him. "You said there was something I could do to help? I really want to."

Shane pushed the map into the middle of the table. "I thought of it after you said you might have found some leads about your family genealogy online. Do you think you could do some research into who might have an interest in this cross and also who might have the power and money to go after it?"

Gillian had stuck her laptop in her case as an afterthought, but it needed a Wi-Fi signal. Her smartphone didn't, though. Maybe they'd be close enough to land the whole way up the coast to keep a steady stream of free wireless signals. "It has to be someone not only with money and power but also completely without morals. Maybe a history of power mongering. Yeah, I can do that. Maybe we can all sit down and—"

Shane looked away from her and frowned, and Gillian followed his gaze to the passageway. Jagger hurried toward them, his long hair loose and streaming over his shoulders. "We need you topside, Shane. Another boat flagged us down—forced Harley to pull up fast. They're lucky we didn't plow right over them."

Shane was already on his feet before Jagger got the last words out. "Is it another marine unit? We should be in Pinellas County jurisdiction by now."

Jagger looked at Gillian, then back at Shane, somber, all traces of boyish charm gone. "It's not police or even Coast Guard. It's two dudes with guns, demanding to talk to either you or Gillian."

14

First, the beast from hell had flattened him. Then he got caught with his hand in the candy drawer by an almost-naked woman and instead of kicking her out of his room, he had wanted to repossess his towel and kiss her. Now, some moron was waving a gun around and asking for him by name.

Shane's calm, reclusive life as a semipermanent member of the marginally employed had been blown to hell in less than seventy-two hours.

No, make that a moron with a gun asking for him or Gillian, which meant it had something to do with the blackmail—but weren't they already giving Tex everything he wanted?

He hurried along the passageway and assumed Gillian was behind him, but when he turned to suggest she go to the pilothouse and retrieve his service weapon from underneath the navigation seat, she wasn't anywhere to be seen, and neither was Jagger.

An air of déjà vu swept over him as he strode through the door onto the portside deck and saw a small white vessel idling alongside *The Evangeline*. This one didn't have a Levy County marine-unit logo on the side or a swaggering blue-uniformed fake deputy on board, however.

Shane assessed the scene quickly, from the last dregs of sunset sinking in the west to the big overhead swing light that Harley had adjusted to illuminate the smaller boat. A young guy wearing a bandana, maybe early twenties, held a wavering shotgun on Harley, who stood with his legs apart and his arms crossed tightly over his chest. Shane's friend looked anything but intimidated.

The second guy on the small boat, wearing a Florida State baseball cap, might be older—maybe late thirties—but he held his shotgun in his arms more like an infant than a weapon. His eyes widened when he spotted Shane, but he still didn't drop the gun into a firing position.

Strictly amateur hour. Of course, amateurs with guns were probably more dangerous than experts. But whatever Tex and his employer wanted, Shane didn't imagine it involved them being shot by a couple of yahoos before they found the treasure.

"Harley, I'll take it from here. Go back in the pilothouse." *And find the pistol, and get ready to move this boat, just in case I'm wrong.*

He walked nearer the side rails of *The Evangeline*. "I'm Shane Burke. What do you guys want?"

Harley turned and headed toward the door into the boat's interior, and the younger guy swerved the shotgun toward Shane, who raised his hands. "Don't get excited. I'm not armed."

The guy reached up to adjust the blue and white bandana, causing the gun barrel to wave precariously. These guys were worse than amateurs; they were idiots.

"I don't want no trouble," Bandana said, his focus darting from Shane up to the pilothouse and back. "We just got an envelope to deliver to you or Gillian Campbell, and then we'll be on our way home."

Couriers, then, which meant they probably didn't know a thing. "Deliver an envelope from whom? Who hired you?"

"I don't know. Gary, give him the envelope."

"Don't use my fuckin' name, *Chris.*" Baseball Cap propped the shotgun against the side of the smaller boat and bent over to pull a thick packet from underneath a seat. He walked to the side of the boat nearest *The Evangeline* and tossed it on board.

The generic manila envelope landed with a splat and slid a couple of feet before coming to a stop, facedown. A metal clasp secured the back. Shane waited to see if it would explode or burst into flames, but from the shape of its contents and the way it landed, he guessed its precious cargo was a stack of papers.

"What did the guy look like who hired you?" Shane made no move to pick up the envelope. If this delivery was the hapless Gary and Chris's only task, they wouldn't be hanging around, so he needed to question them before they took off.

"It was left for us on our boat," Gary said, then turned to Chris. "Put down that dang-fool gun. You look like the redneck you are."

Yeah, well, neither of them would win any IQ contests. "How'd you know what to do with it?" Shane asked.

"Some dude called me, but he didn't give me a name." Chris settled his shotgun on one of the boat's bench seats. "Said he got my number from the marina we use over in Tarpon Springs and knew we fished this area. Offered us a bundle of cash to deliver an envelope, no questions asked."

Shane looked toward shore. Harley had piloted them pretty far out to avoid the shelf of shallows along the coastline in the central part of the state. "You look in the envelope?"

"No sir." Chris answered with enough vehemence to convince Shane he was telling the truth. "The guy with the money said not to, and he didn't sound like a guy I wanted to mess with."

"What *did* he sound like?" Gillian asked.

Shane turned to see her stepping from the passageway and did a double take at the pistol tucked in the band of her jeans. It wasn't his, which meant she'd brought her own. Interesting.

Still no sign of Jagger, but Shane figured he had joined Harley in the pilothouse.

Now that they'd unburdened themselves of the envelope, the couriers were willing to share what they knew. Unfortunately, it wasn't much. "The guy had a deep voice. He sounded kinda like John Wayne in one of them old western movies," Chris said.

"Tex." Gillian's voice was flat. "Did he threaten you?"

"No ma'am, but he sounded . . ." He scratched beneath the edge of the bandana. "Serious. Like he was threatening without actually threatening, you know? I just want to get back to the marina and get the rest of the cash that's supposed to be waiting for us. We gotta be back by nine thirty."

Yet they weren't leaving. Shane walked to the envelope, leaned over, and picked it up. Definitely papers. "What else are you supposed to do to let our friend Tex know you left the papers?"

Chris and Gary exchanged looks. "We need a picture of one of you with the envelope, to prove we delivered it," Gary said. "We don't get the money without it. Just a cell phone shot."

"Take it then." Shane held up the envelope in his left hand, pointed the middle finger of his right hand toward heaven, and gave Chris a shit-eating grin until the phone's camera clicked and the flash left him seeing blue dots. "Where are you supposed to send this shot?"

"To an e-mail address."

Shane's pulse sped up as Gary took Chris's phone, punched a few buttons, and waited. Maybe Tex had finally screwed up. "And before you ask, it's going to one of those free e-mail addresses, to 'CharlieBurke'—all one word."

An itch stole across Shane's shoulder blades. If that son of a bitch Tex had actually brought Charlie into this . . ."You guys better get going then," he said. "And this man who called you is bad news. If he offers you another job, turn him down."

Not that Tex would take no for an answer if he found another need for the hapless Chris and Gary.

The small white vessel, a serviceable little fishing boat about twenty-five-feet long, looped wide around The Evangeline and made its way toward shore. The guys actually waved as they pulled away. Shane didn't feel inclined to wave back.

He handed the envelope to Gillian. "You and Jagger meet me back in the salon to see what our friend Tex sent us. I'm gonna ask if Harley can get us into a riverfront marina in Fort Myers. We'll anchor there overnight."

Gillian had opened the envelope and pulled back the top flap, pulling out a sheaf of papers. "Too dark to see what it is." She looked up at Shane. "Do we really have time to stop for the night? Can't you guys take shifts?"

Shane shook his head. "We could run straight through if we were going all the way down to the Keys to cross from the Gulf into the Atlantic, but it's faster to cut across the middle of Florida through Lake Okeechobee. The crossing needs to be done in daylight. In the long run, it'll save us at least a day or two, or maybe more."

In retrospect, he wondered if he shouldn't have rented a truck and towed *The Evangeline* at least as far as Charlie's, but every state had its own limit as to how big a vessel one could pull. This might not be faster, but it would be simpler and less likely to run into complications unless there were problems filing his navigation plans in the morning.

After working with Harley to find a marina and making the arrangements to refuel overnight, Shane walked back to the salon. Gillian and Jagger sat hunched over the table, sorting papers into three stacks.

"What've we got?" Shane pulled a soda out of the fridge and sat opposite them.

"Clear sailing to Nova Scotia." Jagger handed one stack of papers to Shane. "Those are navigation plans filed with the Coast Guard and with Canadian Customs, clearing our arrival with a three-day window. Already stamped and approved."

Frowning, Shane flipped through the papers. "Everything looks like it's in order. But who filed them?"

Jagger broke into a halfhearted version of "Sympathy for the Devil."

"You did." Gillian said, her voice sarcastic. "Don't you remember?"

Sure enough, each of the forms had been issued in his name, with "Signature on File" on the bottom line. "Who has the kind of pull to do something like this?" He looked at the papers again, more slowly, holding each page up to the light to see if he could see signs of a fake. The documents were watermarked; the seals embossed. "Harley was guessing someone highly placed in intelligence or the military or politics. This makes me think he's right about the big boss being one of those."

"Or all three." Jagger pushed the other stacks of paper across the table at him. "Take a look at those next. I'm going to take Harley some dinner and then spell him for a while before we get to Fort Myers."

Shane looked up. "Yeah, one of us needs to be awake and alert whether we're docked or not. Take it until about 2:00 a.m., and I'll pick it up until we get started through the lake."

"Sounds good." Jagger packed sandwiches from the fridge into a bag and headed down the passageway. He wasn't singing. Bad sign.

"I can take a shift too," Gillian said. "Use me for the times we don't need navigation. I can stand watch as well as the next person."

Shane began looking through the second stack of papers. "Tell me about the gun."

Gillian laughed. "Saw that, did you? I've taken it everywhere with me since all this mess started. I use it when I go on gator calls, and it's not just for looks. I know how to shoot."

Shane's exposure to alligators was limited to zoos. Every once in a while he'd hear about one locally, but Cedar Key was three miles out into the Gulf. "You shoot the gators?"

"No!" Gillian looked horrified. "If they're adults, I catch them, load them in my truck, and eventually relocate them to a gator sanctuary. If they're small, I take them into the wild and release them."

Shane tried to imagine her wrestling an alligator into the back of her pickup and couldn't quite do it. "Where does the gun come in?"

"That's for the humans." Gillian smiled. "People are more dangerous than alligators. A lot more dangerous." She pointed to the papers Shane had been flipping through. "What is all that? It's gibberish to me."

"Somebody's been busy." Shane turned the sheets around so that she'd see them right side up. "Currents and water hazards along the Atlantic coast for this month, all the way from South Florida to Newfoundland. The others show times of high and low tides. Frequencies to monitor on the radio to get the latest conditions. Stuff we'll need to make this trip, in other words."

Gillian shook her head. "They want to make sure we don't waste time. The thing that I keep asking myself is, if these guys have so much pull and so many resources, why don't they just do some investigating themselves and hire divers in Nova Scotia to do their dive? It would be faster."

Shane leaned back, sliding the charts away and pulling the final stack of papers toward him. "I've been wondering the same thing. It's like . . ." He wasn't sure how to describe it. "It feels as if it's almost a game for them, to see how much they can push us. To play god, and see how far their power extends. Because you're right. If all they want is the Knights Templars' cross, there are a lot more efficient ways to get it."

Which meant the person pulling the strings enjoyed the process as much as the procurement. He not only liked winning—who didn't?—but liked the journey.

"We need to try and figure out who this guy is." Shane propped his elbows on the table. "While we're in Wilmington getting the provisions and retrofits, can you do more online research for us?"

"I don't have to wait; I brought my computer with me. Do you have an Internet connection?" She glanced out at the deck, but everything beyond it was black. "I guess not, out here."

Shane laughed. "No, only at the marina in Cedar Key. If we hang closer to shore, we can usually pick up free signals near more populated areas. Otherwise, you might have to go to a coffee shop or library in Wilmington."

"I don't think we'll be in Wilmington all that long." Gillian tapped a finger on the third stack of papers, the ones Shane hadn't yet examined. "Tex has been busier than you realize."

"What?" He picked up the papers that had been secured with a paper clip with a blank sheet on top. Beneath was a copy of a provisions order, setting up *The Evangeline* for the rest of the month, including prepaid fuel stops. The supplies were scheduled to be delivered to the boat in three days' time, to a slip number in the marina nearest Charlie's house.

He got that itchy feeling between his shoulder blades again. "No matter what we do, Tex seems to be a step ahead. I don't like him nosing around where Charlie lives. I don't like him even knowing Charlie exists."

Gillian's laugh was harsh. "If there's one thing to be said for old Tex, it's that his research into his victims is very thorough. I mean, he knew you were a tec diver. He knew about your financial situation— he told me you were on the verge of losing everything. Why wouldn't he know about your uncle as well?"

Embarrassment mingled with worry. "It's one thing for him to know I'm a total fuckup. Another to track down an uncle I haven't talked to in ten years."

"But you love your uncle," Gillian said. "I can see it on your face; you're worried. Which is just the thing Tex preys on. He knows my niece is special to me, that threatening a child was something I'd respond to, and that's where he put the screws."

"Well, I want to keep Charlie out of it. I'm beginning to wish I hadn't even called him. And why would—" Shane was about to ask why threatening a child would be something Gillian might respond to more than anything else, but he'd seen the second sheet in the stack. A work order at Cape Fear Boatyard, also for three days' time, for emergency retrofitting of *The Evangeline*. The name on the work order was followed by a familiar phone number—Charlie Burke's.

Shane had hoped to keep Charlie out of this cluster in the making, but he was too late.

15

Shane's face had done a full lap around the color wheel, from a deep red when he'd gotten embarrassed about his finances to now, blanched white with fear for his uncle. Gillian recognized the signs of a freak-out; the same emotions had fueled her when she'd made that call to Gretchen's. Even though she'd had to lie to her sister, she'd felt better after hearing her voice.

"Call your uncle." Gillian reached out and covered one of Shane's hands with hers and squeezed. "Chances are, Tex did all this stuff without even talking to Charlie and he's clueless about it. As long as we do what they want, he'll never have to get involved."

She had to believe that in order to keep going. She had to believe that Gretchen had bought the story about the stalker and was being watchful—never guessing the true danger.

If there was danger. Gillian had moments when she wondered if Tex and whoever pulled his strings just enjoyed playing with people's lives. To see how high they could make someone jump, but without the intention of ever following through with their threats. But how could one take a chance?

Those moments of doubt had become less frequent since Harley's bar had been destroyed. Still, there was a part of her that prayed Tex would walk away if she and Shane failed. Another part of her feared their failure would bring more ruin, if not death, to someone they loved.

And Shane clearly loved his uncle.

He pulled out his phone and sat looking at it.

"It'll make you feel better," Gillian said.

"We're too far out to get a signal. I can try him when we dock in Fort Myers." Shane not only looked worried, but the skin below his eyes had darkened with exhaustion.

"Stewing over these papers won't help anything. If you're going to take watch at two, why don't you try to get a few hours' sleep? I'll wake you if anything happens."

Gillian thought he'd argue with her, but Shane nodded and pushed back from the table. "Harley's got his stuff in the small room off the starboard passageway—it's noisy because it's next to the engine room, but it's got two bunks in it. We'll take turns using the bed in the master suite. Since we're working in shifts, it should even out."

Gillian followed him down the portside passage and cut across the width of the boat to the master bedroom. "I'll get my stuff out of here or at least shove it in the corner out of the way. Let me take Tank out first; he's a good boy, but every dog's gotta pee."

Shane hefted her bag into the corner and gave Tank a raised eyebrow. "No problem."

Gillian had put Tank's stuff in what she'd deemed the ship's least-used corner, an empty cedar-lined room off the back of the galley whose function she couldn't guess. She'd put his bed in one corner, stainless steel water and food bowls in another, and spread out some plastic-lined pads behind the door in case he had business to do during the night.

Now, she slipped the dog into his full harness to increase her control over him. She'd never walked him aboard a boat in open water, much less at night. He pulled her the length of the deck a couple of times but didn't try to get near the rail.

Brilliant stars littered the inky black sky, and while Gillian didn't have enough sailing experience to gauge their speed, *The Evangeline* seemed to be moving at a fast clip. The rocking motion of the boat was less pronounced out here than it had been in the salon, the movement more gentle. She still had to brace her legs to keep her balance, but thought she'd get the hang of it and maybe even enjoy it in a day or two. She already savored the fresh cool tang of the sea air blowing on her face.

After a few minutes of walking, she took Tank back to the cedar room. "Stay." She pointed a finger at him, then at his bed. He slinked over, turned a few times, and flopped down, giving her an accusatory look.

"I know you don't like it, but get over it. Who knows—I might come back in here and sleep with you. I'm not sure how all this bed-sharing business is going to work."

She left the door cracked in case he got scared and needed to find her, then walked back down the passageway to get her contact lens and makeup bags and move them to Tank's room. Then she'd know where they were, no matter where she was sleeping.

She knocked softly and slipped into the master suite, hoping Shane had already nodded off. Somebody on this boat needed to be well rested. She sure wasn't. Harley couldn't possibly be, and she doubted Jagger was either. They were going to be one ragged bunch of treasure hunters by the time they reached Canada if things didn't change.

But Shane wasn't asleep. He'd taken off his shirt and shoes and lay on his back, green eyes wide open and staring at the ceiling. The bedside lamp was still on.

"Can't sleep? I just wanted to get some of my stuff and put it in that cedar room off the galley—what's that for, anyway?"

"Stay and talk to me a while. I'm too wired to sleep." He slid over a little and patted the bed. "I've never really been sure what to do with that room. The guy I bought the boat from called it a locker room, but it's basically a little cedar-lined box."

Gillian sat next to him, too aware of all that tanned skin over muscle within easy touching distance. As if to prove how easy, Shane reached out a hand and wrapped long, strong fingers around her arm and squeezed. "Stay here with me. I promise not to turn into a horn-dog. I just don't want to be inside my own head right now."

They were adults, after all, in control of their hormones. Gillian would be thirty next month, and she knew from Tex's dossier that Shane was thirty-three. They weren't horny teenagers who couldn't be around the opposite sex without getting naked.

She stretched out next to him and closed her eyes, breathing in the scent she now knew came from his shampoo and shower gel, absorbing the warmth radiating from his skin.

Turning on her side to face him, she propped up on one elbow. "What happened between you and Charlie? Only if you want to talk about it. If not, we can talk about, I don't know, alligators or life on Cedar Key."

He laughed and stretched out his left arm, gathering her toward him so that her head rested on his shoulder. "I don't know about gators, but I have a feeling you could talk about them a long time. A discussion of life in Cedar Key would be a short story. It's a simple place, which is why I like it."

"I understand—it's why I like living out near the reserve, too." It was isolated. Quiet. It carried no reminders of painful times. Had Shane's time with Charlie been painful?

"Did you grow up in North Carolina?"

Shane didn't answer for at least a minute, so Gillian let it go, enjoying the silk of his skin under her cheek, the light sprinkling of blond hair on his chest to which her fingertips had automatically gravitated.

"I was born just outside Wilmington, but my father walked out on us when I was just a couple of years old. I don't even remember him, except from pictures. I look a lot like him." Shane's voice was distant, his gaze fixed on the ceiling; he was probably seeing scenes from a long time ago.

"So your mom raised you alone?"

"She remarried and when she and her husband and new baby moved to St. Louis, I refused to go. I was only five but already felt as if they weren't my family. I was a reminder of a life that hadn't worked out very well. Didn't help that I looked just like a Burke."

Now the story became clearer. Gillian could imagine a little boy who thought his mom loved her new baby more, who maybe even felt guilty because he looked like the man who'd abandoned them. "Charlie was your dad's brother?"

Shane nodded, and the arm he had stretched around her body tightened as he trailed his fingers up and down her arm. "He was a commercial fisherman, a lot like Jagger's dad. He'd travel to Canada to fish during the summer and move down the coast when winter came. He took me in, taught me his love of the water, encouraged me to take up diving."

No wonder Shane loved the water so much and seemed so at home on *The Evangeline*. "What about your mom?"

"She was relieved when Charlie offered to take me."

Just a few short words, but they were loaded with pain. Shane's mother probably hadn't been relieved at all. Gillian couldn't imagine a mother ever being happy to lose her child, even if it was only a geographical loss.

Not a day went by when she didn't think about Ethan and ache for him. Of course her child's loss had been more than geographical.

No, she couldn't believe Shane's mother had been relieved to be rid of him, but it had seemed that way to him, which made his little-boy pain real enough that it had followed him into his adult life. "I'm sorry," she said, her voice no more than a whisper. "No child should ever feel that way."

He shifted to look at her, reaching across with his right hand to wipe a tear away that had escaped before she knew it was there. "Gillian, did you lose a child? Or would you rather not talk about it?"

She'd hoped to get Shane to tell her what happened between his uncle Charlie and himself, but somehow he'd drilled right to the heart of her deepest pain.

"I can't. Maybe later." Maybe never. She'd never talked about Ethan—or Sam, for that matter—with anyone, not even Viv. Only the basics, stated in black and white. *My child died. My husband died.*

She'd told no one about the haunting shades of gray that filled the blank spaces within those stark statements of fact. Gray was the color of blame, guilt, and self-recrimination.

Another tear escaped and she took a deep breath to get herself under control. Slow her breathing. Lighten the heavy pressure against the back of her eyes.

"Okay, we've gotten too damn serious. Let's wipe out the last half hour and start over." Shane wrapped both arms around her, and she felt the press of his lips on her forehead. "Surely we can find something happy to talk about."

All I have to do is tilt my head and kiss him. She shouldn't. Both of them were vulnerable and lonely and, yes, even scared. Kissing him would complicate things between them even more.

Gillian closed her eyes at the soft sweep of Shane's fingers under her chin making the decision for her, and she raised her lips to meet his. Soft kisses, then hard. Sweetness turned to urgency. A dance of tongues and lips and hands honed her focus to him, blocking out the bad stuff.

She could get lost in him so easily and let him erase, for a few stolen minutes, the fear of the last few days and the loneliness of the past five years.

It's wrong. He rolled her onto her back, his mouth training nips and kisses down her throat while his heart pounded in time with hers.

We can't do this. She raked her nails up and down the smooth skin of his back, kneading the flexing muscles as he rocked against her. She moved her fingers as if her fingertips could read the braille of love and want.

He stilled, and she knew his thoughts had tangled with hers. "We can't do this."

"I know." She snuggled deeper into his arms, aching to have him kiss her again.

"But I want to." His voice sounded strained.

"So do I."

"Rain check?"

"Definitely."

Maybe. Depending on how all this played out, and whether guilt or anger or blame would drive them apart just as fear was driving them together. And depending on whether her past was ready to finally be the past.

So instead of making love, of using their bodies to erase the busy work of their minds, they lay together lost in their own thoughts. Gillian wondered where Shane's mind had wandered and whether his body and spirit, like hers, still took comfort in holding and being held.

For now, it was enough.

16

Shane stifled a yawn, looked up the stairs to make sure Harley was more awake than he was, and stepped onto the portside deck of *The Evangeline*. With any luck and the continuation of the perfect weather they'd enjoyed so far, today would be the day they'd reach Wilmington. Or, more accurately, the day they'd reach Southport, on the tip of the North Carolina spit of land below Wilmington.

The day he'd see Charlie for the first time in a decade.

The past four days had taken Shane on a roller coaster of emotions, beginning with the fear that had begun to gnaw at him when he'd learned Charlie had been dragged into this Knights Templars' mess.

He'd tried to call his uncle on and off through the Lake Okeechobee crossing but never got an answer. Not even voice mail. Once they'd exited the St. Lucie River and were back in the open waters of the Atlantic without cell service, he'd accepted that he wasn't going to know what was up with Charlie until he got to the man's house and saw for himself.

The illogical excitement over the coming dive had continued to build as well. Shane had found, on the bottom of the stack of provisions that would be delivered to the boat once it was docked in Southport, a list of diving equipment. Again, Tex, or whoever was working with Tex, had done his homework. Drysuits, tanks, regulators, BCDs. All top-of-the-line.

Shane would use his own equipment, the stuff with which he was comfortable. But his drysuit was ancient since he hadn't done a cold-water dive in so long, and his regulator needed replacing. Between the old diving equipment and the new, he'd be able to give himself an advantage.

The temperatures were already beginning their march toward winter as *The Evangeline* pushed northward. This morning, Shane got goose bumps even with his long-sleeved black T-shirt and jeans. No more shorts- or shoes-optional evenings for the rest of the month, although the days had remained hot and clear.

Once the fresh air had done its job in waking him up, Shane returned to the interior of the boat and ran into his first mate coming out of the master suite.

"I was looking for you." Jagger motioned for Shane to follow him down the starboard passage. "I want you to see something."

The man had driven them crazy with his singing the past four days, as shipboard life had settled into a comfortable rhythm and everyone relaxed a little. Had it not been for nagging worries about Charlie and what form Tex's next surprise would take, Shane might have enjoyed it.

Jagger wasn't singing this morning, though.

Shane craned his neck to see beyond Jagger into the galley. "What's up?"

"You need to see it."

When they rounded the corner to the galley and salon, what Shane saw was Gillian sitting in one of the upholstered booths frowning at her computer screen, Tank at her feet. She'd been hunched over the laptop all the way up the Atlantic coast while they'd had a reliable wireless signal, both researching Duncan Campbell and working up a profile of who their blackmailer might be. She must have found something.

His adrenaline kicked in, waking him up even more. "Have you found the evil genius who's pulling Tex's strings?"

Gillian looked up. "No, but look at this screenshot. It's of an article I found online this morning, from the newspaper in Clearwater."

The screenshot showed a newspaper interior page, centered on one short story: *Investigators Deem Fishing Boat Explosion Accidental.*

Shane's adrenaline took an ugly turn from excitement to horror as he slid the laptop in front of him and read the short article:

The Monday evening explosion of a fishing boat off the coast of Clearwater that resulted in the deaths of two local fishermen has been deemed an accident by Pinellas County investigators. Christopher Miller of Clearwater and Gary Walters of Dunedin were killed when their 24-foot fishing boat, The Buccaneer, *exploded offshore at 9:00 p.m. Monday.*

"Holy shit." Shane sat back, his mind spinning in shock. No way that explosion was an accident. Tex, or one of his buddies, had set it.

"Those two guys were loose ends," Gillian said, pulling the laptop back toward her, tapping a few keys, and then closing the lid with a snap that echoed through the galley like a gunshot. "They probably sent that photo of you to Tex, and after that they were expendable. It would be easy enough to set an explosive with a timer set to go off a half hour before they were due back at the marina at nine thirty. Too late for it to risk damaging *The Evangeline*, but before they'd have time to get docked and raise suspicions with their sudden influx of cash."

Jagger had settled on the bench seat sideways, his arms wrapped around his knees as he stared out at the blue water. "But they didn't know anything." His tone was bleak. "They couldn't have led anyone back to Tex or his boss. They were just . . ."

"Collateral damage," Shane said. His mind conjured up real and imagined images of the casualties so far. Charlie's face fixed in his mind, maybe already threatened. Harley sitting outside the smoking ruins of his life, crying. Gillian's friend, Vivian, her car wrapped around a tree. And now these two guys who probably thought they'd struck the mother lode of all easy jobs. Deliver an envelope for big bucks. Hell, he'd have taken a deal like that.

The comfortable camaraderie that had built up over the past four days sank into morose silence. Gillian's face had settled into a stony stillness, her dark eyes fixed on the floor. Jagger continued to stare out at the water, his expression grimmer than any Shane had ever seen on his friend.

"I'm going up top until we get docked." Shane didn't wait for a response but got up and left without looking back.

He paused at the entrance to the pilothouse, where Harley sat in the navigator's chair, talking on the radio and looking right at home. He liked piloting tight spots and knew the Southport area. Shane trusted him to take them into the marina.

More than he trusted himself right now. He pushed his way onto the deck, then climbed up to the flybridge. The day had turned hot, probably close to ninety, and the breeze had died down as they'd slowed to make the tight turn into the Bald Head Island inlet.

Shane barely registered their location through the fury that coated his mind and thoughts in black ice. If there was one thing Charlie had taught him, it was that true Burke men were slow to anger. But once they were pissed off, they held grudges that didn't die until justice had been served up on a platter like a roasted pig with an apple in its mouth. Shane's dad, Charlie had often opined, wasn't a true Burke man because he ran from things instead of turning around to confront them. The jury, Charlie had also often implied, remained undecided about Shane.

Shane hadn't understood the whole turn-and-confront thing until now. He'd been too busy beating himself up over the past to get angry, too busy wallowing in the idea that he deserved every bad thing that happened to him. Now, after all these years, he finally understood rage as Charlie had meant it. Rage wasn't a hot, fire-in-the-moment kind of anger. It was cold and sure-footed and lethal.

He wanted Tex and his boss. No matter how long it took, he would destroy them. Whatever they loved, he'd kill it unless they killed him first.

Maybe he was a true Burke after all.

The slow sail into the inlet, past the houses and churches and marinas of Southport, seemed to take forever. Once the boatyard was in sight, Shane took a deep breath and climbed off the flybridge, joining Gillian and Jagger on the forward deck. Tank, wearing a red harness with the leash end looped around Gillian's wrist, sat beside them, his head hanging between the rails. All their bags, including the one Shane had packed last night, were stacked against the inside wall.

Gillian turned at the sound of Shane's footsteps. "It's beautiful here. I'm not sure what I expected but it's more . . . something."

"'Picturesque' is the word the tourist brochures like to use." Shane propped on the rail next to her, noting the buildings as they passed and gratified to still recognize most of them. Duffy's Tavern was gone, replaced by Fisher's Cove. The Cod Piece, a restaurant whose name had outraged the local citizenry when it first opened, was now Catch of the Day.

But the old buildings remained, painted in soft pastel shades. The live oaks dripped Spanish moss over the streets lined with beautifully restored Victorian houses. The lighthouses. The wildlife refuge. All were just as he remembered them, and a deep wave of homesickness struck him like an unexpected high tide. Why had he stayed away so long? From this beautiful little town, and from Charlie?

Get a grip, Burke. If he let himself get too sentimental, especially over Charlie, it would hurt all the more when the old man chewed up his ass and spit it out. And it would happen; the only question was when. Charlie had been a grumpy old man when Shane was a kid, even though he now realized the "old man" had only been in his thirties. Now that he was in his sixties, God only knew how cantankerous he'd be.

A tugboat pulled up alongside *The Evangeline*, and Shane lowered the gangway for a local pilot to guide the boat through the traffic of the Cape Fear River. Harley had taken possession of all the provisioning and retrofitting papers and said he'd stay with the boat until everything was squared away for the transport to the boatyard and the delivery of provisions. He might join them at Charlie's later.

The two men had met before during their seafaring days but didn't know each other well, and Harley was a solitary man by nature. Shane suspected he would end up staying in one of the hotels near the boatyard.

"Enjoy the scenery for a minute," Shane told Gillian, gesturing for Jagger to follow him inside.

An eyebrow hike was her only hint at suspicion, but she didn't argue.

Jagger trailed Shane to the master suite. "What's up? Did you finally get in contact with Charlie?"

Shane knelt and pulled a bag from a storage area beneath the bed. "No, he's still not answering." It worried him more than he cared to admit. "I wanted to see if you'd mind staying with Harley, getting the boat taken care of. Gillian needs to go with me so we can get her computer set up for however long we're here." Not to mention the fewer witnesses to whatever hurtful words Charlie had for his nephew, the better.

"Sure." Jagger whistled when Shane handed him a stack of the hundred-dollar bills Gillian had brought aboard with her. "Hell, we should stay at one of the fancy-schmancy places in Wilmington."

"Might as well spend some of it." Shane had thought about sending half of the money to his froggy pals at First Bank and Savings, but if he got his ass killed, which seemed a good possibility, the liquid assets would be of more value than *The Evangeline* to whoever ended up with his stuff, whether Jagger or Charlie or even Gillian.

Jagger folded the notes up and tucked them in the pocket of his jeans. "Call me when you get to Charlie's and let me know what's up.

I might hang with Harley and stay somewhere near the boatyard. Oversee the retrofits."

"Good idea. Thanks." Shane put a hand on his friend's shoulder on his way out. "Thanks for everything."

Jagger broke into a chorus of "Emotional Rescue," and Shane grinned. Trust the Stones to break up an awkward, girly moment.

When he got back on deck, Gillian had taken Tank to the bow. Shane joined them, avoiding the side where Tank sat. "Everything okay?" she asked.

"I wanted Jagger to stay with Harley. Harley doesn't know my uncle very well, and I figured he'd want to stay near *The Evangeline*. I gave him enough of Tex's dirty money to pay for rooms."

Gillian leaned over the rail again. "It might as well come in good for something. So far, Tex has prepaid everything to be done here in Southport. Do you know how long we'll be here?"

Shane shrugged. "Depends on the boatyard schedule and the weather. Assuming Tex paid them enough to put a rush on the job, and assuming the weather stays this good, we could be out of here in a couple of days. Three tops. Or it could take a week."

"A week would be bad." Gillian looked up at the cloudless sky, as if searching for divine answers. Shane hated to break it to her, but whoever was behind this crazy show, he didn't think it was God or anything else divine.

Shane had been doing his own calculations. They'd have a maximum of two weeks to test-dive, find the wreckage of *The Marcus Aurelius*, and extract the cross. Two weeks, that is, if they could be out of here in three days. If they could make it to the coast of Nova Scotia in another five days. If they could find a local to smooth their way with the Cape Breton maritime community. If the weather held.

People's lives were riding on a lot of "ifs."

Once the boat was docked, Shane thanked the pilot, dropped the gangway, and saw him ashore before turning back to Harley and Jagger. "You guys going to be okay here?"

Harley waved the sheets of paper with all the work orders. "Gonna call the boatyard now and see if they can at least get her moved today. It's just past three, so they should be able to move 'er by dark and get started first thing tomorrow."

Shane hated to sound paranoid but, then again, he had a right. "Oversee the work if they'll let you," he told Harley and Jagger. "Look for anybody suspicious hanging around. When you inspect their work, look for bugs—you know, listening devices. Cameras. Anything like that."

So far, *The Evangeline* had seemed like a safe ground for them to talk freely, but this would be an ideal time for Tex and his pals to put bugs in place so that they could monitor what was going on during the dive itself.

"Got it," Jagger said. "Now, go see your uncle."

Shane nodded. Right. Now that he was here, he seemed to have turned back into the foot-shuffling boy who'd dawdle forever on the waterfront to avoid going back to Charlie's boat or, later, his little house a couple of blocks from the water.

Gillian waited by the gangway, her right arm pulled perpendicular to her body by Tank, straining on his leash and harness, trying to reach the shore.

"Looks like the hellhound is ready to get back on solid ground." Shane wondered if Gillian would consider leaving the dog with Charlie. If it didn't occur to her, maybe he'd suggest it. Later.

"No, he saw a cat on the dock and almost had a stroke." She laughed. "I can pretend he's my best friend all I want, but at the end of the day, he's still a dog."

They walked down the gangway with their bags and stopped on the raised sidewalk that ran the length of the marina's waterside pier. Now what? Shane looked around for a taxi, but Southport wasn't a taxi kind of town. "Would it have killed Tex to provide a limo and driver? He thought of everything else."

"I'd rather walk than ride in anything he arranged." Gillian set off down the dock, propelled by the hellhound-turned-cat-hunter, pulling her rolling suitcase behind her.

Only they were going the wrong way. "Tell Tank the best cats are over here."

She managed to get the dog sniffing in the opposite direction, and they strolled toward the treelined streets of the village, pulling their bags. "How far to Charlie's house?"

"Just a couple of blocks." Shane took in the details of his former hometown with a kind of visual hunger, memorizing details, making quick judgments on things that had changed for the better (the old vacant lot full of trash and abandoned boat parts was now a park), as well as things that had changed for the worse (a chain hamburger place had its modern plastic and glass storefront in the middle of a street filled with historic buildings).

Finally, they reached Cape Road, and Shane steered them to the right. "Charlie's is the second house on the left."

He stopped in front, surprised at how much smaller the house looked than it had in his memories. Its tattered shingles were still a faded teal blue, with white window trim and door. But the porch sagged in the middle, and the overhang was propped up with two-by-eights. A rain barrel, painted blue and green, sat to the side of the house, a set of bamboo wind chimes hung from either end of the porch, and an American flag flapped on a pole stuck in a pot with a wild, overgrown plant of some kind.

One thing hadn't changed—the view. Through the gap between Charlie's house and its much-better-tended neighbor, one could see the blue of the river, passing boats, and sunlight bouncing blinding rays off the water.

"Home sweet home," he said softly. "Damn it, I should've come back and helped out here." If he lived through this, he promised himself he'd come back and fix the porch, replace the columns, shore up the roof overhang.

"Charlie will be glad to see you. Don't worry about what's past." Gillian let go of her suitcase handle, grabbed Shane's wrist, and pulled. "Come on."

They walked together onto the porch, and Shane knocked.

No answer.

After a few seconds, he knocked again, harder. Something moved inside the door, but it still didn't open. He looked at Gillian, who shrugged and shook her head.

Something was wrong; Shane could feel it in his shoulder blades. "Charlie, it's Shane. Open the door or I'm going to have to bust it in."

The click of the deadbolt a few seconds later sounded abnormally loud, audible even over the tinkling wind chimes. Shane held his breath as the door opened an inch, then two.

Just wide enough for the double barrel of a shotgun to fit through, pointed straight at them.

17

"Don't shoot!" Gillian shouted the words before Shane could react to the barrel of the shotgun stuck through the door and aimed at his head.

"Goddamn it," said a gruff voice from inside. The shotgun barrel disappeared, replaced by a bloodshot eye with an iris of a familiar shade of green. The eyeball swiveled its gaze from Shane to Gillian and back. "You brought a goddamned woman with you? Well, don't that just figure. Never did have a lick of sense."

The door, covered in white paint so weathered it might as well be gray, eased open a few more inches. "If you're comin' in, do it fast. There's crazy people out there."

She and Shane exchanged glances, and Gillian could tell by his expression this wasn't normal behavior for Charlie—or at least it wasn't the last time Shane had seen him. Of course, a lot can happen in ten years. She was proof of that.

Shane motioned for Gillian to go in first, and she tugged on Tank's leash. The dog was all too happy to be first in the door, not one to be alarmed by shotguns or odd behavior from humans. He seemed happy to be on land again and had, along the walk from the marina, marked half of Southport as his own.

Tank ran straight for the old man, who'd moved to the middle of the room, and Gillian opened her mouth to screech for Tank to stop.

Shane would never forgive her if she let her dog maul his uncle. And why hadn't Shane mentioned that his uncle only had one leg?

As it turned out, Gillian didn't need to screech. Tank stopped and sat in front of the man, wagged his tail, and gave an un-Tank-like happy bark.

Charlie Burke focused on her and raised an eyebrow. "A woman and a dog, too. A regular goddamned family. Well, if you're comin', get on in here and lock the door behind you."

Charlie Burke wasn't what Gillian expected, which was an older version of his nephew. But besides the obvious—white hair, his face a field of wrinkles from sun exposure—he was short and heavyset. He propped on a crutch wedged under his right arm, and the right leg of his worn chinos had been folded up and pinned just below the knee.

The old man thumped out of a living room littered with magazines, newspapers, maps, food cartons, and dust and disappeared through a doorway in the back. Gillian turned to look at Shane, who'd taken on the appearance of a man who'd been hit with a stun gun. His skin was too white, his eyes too wide, his jaw tight. "You okay?" she whispered.

With some effort, he shifted his gaze to her, then up at the doorway Charlie had disappeared through. "What's happened to him?"

Only one way to find out. "Come on." Gillian leaned over and unclipped Tank's leash, and the dog loped through the living room, following his new buddy.

The door led into a dining room, or a space that had once served that function. The openings in the back and side of the room were closed, giving the windowless area the claustrophobic feel of an underground bunker. Charlie sat at the far end of the big square table, his crutch propped against the side. With his left hand, he scratched the top of Tank's head; with his right, he held the shotgun.

Shane cleared his throat. "Charlie, what's going on? It's Shane. You remember I was coming, right?"

Charlie had been staring at Shane since they'd entered, an un-blinking, hard stare. Now, he blinked. "Of course I remember. I got old, but you think I got stupid too, boy? Sit down."

They didn't need an audience for this awkward get-reacquainted session, so Gillian prepared to make an exit. She'd let them talk while she cleaned up that mess of a living room. She had a feeling Charlie wouldn't like it, but it would at least give her something to do. "I'll go and get our bags."

Before she could turn and get back through the door into the front room, Charlie spat out, "Stop right there, missy."

Gillian turned to face him, answering patiently. "Our suitcases are in the front yard, Charlie. They might attract attention if I don't get them inside, and we don't want to attract attention." She'd dealt with enough eccentric Florida recluses on gator calls to know how to address paranoia.

"Good point." He sounded calmer. "Get 'em in, then lock the door and keep the lights off. If you see anybody while you're in the yard, though, don't let 'em inside. I don't want to have to shoot you."

"No, I wouldn't much like that either." Gillian gave Shane a sym-pathetic look and eased into the living room. She stuck her head out and looked in both directions before hurrying into the yard, grabbing the bags off the walkway, and hefting them back inside. Paranoia was contagious.

Once in the house, she locked the door again and, with a regret-ful look at the piles of trash, turned off the lamp as Charlie had or-dered. She didn't think he'd actually shoot her, but then again, things in his life were clearly out of whack.

She paused at the door into the dining room, listening for what she hoped would be a normal conversation between uncle and neph-ew. But there was only silence, so she stuck her head inside. Charlie and Shane sat at opposite ends of the table. Charlie stared at Shane, and Shane fidgeted and looked at everything but his uncle.

"Come on in, girl. Reckon you're a part of this." Charlie reached over and pulled the heavy wooden chair to his left away from the table a couple of inches. Gillian took a seat, leaning over to check on Tank, who'd stretched out underneath the table with his head propped on Charlie's remaining foot. What happened to her antisocial, possessive guard dog?

Shane cleared his throat. "What's with the leg? You have an accident or something?"

"Nah. Blood sugar, or some such nonsense." Charlie thumped the crutch against the table. "It killed off some nerves and it was either lose the leg or die. I wasn't ready to die." He looked back at Shane. "If you'd been around, you might've known that. Happened five years go."

Ouch. Gillian glanced at Shane, but he was picking at a rough spot on the wooden table.

"You're right, and I'm sorry." He looked up at his uncle. "I'm sorry about all of it. I shouldn't have run off. I should've turned and confronted what happened, like Burke men do."

Gillian felt like an observer at a tennis match, looking from Shane to Charlie and back. This was not a conversation she needed to be a part of. It was not one she wanted to witness. But when she moved her chair back a couple of inches, ready to beat a retreat into the dark minefield of the living room, Shane met her gaze and shook his head.

For whatever reason, he wanted her to stay, so stay she would.

After the apology, Charlie had sat back in his chair and almost smiled. Or at least his lips curved up a little at the edges and Gillian thought it was a smile.

"You remember I always used to tell you that about the Burke men, huh?"

Shane gave one somber nod. "I do. I remember everything you told me. I just wasn't very good at doing it."

"That's the goddamned truth." Charlie propped his elbows on the table and let out a ragged breath. "It's good to see you, son. But what the hell have you gotten mixed up in?"

Shane gave her a warning look, one Gillian interpreted as *let me handle this*. Which was fine with her. "We're just heading up to Nova Scotia on a dive. Nothing big."

"Bull-hockey. Try again." Charlie's eyes narrowed in a stubborn look Gillian recognized. Shane had come by it honestly.

"Yeah, okay, it's a serious dive." Shane leaned back. To Gillian, he didn't sound the least bit convincing, so she hoped Charlie's bullshit radar wasn't turned on high.

"Serious how?" Charlie crossed his arms, an eyebrow hiked in a dare for honesty that was lost on Shane, who was busy avoiding eye contact. Gillian had seen it, though.

"There's a shipwreck off the eastern coast of Canada that we were hired to find," Shane said. "One of Gillian's ancestors was on it, along with some treasure. It's an old wreck that's never been found."

Not that Shane had introduced her, but he at least jerked his head in Gillian's direction.

"Who hired you?" Charlie was relentless.

"Some guys from, uh, Texas. Lots of money, not much sense. You know the type."

Gillian noticed Shane had picked at the spot on the table until he had to squeeze a splinter out of his finger.

She jumped at the crash that resulted when Charlie picked up his crutch unnoticed and banged it against the edge of the table. From the vicinity of their feet, Tank gave a low growl. "I never heard so much bullshit in my life. You tell me the truth, Shane O'Connell Burke, or you can take your woman and go off on your little treasure hunt. And the lunatics who are after you can follow you and leave me the hell alone."

Shane sighed and drummed his fingers on the table. A few seconds lapsed before he finally looked up at his uncle. "It's safer if you don't know."

The crutch made a good drumstick, and Charlie seemed adept at hitting things with it—in this case, the empty chair across from Gillian. It clattered to its back with enough noise that Gillian peeked under the table to see if Tank had gotten spooked. He was sound asleep.

"That ship done sailed, Shane. I'm in it whether you like it or not."

Shane's face flushed. "Look, old man. I'm telling you the truth, but I can't make you smart enough to believe it."

Oh, holy cow. This wasn't accomplishing anything, so Gillian decided it was time to get off the sidelines. "Mr. Burke, has someone been in touch with you?"

Charlie looked at her, and his fierce gaze softened a fraction. "Four days ago, it was. Guy showed up at my front door with a bunch of papers he wanted me to sign—work orders down at the boatyard, to outfit a trawler for a trip to Canada. Says he's paying the bills, but if anybody called, I was to say it was me making the arrangements." He looked back at Shane. "That your boat, *The Evangeline*?"

Shane nodded, looking miserable. Gillian wished she could comfort him. He'd hoped Charlie could stay out of this, but Charlie was in it further than they'd imagined. He'd actually met with Tex, or Tex's henchman.

"She's a forty-seven-foot trawler, outfitted as a yacht but with a workhorse engine," Shane said. "Bought her six years ago when I moved to Florida. So what did the guy do? Did he threaten you?"

Charlie nodded. "I told him to go to hell, that if you wanted me to sign papers, you could ask me yourself." He grinned. "The man didn't like that much."

Gillian could imagine. "Did he hurt you?"

"No." Charlie seemed to have relaxed now that they were talking. His shoulders had slumped, and he'd released his death grip on the arm piece of his crutch. "He first said he'd burn me out, and I told him to do it. I got insurance.

"Then he threatened Shane. Said if I didn't sign the papers, Shane wouldn't be able to do a job, and they'd have to kill him." He paused and nodded, almost to himself. "So I signed 'em."

Well, at least Tex was being consistent. Don't threaten directly; threaten the loved ones. It was an effective tactic.

"I'm sorry. God." Shane ran his fingers through his hair. "The last thing I wanted was for you to get dragged into this."

"Well, I wish I could say I was surprised, but after all that shit you were involved with in California, wouldn't nothing surprise me now." Charlie's voice had grown sharp again. Hard. "I figured you got yourself in trouble again and was running away from it. So I signed those papers, considered my good deed finished, and washed my hands of you. Again."

Shane flinched, and Gillian waited for him to defend himself, but he didn't.

Charlie pushed his chair back and reached for the crutch, hoisting himself to his feet. "So I'm done. You can take your lies and go on out. You can take your suitcase and your woman and keep running. I'm too old and sick for this to be the place you run to anymore. You tell your friends to leave me the hell alone."

Gillian stared at Shane, who seemed to have shrunk inside himself. Well, if he wasn't going to stand up for himself, she'd do it for him. More of that anger she'd been stuffing down began to spill out. She couldn't have stopped its progress if she'd wanted to, and she didn't want to.

"You sit back down right now, Charlie Burke." Gillian stood up and pointed across the table at the old man, then pointed at his chair. "You want some truth? Then sit the hell down and listen to it."

Shane looked up, eyes wide. "No, Gillian. It's—"

"No, it's not okay. Your uncle needs to sit his ass down, and he needs to shut his mouth." Shane wanted to keep the peace. He'd probably been doing that his entire life, afraid the uncle who took him in would cast him back out to a family he thought didn't want him.

Gillian didn't know what all had happened between them in the past, and maybe Shane had earned some of his uncle's bad temper. But he didn't deserve to be trashed because of this situation, when all he was trying to do was the right thing.

Charlie looked like a thunderstorm, gray hair and lightning-green eyes and cheeks with rivulets of wrinkles streaking down them. But he returned to his chair and clamped his lips shut.

"Good." Gillian pointed at Shane. "Nothing from you, either."

He threw up his hands as if to say *far be it from me to mess with a crazy woman.*

She turned back to Charlie. "I said I'd tell you the truth, and I will. In turn, once you hear it, you can't unhear it. You'll have to decide what you're going to do with it. Shane was being honest when he said the less you know, the safer you are. Do you understand that you're choosing to take the responsibility of knowing the truth?"

Charlie didn't answer, but kept his stony gaze fixed on her face. She'd have to take that as a "yes."

"I'm being blackmailed by the same people who brought those papers for you to sign. They threatened to kill my three-year-old niece if I didn't help them find a treasure one of my ancestors stole, then lost on a shipwreck a long time ago. To 'help' me, these people dug around and found the only technical diver in the area where we live—Shane—and exploited him into helping me."

She let that sink in for a few seconds, waiting to see if Charlie asked questions or Shane offered to take on the story. Neither did. Stubborn silence obviously ran in the family.

"Since you didn't ask what it was about Shane they exploited, it was financial. They knew he was in danger of his boat being foreclosed on, and offered him a lot of money." Gillian deliberately didn't look at Shane, knowing he'd be embarrassed by it. "Even needing the money, once he heard what the dive entailed, he still turned it down. That's when they threatened him, threatened his friend Jagger, and burned down his friend's bar. He's helping me in order to keep the people he cares about safe—and that includes you."

Gillian paused briefly and softened her voice. "So stop the critical bullshit. Shane is brave and unselfish and . . ." she ran out of steam. "And that's all I have to say."

Sometime during the last part of her tirade, Charlie had looked down at the table. Now he looked up at his nephew. "Does she say true?"

"Yes." Shane paused. "Except for the brave and unselfish part. These people scare the hell out of me."

"There's no shame in being afraid," Charlie said. "Shame is in running from it. Sounds like you have turned and confronted it." He cleared his throat and looked at the stove.

Gillian looked back at Shane, waiting for him to yield, say thank you, smile, do something. He kept his eyes down.

Good grief. "Obviously, you two are too stubborn to talk to each other directly. So, Shane, your uncle's proud of you for facing your fears and doing the right thing. Charlie, your nephew wants to please you, and it means a lot to him that you recognize it."

Men. They were hopeless. "Now, I am going to take a decent shower for the first time in a week if it's okay with Charlie."

He nodded.

She stood up and paused next to Shane. "You okay?" she asked softly.

He nodded, much as his uncle had done.

Fine. The Burke men could sit there and be guys.

"C'mon Tank. Let's go. I don't want you picking up any bad Burke habits." She stopped in the doorway and looked at her dog, who rolled his eyes at her from his position beside Charlie's foot and made no effort to get up.

"Traitor."

18

Shane swore the temperature dropped at least ten degrees when Hurricane Gillian blew out of the dining room. A chill silence settled in. He didn't know what to say to keep the conversation with Charlie going. He'd apologized for being an idiot ten years ago and said a silent prayer of thanks that Gillian hadn't asked what happened between them.

No, he'd just let her ride to his rescue while he sat here with his foot up his ass so far it had his tongue pinned down. She'd very succinctly told Charlie all he needed to know without too many details. Shane was horrified that Tex had been in Charlie's house, had threatened a crippled old man, but he didn't know what to do about it.

He pretended to examine his splinter cut while taking a closer look at his uncle. He'd been so shocked at Charlie's missing leg, he hadn't registered that Charlie, like the house itself, seemed so much smaller than he remembered, his torso lost inside a green plaid shirt that billowed around him like a sail. His uncle still had the booming voice and the intimidating stare and the rough edges, but his hands trembled a little when he reached down to wield his cane like a hammer or pet the dog.

That would be the dog who'd never treated Shane with anything better than benign neglect if not outright hostility, but who had fawned over Charlie from the minute they'd arrived. *Hellhound.*

"There's some bourbon in the cabinet over the fridge," Charlie finally said, as if none of the previous hour had occurred. "You got two good legs. Why don't you pour us a drink?"

Shane found the bottle, smiling at the black Jack Daniel's label. Charlie had had more influence on Shane than either of them realized, even down to the choice of poison. He rummaged around in the cabinets until he found a couple of glasses and set them on the table, pouring each of them a couple of fingers of bourbon.

"Need water or ice?" Shane asked.

"Water is for wimps and ice is for goddamned pansies."

Charlie was nothing if not eloquent. That much hadn't changed.

He waited until Shane was seated before he cleared his throat. "Tell me what you know about these blackmailers."

"Not a lot." Shane went through the story about the money and the blackmailers' uncanny ability to make things happen quickly. "We figure it has to be somebody in the military or government to move things that fast, not to mention highly placed and rich as God. You used to work the waters off Canada's east coast. How long would it normally take to get the paperwork cleared to bring in a boat from the US?"

"Let me see the papers."

Shane walked into the living room and fell over a stack of . . . something. Forget this paranoid crap; he needed a light. Once he'd felt around for the switch to turn on the lamp, he stepped over the stack of old newspapers that had tripped him and retrieved his suitcase. Charlie had always been a slob; they'd lived like one would expect a bachelor and his nephew to live—somewhere between pigsty and hovel. Not quite this bad, however. Shane, in turn, had grown up to be obsessively neat.

He unzipped the front compartment of his bag, where he'd stashed the travel documents after turning over the provisioning and retrofitting paperwork to Harley.

"What did the guy who came here look like?" Shane asked, returning to the dining room.

"Hell, I don't know. Several years older'n you, I guess. Dark hair going to gray a little on the sides."

Sounded like the fake Levy County marine deputy that had threatened him not to leave Cedar Key. It was a different guy than the one who'd set fire to Harley's, who'd been dark-haired and a few years younger than Shane. Shane filed the mental images away to examine later. Charlie's visitor and the fake deputy might be Tex himself.

He took his seat and slid the papers across the table to Charlie. "They filed the itinerary and navigation plans with both the US Coast Guard and Canadian Customs. Everything looks legitimate to me, but you've done a lot more border crossings than I have."

Charlie took his time, reading each document top to bottom, holding it close to his face so that he could see. If Charlie's diabetes was bad enough to have cost him a leg, Shane figured it probably had screwed with his vision as well. "You need glasses?"

Charlie squinted over the top of a pink sheet of paper and muttered, "Got some. Don't like 'em."

What a surprise. Shane nodded and kept his mouth shut until Charlie finally set the papers down. "They look real enough. The nav route they filed for you was done by somebody who knew the waters between here and Nova Scotia and what to look for in September, which means they hired it done and paid to get it done fast. And they got that go-ahead from Canadian Customs in less than twenty-four hours. Who the hell can make government offices jump like that?"

Shane shrugged. "That's the million-dollar question—literally. When they, whoever 'they' are, first approached me about this dive job, working through Gillian, they offered me a million under the table plus expenses."

"*Humph.* Now that they're using threats instead of bribes, do you still get the million if you find this thing they want? And what the hell *is* it they want so bad?"

"It's an old ruby cross that supposedly belonged to the Knights Templars—you know, from the Crusades. Middle Ages. If I can manage to find it, I'll be damned sure they pay the million if they want their precious treasure, because I'm guessing it's worth a hell of a lot more than that. I want the money, and I want some kind of believable guarantee that they'll leave all of us alone."

He hadn't quite figured out what kind of guarantee he'd find believable, but if they survived this venture, all of them—he and Gillian and their friends and family members—needed to go on with their lives without wondering when someone would creep out of the dark with a can of gasoline and a match, or set an explosive inside their boat or car.

"As for where the cross might be, Gillian can answer that question better than I can." Shane had heard the water from the shower cut off a few minutes earlier and hoped she'd rejoin them. "I think she also can give us a clearer idea of when the ship sank. Otherwise, I don't have a lot of hope of finding it. The North Atlantic's a big place." *And not a safe place to dive.*

"You screwed up by getting involved with the woman."

What was Charlie smoking? "I'm not—"

Charlie made an alarming noise that sounded like a cross between a wheeze and a honk. Shane pushed his chair away from the table, ready to rush over for a try at the Heimlich maneuver or at least to pound his uncle on the back. Then he realized Charlie was laughing. If the old man would do it more often, it might sound more natural. Shane slumped back in his seat and gave Charlie a sour look.

"That expression of yours was worth a million bucks by itself," Charlie gasped. "Don't deny it. If you and that Gillian girl ain't knocking knees yet, you will be. But it's still a mistake."

Knocking knees? God Almighty, did people still talk like that? Shane had fallen into a time warp without knowing it. "Even if it were true, which it isn't, it might not be a mistake."

Of course it was a mistake, but he was admitting nothing.

"There might come a time when you have to choose between her and surviving." Charlie's voice softened. "You been in that place before, son, and it almost destroyed you. In fact, until today, I thought it *had* destroyed you. Was convinced of it. If it happens again, you make the same choice as last time, you hear me? You choose to live. Just don't let it eat you up from the inside."

Shane found himself back in a dark place he rarely let himself visit, a dark, cold emptiness where death lay above him and life, in the form of a single rope, lay clutched in his hands. He shuddered as the familiar, icy tendrils of panic took him by the throat and squeezed.

"Shane—you okay?" Gillian's hand rested on his shoulder, and he looked up at her. Warm. Real. Alive.

The panic subsided and left Shane feeling akin to melted Jell-O as the adrenaline drained from his muscles. "Yeah, you up to talking about our friend Duncan Campbell?"

Her wet hair swept her shoulders, leaving damp spots on her dark green Scrub State Reserve T-shirt. She looked from him to Charlie and paused at the navigation sheets. "Yeah, let me get some stuff out of my bag."

By the time she returned, Shane had poured a couple of fingers of bourbon for her and set it on the table.

"Thanks." She pulled out a map and some typed sheets. "I found out a few things by talking to one of my great-uncles, but most of what I've learned came from one of those online genealogy sites."

"You've been holding out on me." Shane bit back the urge to grouse at her. He'd suspected she knew more than she'd told him, and that she'd planned to use it as leverage to get herself included on the dive. Now that she'd proven useful on shipboard, she figured it was safe to trot it out. He reached out and grasped her wrist. "Just so we're clear, no more holding back information. The time for playing games with each other is done. We're either all in or we're not. Agreed?"

At least she had the good grace to look embarrassed, even to blush a bit—which looked damned good on her. "Agreed. I'm sorry. I'd planned to tell you when we left Cedar Key, and then . . . I just didn't."

He nodded. She didn't tell him for the same reason he hadn't pushed himself too hard to develop a preliminary dive plan. It was easier to enjoy those past four days of peace and pretend they were together by choice and not under duress. "So, what can you tell us?"

Gillian sorted through her papers and pulled one out. "Okay, here's what I know of Duncan Campbell. According to the genealogy site, he was in his middle twenties, the youngest son of a youngest son who'd grown up near Glasgow. That pretty much meant he had no social prospects. He was married and had a young son himself when he took a job with a family, the Sandilands, who were tied in with the Knights Templars. Not knights themselves, I don't think, but some kind of patrons. I'm guessing the Campbells were part of the household staff. Maybe even servants."

Shane could imagine how Duncan, with a young family and no way to move up in a society that rewarded people for their birth order, would be tempted if surrounded by riches. "So he helped himself to some Templars' treasure and hopped a ship?"

"Sort of." Gillian rustled through her papers. "One branch of the Sandilands moved to France, and Duncan and his family went with them. I couldn't find out why they moved, but that was where Duncan allegedly stole the ruby cross and caught a supply ship, *The Marcus Aurelius*, that was headed to a place in Nova Scotia called Port Royal. Slipped his family out in the dead of night."

She set the papers back down and looked off into space. Shane had learned to recognize it as her thinking pose.

"The genealogists were full of theories about how the Sandilands sent the cross with Duncan to get it out of France. They think the plan was for the Sandilands to follow along later, help sell the cross to the British, and then split the profits." She shrugged. "I don't know how any of them would know that; it's probably guesswork."

"I know where Port Royal is, or was." Charlie spoke up for the first time. "It's on the northwest side of the province. Hard to get to, but a good place to harbor once you navigate in. That's where Duncan's ship went down?"

As badly as Shane felt about Charlie getting dragged into this mess, he was thankful for the man's experience. He might be able to help them in ways they didn't know.

Gillian shook her head. "No, the ship Duncan was on didn't make it as far as Port Royal. That's where it gets even more dicey." She rustled through some more papers. "I couldn't find any official documents on *The Marcus Aurelius*, but there were several accounts of the shipwreck from Duncan's descendants, stuff written down in family Bibles from different generations and different branches of the family. I guess the original story had been passed down by Duncan's son—who survived the shipwreck—to his children, and so on. But all the written accounts agree that the ship foundered off the coast northeast of what's now Louisbourg, Nova Scotia, on the farthest eastern point of Cape Breton Island."

She pulled out the provincial map of Nova Scotia and pushed it to the center of the table, pointing to a spot on the eastern shore.

"I don't need to see that map." Charlie leaned back. "That's the death coast, from Louisbourg all the way up to the tip of Cape Breton. Locals say there's shipwrecks stacked one on top of the other on the ocean floor off that whole area. What year did your ship go down?"

"About 1670, give or take a few years—originally, I'd thought it was earlier. That's the most I could narrow it down."

Charlie shook his head. "Chances of finding a ship that old in those waters aren't good at all. Shane, you're a talented diver, or at least you used to be. But you can't find what can't be found. It would take a miracle."

Shane pulled the map to him and studied it. The jagged coast-line of Cape Breton protruded far into the North Atlantic, dotted with various small islands and one or two larger ones. He found Louisbourg, tucked on the south shore of the peninsula, and traced his finger eastward to open water.

A ship coming from Europe would've been following the old Viking trade routes. If it wanted to navigate to the St. Lawrence Seaway, it would have to skirt the coast where it jutted out. One slight miscalculation or renegade wind would mean disaster. That largest outlying island would've been a definite hazard in a day where nav-igators didn't have conveniences like sonar or even freaking light-houses.

He tapped a finger on the big island, which was shaped kind of like a bird with its wings outstretched, flying to the west. "My guess would be that this is the most likely trouble spot for a ship that got caught in bad weather trying to round that cape."

Gillian stood up and leaned over the table so that they could both see the map. "Yep, that's the one. The closest community to it now is a place called Main-à-Dieu. The island is called . . . wait a sec-ond." She sat back down and rifled through the papers.

"Scatarie," Charlie said, his voice flat. "Scatarie Island. Last I heard, she was still bringing ships down. There's a big old tanker sit-ting on the rocks right now. Ran aground back in 2010 or 2011, I think, and sits there while everybody fights over what to do with her."

"You know anything about diving that area?" Shane slid the bourbon bottle across the table and Charlie caught it without a fum-ble. The man might be paranoid, and with good reason, but his re-flexes were still sharp.

"A little. It's a hard dive, or so I've heard. And your chances of finding something aren't good. Most of the wrecks that've been cata-loged around there are in fairly shallow water, but it's rough. Lots of wave action. Hard to handle a boat even during the calmest time of year, in June and July." He shook his head. "And this is September. Up there, it's not summer anymore."

Shane cursed inwardly, not wanting Gillian to see how concerned he was about this dive. Even the map looked menacing, and without an exact idea of where the ship went down, he was going to eat up a lot of time doing scouting dives. "I don't guess you know anybody in the area who could help us, do you?" he asked Charlie. "A local? Somebody who knows the legends and rumors and where the bodies are buried. Somebody who might be willing to help a guy who's diving for something not quite legal?"

The navigation plans said Shane Burke and his boat *The Evangeline* would be taking a pleasure trip, not trying to locate a shipwreck and recover treasure that legally belonged to Canada and the province of Nova Scotia.

Charlie tugged his crutch under his right arm and hoisted himself up with a dexterity that both surprised Shane and shamed him—clearly, his uncle had had time to learn how to get around with one leg, but he'd done it without the help of the closest thing he had to a son.

"I got the perfect person to help you." Charlie thumped toward the living room, and Shane and Gillian exchanged startled looks and scrambled to help him. But he'd managed to maneuver the heaps of junk just fine without them. Guess he'd had lots of practice.

"Who is this person?" Shane said, catching Gillian by the arm when she tripped over a footstool hidden beneath a pile of papers.

Charlie's voice floated toward them from the back of the house, where they found him pulling out drawers and opening cabinets in the room that used to be Shane's bedroom. The same little window looked out on the water, and the same dresser Shane had used was the one Charlie now ransacked. Finally, from a bottom drawer, he pulled out a small address book with a blue and white lighthouse on the front.

He held it up and grinned. "I'm going to introduce you to the most ornery old fisherman who ever walked the earth. His name's Chevy."

Great. Shane thought he'd grown up with the world's grouchiest fisherman. Nice to know there was someone even Charlie found ornery.

19

The number of people buying groceries in the Southport Sav-A-Center on a Friday night totaled three, counting Shane and Gillian. She had identified their fellow shopper as a college kid by the piles of ramen noodles and boxed mac and cheese in his cart.

After discovering Charlie's food supply had dwindled to a couple of frozen dinners and some canned tuna, Gillian had suggested putting some of Tex's money to use and stocking up.

Shane had been quiet since their discussion about the dive took place, and Gillian could tell he was bothered by it. She'd also overheard more than Shane realized of his conversation with Charlie about their past, and about how if he had to choose between saving Gillian and surviving, he should choose to live. She hadn't been eavesdropping, but sound carried in the little house and she'd been putting her dirty clothes in the back compartment of her suitcase when they were talking.

Jagger had hinted at something in Shane's past that had torn up his self-confidence, and while Charlie's tone was gruff, he was clearly worried that history might repeat itself.

When she'd gone back into the dining room, Shane's face had looked haunted. It was the only word Gillian could come up with to describe it. Both scared and anguished. She was torn between leaving the festering wound alone and asking him to tear it open so that she'd know what kind of issues he was dealing with. So much depended on his ability to do this dive.

"Think Charlie would cook a vegetable?" She picked up an eggplant and waved it across the aisle at Shane.

He frowned at it. "Not on a bet. Get stuff he can eat raw that's already chopped up."

Gillian watched him plow methodically through a shelf of peanut butter, reading labels and trying to decide what his uncle might eat. His hair was still damp from his own shower, and the fluorescent lights of the store gleamed off the blond highlights a person could only get from genuine sunlight and not from a bottle in a salon. The forest-green shirt he wore untucked emphasized his broad shoulders and trim hips.

Even from the back, he was too sexy for his own good. Yet he didn't seem to know it, which was the thing Gillian liked about him. Oh, he had that arrogant male thing going at times (and she certainly saw that he'd learned at the foot of a master), but it was based on what he could do and not how he looked.

She asked herself again: Why had Shane Burke been wasting away in Cedar Key, drinking at Harley's and taking just enough day-tour work to survive? Barely survive. The answer had to be tied to whatever had happened with that life-and-death decision he'd had to make.

By the time they finished shopping, they'd managed to spend several hundred of Tex's dollars on food and toiletries and cleaning supplies—at Gillian's insistence—and filled the back of Charlie's old blue van. The haul was heavy on nonperishables, but Shane insisted that he'd grown up on that stuff and he doubted, based on the containers strewn around the living room, that Charlie had developed a taste for cooking.

"Mind if I take a detour?" Shane steered the van around a pothole, but Gillian still felt as if she were on a carnival ride—or a wild mustang.

"This thing must have no shock absorbers on it."

Shane laughed. "Hell, I don't even know how old the van is. I learned to drive in it when I was fifteen, if that gives you a clue."

Gillian had to smile at the mental image of the beanpole Shane had probably been at fifteen, bouncing around town in his uncle's blue van. He'd probably thought he was one hot-chick magnet. "So what's this detour?"

"I thought I'd circle around by the boatyard, see if *The Evangeline*'s out of the water yet. I talked to Jag earlier, and he and Harley were headed to dinner. He thought they were gonna move her about now."

"What are they going to do, exactly?" "Retrofit" was one of those words that, it seemed to Gillian, covered any multitude of activities.

"Sort of like winterizing a car. But if we have to work in open water out of season in that area, September's probably a decent time." Shane slowed down, minimizing the bounce as he maneuvered the van around a tight curve. "But to answer your question, what the work orders included was checking the hull for cracks or weak areas and reinforcing it. *The Evangeline*'s got a fiberglass hull, so the good news is that it's pretty impervious to cold."

Whenever anyone pointed out the good news in a given situation, the bad news inevitably followed. "But? I'm sensing a 'but' there."

Shane nodded. "But the area's rocky as hell, and fiberglass doesn't dent like metal. It's really durable, but if it does get a big hit, it breaks like, well, glass. So they'll reinforce it. Double-check all the seals and joints. Go over the engine and fuel systems."

It did sound like winterizing a car or giving it a seasonal tune-up. Not as extensive as she'd feared, so maybe not as time-consuming, either. Thinking of time reminded her of their deadline, which had dwindled to twenty-one days. So much was at stake. "I think I should call Gretchen tonight and make sure things are OK." She looked out the window at the boats docked in the vast marina, many probably tucked in for the winter now that Labor Day had come and gone.

"It's probably a good idea." Shane reached over and squeezed her knee, and she covered his hand with hers. "We might not have another chance until this is all over, and it will make you feel better to know they're fine."

"Are you comfortable leaving Charlie here by himself?"

Shane retrieved his hand to take another tight turn, and Gillian mourned its absence. She could get used to touching him and being touched by him.

"No, I'm not at all comfortable leaving him behind. I thought about taking Charlie with us, but that was before I saw him. He's in no condition to go on that kind of trip, so I'm not even putting that idea in his head."

Gillian could understand why. Charlie would want to go, given the least bit of encouragement. But the boat was already crowded with the four of them, and one more—one with a mobility issue, at that—would complicate things even more.

"Is there anywhere else he could go? Family or friends he could stay with?"

Shane shook his head. "None I know of, and I seriously doubt he'd leave that house, especially if he thought he was being forced out. I did think of one thing, but . . . no, forget it."

Was he joking? "Well, now you *have* to say what you were thinking. It's a rule."

He smiled. "I was going to ask if you'd consider leaving Tank with him, but I know he's like your kid. It's not a fair thing to ask."

She looked out the window as they slowed in front of the entrance to the boatyard. Two vessels sat atop metal stands of some kind, tall enough for their keels to clear the ground by several feet. Arching high overhead was a covering that looked like a giant's greenhouse. "There it is—the second one down."

The Evangeline didn't look that big sitting in the water, but up on stilts she looked enormous. "I didn't realize how much of the living space was below the waterline," Gillian said, trying to mentally place where the salon and lower rooms were located. She kind of wished she hadn't seen it out of the water.

Shane stopped and looked at the boat a few seconds, then nodded. "Looks like they have her secured really well, and there's only one other boat in the work area. Hopefully, that means they can get the work done in a couple of days max."

He did a tight U-turn and drove back toward the marina while Gillian gave more thought to his question about leaving Tank behind. On the one hand, it broke her heart. After losing Ethan and Sam, she'd bought the pickup and moved into the trailer, and a couple of months later, she'd found Tank abandoned on the side of Highway 24, a fur ball of a puppy with a bad attitude. They hadn't been separated more than a day in the past five years.

On the other hand, shipboard was not the place for a dog, especially under these conditions. She didn't know what lay ahead for any of them, but she sensed Tank would be safer here than traveling with them. Plus, she'd seen Charlie drop his hand beneath the table several times, touching Tank, and she'd never seen her big old guard dog take to anyone but her like he'd latched onto Charlie.

"Yes," she said, knowing it was the right choice.

"Yes what?"

"I'll leave Tank with Charlie." Tears welled up and she turned toward the window again before Shane could see them. "I think it'll be better for both of them."

Shane pulled into Charlie's driveway a few minutes later but made no move to get out. He reached out and took her hand again. "I know that's not easy, so thank you. Charlie likes the hellhound."

Gillian chuckled. "Yeah, you're just glad he's staying because you knew he'd bite you one of these days."

He leaned over and kissed her cheek. "You're right. But thank you anyway."

She turned and curled her fingers around the back of his neck, holding him close to her, their foreheads touching. In the dim streetlight, his face was formed of shadows and light, but she saw his gaze drop to her lips before he angled his head and moved closer. She'd kiss him once, and then they'd go inside.

His lips were soft against hers, but as she opened her mouth to his, he angled in deeper. When he moved to kiss her jawline, her neck, her earlobe, she pulled him back to her mouth. She'd kiss him once more, and then they'd definitely go inside, because this was a bad idea.

He sucked gently on her lower lip before setting up a gentle rhythm to his kiss, one that shot straight to her guts and damned if her toes didn't curl involuntarily inside her tennis shoes. Okay, this would be the last kiss, and then—

Bright light flooded the front seats of the van, propelling them apart. Shane scowled at the open front door, where Charlie and Tank could be seen standing side by side. Gillian groaned. "Why do I feel like I'm sixteen again and just got caught making out with my prom date?"

Shane grinned at her. "Did that happen?"

Yeah, it had. "His name was Bobby Harper and he had a lisp." He'd also grown up to be a senator, last she'd heard.

"I'm not saying a word." If Shane's cough was an attempt to hide the fact that he was laughing at her, he needed a new tactic.

They walked to the back of the van and began to unload groceries. "At least Charlie was so intent on catching us, he forgot to be paranoid about opening the door," she said.

"Or maybe Tank's already distracted him. He didn't even have his shotgun."

Well, not within view anyway.

They got the groceries put away and then found there was nothing they'd bought that either of them considered fit to eat. Charlie, however, was pleased and immediately set about the task of making himself two peanut butter sandwiches.

"Where's the best place to eat around here?" Shane asked, watching as Gillian emptied some of Tank's food into his bowl. She'd restocked his supply at the Sav-A-Center while they shopped for Charlie, so at least the older man wouldn't have to worry about what to feed him. She'd have to give him the "no people food" lecture before she left, although she doubted it would do much good. She'd already caught him dropping a peanut butter–covered bread crust onto the floor for the dog to gobble up.

"I heard the old Cod Piece is pretty good," Charlie said, leaning down to hand Tank his peanut butter crust in person this time. Gillian bit her lip. She wouldn't chastise him, not when she was going to ask him to take her dog in case this mission failed and she never came home. Not that Shane had said it that way, but it was the truth, and they both knew it. If Charlie wanted to feed Tank peanut butter, so be it.

Then the restaurant name sunk in. "Um, there's a restaurant called the Cod Piece?" She so did not want to eat there.

Shane laughed and opened the door, motioning her back outside. "It's a long story. I'll tell you about it on the way."

To Gillian's relief, the Cod Piece had undergone both a name and menu change, and by the time they finished their appetizer of crab cakes swimming in rémoulade sauce, Gillian felt herself relax for the first time since they'd arrived in Southport. Shane had regaled her with stories of the Cod Piece and other bizarre tales of coastal Carolina life until she'd actually giggled, which hadn't happened since long, long before Tex came into her life.

Conversation died down when the entrées came, and Gillian picked at her shrimp and grits. The thought of Tex had sobered her again, reminding her that even if she were interested in dating anyone, which she wasn't, this wasn't a date. She thought again of the conversation she'd overheard, and whether it was fair to ask Shane to talk about his vulnerabilities when she hadn't shared hers.

Tex had found the right strings to pull in order to control both of them. Now, maybe it was time for both her and Shane to come clean. As he'd said back at Charlie's, the time for playing games was done.

20

Shane didn't understand women. He wasn't sure any man did, but if so, he wasn't one of them. One minute he'd had Gillian laughing at his admittedly embellished tales of growing up in Southport. The next, she looked somber and jittery, and he suspected it wasn't because she didn't like the shrimp and grits she'd been picking at since the entrées had arrived.

He mentally girded his emotionally deficient loins and waded into the deep pool of feelings women seemed to comfortably occupy. "Okay, out with it. What's wrong?"

Yeah, soul of sensitivity, thy name is Shane. The Burke men were known for it.

She took a deep breath and set her fork down beside her plate, so Shane did the same. This was going to be bad; he could tell.

"I overheard part of your conversation with Charlie earlier. I wasn't eavesdropping, I swear."

He had no idea what she was talking about until a cold realization hit him. *That* conversation. About California. He thought frantically, trying to remember exactly what Charlie had said and how he could spin it in a way that would satisfy her curiosity and spare him the pain of reliving his soul's darkest hour. Right now, Gillian liked him. She liked the Shane he presented to the world. If she heard that story, she'd not only dislike him but be very afraid to know the fate of her niece was in his shaky hands.

"I can tell by your expression you know which conversation I mean." She studied his face with brown eyes that apparently saw way too much. "Here's the deal. You said earlier that we needed to stop playing games, and I think you're right. One of the games we've been playing has been to keep our private stuff private."

Damn straight. That's why it's called private stuff. He didn't want to be a smart-ass, however, at least not until he was backed into a corner. "Okay."

She speared a shrimp and stuck it in her mouth. Shane got distracted by that mouth. She was even sexy chewing up a crustacean. "Okay. I think we should tell each other what it is that Tex is using to control us. We might be able to help each other. At the very least, I'll know where you're vulnerable, and you'll know the same about me. It might help us figure out how to fight back."

Despite his intense urge to cut and run, Shane had to admit her logic was sound. Following through was another matter. "Did you ever think you might be better off not knowing some things?"

Those eyes dug deep into his brain again; he could feel the tentacles of her curiosity clawing their way inside, trying to pull out feelings he didn't want to acknowledge, much less share with a woman that—okay, he admitted it—he hoped to get into bed one of these days. Assuming neither of them died first.

Strong, smart women like Gillian Campbell didn't want to have sex with cowards.

"Is it that I'm better off not knowing, or that it's easier for you if I don't know?"

Well, when she put it that way. "Both?"

She smiled and looked down at her bowl, stirring the tines of her fork idly through the grits, forming figure eights of corn and butter. "How about I go first?"

Curiosity quieted Shane's inner whining. As near as he could tell, the thing that brought Gillian firmly under the evil thumb of Tex and his employer was the threat against her niece. She'd gotten her friend Vivian out of the country, but it was the threat against the little girl, Holly, that had rattled her. He'd asked her once if she had lost a child, but she hadn't answered.

"It has something to do with a child, doesn't it?"

She stirred the grits some more before finally letting go of the fork and pushing the bowl away. "Five years ago, my son and my husband died in a car wreck. Ethan was three—the same age Holly is now. And I killed him. Killed both of them."

Shane looked down at his own plate, where the grilled oysters looked back at him like dark, soulless eyes. "Tell me what you mean." It was ludicrous, of course. Gillian would no more kill a child than he would. The woman wouldn't even kill an alligator, for God's sake, which Shane didn't think he'd have any qualms about at all.

"I was in grad school at Florida, but we lived in Ocala instead of Gainesville. I had finished my master's degree except for the formalities." She looked out at the crowded restaurant dining room, but Shane didn't think she really saw it. "My husband Sam and I had been arguing for weeks. I wanted to stay in school and go for my doctorate so I could teach college, and Sam wanted to move up to Pensacola where his parents lived. He'd work at the bank, and I'd stay home and raise Ethan the way both of us had been raised. Maybe teach high school once Ethan got in school himself."

The waitress came and refreshed their sodas, and Gillian waited until she left before resuming. "The night it happened, I was supposed to pick up Ethan at day care, but I got held up at the lab and then my car wouldn't start. Sam had to drive from Ocala to pick Ethan up, and then me. The rain was horrible. We stopped for dinner, and he drank a couple of beers, so I insisted on driving."

Shane saw where this was headed. "You were driving when the wreck happened?"

She nodded, and while her eyes looked a little shiny, she didn't cry. She just looked incredibly sad. "Sam and I were arguing. Ethan was asleep in the back in his baby seat. Sam grabbed the wheel, and I took my eyes off the road for a second." She closed her eyes, and her voice grew so soft that Shane had to strain to hear her. "Just for a second. I don't remember anything else until I woke up in the hospital and they told me my baby was dead."

She swallowed hard and looked up at Shane. "So Tex knew exactly what would keep me in line. He even said it: 'Do you want to be responsible for the death of another little kid?'"

Shane wanted to hold her tight and tell her over and over, until she finally heard and believed, that what killed her family was an accident. That if anybody was at fault, it was her damn-fool husband, may he rest in peace, who drank too much and grabbed the steering wheel. And he wanted to use Tex's balls for target practice, for using such a painful thing as ammunition.

"I'd kill Tex if I could get my hands on him." Shane found it hard to look at Gillian, the pain in her face was so stark and etched into every line, every freckle, every one of the few damp tears that managed to escape.

She gave a bitter laugh. "Get in line behind me. But that's the worst thing. Every time I've wanted to tell him to go to hell, I have to swallow down those words. I hate bullies more than anything, and I've had to let myself be bullied. When Ethan died, I bought the truck and the trailer. I found Tank, and I moved to a place where I thought I'd never have to be afraid again. Never have to worry about losing anyone because I'd keep everyone at arm's length. And then here comes good old Tex."

Yeah, good old Tex knew where to put the screws. Ironic how similar their situations were in a way. They both had hidden themselves away—Gillian in her trailer and Shane on *The Evangeline*—to avoid ever being responsible for another life. And now they both were performing like trained seals to keep the people they cared about safe.

"Anyway," she said, folding her napkin and setting it on the table beside her plate, "that's how Tex has been able to control me so easily. By reinforcing the guilt over my son."

She had no reason to feel guilty. "I'm just gonna say this once because it's something you know in your heart. You're a smart woman." Shane chose his words carefully. She was too fragile for a misstep. "You know that accident wasn't your fault. It was just that—an accident. If you want to blame anyone, it's okay to blame your husband."

Careful, Burke, careful. "You talk about losing Ethan, but you don't mention Sam. Why is that?"

Gillian had been watching him with the same tired, sad expression she'd worn throughout her story, but now her eyes widened. "I don't mention Sam?"

Shane shook his head. "It makes me wonder if deep down, beyond that part of you that's hanging onto your guilt, you're not mad as hell at him?"

Gillian made a dismissive gesture. "That's silly. How can I be mad at someone who's dead?"

Shane didn't answer, but watched as she processed the answer to her own question, her brows drawing together in thought. She raised her hand to her mouth and stifled a sob.

Oh hell, he hadn't meant to rip her wide open in public. That was classic Shane. He starts out well, then takes things a step too far.

"You can think on that a little later," he said, desperate to divert her attention. "I'll match you one on the guilt scale, and raise you one."

The ploy worked. She wiped away a couple of stray tears and looked up at him. "What?"

"The conversation with Charlie." Was he going to do this? Spill his guts in the restaurant formerly and known to him forever as the Cod Piece? It seemed the least he could do since she'd just eviscerated herself to get him talking.

"What Charlie said, the part I heard, was that you shouldn't get involved with me because you might have to choose between me and survival, like before. Is that why you hadn't seen him in ten years? Because you had that kind of choice to make?"

He nodded. "I was twenty-three and had been in the Marine Corps three years, stationed in San Diego. With Charlie's help, I'd gotten my tec diving credentials before I enlisted, so I took to combat diving right away. It's brutal. Imagine scuba diving in full combat gear, carrying a shitload of weapons. But I was some hot shit, at least in my own mind."

She dug a shrimp out of her bowl with her fingers and popped it in her mouth. "I can't imagine diving like that. It's hard enough with double tanks."

Shane thought back to the dive training, how they stayed under until their lungs and muscles caught fire, then forced themselves to surface slowly and change gas mixtures to avoid decompression problems even as their bodies raged for oxygen. "I got a charge out of it, the adrenaline rush, the feeling of having cheated death every time you took a deep dive or went on a hard maneuver and came out whole. I was good enough, I guess, that I started helping train the newer dive recruits, both Marines and SEALs."

He was silent for a while as he thought back to those days. Everything in his life had been spread out before him the way he'd always dreamed of it. He was happy to stay in the Corps and live cheaply until he saved up enough to open his own dive shop with Jagger.

"When I first came to talk to you about the dive, you said you always dive alone," Gillian said. "Is that because of something that happened then?"

"Yeah." Shane blew out a breath he hadn't realized he was holding. "My CO—commanding officer—asked me to take one of his baby Marines down for a private lesson one day, off the books. The kid was the son of one of his old college buddies and he was one more failed dive away from getting kicked out. So I took him up to La Jolla, thinking I'd show off a little, take him on a cave dive that would be so damned interesting, he would forget to panic."

Shane laughed softly. "It didn't work out that way. We dove together and had Jagger up top in a dive boat with a decompression line so we could come up slow. The kid's name was Kevin. Kevin was doing great until he swam between a couple of rock formations in the cave, misjudged how close together they were, and got stuck. He freaked."

Gillian nodded. "Panic's the worst thing a diver can do. That's basic."

Basic, but the brain was its own worst enemy when it came to panic. "He'd used up all his air by the time I cut him loose, so I was sharing with him. But we had to go up the line in stages to avoid decompression sickness. It's a slow process, and although we were running low on gas, we had enough to make it. But he let go and shot for the surface."

"Ah." Gillian took another sip of her soda. "And you had to either go up too fast with him, or keep going up the line to keep yourself safe."

Shane felt the heat of embarrassment spread over his face. "What a selfish bastard. By the time I got to the top, he was talking crazy shit. By the time I rolled into the boat, he was having seizures. By the time we got to shore and called the EMTs, he was dead."

Gillian folded her napkin and unfolded it, but kept her gaze fixed on Shane. He forced himself to look back at her. "A wise man I know recently told me something," she said. "So I'll say this once. It was an accident, and you did nothing wrong. You did exactly what you were supposed to do. This kid shouldn't ever have been training as a combat diver, and your CO should've been able to see that and moved him somewhere else. Did the Marines find you at fault?"

Shane shook his head. "No, it was ruled an accident. But I could've done something different. I know I could have."

Gillian reached over and took his hand. "And I could've kept my eyes on the road that night. We don't get do-overs, do we? But think of it this way. If you'd let go of the line and followed Kevin, he'd still have died. The only thing different would be that you might have died as well, and for nothing."

Shane looked at his fingers twined with hers and felt a rush of gratitude. He'd told the story and survived it, or at least he'd told part of it. His own diving panic wasn't real; it was a sick game his mind played with itself. He didn't panic at the idea of diving. He panicked at the idea of panicking while diving. Subtle difference, but it screwed with you.

"Let me guess the rest." Gillian smiled at him. "You were reeling from guilt, showed up on Charlie's doorstep, and he treated you to some good old-fashioned Burke-style tough love."

Yep, that summed it up. "Very tough. I tucked tail and ran back to California, thinking I was just like my dad, who wasn't a real Burke man because he also ran from his problems. Jagger rescued me and hauled me off to Cedar Key."

"We're both pretty pathetic, aren't we?" Gillian laughed, and he surprised himself by laughing too. "But I'm glad I know and glad I told you the truth."

"Me too." He didn't feel a proverbial weight lift off his shoulders, but he did feel relieved that she hadn't judged him. He still did enough of that for everyone, but maybe that old habit would eventually die. And he prayed this dive would help him prove to himself that he still had it—the legendary nerves of steel and steadiness of mind to be the best.

The waitress arrived with a dessert menu, and Gillian held it in front of her face and ordered where he couldn't hear her. "It's a surprise," she said. "And Tex is paying."

He'd seen some chocolate monstrosity on the menu and would lay odds she'd ordered it. "And so he should pay for it. In fact, Tex should—"

Damn, his pocket was vibrating. Shane dug out his cell phone and looked at the screen. "It's Jagger." He punched the talk key just as the waitress reappeared with the biggest damn piece of chocolate cake Shane had ever seen, let alone eaten. Make that chocolate cake with chocolate icing and chocolate ice cream. He wanted to drool on it and call it "precioussss."

He held the phone to his ear. "Hey man, what's up? I saw *The Evangeline* at the boatyard."

Jagger's voice cut in and out, and Shane couldn't make sense of what he was saying.

"Wait, slow down and start over."

Jagger sounded drunk, except the man rarely drank unless Shane was egging him on. "Hang on," he said. "Let . . . have . . . move." The phone banged against something but when Jagger came back on the line his voice was clearer. "This better? Need you here. The Tradewinds, next to the boatyard. Room 24. No, that's not it. Wait. Room 34."

Shane shrugged at Gillian and motioned for the waitress. "We're on our way, but what did you say about Bob Marley?"

"Nothing." Jagger's voice sounded strained. "I said they got Harley. And bring your first-aid kit."

21

Gillian dug in her wallet, grabbed a hundred-dollar bill from Tex's stash, and threw it on the table. She didn't know what had happened to make Shane bark "We've gotta go" and stalk toward the door, but she shrugged apologetically at the bewildered waitress and got up to follow him.

"Sorry, just keep it. I left the money on the table," she told the waitress on her way out. "We've had an emergency."

"Let me box it up for you."

Gillian looked longingly at the mounds of chocolate on the tray, then at the entrance to the restaurant. Shane was nowhere in sight.

"No time, but thanks—it looks great. And keep the change."

She hurried out just as Shane screeched the old blue van to a stop in front of the restaurant. Barely had she jerked open the passenger door and slid onto the seat before he stomped the gas pedal, the squeal of the tires echoing across the parking lot.

"What happened?" Gillian struggled to close the van door as it bounced off the curb when Shane took the corner too hard.

"Something's up with Harley. Jagger wasn't making a lot of sense, and that was before it sounded like he dropped the phone and disconnected."

They reached the parking lot of the Tradewinds in less than five minutes. Gillian had seen its clone in just about every town she'd ever driven through—a single line of rooms stacked two stories high, a rusted iron rail spanning the second-floor walkway, and a small, dimly lit reception area in front. She could guarantee a slime-festooned ice machine and a couple of vending machines lurked in a shadowy corner beneath the stairway. The hotel was within walking distance of the boatyard, though, which ensured it a steady clientele.

"Help me look for room thirty-four." Shane slowed down and squinted at the doors' almost-illegible room numbers, no doubt the victims of age and neglect.

Gillian spotted a yellow glow of light spilling from an open door at the end. "Go all the way back. The door to the last room's open, but there are no cars parked in front of it." Harley and Jagger had taken a taxi to the boatyard but had likely walked to the hotel.

"Damn it. I don't like the looks of this." Shane jerked the van to a stop at a diagonal across two parking spaces near the last room, and was out the door before Gillian could unstrap her seat belt.

By the time she reached the doorway and peered inside, Shane had knelt on the floor next to Jagger, who was sitting up with his back against the foot of the bed, his face bloody and bruised. Gillian had seen category two hurricane sites with less damage than the little hotel room. The phone had been dragged off the desk and rested near Jagger's leg. A lamp lay overturned on the cheap particleboard dresser, and chairs rested on their sides. A mattress hung off the edge of one of the beds, its vaguely nautical blue-green bedspread fanned across the floor.

There was no sign of Harley, but at least Jagger was conscious. Shane helped him to his feet while Gillian closed and locked the door and then smoothed out a spot on the bed so that he could lie down. Next, she went into the bathroom to run hot water over a washcloth.

"We've gotta go after them," Jagger was saying as she came back into the room. "Tex has Harley."

"Goddamnit." Shane ran to the door and wrenched it open, but stopped on the threshold. "If this happened right before you called, they had at least ten or fifteen minutes' head start. We've got to think about why they took him. What were they driving?"

Jagger touched a finger to his busted lip and winced. "Hell, I don't know. I wasn't exactly standing in the parking lot watching it all go down. Ah, thanks. That feels good." Jagger closed his eyes as Gillian eased the warm, wet cloth over his face. The cuts looked minor, but he'd kept a hand pressed against his rib cage when Shane helped him up.

"Are you hurt anywhere else?"

"I feel like Shane ran over my gut with Charlie's old van, but nothing's broken." He took the cloth and pressed it against his jaw. "But it was Tex, or at least it was the same guy we saw on *The Evangeline* that day in the harbor, posing as a deputy. The guy that burned down Harley's bar was the one we saw first, though. He was lurking around at the boatyard."

Shane prowled the length of the room, back and forth, fists clenched and jaw tight. "How'd they know you were at this hotel?"

Jagger handed the cloth back to Gillian. "No idea. How do they know half the shit they do? Harley spotted the firebug at the boatyard, though." He smiled, which split his busted lip again and sent a trickle of blood down his chin. Gillian handed the cloth back without comment. "You know Harley—he took off after the guy like he was sixteen, not sixty, damning him to hell six ways to Sunday. I had no choice but to chase them."

Gillian frowned and sat next to Jagger on the bed. Something didn't add up. "So when did Tex get involved?"

"That's just it." Jagger looked from Gillian and back to Shane. "We chased the firebug here, to this room. The door was standing open and Tex was in here, going through our overnighters." He shook his head. "Did we stop and think before we raced into the room after the firebug? That would be a 'no.' So we surprised Tex, but he surprised us, too."

"You and Harley should've been able to beat those guys in a fist-fight. I've seen you take down guys twice your size." Shane shoved the dislodged mattress back on the other bed and sat on the edge. "How did it go down?"

"We were knocking the shit out of them until Tex pulled a gun. He shot Harley and bashed me in the mouth. I crawled into the bathroom to call you, and when I got back, nobody was here. It was less than a minute, and Harley had still been fighting, even with the gunshot wound."

Gillian met Shane's gaze; his narrowed eyes and clenched jaw echoed her own. "We told him the truth to keep him safe," she said. "We brought him with us to keep him safe." She didn't need to add the rest: they might have gotten him killed instead.

But if he'd been dead, Tex wouldn't have taken him. That rationale was enough to slow down her jackrabbit heart.

"Jagger." Shane's voice was low and even, a tone that Gillian, even with her limited experience, recognized as barely controlled fury. "You said they took him. Now you're saying they shot him. Get your story straight."

"We fought the best we could, and it happened fast. He just had a shoulder wound." Jagger sat up, holding his ribs. "And until you've had your teeth knocked loose by the butt of a forty-five you can drop the judgmental attitude, asshole."

"How the hell are we sup—"

A loud crack echoed through the room, and both men looked at the cheap red-covered Bible that lay on the floor surrounded by glass. One large shard of tinted glass fell on top of it with a final splintering *thunk* like an exclamation point.

Gillian had eased open the nightstand drawer, intending to throw the book at Shane's head, not at the TV. But at least she'd gotten them to shut up.

After a few seconds, Shane shifted his glare from the broken glass to Gillian. "Are you insane?"

"Stop arguing with each other and think about Harley."

Shane slumped back on the mattress. "We're arguing because we don't know what to do about Harley. They could be anywhere. We don't know what they're driving. We don't know where they're staying. Wilmington's a pretty big city, and there are a dozen outlying spots like Southport.

"We don't even know what they want. Why the hell was Tex searching the luggage?"

Good question. Gillian looked at Jagger. "Any ideas?"

"While I waited for my head to stop spinning or for you guys to get here, whichever came first, I was wondering the same thing," Jagger said. "Maybe they were trying to see if we had any information on the cross or the dive that we weren't sharing with them."

Tex had never been shy about voicing his opinions before, so Gillian wasn't startled when her cell phone buzzed in her pocket. She pulled it out slowly, knowing what the screen would say: "Private Caller."

22

Gillian leaned over the rail near the bow of *The Evangeline*, scanning the night horizon for a light. Just a light. But everything around her, except the foam atop the waves as the boat cut through them, was black. Black sky, black water, black horizon. Black future. The wind sweeping off the ocean, pelting her face with cold spray, made the air feel closer to low thirties than high forties.

Eight days had passed since Harley disappeared. Eight days since Tex had taken his hostage; Harley was a "reminder," he'd said, that they needed to work fast and keep their mouths shut.

Seven days since they'd sailed out of Southport, bound for the eastern coast of Nova Scotia with a lucky wind at their backs.

Two days since Shane had last been able to reach Charlie.

One day, Jagger promised, until they reached Main-à-Dieu, the fishing village on the eastern edge of Cape Breton, Nova Scotia, where an old fisherman named Chevy McKnight would be waiting for them.

The week had flown by in a blur of routine. Jagger and Shane took six-hour shifts in the pilothouse. When he wasn't sleeping or navigating, a tuneless Jagger obsessively reorganized supplies and dive equipment. Shane alternated solitary meditation with long, intense workouts—running laps around the deck with weights tied around his ankles and upper arms, climbing the stairs to the flybridge in sets of ten, or riding a stationary cycle, again wearing weights.

Gillian caught herself watching him, learning how the different muscle groups flexed under his tanned skin as he worked through his reps. Seeing the utter stillness he managed to achieve when he'd sit on the flybridge with his eyes closed, a god of calm and strength unmoved by the buffeting winds of ocean or fortune.

Then she'd feel guilty, reminding herself where they were going— and why. She had no business entertaining lustful thoughts about Shane Burke. Still, every time he appeared on deck, she'd end up watching him, thankful he was too focused to notice.

To be fair, Gillian hadn't been lying around the deck and day-dreaming about Shane. Knowing he'd bought plenty of diving equipment in Southport to supplement what he already had, she'd sneaked around in town and bought a heavy-weight wetsuit for herself. With Jagger manning the dive boat and Charlie's friend taking the helm of *The Evangeline*, there was no reason she couldn't dive alongside Shane—no reason except his pigheadedness.

Then again, she had no intention of asking for his permission. She'd been doing her own exercise routines when Shane was asleep or navigating, building up her lungs and her flexibility. If Jagger had noticed, he hadn't commented. Then again, Jagger wasn't talking much these days.

Whenever she could get an Internet connection, she'd also been tied to her laptop, saving pages of information about diving around Scatarie Island and scoping out possible leads on Tex's boss—assuming Tex wasn't lying about someone else being in charge. Her list of names had been long until Shane suggested that if she was so sure of Tex's accent, she should pull out the people with ties to Texas or its border states. This afternoon, she had decided to hone it further and create a subset of people known to have a lot of money, connections, or both, as well as the Texas link.

She now had a list of five names, a couple of which scared the hell out of her.

"You won't see anything out here tonight." Shane joined her at the rail, stretching his shoulders by pulling one arm up and over his head, then the other.

"Jagger taking over for a while?"

"Yeah. I want to take her into the harbor tomorrow and meet this Chevy guy. Maybe he's heard from Charlie."

Shane's uncle had stopped answering his phone two days ago, and while they were a bit worried, they also knew Charlie was eccentric. If he didn't feel like chatting, he wouldn't answer.

Gillian looked down at the sea foam again, stark white against the black of the water and sky. It was hard to look into all of that yawning emptiness and believe anything was out there. No wonder so many ships, sailing without today's high-tech equipment, ended up on the ocean floor. One tiny error in direction, one failure to compensate for wind speed, and it would be easy to run aground or rip open a hull as it scraped across a rock. Or an iceberg.

A chill spread up her spine. "Where did *The Titanic* go down?" Suddenly she felt spooked by the vastness of her invisible surroundings. *The Evangeline*, which looked so big and solid and sturdy in a sheltered harbor, was in reality a very small blip in the ebony sea that stretched thousands of miles around them.

Shane glanced over and smiled when he saw her expression. "A few hundred miles due east of where we'll be diving. But it's September; we won't hit an iceberg."

What about rocks? Rogue waves? Freaking sea serpents? She closed her eyes and forced herself to slow her breathing and swallow down the fight-or-flight response threatening to kick in. Acting like a hysterical woman wasn't going to help anyone. Besides, her flight options were limited and there was no way to fight the ocean.

"Hey, don't go there." Shane wrapped an arm around her shoulders and pulled her into a hug. He was everything this night wasn't:

warm, solid, steady. "You can't let yourself start thinking too much about the things out there that you can't see."

She looked up at him. "How did you know that's what I was doing? You could tell I was wondering about sea serpents?"

He blinked and almost smiled again. This was the closest to relaxed that she'd seen him since their almost-dinner date. "Sea serpents? Well, hell, maybe so. Don't sweat it. For people who aren't used to spending days aboard a ship in open water, shipboard madness is pretty common."

Gillian wasn't sure if knowing her fears were common made her feel better or worse. "And I always thought I was special. Even my madness is common."

The wind whipped a strand of hair across her face, and Shane smoothed it back, then traced his fingertips across her cheek. "You are special." His voice carried strains of sadness and regret. She imagined an unspoken *Too bad we didn't meet in another time or place* attached to that expression.

A surge of fierce anger spread through Gillian's heart and zinged straight to her gut. She accepted that there was a good chance she was going to succumb to the Campbell curse. If she didn't die on this trip, Tex or his boss would kill her. And she'd die with regrets. So many regrets.

But she could avoid at least one of those regrets if she choked down her fear and acted on her impulses for a change. If she reached out for Shane before they landed again on solid ground, within the grasp of Tex and his infamous reach.

If she had the guts to let go of her guilt and anger over Sam and admit she was ready to move on and let the albatross of her past slip from around her neck.

She simply had to let Shane know that she wanted him, no matter how they'd met and no matter what the future might bring. If he didn't want her, that would be his regret to face, not hers. At least not hers if she tried.

As if he sensed her change in mood, Shane's hands slid down to her waist and his gaze dropped to her mouth. But he didn't move to kiss her. Instead, his brows met in a perplexed frown.

Great. She was trying to look lustful and bold. Instead, she was confusing the man.

Here goes nothing. Arching her body against his as if she could absorb his warmth through her skin, Gillian stood on tiptoe and swept her hands up his chest and around his neck. The thick fibers of his blue sweater tickled the pads of her fingertips before they reached the soft skin beneath his hair.

He remained still, but she felt the thud of his heartbeat quicken against her chest, the press of his arousal growing hard against her belly. Stifling the urge to grind against him, she settled for a handful of hair to tug his head downward. She pressed her lips to his, once, then again. He kissed her on reflex but didn't pursue it. In the shadows, his eyes were dark pools, as fathomless and unreadable as the invisible horizon. But his body was responding to her, even if his mind wasn't going along.

"Stop fighting me, damn you." Gillian pushed him toward the rail and pinned him there.

Shane reached up to wrap his fingers around her upper arms but didn't try to move her back. He was breathing harder, determination visible in every shadow and plane of his face in the dim deck lighting. He spoke low, through clenched teeth. "We can't do this."

If she'd thought he didn't want her, she would've backed away and hidden herself in shame for the rest of the voyage. But whatever Shane's mouth said, his body didn't lie, and that pounding heart and hard heat gave her courage to reach between them and stroke him through the denim of his jeans. "Tell me you don't want me."

He groaned and pulled her hard against him, his hands cradling her face, his kiss no longer unresponsive but hard and demanding. He tasted of mint and citrus and ocean air, and every sweep of his tongue offered the promise of obliteration. For a while, he could make her forget everything and everybody but him. She wanted to forget.

His lips softened, the kiss slowed, his tongue stroked hers more gently, and then he pulled away, resting his forehead against hers, eyes closed. "That's to convince you how much I want you. Enough that it hurts. But it's wrong for us to . . . when your niece and Harley and . . ." He shrugged. "It's wrong."

Nobility was an admirable trait in a man, but his was misplaced. "How will our being together make their situations better or worse?"

He opened his mouth to answer, then closed it again. For a few seconds, he looked past her, into the blackness. Again he took her upper arms in his hands, but this time he moved her back a couple of unwilling steps. "I have to go and shave for the dive."

What? Gillian propped her hands on her hips and watched, openmouthed, as Shane gave her one last, hard look, opened the door to the boat's central passageway, and disappeared.

Suddenly, there was one more regret she could get out of the way tonight: telling Shane Burke where he could stick his razor.

She jerked open the door and stomped up the steps to the cross-way, then down to the hallway that led to the master bedroom suite. The door was closed, and Gillian paused. Did she really want to do this?

The old Gillian would have walked back to the salon, played on the computer, and felt sorry for herself.

The Gillian who was determined not to go gently into the good night of the Campbell curse won out, however, and she grasped the handle and turned it.

Easing open the door, she was surprised to see the room bathed in dark shadows, illuminated only by the light pouring from the open bathroom door. Good. She could take him by surprise.

She closed the door behind her and walked softly toward the light—only to find the bathroom empty. "What the hell kind of game are you playing, Burke?" she murmured.

"Looking for somebody?"

She spun at the sound of his voice behind her and eeked when her back hit the wall less than a second later. This time, Shane was on the attack, his big body pressing hers into the wall, holding her in place.

Damn it; he'd tricked her. Gillian knew she needed a good comeback, an *Is this what you mean by a close shave?* or *Is that an electric razor in your pants or are you happy to see me?*

But damn if he didn't take her breath away, and she couldn't get the words out.

"Are you sure you're ready for this, Gillian?" His breath tickled her ear, and while his tongue and lips and teeth made their way down the side of her neck, he slid his hand the length of her body and between her thighs, pressing against her core.

Some rational part of her brain thought she should be embarrassed that he could feel how wet she was through her jeans, but the prehistoric brain had taken over and erased her higher-brain language skills.

He laughed, hot puffs of air against her collar bone. "Oh yes, ma'am, I do think you are ready."

"Uh huh. I . . . oh." Gillian hadn't felt him unzipping her jeans, but suddenly his fingers were pressing and stroking again, and there was no denim barrier to prevent them from reaching their target. He kissed and stroked until her knees gave way.

"Damn, I'm good." Shane scooped her up and carried her to the bed. For a second she envisioned a lovely scene from one of those cheesy made-for-television romance movies that Viv made her watch when Viv wasn't parked on a shopping channel.

The vision quickly morphed into a romantic comedy when Shane tossed her on the bed like a load of laundry.

"Hey, watch it." She struggled to a sitting position, her sweater twisted beneath her and momentarily trapping her.

"I am watching it—that's a good look for you."

Her sweater had skewed sideways, her pants were unzipped and hanging off, and thanks to Shane and his wandering fingers, her panties were bunched around her thighs. It was not a good look for anyone who was sane.

He'd shucked his own sweater and that sight pretty much silenced anything else she might say. Damn but she wanted her hands all over that.

Gillian figured she'd regret doing it, but she had to ask: "What changed your mind?"

Shane sat on the bed, leaned over, and wrenched off her misshapen sweater. His gaze drank her in, his expression almost hungry, and she felt beautiful for the first time in longer than she could remember. She hadn't been with anyone since Sam, and Sam hadn't looked at her this way . . . maybe ever.

He took her hand and held her knuckles to his lips for a second, his eyes closed. "What you said was right. Denying this thing between us, whatever it is"—he turned her hand over and kissed her palm—"it doesn't accomplish anything. It doesn't help the people who are in danger, and it sure as hell frustrates us. Well, me anyway."

Who knew Shane could be such a romantic? She twined her fingers through his, and, again, wasn't sure what to say. She'd been so focused on knocking down his barriers, she hadn't given much thought to what she'd do when they fell. Her inner vixen had gone mute.

"What was the whole shaving thing about?" Obviously, her inner dork was wide awake and chatty. "Just a way to trick me into following you inside?"

"I was serious. You ever see a diver with body hair?"

Oh, that kind of shave. She laughed. "I was on the national champion swimming and diving team in college. And yeah, those guys shaved off anything that might slow them down. Never seen a scuba diver do it, though."

"Call it superstition. A dive doesn't feel right until I go through the ritual." He gave her an appraising look. "I didn't know you were a competitive swimmer."

There was a lot he didn't know about her, and vice versa. Whatever their relationship might be, they'd skipped over the small-talk-get-to-know-you phase and dived straight into the deep water.

Gillian wondered if he'd done his shaving ritual the day Kevin died, but she didn't plan to resurrect that ghost tonight.

Instead, she reached up and ran her fingers through his sun-lightened hair, grown just long enough to curl a little at the nape of his neck, then trailed them down to the light sprinkling of blond hair on his chest. "You're gonna be suited up, so it shouldn't make a difference. It would be a pity to lose this." She looked pointedly at his jeans. "Although playing with shaving cream and razors could be interesting."

He groaned in mock horror. "Lady, there are some places you will not be going with a razor."

She reached out and stroked the pronounced bulge in his jeans before fumbling with the zipper. "Only if you're still wearing chocolate boxers."

He lay back on the bed, his breath coming faster, and if he minded that she was clumsy, he didn't show it. He raised his hips and let out a slow hiss as she eased the jeans down and brought the source of all that heat one step closer to freedom.

Except what the hell was he wearing? Sexy little black boxer briefs covered with—? She leaned over to see better. "Shane, there are dogs on your underwear. Dogs." Obviously, the man had a weird underwear fetish.

Although those dogs were getting larger by the second and were pretty impressive.

"They're not just any dogs. They have special meaning to me." His voice was somber, and she looked up, bracing herself to hear an

Old Yeller–like tale of a boy forever looking to replace the special dog that died tragically and broke his heart.

"What meaning is that?" Gillian hoped it wasn't a total mood killer.

"They're chocolate labs." He tried to keep the serious look on his face but failed and burst into laughter. "You should see the look on your face. You were waiting for me to tell you a pathetic dog story."

Yeah, she'd see how long he laughed. She tugged off her jeans and that shut him up. Then she walked to the nightstand and pulled out the chocolate drawer.

"Uh, you need a snack?" He raised an eyebrow as she rummaged through the drawer looking for . . .

Aha. Found it. She held up two large foil-wrapped balls of chocolate she'd spotted on her earlier plunder and walked back to the bed, letting them rest on her open palm. "Let's see. What can I do with these? Oh, I know."

She sat down, leaned over, and grasped the waistband of the chocolate labs. "Sorry, chocolate is very bad for dogs. These boys've gotta go."

His slight intake of breath was the only audible response she got to the gentle stroke she gave him as the dogs hit the floor. He'd propped on his elbows and watched her with hooded, glazed eyes as she slowly unwrapped the first ginormous chocolate-covered cherry, then the second, admiring them from all angles before bringing the first one to her mouth.

She bit off the end of each one, then held them over his cock.

"Holy shit." He groaned as she turned both candies over and let the cherry-flavored liquid pour onto him and drizzle down the sides of her new chocolate-cherry candy cane.

"Now, I'm ready for a snack."

"You are sick. Twisted. Oh my God, brilliant." He finally lost the ability to verbalize, leaving Gillian free to lose herself in the best damned chocolate-covered cherry she'd ever eaten.

She'd just settled in for her final assault when he quit thrashing and lunged for her, rolling her onto her back with enough force to squish the rest of the chocolate balls under her hip.

He kissed her once, twice, and licked a dab of chocolate off his lower lip. "I hated to see you having all the fun." He retrieved a chunk of chocolate from the bed and smeared it across her breasts, then proceeded to get even.

God, but revenge was almost as sweet as chocolate. She held on to his head as he brought her to the edge again and again, seeming to know the second she was on the verge of coming and then pulling back and moving to a different spot.

"You're killing me." She writhed as his fingers slipped inside her, trying to get closer or to get away, to find release.

He trailed kisses down her belly, slid a hand beneath her hips . . . and stopped. "What the . . ." He looked down at his right hand, which had found the rest of the chocolate—at least what wasn't stuck to her butt.

"I didn't say my methods weren't messy." Damn it. She'd been almost there, almost there.

He stood up and pulled her to her feet. "I think we need to continue this in the shower."

"Good idea. No, bad idea. One person barely fits in that shower."

He herded her ahead of him into the tiny room and only managed to get the door closed behind them by herding her into the shower stall as well.

"I'm not sure about this." Gillian backed against the wall as he flipped on the faucet, directing the spray against the far wall until it warmed up.

"One last thing." He opened the medicine cabinet hidden behind the mirror over the sink and pulled out a box of condoms. He held up the little packet. "Chocolate."

She laughed until he rolled it over his erection and stepped into the shower with her, kissing like sin. Kissing like he might devour her, and knowing she would let him—help him, even.

Kissing like they might have no tomorrow.

The laughter turned to heat as he scrubbed her clean, their bodies touching in the tight space, his hands roaming and stroking. If he didn't get inside her soon, she was going to explode.

"Now. I need you now." She wrapped her arms around his neck and hooked one leg around his, trying to bring him even closer.

Finally, with a gruff moan, he lifted her so that she could wrap her legs around his hips and settled her down, entering her with excruciating, delicious slowness until she was holding him inside her. She cried out as he lifted her again, and then let her fall, pinning her to the shower wall and setting up a hard, steady rhythm.

"Fuck." He clenched his teeth as he took the brunt of water. It had turned to ice, and then it stopped. "I've gotta disable that damned shower monitor."

She squeezed her inner walls around him as hard as she could, then released, then squeezed. "Is that warming you up?"

He uttered something unintelligible, lifted her again, and set up a pounding rhythm. "Sorry, I can't slow . . . can't."

"Don't stop." Gillian held on, the drag of each thrust across her clit sending her closer to the edge until she finally went over, clutching him both inside her and in her arms until he came with a final jerk, his muscles straining, his head thrown back in total abandon.

For a long time, they remained together, their breathing finally evening out. Shane seemed as reluctant as she was to have the moment end.

But Gillian knew one thing with certainty. If tonight was all they had, if tomorrow was the end, or the next day, or the next, she'd have no regrets.

23

Shane sat cross-legged on the flybridge with his eyes closed, reaching out with every sense but sight. Petrels flew overhead, squawking as they trolled for food around the half-moon harbor of Main-à-Dieu. A horn from another boat as it maneuvered through the light fog that had cloaked everything in a soft-focus coating of gauze. Salt-tanged, steady wind from the east that brought a touch of chill, but not enough to spoil the soft sunlight heating his face.

The way the wind moved across his scalp with no hair to push around made him think of Gillian and her antics with shaving cream, which were not as hot as her antics with chocolate-covered cherries but still made him smile. He let his mind linger on her, surprised that last night had happened but glad of it. Surprised that this morning, he hadn't felt guilty. Surprised that all last night had done was make him want her even more. He'd intended to scratch an itch; instead, he'd kindled a fire.

He took a deep breath and let his senses talk to him again. The point of this exercise was to empty his mind, but if stray thoughts came in, he'd been taught to let them come, give them a few moments' attention, and let them go.

That wasn't Marine Corps training, but the "Charlie Burke Guide to Life." *Clear your mind before you do serious thinking, son.* He could hear that voice in his mind, even if he hadn't been able to get it on the phone in a couple of days.

And Shane had some serious thinking to do. Despite all appearances to the contrary, he was not a spontaneous kind of guy. He needed a plan. Maybe more than one. And all the ones he'd come up with so far ended up with somebody dead.

They'd reached the small harbor of Main-à-Dieu early that morning, found the spot where Charlie had told them to anchor, and set foot on land for the first time in a week. What they didn't find was Chevy McKnight, but only a note left with a guy named Ricky at the building that serviced the busy little harbor.

Chevy and his wife had gone into Sydney for supplies and would meet them at the dock at six. And if he were feeling adventurous, the note said, Charlie Burke's son could take a look-see at the waters off Scatarie Island nearest Moque Head. Shane didn't know if the "son" part was a mistake or if that's how Charlie had described him, but he liked it. Charlie *was* his father in every way except for a few strands of DNA.

"Can you tell me the best route to get to Scatarie, nearest Moque Head?" he'd asked Ricky.

"Sail east hugging the coast and you'll run into it. Kind of late in the season to be diving." Ricky, who was manning the combination marina, tourist center, dive shop, and general store, was bald but for a tuft of white hair on top. "Never knew old Chevy McKnight had a nephew in the States, but he says you're a hotshot diver from Florida, one of those that like the adventure, eh?"

"That I am." Shane wondered what else Chevy had said to explain their out-of-season appearance, but the man didn't ask anything else.

An hour and a sandwich later, they'd headed back out with Jagger at the helm of *The Evangeline*, Gillian in the salon working on her computer and Shane on deck, watching as the relatively flat land of the harbor area gave way to rocky outcroppings and jagged, tree-covered cliffs. They sailed along the coast toward Moque Head, the easternmost point of Cape Breton.

Today, he would dive. Get a feel for the currents. For the ocean floor. For the visibility. Old Ricky had laughed when he asked about the fog. "Not a question of whether there'll be fog," he said. "Just whether it'll be easy like today or whether it'll be so thick you can't see far enough to spit. Why, today's practically sunny."

Shane had spent the last hour in the stirrings of a predive adrenaline rush, and thus his attempt at a Zen moment on the flybridge. Today's dive would be for reconnaissance, and he had to be hyperalert, hyperobservant, and the opposite of hyperactive.

"Sorry to interrupt, but can I talk to you for a minute?"

Shane looked behind him, where Gillian had climbed the ladder enough for her head to stick over the edge of the bridge. Her hands gripped the ladder rail so tightly her knuckles had turned white, and her bright red sweater flapped in the wind. She'd braided her hair and pulled it back.

"Sure, come on up." He grinned as she managed to ease off the top ladder rung and crab-walk in his general direction. "Not afraid of heights, are you?"

She gave him an eat-dirt-and-die look and pushed herself into a seated position. "No, sitting unprotected atop a wave-tossed ship in a fog bank comes naturally to me. Can't you tell? Where are we going, anyway?"

"Moque Head. We can see Scatarie Island from there. Well, maybe." In the fog, maybe not. "I'll do my first recon dive from near Scatarie, maybe two dives if the weather holds. And you'll love this— Moque Head is halfway between Burke's Point and Campbell's Point. How ironic is that?"

Gillian laughed. "I wonder if that's a good sign or bad?"

A good sign, Shane thought. He liked the feel of this place. Not the sea itself—it was going to be a bitch of a dive. But Main-à-Dieu, and this little corner of Cape Breton. It had the same vibe as Cedar Key in its own way. Small, fierce, and unapologetic.

"What did you want to talk to me about?"

"About the research I've been doing." Gillian tensed when a gust of wind swept over the flybridge, then relaxed when she seemed convinced that she wasn't going to get blown off. "I did what you suggested and narrowed my list of prospects for Tex's boss down to people with ties to the Southwest. Then I went ahead and threw out the people who didn't look rich enough or powerful enough. Finally, I narrowed it to people with direct ties to Texas."

That was a hell of a lot of speculation. "You're that sure of Tex's accent? And what makes you think his boss is from the same place?"

"Well, I don't know for sure, of course." She closed her eyes as another gust of wind blasted across them. "But I have a lot of relatives who live around Dallas, and I know that accent. It's different than Oklahoma or even West Texas or Houston. And think about it. If you're filthy rich and up to your neck in this kind of crap, who would you trust to do your dirty work? If you wanted to commit blackmail, extortion, kidnapping—even murder—and can't get your own hands dirty, who would you trust not to rat you out?"

Shane stared out at a landmass barely visible through the fog—probably Scatarie—while he considered the question. "Somebody I'd known a long time," he finally said. "Maybe someone I grew up with, or a family member. Somebody I knew would never sell me down the river." He smiled at her. "She's sexy and smart too. Gotta like that in a girl."

"And there you go, being a guy." She shook her head. "Okay, let's accept that we're making a lot of assumptions. I came up with four men and a woman who fit that profile."

"It's not the woman." Shane would bet on it.

Gillian raised an eyebrow. "You think a woman isn't capable of this?"

"Not this particular mess. This kind of bullshit is too heavy-handed and artless to be a woman. A woman would be smarter about it, less"—he struggled to find the right word—"blunt. She'd use a chisel, not a sledgehammer. Who're the guys on the list?"

Gillian reached into her jeans pocket and pulled out a folded sheet of paper, only to almost lose it to a gust of wind. "Can we go inside?"

"Sure. Here's the easiest way to climb down." Shane swung his legs off the edge and did a practiced pivot on the third step down, putting him in position to descend the ladder.

Gillian followed. He didn't wish her ill, but he half hoped she'd slip so that he'd have an excuse to catch her. Touch her. Instead, he just admired the view as she climbed down much more gracefully than she'd gone up.

"Stop looking at my ass." She hopped off the last rung and treated him to the same devilish smile she'd worn just before the attack of the chocolate-covered cherries. His balls tightened in honor of the memory.

"Yeah, I'm busted." And since he was busted, he enjoyed the view all the way down the side passage and into the salon—until she turned and handed him the paper. Her expression had turned worried.

He unfolded and scanned the list of names, and saw why. He didn't recognize the first two names. The third and fourth made his scalp crawl.

"Holy shit." He sat on the bench, staring at the names, then took out his cell and called Jagger. "How close are we to Moque Head?" He paused and listened. "Okay. Take us out toward Scatarie and drop anchor. We need to meet on deck and plan today's dive."

"Why on deck?" Gillian got sodas for each of them from the fridge and brought them to the table. "Wouldn't it be easier to talk in here?"

Hell yes. "Not really. I've just heard the currents here are volatile. This will give us a good chance to get a look at the water from a stationary position before I go in."

He drew a fair approximation of a cockroach on the back side of her paper, then tapped his ear. Under the guise of cleaning and organizing, Jagger had been combing the boat for bugs or even little surveillance cameras. He hadn't found anything, but that didn't mean they could be careless. *The Evangeline* had been out of their hands for thirty-six hours in Southport, and if Gillian's research on the identity of Tex's boss proved true, anything was possible. They'd be harder to hear topside.

"Gotcha." She nodded. "I wonder if we'll be able to see the old lighthouse on Scatarie from here?"

"I'm not sure which side of the island it's on. Or how much the fog will obliterate."

They sat in uncomfortable silence for several minutes as the boat moved closer to shore. When the sound of the anchor line being released filled the salon, Shane nodded to Gillian and they headed to the deck.

Jagger waited for them, sitting near the bow with his back against the rail. He'd tied back his dark hair and then stuffed it inside a fedora of green and gray Cape Breton tartan. He'd bought it at the harbor shop at Main-à-Dieu, and Shane couldn't decide if he looked rocker-cool or dorky-psychotic with his hat, his hippie hair, and his black "Keith Richards Makes Goat's Head Soup" T-shirt. Balancing that fine line was something his friend did well, so he'd learned to give him the benefit of the doubt.

"What's up? You've already planned the dive, so I guess we're gonna talk about something Tex can't hear." He kept his voice low.

Shane handed him the paper. "Gillian has narrowed our top possibilities for Tex's boss down to these names. I eliminated the woman; I think this has to be the work of a guy. A really arrogant guy."

Jagger took the paper and Shane could tell exactly when he reached the final two names by the way his eyes widened. He looked at the list again, then ripped it into tiny shreds and tossed them into the wind. "Sorry for the litter, Canada. Okay, if we ditch the woman, that leaves us with four. I don't know those first two guys, but you can strike off number three."

That would be the famous oil tycoon who'd parlayed his family millions into billions through savvy investments. He had a reputation as a renegade and a ruthless boardroom tyrant. Shane didn't know much about the guy except when he'd make the news either because his company had gobbled up a competitor or he'd dumped another supermodel girlfriend.

"Why?" Gillian asked. "He seems powerful and rich enough."

Jagger shook his head. "I read this article on him not long ago in a magazine—*Forbes*, I think. Hey"—he kicked Shane's shin with the toe of his worn blue-and-white Nikes—"I was in the dentist's waiting room and it was just sitting there, okay? Anyway, the story told about how he had this brother with a rare form of leukemia who died when they were kids. Now that he's loaded, he pours tons of money into children's medical charities. Even has a foundation set up for it."

"Ah." Shane saw his point. "He might threaten us, or even burn out Harley, but he wouldn't threaten Gillian's niece." He turned back to Gillian. "What can you tell us about the two we don't know?"

"Not much, so I need to do some more digging around. Like the others, their families made their money from oil. Both are pretty reclusive but given a little more time, surely I can find out something."

Shane nodded and looked out over the cliffs and rocky shoreline of Moque Head and, to their port side, the fog-shrouded rise of land that made up the western shore of Scatarie Island. The sea had grown choppier and the fog heavier. If he were going to do a dive today, it needed to be now.

He looked back at Gillian. "You research while I do a recon dive."

They all got to their feet, but Jagger grabbed the sleeve of Shane's sweatshirt. "You don't want to talk about who's behind Door Number Five?"

He met Jagger's gaze, then Gillian's. "No, because it scares the hell out of me. Trying to find a way to outmaneuver your average ruthless billionaire is bad enough. I want to disqualify everybody else before I even think about the fucking secretary of state."

* * *

The Evangeline was rocking and rolling in rougher seas by the time they anchored a quarter mile off Scatarie in the spot closest to Moque Head and clear of the shoals they'd studied on sonar. Shane paced the master suite in his drysuit and boots, getting a feel for the weight and flex of the black neoprene. He hadn't done any cold-water diving in a while, so the heavier suit, with tight seals around his wrists and neck, would take some getting used to.

He made his way to the aft deck where he and Jagger had laid out the rest of his equipment before Jagger moved anchor. Regulator, buoyancy control vest, weight belt, steel tank, gloves, hood, mask, dive computer, fins, light, pony bottle, knife. He might sink like a boulder with all this stuff.

He was studying the dive computer when the hatch door opened. "About time you got here," he said, not looking up. Jagger would play the role of dive master today and help him finish suiting up.

"You were expecting me?"

"Hey, Gillian. You found anything on our . . ."

He turned and lost his train of thought. She'd poured herself into a wetsuit. Royal blue, skintight—and not going anywhere near his ocean.

"You must have missed the memo. I dive alone." He pointed to himself. "Me, dive." He pointed to her. "You, research. We agreed."

"Actually, we didn't agree to any such thing. You assumed."

"I assumed you were a smart woman. Guess I was wrong." Even if he dived with partners, which he didn't, he needed to concentrate, not worry about what trouble she was getting herself into. "You aren't qualified to dive here."

Her brown eyes narrowed and she got that pouty look he found sexy when it didn't involve interfering with his dive. Now, it was annoying as hell.

"I have my certification card and have logged a lot of open-water dives. I have a seven-millimeter wetsuit approved for this water. This is not a deep dive, so I'm not worried about decompression. There's no reason for me not to go down with you."

"There are so many reasons I can't count them." He took a couple of steps toward her, and she backed up. He should toss her into the North Atlantic and let her learn the hard way that this water was not what she'd encountered in the Gulf. She could take her C-card and shove it. Well, okay, he wouldn't actually throw her in, but he could make her *think* he was going to do it.

The green-gray water heaved and foamed beneath *The Evangeline*, pitching him forward to pin her against the rail, then away, then forward again. His mind wanted her away from his dive; his body was all excited at the prospect of another round of body bumps with Gillian Campbell.

Judging by her narrowed eyes, she noticed. "Should I be afraid of that little display of affection?"

Little? Hardly. He gave her an extra bump with his rapidly growing display of affection. "You had no complaints about it last night, babe."

His attempt at humor was an utter failure; she looked more pissed off than before. "I'm going in the water, Shane. I can go with you or I can go by myself." She shoved him away from her. "And really, there's nothing you can do about it."

"I cannot save your ass when you get in trouble."

"Fine. I won't save you, either."

"Fine." He reached down and retrieved his hood from the deck, slipped it on, and tucked the bib inside his suit. Then he turned his back to her. "Zip me up, if you can find the time before you jump to your death."

She closed the waterproof shoulder zippers, then wrapped her arms around his waist. Resting her head on his back, she gave him a bear hug. "Sorry. Let's not even joke about dying, okay?"

Nice going, Burke, you fucktard. He turned around and pulled her to him. "Nobody's going to die. Not today, anyway."

He sighed, cursing his inability to say no to her and mean it. "How about a compromise? I'll go down alone, run through a tank, and scope things out. If the current's okay, I'll get a new tank and then we'll go down together on the second dive."

He slapped a hand over her mouth before she could say anything. "And I mean just for today. Not for the real wreck salvage, assuming I can find any signs of the damned thing. Today, we're just scouting the environment and getting a feel for the new equipment. And you're gonna get cold even in that heavier wetsuit."

She bit his fingers, and he snatched them back, examining his hand for blood.

"Aye-aye, cap'n." She grinned. "Stop being such a baby. I didn't even break skin."

"Whatever." He turned as Jagger exited the hatch. "Where've you been?"

"Checking on the tides, weather, currents. You should be okay for a couple of dives, but we'll reassess after the first one. There's a front blowing in later." He picked up the buoyancy control vest with the single steel tank already attached and held it up for Shane to slip inside. Tomorrow, he'd go down with two tanks.

"Think you have enough equipment?" Gillian had knelt beside the pile of gear, looking through it while Jagger fitted Shane with a pony bottle and Shane strapped on his weight belt and strapped the dive computer around his forearm.

By the time everything was attached, he was sweating inside the watertight suit. A little fifty-degree water was going to feel good. When Shane donned his mask and fins, Jagger opened the gangplank door and nodded. "You know the signals."

"Yep. See you on the other side." Shane popped in his regulator, took a giant step off the edge of *The Evangeline,* and hit the water feetfirst. Perfect. He surfaced and gave an "okay" sign to Jagger and Gillian, then let himself sink slowly along the anchor line, swallowing to help his ears adjust to the change in pressure and adjusting his buoyancy to compensate for the extra layer of gas bubbles in the drysuit.

With the day cloudy and the currents strong, Shane also wanted a slow descent to adjust his vision. He doubted the daylight reflected more than fifteen feet, and at twenty feet he turned on his dive light, illuminating the area around him in eerie green. At seventy feet, he touched bottom. Shallower than he expected.

This section of the North Atlantic was a geologist's dream. Shane made note of the anchor line's location on his compass, marked it on his dive computer, and swam in the direction of Scatarie. The ocean floor, like the edges of the island itself, was bedrock, cracked and broken by millennia of rough seas and icy winters. Boulders the size of pickup trucks littered the floor, but worse were the uneven shoals that reached almost to the surface in spots. No wonder so many ships had gone down in these waters. From the deck of a ship, what looked like deep water would be a foot of murky water hiding a deadly rock.

In these shallow waters, the kelp forests were impressive, and Shane maneuvered among their brown, wavering fronds, small schools of silver and orange fish darting out of his way.

He did a one-eighty and headed back in the direction of the mainland. In a few yards, on his right, he spotted an oblong lump lying on the ocean floor. He swam to it and began sweeping aside marine growth. Concretions had formed around the edges, effectively attaching it to a small rock formation. After a couple of minutes, Shane realized with a rush of adrenaline that it was the barrel of a cannon.

Closing his eyes, he slowed his breathing and checked the dive calculator. He had a good twenty minutes of air before he needed to begin his ascent. He made note of the cannon's location on his computer, cursing at his lack of dexterity in neoprene gloves. The computer gauged the water temp at just over forty-five degrees, so he slipped the gloves off and tucked them beneath his weight belt.

Adjusting his BC to lift him above the cannon, Shane used a small underwater camera he'd bought on impulse, and took a couple of shots. Then he swam in a pattern in the shallower water toward Scatarie, examining the areas adjacent to the relic's location. Twice, he spotted what he thought might be wreck detritus of some sort, but turned out to be junk. A glass bottle tangled in a kelp forest. An aluminum can. Even a freaking rubber-soled athletic shoe, although at least it was being used as a home for tiny fish.

He was just about to write the cannon off as a fluke, something washed far afield by the currents, when he spotted something that glinted when his light swept across it. The object had been encased in the concrete-like materials that built up over the years from silt and sand and shells, but as Shane fanned the water and kelp away from it, he could tell it was the edge of something metallic. He adjusted his buoyancy so that he could work at freeing more of the object, cursing as the wave action at this shallow depth kept washing him away just as he'd reach for it.

The current had been tugging at him with increasing pressure over the last ten minutes. Gillian would be disappointed, but he doubted they could do a second dive today. And tomorrow morning, the real work would begin.

With an eye on his dive computer, Shane used another five of his remaining fifteen minutes working at the small piece of metal. Finally, he was able to clear enough of the concretion around it to get a light on it. The small, curved bit was crusted and corroded, but he'd swear it was the bowl of a spoon. Looking closer at the concretion, he spotted other bits of metal and, a few feet farther toward the island, another piece of a cannon—maybe a trunnion.

These items might or might not be from Duncan Campbell's day, but by God, Shane had found a shipwreck.

24

Gillian looked out the window of the salon for at least the hundredth time since Shane dove. As near as she could calculate, figuring he could get forty-five minutes of dive time on a hundred-pound tank depending on his depth, he probably had only another twenty minutes of air. Jagger had stayed on deck, ready to help him aboard.

She'd tried researching the first two names on the list for Tex's boss, but in this location she had to use her cell phone signal to access the Internet, so it was a lesson in aggravation. Plus, she kept looking at the last name on the list: U.S. Secretary of State Weston Flynn.

It couldn't possibly be him, and yet if anybody had "reach," it would certainly be Flynn. She began an online search and, as expected, found thousands of articles and photos. He was a nondescript man in his midfifties, graying, slick-talking, and seen as a moderate conservative, whatever the heck that meant.

Gillian had often heard his name included in conversations about presidential hopefuls, although her impression from the Sunday morning news shows was that some felt he was too privileged and insulated to identify with the average American.

Weston Flynn wanted to be president, though. Surely a man with that much to lose wouldn't risk playing such an evil game.

And yet. And yet . . . Gillian couldn't quite shake the bad feeling she got when she thought about him.

She stared out the window again, scanning the water for a sign of Shane. After a couple more attempts to read about Flynn, she grabbed her phone and headed for the locker room off the kitchen, the little room she still thought of as Tank's. She was way too restless to read; she wanted to dive, and she'd hidden the rest of her gear behind the door.

For at least the dozenth time today, she prayed that Tank and Charlie were safe. They'd all agreed that Charlie was most likely being cantankerous and paranoid. If Tex had Charlie, he would have called with more threats. But their tormenter had been silent. Gillian's guess was that he was either en route to Main-à-Dieu or already here, watching them.

Tex could watch her dive, then. She'd be on deck and ready when Shane came back up. She attached her aluminum tank to her buoyancy vest, grabbed her dive bag and fins, and headed toward the aft deck.

Jagger was leaning on the rail, using binoculars to watch a boat sitting close to shore off the north corner of Scatarie Island.

"Think that's Tex or one of his flunkies?" She couldn't tell much at this distance. The fog had lightened a bit, but the wind had picked up and the water was choppier.

"I don't know—maybe. The name painted on it is *The Breton* and it's a workboat, but we're well out of lobster season. Could be hikers who've hired a fisherman to bring them out here. Scatarie's a protected wildlife preserve and the weather's still mild." He turned and frowned at Gillian's gear. "It's gotten too rough for a second dive. Once Shane gets in, we need to get back to Main-à-Dieu harbor. We'll get an early start tomorrow after this storm blows through."

And tomorrow, she'd have to fight with Shane all over again. "Then I'm going in now. I'll just get wet and come back with Shane."

Jagger grinned. "I could make all kinds of sexual innuendos."

"Not if you're smart."

He picked up Gillian's BC vest and began singing "Play with Fire" while he helped her slip it on. She went through her predive ritual, checking gauges. "What's the water temperature?"

"Last time I checked, just under fifty. I'd say to wear the hood and gloves if you were going in longer, but Shane's only got about five minutes left, ten if he pushes it. You should be okay without them."

"Does he usually do that? Push it with his time?"

Jagger scanned the water. "Yeah, but not enough for it to be risky. He's carrying a pony bottle and he has the dive computer. Plus, I've been monitoring the sonar; it's not that deep here. Forty to sixty feet, deeper in a few spots. It doesn't get really deep until you hit the middle of the channel."

Gillian decided to wear the gloves but not the hood and pulled on her mask. "Anything else I need to know?"

Jagger turned her around and checked her tank, then her regulator. "Go down slow, and hang on to the anchor line. Don't leave it or we'll have a helluva time finding you if you get in trouble. The current's strong, so be prepared to get tossed around." He grinned. "Oh, and have fun."

Right. "Great to hear you singing again," she said, then took a giant step off the side of *The Evangeline*. The water enveloped her like a cold, wet blanket and she floundered a little before finding the anchor line, surfacing, and giving Jagger the "okay" sign. He waved and closed the gangway door, and the last thing she saw before biting down on her regulator and submerging was Jagger resuming his position at the rail, his eyes back on the other boat.

Gillian took a few seconds to get acclimated before beginning her descent along the anchor line, adjusting her buoyancy. She was glad she'd decided to wear the gloves. Especially near the top of the line, the current tossed her around like a Raggedy Ann in neoprene. It settled a bit as she slowly descended, pinching off her nostrils hard every foot or so to equalize the pressure in her ears.

Gradually, her vision adjusted to the turbid world into which she'd immersed herself—well, it sort of adjusted. Her dive time had been limited to Florida and Louisiana, where the water was relatively clear unless a storm was brewing. Here, everything was murky green and after ten feet, she knew Shane had been right. She couldn't see crap, and the current had her holding on to the line so tightly her fingers had probably turned white inside the blue neoprene gloves. She wasn't experienced enough to dive here.

Until now, she figured she'd dive today and then talk Shane into taking her with him tomorrow, after they'd spoken to Chevy McKnight and began the real hunt for *The Marcus Aurelius*.

Time to rethink that strategy. Shane would end up having to babysit her, which wouldn't make either of them happy. She'd have to admit that she was wrong and he was right.

Damn, but she hated that.

Gillian reached the ocean floor, amazed at the rock formations brought to life by the swaying kelp forests. She checked her dive calculator and saw that she was at seventy feet, and by her calculations, Shane should be arriving back at the line soon.

If she were the stupid and impulsive woman he thought she was, she'd swim off in search of him, maybe even surprise him. But when he arrived back at this line, he was going to find stubborn—but ultimately sensible—Gillian hanging on to it for dear life.

Instead, she practiced adjusting her buoyancy, seeing how long she could remain motionless before the current turned her sideways.

And she thought about Weston Flynn.

Cursed though they might be, the Campbells had good instincts. Well, except when old Duncan's instinct told him to steal the damned Templar cross in the first place. But Gillian had learned to trust her gut, and her gut kept leading her brain back to Flynn.

It could be as simple as the fact that he was an avid hunter and she was a biologist, which put them on opposite sides of a lot of social issues. If he ran for president, she was pretty sure she'd vote for his opponent as long as he or she wasn't a three-headed troll.

But her fixation with Flynn as Boss-of-Tex material went further than politics. She'd never admit this to Shane, but a lot of her distrust had to do with the guy's eyes. Gillian had spent a lot of the past twenty-four hours looking at pictures of the secretary of state, and he was colder than Cape Breton in the dead of winter. He saw the world through irises of a hard, flinty blue-gray. They made him looked distinguished, along with his graying hair and his expensively tailored navy suits. But even in pictures with his immaculately groomed family—the pampered, anorexic wife with big hair and the two blandly handsome grown sons—he looked detached. No, more than that. He looked bored.

If one were filthy rich and incredibly powerful, how long before everything seemed boring? If one held a public office where every action was scrutinized, how tempting would it be to stretch the limits? To see how far one could go?

Testing boundaries wouldn't be boring. It would be exhilarating.

Gillian's gut told her Weston Flynn might well be the wizard behind the curtain of Oz, working the controls of Tex and however many flying monkeys he employed, seeing the extremes to which he could push poor, stupid people to do his bidding.

Poor, stupid people like her. Like Shane and Jagger and Harley.

It really pissed her off.

A clanging noise sounded from behind her, startling her so badly she momentarily let go of the line and had to scramble to get back to it. Shane had slipped up behind her while she was focused on Weston Flynn and had begun banging his light against his pony bottle to get her attention.

She shot him a big, blue, neoprene-covered bird, and got a grin in response. Life wasn't fair; the man even looked sexy in a bulky drysuit covered head to toe in diving gear.

He held one hand out to her and motioned with his other for her to take it. He pointed to himself, to her, and then back over his shoulder. He wanted to show her something.

Well, it was better than having him pissed off at her for diving alone after him, which she'd more than half expected. She reached out and grasped his wrist, and he pulled her away from the line.

Okay, you can do this. No holding your breath. No hyperventilating. She gave him an "okay" sign, swimming beside him. Progress was slow. They'd swim a few feet, then get swept back by the current. Rinse and repeat. Finally, he pointed ahead at a long, kelp-covered object.

A cannon barrel! She nodded at Shane as he watched to see if she understood, and he grinned again. He pulled her past the cannon to a big assortment of boulders that had what looked like concrete between them at the bottom. Shane pointed to some kind of metal object wedged inside the material, but she couldn't tell what it was.

Gillian let go of his hand and fanned the kelp from the area. She still couldn't make out the metal object but spotted something on the ocean floor, moving past them with the current. She got Shane's attention by banging on his tank, and pointed to the spot. It looked like a coin, and she wanted to see it.

A cannon and a coin and an unidentified metal object had to mean a shipwreck. No way it could be *The Marcus Aurelius*—that would be too easy. But Chevy McKnight had left them instructions to dive in this spot, and there had to be a reason.

Gillian descended to the ocean floor and reached for the coin, lost it, and finally grabbed it, along with a handful of marine growth. She turned back to Shane and held it up, not understanding his sudden expression of alarm and his outstretched hand until the current swept her sideways and straight at the rocks.

She tried to reach out her arms to break her crash, but they might as well have been pinned to her sides. Twisting her body at the last second to shield her head, she looked stupidly at the pattern of cracks in the safety glass of her mask, wondering what had happened. A split-second later came the pain shooting through her temple, then darkness.

25

Shane's body grew as sluggish and frozen as the water pressing in on him. He gulped down big breaths of gas he couldn't afford to use trying to lunge toward Gillian.

She was too far away, and he was too slow. At the realization that he couldn't save her, the damaged part of his heart, the fractured, rusted part that had begun a fragile healing over the past few weeks, cracked like the crevice-riddled bedrock beneath the North Atlantic.

He was useless as he watched her hit the jagged boulder head-first. Numb and detached, as the safety glass on her mask spread into an intricate web of cracks before crumbling into diamonds around her. Unable to hold on to a rational thought when the regulator fell from her lips, whipping in the current like a black and silver eel.

His dinosaur brain told him to kick for the surface. To run, and to keep running. He hadn't asked to get involved in this shit. He'd been minding his own business, living on the water in Cedar Key. He'd been happy.

Wrong, asshole. You were drowning in self-pity, and she threw you a lifeline.

He reached for her again, and this time, the current that had propelled Gillian into the rocks swept Shane toward her, moving him far better than his cumbersome arms and legs.

Breathe. She has to fucking breathe.

Trying to ignore the blood washing from her temple, staining the water around her head, he grasped the regulator, forced it between her teeth, and clamped his hand over her mouth and jaw to hold it in place. He prayed like hell she hadn't swallowed a lungful of salt water. How long had it taken him to get to her? How long had panic held him immobile? Five seconds? Ten? Thirty? The larynx's first reaction to immersion was to spasm, keeping water out, but then she'd instinctively breathe it in and suffocate.

Shane struggled to pull gas into his own lungs and knew if he didn't get his short, panic-driven breaths under control, he'd run through the last of his tank in no time.

Fighting the current, he rolled Gillian to her back. His gaze kept straying to her face, slack and ghostly white where his diver's light penetrated the green darkness. He wrapped his left arm around her back, under her left arm and up, clamping her tightly enough to swim and keep the regulator clamped over her mouth at the same time. At least that was the plan.

His dive computer sent a warning vibration tingling across his arm. He had to get them to the surface, and fast, but he was still pulling too hard off his emptying tank, each breath more labored than the one before. He had to slow down his breathing.

He closed his eyes and thought about *The Evangeline*, envisioned himself atop the flybridge hearing the gulls and the soft slap of water against the hull. Visualized himself warm and safe, with his skin soaking in the warm Florida sun. The sensory memories penetrated his nervous system, slowed his heart rate, calmed his breathing.

With it came a clarity he hadn't felt in a long time. He could save Gillian. This wasn't California, and she wasn't Kevin. He was the only one panicking here, and that panic he could control.

Tightening his hold on her, he reached down with his right hand and, after a few seconds of fumbling, unfastened her weight belt and let it fall to the ocean floor. They began rising immediately, but the more they rose, the worse the whiplash effect of the current became.

Another ten or fifteen feet, and they'd be at the full mercy of the waves.

He fought the instinct to rip off his own weight belt and barrel to the surface and, instead, adjusted his BC to control their ascent. Keeping her in a firm grasp, he swam with the current and let it take them back toward the anchor line. Finally, he spotted the yellow line through the whipping, leathery kelp. The weather up top must be deteriorating fast; even the line was lashing back and forth, pulling at the anchor.

He'd staved off the panic that had almost caused him to hyperventilate, but he couldn't do much about the exertion of carrying an extra person. Breathing heavily and holding Gillian in place with his left arm, Shane paused at the anchor line long enough to rip out his heavy regulator and unhook the one attached to his pony bottle. It would buy him an extra fifteen minutes of air. Shoving it in his mouth, he made sure Gillian's regulator was still functioning, the bubbles from her breathing still escaping. So far, so good.

Pulling both of them up the dancing anchor line drained energy from his aching arms and shoulders. It was excruciating business. Slow business. Shane extended his right arm, grasped the line and doubled it around his fingers, kicked with his fins and strained his biceps to drag them upward. He timed their progress between waves, only letting go of the line to move his hand higher when the waves ebbed. Every few feet, he adjusted his own BC to keep their progress steady.

Repeat.

Repeat.

The muscles in his right arm and shoulder twitched and burned as if someone had set a match to them and his veins carried gasoline. But they were making progress. He could see again, the dim light from above finally penetrating the waves. The dark hull of *The Evangeline* rested overhead.

Now he hoped like hell Jagger could get them out of the water.

He let go of the line and pushed for the surface at an angle from the boat, finally breaking through a few yards off the starboard side. He spat out his regulator and promptly got a mouthful of seawater, but he had Gillian in such a headlock, they'd have to pry his fingers apart to get them unclenched from her mouth and jaw.

Jagger spotted him almost immediately, raised his binoculars, and Shane saw him mouth a few curses as he threw the binoculars aside and ran for the gangway hatch. It was already open, the ladder already down, but the boat was pitching wildly. Jagger hit the rail, then the side of the wheelhouse, careening like a pinball on a tilted machine until he finally reached the opening.

He yelled something, but Shane couldn't understand. The wind and waves and slashing rain had their own voices, and their chorus was deafening.

A sharp pain shot through his calf, and only when Gillian tried to twist out of his grasp did he realize she was conscious and kicking him, instinctively trying to break free.

Shane hadn't prayed in a long time. He figured he had no right. Now, though, he sent up a relieved message of thanks. She was disoriented, but she was breathing and moving and awake.

Her elbow smashed into his gut, reinforcing that diagnosis. He let her go for a moment, but when he was sure she could stay afloat, he put a hand on either side of her head and forced her to look at him, keeping them both afloat with his legs. Her glazed blue eyes didn't see him. They were fixed on *The Evangeline*, on the clouds overhead, on the waves knocking them aside.

Finally, her gaze skimmed past him, then snapped back to his face. "You're okay," he shouted. "Do you understand? We're okay."

A wave knocked them apart, but Shane saw with relief that Gillian had removed her regulator on her own and was trying to swim back to him.

"Let me tow you." His shout sounded weak and thin against the gale. "Save your strength for the ladder." He used his hands to mimic climbing. When she nodded, he reached out, got washed away, started over. On the third try, he managed to hook an arm around her from behind and begin swimming toward *The Evangeline* as hard as his legs could work against the current.

Once he finally reached the boat, he said another prayer of thanks. Jagger held up a knotted line and threw it out lasso style. It sailed over Shane's head in a wild spray of wind and rain, but he was able to grab hold of it in the water. "Under your arms," he shouted to Gillian, slipping the loop over her head. She pulled her arms through, and Shane gave Jagger the "okay" sign.

Jagger was strong, but he wasn't a big guy. Shane held his breath until Jagger hauled Gillian against the side of the boat, then Shane swam for the ladder. It hit him in the head on his first few approaches, but eventually he jerked an arm through the bottom rung, and hung there, whipping against the side of the boat while he maneuvered out of his fins.

They were damn fine fins and he'd had them a long time, but there was no way he could carry them up. He let them go and grasped the ladder with his right hand, maneuvering himself into position to climb. By the time he finally pulled himself to the top rung, he barely had enough strength to heave his body over the rail onto the deck. The pitch was so bad, he rolled halfway to the pilothouse hatch before making it to his knees and shucking the bulky buoyancy vest.

Jagger still hadn't gotten Gillian onto the boat, so Shane slipped and slid his way aft, took hold of the line behind Jagger, and tied it around his waist. Leaning into the wind, he took one laborious step after another until the line slackened behind him. He twisted around enough to see Jagger helping Gillian out of her BC and finally gave himself permission to collapse.

The rain pelted his drysuit like drops on an umbrella and sent icy rivulets running off his hood into his eyes and mouth, but he didn't care. No feather pillow had ever given him as much comfort as the worn wood of the wet deck against his cheek. He lay on his stomach and let it rain, only moving when the pitch of the boat threatened to send him sliding back toward the rail. He couldn't remember ever having been this exhausted, mentally and physically, but Jagger might need him to navigate back to Main-à-Dieu or Scatarie, whichever looked safest. He'd rest for just a few seconds more . . .

* * *

"Ow." A pain shot through the back of Shane's head; it felt suspiciously like being hit with a baseball bat. He opened his eyes to an expanse of white steel that, when he turned his head at an awkward angle, looked like the top of *The Evangeline*'s entry hatch. Another shift and he could see the storm raging outside the open door. And he was moving.

He tried to shift his legs, but they weighed at least two tons apiece. His skull took another brain-jarring thump, and he craned his neck upward to see Jagger with his hands hooked under the shoulders of Shane's inappropriately named drysuit, dragging him up the steps toward the pilothouse. "What the hell are you doing?"

"Trying to haul your wet, shaggy ass out of the storm so I can get us out of here, since you decided to take a nap." Jagger panted from the exertion. "Man, you need to go on a diet."

Shane's head bounced on another step, and he decided he'd better try to make it on his own, or else he'd end up with a concussion. "I got it from here. How's Gillian?"

Jagger stepped around him and closed the hatch against the weather. "She's shaken up, but I think she's okay. Go in the master suite and do whatever people do for head injuries. You know. Keep her from going to sleep or something. I have a boat to rescue."

He wheeled, trotted up the remaining stairs, and closed the pilothouse door behind him.

Not a single Rolling Stones reference. Guess Jagger's day hadn't gone any better than Shane's or Gillian's.

Shane climbed to his feet, only to be knocked on his ass again when *The Evangeline* took a sharp roll. When the world stopped tilting, he tried again and made it upright. Walking up the remaining two steps to the crossover landing convinced him mountain climbing was not in his future. His body parts were competing to see which one could cause the most misery. His shoulders had a narrow lead on his thighs, but many more stairs and the thighs could make a last-second surge for the win.

He paused next to the door into the pilothouse. He liked to be at the controls in bad weather, but "too many pilots ruined the navigation," or something like that. As badly as he hated to admit it, Jagger was at least as good a navigator as he was. Maybe better. He'd trust his friend to take them to safety, either on Scatarie or back to Main-à-Dieu.

Holding on to the wall for balance, he staggered down the steps on the other side of the landing and eased open the bedroom door.

Gillian lay on his bed with her eyes closed. Jagger had spread a tarp over the mattress to keep it dry, but Gillian was soaked. Shane pulled a blanket off the closet shelf, wincing at the pain that shot through his shoulders. He'd be lucky if he could even move tomorrow, much less dive.

But they'd found something, and he couldn't wait to talk to Chevy McKnight and see why he'd directed them to that particular spot.

Gillian's face was pale, like that of a china doll that might break if you looked at it too hard. Shane thought about getting her out of the wetsuit, but the layer of water in it would keep her warmer than regular clothes if they ended up having to take refuge on Scatarie. He spread the blanket over her and sat on the bed, wondering if he should wake her. Her breathing was steady, but she probably had a concussion. At least she'd stopped bleeding.

She'd scared the hell out of him, but not for the reason he would've expected. Sure, he'd panicked and endured a brief visit of a ghost from his past, but he'd been able to push that aside and act.

Bottom line: Gillian had been the one who helped him do that. Even a month ago, he would have frozen and then would've run away. That's the fright he'd expected.

What had scared him about losing Gillian wasn't the guilt he might carry with him but the lonely, empty hole in his life without her in it. She'd filled a role he hadn't realized needed filling. He didn't know if it was love; they hadn't known each other long enough, and their whole relationship had been built out of a need to survive. Did foxhole love survive when the war ended?

All Shane knew was that whatever happened to him in the next two weeks, he had to come up with a scenario where Gillian survived.

He grasped her left wrist and stripped off the blue neoprene glove, rubbing her hand between his to warm it, noticing for the first time the raw skin on his own palms. That would teach him to remove his gloves, no matter what he'd found; one never knew when a hard climb up an anchor line might be imminent.

He didn't notice until he reached for her right hand that she'd opened her eyes. Smiling, he finished removing the second glove. "Hey there. You sure know how to finish out a dive."

Her smile was brief, but it warmed her eyes. "Yeah, too bad I wasn't around to enjoy it." She squeezed his hand. "Thank you. Guess that's the end of my career as a salver. Feel free to say 'I told you so.'"

Shane stretched out next to her on the bed, stifling a groan at the burn that set up in his thighs now that his muscles were cooling. He was seriously slammed and wanted nothing more than to sleep. But now that Gillian was awake, he needed to keep her that way. He also needed to talk to her about the game plan he'd been pondering while he lay on the deck being hammered by rain so hard it put Florida to shame.

"Let's talk about your diving." He tried to figure out a way to eat a big old dish of crow without choking on it, because he was about to serve one up.

"I know, I know. I'm not qualified to dive here." Gillian coughed, then groaned, and rubbed her eyes. "I got that message loud and clear."

One big bowl of crow stew, coming up. "I was wrong to say that. I was wrong about the whole dive plan. What I should've done was get you ready for these conditions. You need to be diving with me."

Gillian rolled onto her side to face him, pulling the blanket more tightly around her. "Could you repeat that? I thought I heard you say you wanted me to dive."

Well, no, he didn't *want* her to dive. She was way out of her depth, no pun intended, and they both knew it. But he did need her. "I realized today that it's going to take both of us if we have any chance in hell of finding the Templars' cross. Jagger's no diver, plus we need him to handle the boat. Now that I've seen what it looks like down there, I can get you prepared."

Gillian didn't respond, so he turned his head to look at her; his aching shoulders would never forgive him if he tried to roll on his side. He took in the narrowed eyes, the single, determined vertical line between her brows, the way she'd sucked in her lower lip.

He'd like to chew on that lower lip himself. Guess if he was thinking about sex, or at least kissing, he was gonna make it.

Screw the shoulder. He rolled to face her, leaning close, touching his lips to hers. She tasted of salt water and sea air and home. He was where he was supposed to be. "Just don't scare me again."

"I won't." Still, she looked troubled, even when she kissed him back.

He'd expected her to be happy about his decision, but maybe today's scare had changed her mind. She wouldn't be the first diver to avoid the water after a close call, but it was a mistake. When you get thrown, you get back on the horse at the first opportunity. "You don't have to dive if you don't want to. I mean, a doctor might take one look at your head and tell you to stay out of the water anyway."

"I do want to dive, and no doctor—for that very reason. I need to go back in. If I don't dive again now, I'll start being afraid of it and I've wasted too much time on fear and guilt." She paused, frowning. "But what a freaking idiot! I came down with gold fever and almost got us both killed chasing after a coin."

Her eyes widened, and she struggled to sit up. Her gaze pinballed around the room. "Where did Jagger put my BC? We didn't lose it, did we?"

Shane was sure she'd been wearing the buoyancy control vest when they pulled her aboard. He even vaguely remembered Jagger removing it. "It's probably still up on deck. Why? We can get you another one in Sydney if there's nowhere in Main-à-Dieu to buy one." Which he doubted, especially out of season.

"The coin. I know it's illegal to take it, but I think I stuck it in one of the pockets of my vest. I want you to see it."

Depending on where Jagger had stashed it, the vest might or might not still be on deck when they got in. Speaking of which . . .

"Hey." He raised up on his elbows. "I think the boat's settling down. Either the storm is dying or Jagger got us to a sheltered spot."

The harbor at Main-à-Dieu was wide and relatively shallow, edged in breakwaters, and he hadn't seen anything off Scatarie that would offer much protection for *The Evangeline* against the brunt of a serious storm. So with any luck, this blow had played itself out quickly and moved on.

He glanced at Gillian. "Think you can walk?" Hell, Shane wasn't sure he could walk.

"I think so." Gillian's neoprene suit slid along the tarp as she struggled to her feet, using the wall for balance. "I'm good."

Shane swung his legs off the bed and stood with his arms out, ready to break his fall if he tumbled. *The Evangeline*'s pitch and roll had settled to a gentle sway, though, and by the time he made his way around the bed to help Gillian, he felt the vibration of the anchor being released.

"I'm okay, although I'd hoped to be wearing clothes when I met Charlie's friend. And maybe have dry hair." Gillian's walk to the door was slow, but steady. Shane followed her into the hallway, ready to catch her if she looked in danger of collapse.

By the time they traversed the crossover landing and started down the steps to the outer hatch, Jagger had lugged out the bags they'd packed before reaching Main-à-Dieu this morning. It had turned out to be a longer day than Shane could've imagined.

He grabbed his duffel and Gillian's small rolling case, stopped on deck long enough to locate her buoyancy compensator, and followed them off the gangway and onto a short dock.

A man stood at the end of the worn wooden pier, watching them with his hands stuffed in the pockets of heavy chinos. He wore a dark blue nylon jacket, a baseball cap, and a grumpy-old-man expression that made Shane feel right at home. Charlie had described Chevy McKnight as the most ornery fisherman to ever walk the earth, and this guy fit the part. He was every curmudgeon ever played by actors like Ed Asner and Ernest Borgnine come to life. A hell of a lot like Charlie, in other words.

Shane bypassed Jagger and Gillian, set down the bags, and stuck out his right hand. "You must be Chevy. I'm Shane Burke."

The old man looked at Shane's hand, then jerked his head toward the central harbor. "No sir, you're trouble in a diving suit. That's who you are."

Shane turned to see a boat anchoring not far from them, and his heart jumped to his throat. He'd noticed the red-hulled workboat offshore at Scatarie just before he dived and hadn't thought much about it. The hull read *The Breton*.

He should've paid more attention before. Standing on the deck of *The Breton* was a guy who appeared to be watching them through a rifle scope.

A guy who looked a hell of a lot like Tex.

"Better hit the wood." Chevy's voice was gravel and concrete, more growl than statement.

"What?" A blow between his shoulder blades sent Shane face-first into the pier just as a boom sounded above him. It was followed by another blast, this one from the south.

Gillian, who must have tackled him since she was now lying on his back, facedown, whispered, "Holy shit, I think Chevy just started a war."

26

Gillian waited for a full-fledged gunfight at the Main-à-Dieu harbor to break out, but after the second shot, silence fell. She'd knocked Shane over, covered him like a wet neoprene blanket, and tucked her head down next to his. But now she hazarded a look up. People had wandered out of several of the buildings nestled around the harbor, looking toward them on the dock and toward *The Breton*, anchored nearby.

It wasn't exactly a crowd, maybe five or six people, but it was enough that when she rolled off Shane and craned her neck, Gillian saw *The Breton* chugging away from them. There was no sign of Tex.

Chevy uttered his first words since the gunfire: "Damned communists."

Shane sat up, wiping blood off his face from the scratches he'd gotten when he hit the pier. Gillian reached up and pulled out a splinter. "Sorry about that," she said. "I wasn't sure you saw Tex."

"I almost didn't." He looked up at the old man, who was tucking a small pistol back in the pocket of his pants. "I was watching Gary Cooper over here, trying to reenact *High Noon*."

Chevy looked down at them for the first time. "The hippie got shot. Might want to help him instead of worrying about me."

Jagger! Gillian hadn't even thought about him. She twisted around and found him sitting on the deck behind her, holding his

Goats Head Soup sweatshirt out to look at the source of the spreading bloodstain near the front of his left shoulder.

"Are you okay?"

He treated her to the first genuine smile she'd seen out of him in a few days. "I always wondered what it would feel like to get shot." He sounded genuinely pleased.

Obviously, he was suffering from shock. "Well, how *does* it feel to be shot?"

"It hurts like hell."

"Here." Shane climbed to his feet and held out a hand, grasping Jagger's left wrist and pulling his friend to a stand. Jagger swayed once but found his balance.

They all faced their host, who had crossed his arms over his barrel chest, his weathered face a study in neutrality. Gillian had no idea if he was going to yell at them or inquire after their health.

"Well, come on then," he said, turning and walking toward the junction of the pier and the wooden boardwalk that circled a wide swath of the town's harbor front. "Truck's over at the store, and I don't have all evening to waste on you. I'm hungry." Gillian thought she heard him mutter something about "damn fool Americans" before he got out of earshot.

Shane picked up his duffel and Jagger's pack. Gillian grabbed her bag and BC vest before he could be gallant and try to tote everything like a mule. "Did you pack your gun?" He eyed her rolling case. "I have mine in my duffel, but we might need both of them if that little adventure was any indication of what's to come."

"I got it." She walked alongside Jagger down the boardwalk, with Shane trailing behind. *The Breton* had almost reached the wide mouth of the harbor but was slowing down near the southern breakwater. "Looks like he might be planning to drop anchor over there. Reckon where he got the boat?"

"Probably leased it at . . ." Jagger trailed off and stopped at the sound of Gillian's ringtone—a tune they'd all come to dread.

She dug her phone from the front pocket of her bag. "What a surprise—'Private Caller.' I'll put him on speaker."

She punched the talk button and held the phone up. "Hiya, Tex." The more she thought about him shooting into this little town, the more pissed off she got. He could have killed an innocent bystander. Never mind that Chevy had started it. "You do realize that if you shoot your divers, your boss's chances of getting that cross in the next two weeks fall to zero."

Never mind that it was little better than zero anyway. Despite her excitement over that coin, today's adventure had shown her what a needle-haystack situation they were in.

"If I'd wanted to shoot Mr. Burke, I would have. Mr. Mackie is expendable. He's lucky people started coming outside or I'd have finished the job."

"Harsh." Jagger pulled his jacket around him more tightly, glancing down at the rip in the nylon made when the bullet passed through. He no longer looked amused.

"Yeah, lucky," Gillian said. "And to answer the question you haven't asked yet, no, we didn't find the cross today."

"Then I suggest you work harder. I've made arrangements for you to stay at . . . hold on." Tex spoke to someone in muffled tones in the background. Son of Tex, maybe? "At a guest house on the outskirts of town, the Brown Seal. You will not stay with that old fool Clarence McKnight."

Gillian looked at Jagger and Shane, eyebrows raised. "Sorry, Tex," Shane said. "We've made our own arrangements, and if you want me to dive for you and your boss, you'll live with it."

Gillian nodded her approval. If Tex didn't want them with Chevy, it made her more determined to stay with him. "We think Mr. McKnight's knowledge of the local waters and all the shipwreck legends will help us," she said. "You do want us to succeed in this mission, don't you?"

The long pause told her they'd won this round. "I'll be in touch," Tex finally said. "And tell that lunatic McKnight that if he takes one wrong step, I know where he lives. It'll take more than that fortified lighthouse to keep him safe."

"Duly noted," Gillian said, ending the call without waiting to see if Tex had more to say.

"Fortified lighthouse?" Jagger asked. "Oh, this is going to be interesting."

Yeah, maybe too interesting.

"And if Tex thinks Chevy is a lunatic, does that mean the guy's really smart or really crazy?" Shane asked.

"The two aren't mutually exclusive." Gillian stuffed the phone back in her bag. "Guess we'll find out soon enough."

Down the boardwalk, the old man already had a hundred-yard head start and showed no signs of slowing down. An ancient green pickup sat near the harbormaster's office, and Gillian suspected it would be their ride. She hoped Chevy lived nearby. Her wetsuit had been a good-enough choice for the dive, but now that the gunfire adrenaline had drained, she couldn't stop shivering.

Jagger walked alongside her, and Gillian was worried both by his silence and his downcast eyes. Unless the bullet had gone all the way through his shoulder—and she hadn't spotted any damage to the back of his jacket—he'd need it removed. Gillian suspected Main-à-Dieu didn't have a hospital. That would be a question for Chevy.

She didn't want to walk too fast herself. She'd had a couple of waves of dizziness she didn't dare let Shane know about, or he'd never let her back in the water. A hot shower and a nap would work wonders. After that, if she still felt wonky, she'd put away the wetsuit and leave the diving to Shane without an argument.

Shane had surprised her with his decision to let her dive, and she'd surprised herself by admitting that he had to make the call. She'd been stubborn, stupid, and rash to go in the water alone in those conditions. She could have killed them both, and it wasn't a lesson she planned to forget. This was no vacation.

If Shane said dive, she'd dive. And if he said she needed to keep her feet planted on *The Evangeline*, she'd respect that.

"Okay, that's enough." From behind her, Shane stuck a foot out and knocked the suitcase handle out of her hand. "You guys are creeping along like old ladies. If you go any slower, you'll be going backward. Stay here with the bags, and I'll get old Speedy up there to pick you up at the nearest corner in the truck."

Gillian turned to argue but stopped when she got a look at Jagger's face. He was shivering worse than she was, and for the first time she thought about what a stressful day he'd had, even before he got shot. She'd been so focused on her own drama, and Shane's, that she'd given no thought to what it must've been like for Jagger with the weather worsening, Tex nearby, and both divers staying down too long. Then navigating through that storm. He'd done it all with no fanfare and no complaints.

"Good idea," she told Shane. "Make sure Chevy doesn't leave without us."

Shane edged past them and started off down the boardwalk at a weary-looking trot, his navy duffel and Jagger's heavy green knapsack bouncing over his shoulder. They all needed some rest.

By the time she and Jagger reached the nearest thing that could be called a road, she'd had a chance to get a better look at Main-à-Dieu. Its French name translated to *Hand of God*, and Gillian thought it was pretty enough to have been crafted by God's hand. The shallow half-moon harbor featured a narrow beach and scrubby growth that gave way to rolling hills. Farther up the coast, the terrain grew dramatically rugged, with cliffs and rocky highlands, but here it was gentle. Or it seemed that way in the sweet freshness that always seemed to follow a violent storm, as if nature had worn out its fury and felt the need to atone.

Most of the two dozen or so buildings in sight of the harbor were neat white one- or two-story clapboard rectangles, and a colorful fleet of workboats gathered near the water's far end. Chevy was a lobsterman, Shane had told her, and he and Charlie had struck up a friendship back when the elder Burke was an itinerant fisherman traveling with the seasons. Summers belonged to Nova Scotia, and she figured Main-à-Dieu was probably a lot like Southport fifty or sixty years ago. It reminded her of Cedar Key, only smaller and colder.

"You look as wracked as I feel. Let's wait here." Jagger sat on a boulder next to the road. "How's your head?"

Starting to pound like the surf hitting the sunkers offshore, but part of that could be attributed to hunger. It had been a long time since this morning's sandwich. "It's been better. How's your gunshot wound?"

He smiled and broke into a warbly verse of an old Stones song: "He shot me once, but I shot him twice." Jagger's smile faded as he stared at the edge of the harbor, where *The Breton* sat like a harbinger of doom. "Nice to know I'm expendable."

"Tex is an asshole." Gillian's heart lifted at the sight of the green pickup bouncing down the street toward them. "When it comes right down to it, as far as Tex is concerned, we're all expendable once our two weeks is up."

Jagger didn't answer, but he didn't need to. There was nothing to stop Tex's boss from ordering them all killed as soon as he had what he wanted. If it was Weston Flynn, letting them live was too risky. He had too much to lose. Their only advantage right now was that if their culprit was the secretary of state, he didn't know they suspected him.

For now, all they could do was play along, buy time, and hope for a brainstorm about how they could keep everyone safe. A lucky break would be nice, or an intervention from the real hand of God. Too many people had already been hurt. Harley. Viv. Now Jagger.

Whatever happened, Shane and Jagger had to survive this. Even if Gillian had to call the freaking *New York Times* and publicly declare the secretary of state a blackmailer and would-be murderer. The only thing that had stopped her from doing it already was lack of evidence. They had to tie Tex to Flynn somehow more than being born in the same Texas town. If she found a way to expose Flynn and Tex, by the time they tracked her down and had her killed in a way that didn't throw any suspicion toward Washington, Shane and Jagger could be long gone. There was enough of the initial money left for them to disappear to somewhere like Montana or Wyoming—or Nova Scotia.

Not that they'd ever agree to run, so she'd have to find a way to convince them.

The pickup lurched to a stop, and Shane stifled a grin when he opened the door and climbed out. Something about Chevy had amused him. "Gillian, why don't you ride in the back with me? Jagger looks like he needs some heat."

She agreed, although she was freezing and could do with some heat herself. A temperature drop had followed the storm, and her wetsuit had stopped trapping in warmth and begun trapping in cold.

While Shane helped Jagger into the passenger seat, Gillian walked to the back of the truck and looked into the ridged bed. There was no graceful way to do this, so she shoved her bag and BC ahead of her and rolled herself in. The hard plastic liner was cold and smelled like eau de fish. Awesome.

Shane slammed the passenger door and had to make an awkward leap to get in the truck bed before Chevy pulled away. He settled into the corner with his back to the cab, and held out an arm. "Come here; I have some body heat to share."

"Well, how could I pass up a romantic invitation like that?" Gillian slid next to him and had to admit his arm felt good around her shoulders even through his bulky drysuit, which might be dry on the inside but was cold and damp on the outside. "Is our host as cheerful up close and in person?"

Shane smiled. "Yeah, he reminds me of Charlie. Heart of gold trapped in a body of barbed wire. Except he makes my uncle look, well, normal. He thinks the aliens and communists are in league."

Great. "Still, if Tex doesn't want us with him, there must be a good reason to stay with him."

Shane pulled her closer. "Damn straight. How's your head?"

"Never mind me. Jagger needs a doctor."

Twisting around to look in the cab's back window, Shane nodded. "Chevy wants to let his wife take a look at him and if she can't help, they'll drive Jagger to Sydney. Problem is, Canada has the same law as the US. A hospital or doctor has to report a gunshot wound to the police. I'm not sure we want anybody looking at our customs status that closely."

Damn Tex and his assessment of who was expendable.

"How much does Chevy know?" Gillian wanted to get her story straight before they got to wherever they were going—which apparently was uphill. The truck took a sharp curve onto a winding, unpaved road barely wide enough for the pickup. If the grade got any steeper, she and Shane might slide out the back.

"Everything," Shane said. "Charlie told him everything. And Chevy knows it'll put him in danger—thus, him coming to the harbor armed."

The truck had continued its steady climb, but now Chevy made a sharp hairpin turn and Gillian leaned forward. "Look—it *is* a lighthouse."

Shane whistled. "Sweet. That's even cooler than living on a boat. Wonder if it's still in use?"

Chevy cut off the dirt and gravel road and drove along a dirt trail toward the lighthouse, circling it and pulling the truck into a steel detached garage behind the building. He got out and slammed the door behind him. "Help your friend out and bring him to the second level," he told Shane. "We talk after dinner." He strode toward the lighthouse without a backward glance.

Shane grinned again as he walked around the truck. "Quite a character, huh?" he asked Jagger, who struggled to stand and finally let Shane help him. "Did he talk to you about aliens or his other visitors?"

"Yeah, they're in league with the communists and politicians. Can't wait to hear what he thinks of our buddy Weston Flynn." Jagger waved Shane away and winced as he rounded the truck and joined Gillian on the path to the lighthouse entrance. They stopped to wait for Shane, who was collecting Jagger's bag.

Gillian stared up at the lighthouse. It was a classic cylinder, wider at the base, maybe seventy or eighty feet tall, and painted white with red stripes around it. Three stacks of windows rose up its side, probably each belonging to a separate floor. What looked like a glassed-in observation tower circled the top. It was a beauty, and she couldn't wait to see what it looked like inside.

Gillian glanced back at Shane but her comment about the lighthouse faded when she looked over the cliff beyond. A golden-orange sunset cut through a fog bank that was rolling toward them across the Atlantic. It was beautiful, mystic, eerie. A wooded island in the distance looked familiar. "Is that Scatarie?"

Shane nodded. "We're not far from Moque Head. I'm anxious to see why Chevy had us dive there, but first I guess we better make sure Mrs. Chevy doesn't kill Jagger."

* * *

"They're kind of sweet, aren't they?" Gillian sat curled up on a sofa next to Shane, and his arm around her was as warm and comforting as the room around them. It felt wrong to feel so content when the world was going to hell in a clamshell.

It was hard to be anything but comfortable here, though. The high-ceilinged, round living area on the second level of the lighthouse managed to be cozy, thanks no doubt to the earthy touch of

Cleopatra Huckaby McKnight. Cleo and Chevy were huddled in the adjacent kitchen and dining area, whispering furiously. Jagger was asleep in one of the bedrooms on the third level.

"Sweet?" Shane made a scoffing grunt. "They're like a geriatric Mr. and Mrs. Smith, only Cleo's a lot scarier than Angelina Jolie. They're probably planning World War III in there."

"I like her. And she patched up Jagger." Cleo Huckaby had been a nurse before she decided on a career as a lobsterwoman and got a job on Chevy McKnight's crew. He'd hired her to prove a woman couldn't last a season and ended up marrying her. She'd worked alongside him ten more seasons before she hung up her lobster boots. They'd just celebrated their thirtieth anniversary.

She'd poured Jagger full of whiskey until he passed out with "Hand of Fate" on his lips, heated water to sterilize a wicked knife, dug around in his shoulder until she pulled out the bullet just as he woke up, plied him with more whiskey, and finally stitched him up. She kept antibiotics on hand for the odd injury, and he'd be taking those to ward off infection. Apparently, lobstermen had a lot of accidents involving hooks.

Gillian yawned, wanting to sleep now that she'd had the hot shower and enough home-cooked food to fill her up for days. Cleo had prepared enough hearty fare for a week, with thick chowder full of local mushrooms and briny oysters and corn, served with bread she'd baked herself. They'd even drunk mead, a brew Cleo concocted from her own supplies of honey, then bottled and sold during tourist season.

Gillian couldn't sleep yet, though. They needed to come up with a plan to find the cross. An hour after they'd arrived at the lighthouse, she'd gotten an e-mail from Tex using the "Charlie Burke" e-mail address: a photo of Holly, this time not at day care but playing on her backyard swing set. Gretchen could be seen in the background, sitting in a lawn chair. The message contained only one word: *Remember.*

A quick phone call to Gretchen assured her they were okay and nothing weird had happened except she'd noticed a guy in a van parked on their street for several consecutive days. Three or four days ago, he'd disappeared.

Gillian would lay odds the van driver was Son of Tex, and that he'd disappeared because he was here with Tex. At least it made her feel better to think they'd followed her and left her family unwatched. Shane had checked in with Charlie, and he'd finally answered his phone. He hadn't seen anything amiss—but was keeping his shotgun by the door just in case. Tank had settled in and taken over the house.

Chevy and Cleo joined them in the living room, with Chevy taking the recliner and Cleo perching on the black wrought iron staircase that spiraled the full height of the lighthouse from the first-level mudroom all the way to the lantern-room-turned-observation-deck. They'd finished watching the eerie, fog-shrouded sunset up there before dinner. Chevy had encased it in insulating hurricane-safe glass, and Cleo had furnished it with comfortable chairs and a wet bar.

"Where do we start?" Cleo asked. She was a tall, slender woman with graying hair, as warm and sweet-natured as her husband was crusty. They both had a lot of laugh lines, though, and Gillian found herself envying their easy affection.

"Tell us what happened today," Chevy said. "None of the bullshit, either. Why'd you end up coming ashore still in diving gear and hurt?"

They all looked at Shane, and he blushed under the scrutiny. Gillian loved that about him. He genuinely didn't like to be the center of attention.

He went through the story quickly, not mentioning the fact that Gillian had dived against his wishes, or that she'd been injured after getting distracted by a coin.

"Hmph." Chevy scratched his head, causing a clump of white hair to stick up. "Find anything of interest besides the silverware?"

Gillian wanted to show off the coin and hoped Chevy and Cleo wouldn't report her to the authorities for taking an artifact from its watery resting place.

From what she could tell so far, though, the McKnights weren't exactly the authority-loving type. They lived up here in their rehabbed lighthouse—built in the late 1800s and never put into commission. They minded their own business, made a decent living by brewing mead and catching lobster, and thought politicians were minions of Satan. No one had mentioned aliens again. She decided to take the plunge.

"I did find something, and it was the reason I got blindsided by the current." She reached into her pocket and pulled out the coin, which she'd been relieved to find tucked safely in her BC. "I'm sorry; I know it's illegal to take things off of wrecks, but it had been washed free and I grabbed it without thinking."

Chevy walked over to retrieve the coin, turning it over and rubbing it. Then he took it to a desk in the corner, turned on a lamp, and pulled out a magnifying glass.

"We don't think much of treasure hunters trying to get rich, but we also don't think much of what they call *in situ* preservation," Cleo said. "The government should let scientists remove and save as much as they can from the wreck sites. They're pieces of our history that the ocean will eventually destroy, what it hasn't destroyed already." She sounded as if she'd made that speech a few times before. "Besides, that coin of yours didn't come off a wreck site; you said you found it on the ocean floor. That probably makes it fair game."

Gillian relaxed. Neither of them seemed to be bothered by her theft.

Chevy rejoined them, handing the coin to Cleo. "Looks like French silver, with a date of 1688," he said. "Worth a bit of money."

Gillian didn't care about the money. She might one day, but not now. "Does that, plus the silverware, mean we were on a wreck site?"

Chevy returned to his recliner and sipped his mead. "This damn batch is too sweet, woman. Don't put so much honey in it next time." He didn't wait for his wife to respond, which was just as well. "Woman" was examining the coin and ignoring her husband.

"Scatarie itself is a wreck site—all around it," Chevy said. "Shipwrecks are piled two, three, four deep out there, one on top of another. Newest ones are usually on top, but not always—depends on storms and currents. Last estimate I heard was that only twenty percent of the wrecks off Scatarie had been found."

"Most of them would be gone now, right?" Shane leaned forward and propped his elbows on his knees. "I mean, the wooden ships . . ."

"Wooden ships were kindling before they had time to sink." Chevy got up again and retrieved a map from the desk. "Come in here and let me show you a few things."

They gathered around the table, where Chevy spread the map showing Cape Breton's east coast. Gillian recognized the Main-à-Dieu harbor, with its breakwaters extending on the sides to help protect ships and residents both. And the largest of the many offshore islands: Scatarie.

Chevy tapped a spot with his finger. "This is where you went in today. Current's bad on that passage between Scatarie and the mainland, and I wanted you to get a feel for it so you could decide how you want to do your real dive." He slid a finger to the east. "Here's where I think your best chance of finding that old wreck you're looking for. If it's there to be found."

Gillian looked at all the circles and lines and numbers on the map, showing depth and geological formations. "What makes you think it's there?"

Chevy tapped his finger on the map again. "This here's a ship-kill zone. You got two big sunkers offshore, with a narrow passage in between. Ship wanders into that passage, it's done for. You ever heard of *The Feversham*?"

They hadn't, so for the next half hour, Chevy told them about the *HMS Feversham*, a thirty-two-gun British warship that left Quebec in 1711, bound for New York and followed by three supply ships. "They all sank in this corridor during a storm," Chevy said. "*Feversham* hit the rocks, and it was too late for the supply ships behind her to change course. More'n a hundred died, but there were enough survivors that made it to Scatarie to know what happened."

It was an interesting, haunting story, but Gillian didn't see the connection. "What does that have to do with *The Marcus Aurelius*? It sank years earlier, and as far as I know there were no records that survived."

Cleo poured Chevy another glass of mead and if he thought it too sweet, it didn't stop him from taking a big swallow. "My grandfather grew up on Scatarie." He led them back into the living room. "The island had quite a few residents back then. Now, of course, it's uninhabited. But I remember taking a boat out there to visit him, and I spent a lot of time rambling around on those rocks. There were stories, too. One of them was about an old wreck that lay beneath the British warship. There's an even newer one on top of *The Feversham* now. But in that old wreck below it, the old folks would tell us, almost everyone died except a couple of children."

Gillian's heart rate sped into overdrive. "That could be it! Has anyone recovered anything from it?"

Chevy shook his head. "No, and I don't know if it's even true. Tales get taller as they get told, eh? And if I remember the stories, there are bound to be lots of other old-timers who remember it as well. Could be there's just nothing left of it."

Shane had pulled the map closer to study the site of *The Feversham* wreck. "This is a really shallow dive, but it looks like the ocean floor takes a big dip not too far behind it, down to one-hundred-plus feet. Has anyone dived that area?"

"That, I don't know." Chevy finished his drink and set the mug back on the table with a smack of his lips. "Folks're still fighting over that freighter that ran aground on the island a few years ago. Still sitting out there on the rocks, it is. But deepwater diving's come a long way in the last few years. Could be a man with the proper equipment . . ." He shrugged. "Maybe he could find something back there."

"Or her," Cleo said, giving her husband a narrow-eyed smile, and Gillian spotted his smile before he pasted on his stern look again.

"How long before Jagger can sail *The Evangeline*?" Shane asked. "We have less than two weeks to come up with either a cross, an idea, or both."

"Not for at least a week," Cleo said, and her voice brooked no argument. "He needs to stay still and let himself heal."

Gillian sat back in her chair, deflated. "We can't wait that long to start." She looked at Chevy, trying to put as much beseeching charm into her expression as she could. "Could you take us out?"

"Hell, no. I have business to tend to." His voice brooked no argument either. So much for Gillian's questionable charm.

Cleo cleared her throat. "What is wrong with you people? The answer's obvious."

They all looked at her, and Gillian had a dawning suspicion of what she meant.

"I'll take you."

27

Shane stared at the clouds moving in from the southeast, threatening a squall. Make that another squall. He sat opposite Gillian on the inflatable Zodiac they were using as a dive boat. Once Jagger had recovered enough to get back on the water, Cleo handled *The Evangeline* and Jagger took over the inflatable, which could get in and around the rocks more easily. Today, with Cleo off to purchase her supplies for the week, they were leaving *The Evangeline* at anchor untended.

For the past twelve days, he and Gillian had been diving in and around *The Feversham* wreck site, fanning farther out each day, dodging the worsening weather. The storms were coming more frequently, lasting longer, and stirring up more of the ocean floor each time.

They'd found a lot of artifacts, mostly pieces of cannons or silver or coins embedded in the concretions between and below the forest of underwater boulders. He'd even taken Gillian into the deeper water farther out, where it was darker, colder, and decompression issues came into play. She'd handled it well, but her nerves were on edge the closer they got to their deadline.

Hell, his weren't much better, and even Jagger—the most stoic of them all—had gotten twitchy.

Shane turned to Gillian. "Okay, a storm's coming in tomorrow, so we're going to make today count. You clear on protocol?"

She nodded, tugging at her collar. When Chevy had gone to Sydney to replace Shane's fins, coming back to surprise them with the Zodiac, he'd also gifted Gillian with a drysuit. She hated it. "Get over it," Chevy had told her. Shane agreed that they were bulky and not as comfortable as the wetsuits, but even the shallow waters had grown cooler. The deep water was downright frigid.

He moved to the edge of the boat, strapped on his mask, and went through his short predive ritual. Closed his eyes, steadied his breathing, calmed his system. Then he stuck in his regulator mouthpiece, rolled backward into the water, got his bearings, popped up and gave Jagger the "okay" sign. Gillian followed a few seconds later.

Then they swam. Shane hadn't had a dive buddy in ten years, and even before the incident with Kevin, he'd done most of his diving alone. He'd been surprised to discover how much he enjoyed diving with Gillian. She was curious and observant and careful.

Careful was key out here. Shane had dived from the Zodiac earlier and secured a line from the boat to a big piece of iron they'd found concreted onto a rock formation behind *The Feversham* site—maybe part of an old ship railing. Now, as they approached it, he pulled a long, coiled red line off his weight belt and held it up so that Gillian would take hers off as well.

These were their tethers; he'd insisted on them once they began diving into deeper water. If the seas got rough or they got disoriented, all they had to do was follow the line back to the ship railing and then follow the anchor line up to the inflatable boat.

He tied his line around his weight belt, checked his knots, then checked Gillian's. They'd been splitting up the past few days to cover more territory. He turned to leave, but twisted back when she grasped his arm. Once she caught his gaze, she pressed two neoprene-gloved fingers to her lips and then placed them on his.

They were both still smiling as they gave each other the "okay" sign and swam in opposite directions. They'd been together every night of the past two weeks, not saying anything when Cleo made the assumption that they wanted one room. Jagger hadn't commented, either, and Shane kept thinking he should bring the subject up. The more he was with Gillian, the more he wanted her.

But what could he say? He didn't know if he loved her, but thought he might. He didn't exactly have a wealth of successful relationships to use as models. He hoped they'd survive this mess and have a chance to see if what they had could survive outside crisis mode, but surviving felt like a long shot right now.

At least he'd come up with a plan, and Jagger had agreed to it. If they didn't find the cross by tomorrow night—or earlier if the weather shut them down before their deadline—Jagger was going to take Gillian and hide out while Shane acted as the decoy aboard *The Evangeline*. He'd wait until the storm hit, run the boat onto the rocks off Moque Head, and sink her, hopefully giving himself enough time to dive to safety and rejoin the others.

By the time Tex and his boss figured out there were no bodies to be found, Shane hoped they could all be in hiding somewhere—Charlie and Chevy and Gretchen and the whole lot of them. Until they could find some leverage on Weston Flynn. If Flynn was even their man.

That plan had more holes in it than a bag of doughnuts, but it was all they'd been able to come up with. It would kill him to lose *The Evangeline*, but at least it would be on his terms. It would kill him more to lose Gillian—or any of them.

Shane finally reached the farthest area he'd explored on his last outing, at just over a hundred feet deep. A few yards into the deeper water stood two tall rock formations that would easily reach the top of a two-story building. Glaciers had carved this ocean bottom out of solid bedrock, and he couldn't help but be awed by the millennia it had taken to create such a vista.

A narrow opening ran between the tall formations, and he was surprised to see it was wider than he'd originally thought. He approached it with caution. They'd seen some brown seals on the rocks around Scatarie, but so far they hadn't run into any sharks or other big nasties. Generally, a shark had no interest in a diver who left him alone, but Shane didn't want to surprise one.

He eased through the narrow opening and shone his light into the blackness, so surprised he almost lost his regulator. He'd expected to run into more rock, but there was only more water. After looking around a few minutes, he saw why this area had shown up as solid rock on their sonar. The passageway led into a box canyon that was surrounded by rock on not only three sides, but above. It was basically a cave. Things that got washed in here would stay here, even for hundreds of years.

With growing excitement, Shane came to rest on the floor of the cavern and used his light to try and gauge the dimensions. He checked his dive calculator. He had forty-five minutes before he was due to meet Gillian at the anchor line. Normally that would give him thirty minutes to search, but because of his depth, he'd have to make a decompression stop along the way, plus he could tell he was running through his tank faster than usual. So twenty minutes of search time, tops.

Beginning at the opening into the cavern, he swam right along the rock wall, making a mental note of where it curved in, or where the rocks were split. Concretions were deep around the base of the rocks, and he inspected the surface of each one with his light.

On his third stop, he spotted a glint of metal. He fanned the water and silt away from the concretion, but couldn't see anything. *Damn it.* He needed to know if this spot was worth coming back to. Asking forgiveness from the Canadians and the Nova Scotia government, he unstrapped his knife from its sheath on his calf and hacked into the concretion. Despite the cold water, he was sweating inside his drysuit by the time he chipped away enough to expose the edge of a coin. Not just a coin, but a gold coin. Seawater didn't damage gold; and its gleam sent Shane's pulse racing. Where there was one coin, there would be more. Maybe a lot more.

Maybe a ruby-encrusted gold cross.

Shane took the small underwater camera he'd strapped to his gear, took a few shots, and checked his watch. He'd spent eight precious minutes uncovering that coin; he needed to see how big this place was and what else was here, then get back to Gillian. If the weather held, they'd return to *The Evangeline*, strap on new tanks and both come back to this spot. Maybe even move the Zodiac closer.

Suppose you do find the cross, asshole. Are you really going to turn it over to Tex? Do you trust him to keep his word?

Fuck no. But he'd find the cross first, then figure it out.

For the next twenty minutes, Shane skirted the edge of the underwater cavern. As near as he could tell, it was about half the length of a football field and about the same width. He found no ways in or out other than the passage he'd entered through. The rocks across the top of the cavern were at about fifteen or twenty feet, and what in an aboveground cave would be stalagmites and stalactites were columns of rugged, reddish rock.

By the time he completed circling the cavern, he'd found at least thirty more glints of metal—quite a bit of it gold. *The Marcus Aurelius* had been bringing money and supplies for the early French settlement near Louisbourg, so they would've had gold aboard. Maybe a lot of it. Duncan Campbell might have been a larcenous ne'er-do-well, but his employer wasn't.

As Shane swam back toward the passage leading out of the cavern, he caught a glint of silver he'd missed earlier, embedded near the edge of the rock wall. He stopped to look at it, even though it was probably another piece of silverware. It had a flat, curved edge that looked wrong for silverware, though, so he took out his knife again and dug into the hard marine matter.

It was a plate, and plates in those days often had maker's marks. The concretion here was softer, being exposed to more current, and it didn't take him long to free the plate enough to pull it out.

He fanned his hands over the metal disk, rubbing to try and remove the concrete and rocks and shells that covered it, but they were crusted on too hard. If it had an identifiable mark, it could be enough to confirm that these relics were of the right sort to be from *The Marcus Aurelius.*

His dive watch told him it was time to meet Gillian, though. He unzipped the front of his BC and slipped the plate inside it, then rezipped. After slipping out of the cavern entrance, he began to coil the tether line around his arm as he followed it back to the ship railing they were using to anchor the Zodiac.

His head spun with ideas. He couldn't swear that cavern held some of the remains of *The Marcus Aurelius,* but his gut told him he'd found it. Whether he'd uncover the cross was another matter, but with any luck and cooperation from the weather, they could come back today or early tomorrow and find out before the storm moved in. This time, they'd bring something to dig more effectively into the concretions. If the cross was here, it was embedded in that stuff; it wasn't floating around on the ocean floor, waiting to be found.

With this solid a lead, maybe Tex would even give them an extra day to look.

Yeah, because Tex is such an understanding guy.

When he got back to the anchor line, Gillian was waiting. She pointed at her watch and shook her finger at him. He grinned. She wouldn't be so fussy when she heard what he'd found. He took her hand and brought it to his chest, pressing it against the hard metal plate that rested beneath his vest.

She gave him a flirtatious crinkle of her eyes behind her mask until she realized, eyes widening, that he was trying to show her more than his love and affection. She felt around the edges of the plate, then looked back at him. He nodded and pointed upward. First they'd ascend, then they'd play with the plunder.

They secured their tether lines to their weight belts and began the ascent. Shane wasn't sure how deep Gillian had dived, but he would need to make compression stops. He hadn't been extremely deep but didn't know what the cavern had added to his perceived depth. The water had been colder. It had been darker. He'd run through his gas faster.

Figuring he'd been at about 120 feet, he divided it in half and stopped at the sixty-foot mark. He pointed at his watch and held up three fingers. He had to wait three minutes before ascending farther, to give his body a chance to adjust to the change in compression.

It was slowgoing when he wanted to get topside so badly, but he knew to take the rules seriously. Every year, a few divers miscalculated or ignored the deco rules and ended up dead. So he stopped every ten feet, waited a minute or two, and pushed on. Gillian stopped with him.

The last deco stop was at ten feet. In such shallows, the waves battered them around, but they could see and, by holding on to the anchor line, could keep their position somewhat steady. The dark oval of the Zodiac floated above them and, far beyond it, outside the range of the sunkers, lay the deep, smooth hull of *The Evangeline*.

A deep boom sounded from beyond them, and Shane looked up and around. They might hear thunder at this depth, but he saw nothing that—

He barely had time to turn a questioning look toward Gillian when a wall of water hit him with enough force to blow the anchor line into the air with him still clinging to it.

He hit the water hard when the line came back down, and he thought he might have lost consciousness briefly. The only certainty was that when awareness returned, he still had the anchor line wrapped around his wrist, but it no longer had any tension on it. The Zodiac wasn't at the other end.

His heart pounding hard enough to make his buoyancy vest feel too tight, Shane surfaced and looked around, pulling his regulator out of his mouth and gulping in air. He breathed a sigh of relief when Gillian popped up about ten yards away.

He continued to spin and finally spotted the Zodiac. Whatever had happened, the inflatable boat had been blown fifty yards to the east but was still upright. As soon as he saw Jagger in the water, grasping the edge of the inflatable, Shane said a prayer of thanks and turned to swim toward Gillian.

She'd taken out her regulator as well and was looking back toward the mainland with a horrified expression. Shane followed her gaze to where *The Evangeline* was anchored.

Only then did Shane understand what had happened, because *The Evangeline*, his beautiful boat, his home, his place of safety, was nothing more than a smoking hull. The explosion—because only an explosion could cause that kind of damage so quickly—had sent a miniature tsunami fanning in all directions.

Now, flames licked from the engine room and spread across what was left of the foredeck. The aft deck had already begun sinking, ready to join the layers of wrecks off Scatarie Island.

At first, Shane thought the smoke from the explosion had irritated his eyes. Only when he jerked up his mask and propped it on his head did he realize he was crying. He couldn't stop, even when Gillian swam beside him and put a hand on his shoulder.

What the fuck had happened?

"Shane!"

He blinked and looked at Gillian. "It's Jagger," she said, and he hated the pity on her face. Hated it. He spun in the water and looked back at the Zodiac. Why wasn't Jagger coming to get them? Instead, he was lying almost flat in the boat and yelling.

"What's he saying?"

A high-pitched whine sounded next to Shane's ear, and the water in front of him splashed as if something had hit it. Jagger pointed behind them, so they turned again.

In a split second, Shane's combat training kicked in. He spotted the distinctive red hull of *The Breton*, and the distinctive outline of a man with a rifle pointed at him. Grabbing Gillian's weight belt, he jerked her underwater while using his fins and his heavy thigh muscles to propel them backward just in time for the next bullet to pass where they'd been a few seconds earlier.

Tex seemed to have decided they were all expendable, but why?

28

Why the hell was Tex trying to shoot them now? Shane blocked the whole issue of *The Evangeline* out of his mind; he'd have to mourn later. Their deadline had at least thirty-six hours to spare, a solid lead to the Templars' cross had finally popped up, and *now* Tex was trying to kill them?

Something had happened to change the rules. Something bad.

Another shot sliced into the waves a few feet in front of them. Next to him, Gillian lowered her mask, slipped her regulator back in her mouth, and flipped on her gas. Good idea. They both had a little time left on their tanks, and full pony bottles as well. Shane got back into his gear and motioned for her to follow him toward the Zodiac—or at least where he thought the Zodiac was. The fog had gone from chicken broth to pea soup, which would work to their advantage. It was hard to shoot a target you couldn't see.

Jagger had taken refuge in the water and floated the inflatable in front of him like a big rubber shield. If Tex had been smart, he'd have sailed close enough to shoot a hole in the Zodiac and sink it, or he'd have hit the portable gas tank and blown the damn thing up before tackling *The Evangeline*, ruining their escape options.

Shane had doubted Tex's humanity, but never his intelligence. So not only had the rules suddenly changed, but Tex wasn't thinking things through carefully.

He and Gillian swam underneath the Zodiac and surfaced next to Jagger. Shane ripped out his mouthpiece. "You okay?"

Jagger nodded, but he looked like hell. His shoulder had healed enough over the past two weeks for him to operate the inflatable, but not enough for swimming. He needed to get back to the mainland.

"Why's he shooting at us?" Gillian had raised her mask and peered over the edge of the Zodiac toward *The Breton*.

"I don't know, but I'm going over there to find out. Something's changed and we need to know what it is." Shane had no idea what he'd do when he got there, unarmed, but he could at least provide enough diversion for the others to get help.

"That's a really b-bad idea." Jagger's voice was shaky, and Shane took note of his blanched face and too-bright eyes. "You're not even ar-armed."

"If I can surprise him, his gun won't matter." Tex had to be alone on that boat. Otherwise, Son of Tex would have been on deck with him, watching the fireworks and playing *shoot the diver*.

"You're right," Gillian said, although she didn't look as if she liked it. "If you can create a diversion, maybe get the jump on Tex, then Jagger and I can start up the Zodiac and get to the mainland for help."

Shane looked over his shoulder. From surface level, the mile and a half of choppy water to Main-à-Dieu harbor looked impossibly far—at least as much as he could see in diminishing visibility. The fog moving in would help camouflage the boat, though, and Jagger could navigate in pitch-dark as long as he had a compass. Gillian had one clipped to her drysuit. This could work.

Of course, unless he managed to sneak up on Tex and get the rifle away from him, he might not live to enjoy it.

"Assuming the best, I'll get control of *The Breton* and sail her back to Main-à-Dieu. I'll meet you at Chevy's lighthouse."

Shane reached for his regulator, but Gillian laid a hand on his arm, her brown eyes serious. Worried. "What do you think this means?"

Shane gave her a salty kiss, and then another. "I don't know. But I'm damned sure going to find out."

He looked at Jagger and nodded toward the Zodiac. "Let me help you back in before I leave. Fog's too thick for you to be much of a target." Normally, Jagger wouldn't need help. Normally, Jagger would've reamed him one for even suggesting it. But they'd passed normal a long time ago, and his friend only nodded.

After a struggle, Jagger positioned himself by the short portable ladder and Shane heaved him over. By the time he had struggled to a seated position on the bottom of the inflatable, Gillian had removed her tank and BC, thrown them in, and climbed up the ladder next to him.

She looked down at Shane and he smiled, thinking of the corny things he wanted to say. *Be careful.* Or, *No matter how this turns out, I'm glad I met you.* Maybe even the *L* word.

Instead, when she returned his smile, he just wrapped his mind around it to hold on to, crammed in his mouthpiece, and flipped backward and ass side up, thrusting his legs to propel himself downward and away from the boat.

They'd been diving with the Zodiac moored off Ragged Rocks Cove, on Scatarie's south coast, but *The Breton* had stayed in the deeper water one cove to the west, nearer the Main-à-Dieu passage. As he swam, Shane visualized the position of *The Breton*, and where he'd last seen Tex on deck. Chances were, unless he was preparing to pull up anchor and head back to the mainland himself, the murderous asswipe was still trying to get a better shot.

Halfway there, Shane found himself pulling hard on his regulator and checked the gauge. Gas was down to the red zone, so he switched to the pony bottle hung in a sling over his left rib cage. The water had grown rougher, and he guessed the time at around 3:00 p.m. Whatever happened, it needed to happen before dark.

He finally spotted the back end of *The Evangeline*, steadily sinking near a massive rock that had broken its fiberglass hull like an eggshell.

It's just another obstacle. Ignore it, and go around. Shane cut to the portside of his dying boat and, once past it, immediately saw the dark shadow of *The Breton*, still sitting in place. He located its anchor line and followed it up, trying to think of the different scenarios he might encounter.

Best case: Tex was still on the foredeck with his binoculars, giving Shane enough time to climb up, ditch his dive gear, pull out his knife, and give old Tex the surprise of his miserable life.

Worst case: Tex had spotted him leaving the others, had figured out what Shane was up to, and was sitting up top like a big, ugly spider, leaning over the rail with his rifle and waiting for Shane to surface. At which point it would be *Adios, Shane.*

Chances were good that reality would fall somewhere in between, so as Shane neared the fixed starboard-side ladder of *The Breton*, he peered through the water before surfacing. No Tex leaning over the rail, at least not that he could see.

Holding on to the bottom ladder rung, he next pondered his equipment. He'd need it to dive again for the cross, but he didn't want to make his boarding more difficult than it already was—never mind more noisy—by clanking up the ladder with tanks and hoses. He decided to risk a few extra seconds on a compromise, rigging up an awkward bundle of BC, mask, regulator, tanks, mask, and weight belt. Once they felt secure, he tied the whole mess to the bottom ladder rung using his tether line. The compass he kept, along with his knife.

With regret, he reached down and unfastened his fins and kicked them off. Fins and ladders? Bad combination.

Even without his gear, Shane struggled to make it up the ladder with the waves tossing the boat like a toy. If he lived through this, he'd have to write an endorsement letter to the company that made the neoprene dive gloves. Without them, he'd have lost his grip and drowned while he looked at his gear bobbing just out of reach.

He finally ascended high enough to peer over the rail and take stock, only then realizing the ladder led right to the pilothouse door. *Shit.* He went back down a rung, held on tight, and considered his options. Entering the boat from this ladder would put him not only in view from the pilothouse but also from the foredeck where Tex had been standing earlier. But the seas were too rough for him to reach the ladder near the stern. He could go back into the water and hope to struggle back into his dive gear, but he didn't have enough air to swim to the mainland underwater and the seas were too rough to swim conventionally. In other words, his options sucked.

Shane had flirted with prayer the last month, and he still wasn't convinced anyone heard. But he sent up a few pleas anyway, just in case. He didn't want to die. Now that death could be close at hand, he realized all his fucked-up thoughts about suicide had been nothing but the whining self-pity of a selfish man.

He didn't think he was that man anymore, and even if Tex was waiting in the pilothouse door with a rifle, he was glad.

Amen, and let's do it.

He eased up the next-to-last step on the steel ladder, took a quick look at the open—and empty—pilothouse doorway, and hoisted himself over the rail. He scuttled across the narrow deck and pressed himself against the wall.

The Breton was a bit longer than *The Evangeline*, maybe a forty-eight- or fifty-footer. A bit shabbier, but still a basic workboat. From what Shane could see, the pilothouse was broad and deep, and any access to belowdeck areas likely led from inside it. This boat wasn't outfitted as a liveaboard.

A vibration underfoot told Shane he'd made it just in time: the telltale feel of an electronic windlass pulling up anchor. Either Tex was going to try closing the distance to the Zodiac, or he was giving up and returning to Main-à-Dieu. Probably the latter. Even a local who knew the waters wouldn't try to locate an inflatable off Ragged Rocks Cove in this fog. But it also meant Tex was in the pilothouse and could have seen Shane slip aboard.

Time to renew his acquaintance with Tex.

Shane moved quickly but quietly, his combat training coming back to him, albeit with a bit of mental rust. Locating the hatch that led to the pilothouse, he reached down and unstrapped his dive knife before taking a cautious look inside the open doorway. Tex sat at the controls, his back making a tempting target. Shane looked around for any sign of Son of Tex, but saw nothing. Was it really going to be this easy?

"Come on in, Mr. Burke. I thought I'd lost you when you stuck your head over the rail and went back." Tex swiveled in his leather captain's chair, and only then did Shane see the rifle. The man had been holding the goddamned thing, waiting on his prey to get close. "We need to have a talk."

He hadn't seen Shane's knife—or at least Shane didn't think so. "I think you're right. Mind if I sit? I've had a long swim."

Tex kept the rifle in place while he reached out with his left hand and flipped the switch to stop the windlass from drawing up the anchor. He jerked his head toward a doorway in the back. "Through there. I'll be right behind you. If you think I won't shoot you before your deadline is up, you're wrong. Waiting another thirty-six hours is a formality. You were destined to fail from the beginning. After failing at everything else in your life, why would you succeed now?"

Shane had already started down the stairs, slipping his knife into a pouch on the front of his drysuit. But Tex's words dug into the anger that he'd been pushing aside for most of the past twenty-eight days. He turned, ignoring the rifle barrel less than a foot from his nose. "If you thought we'd fail from the beginning, why the fuck have we even been playing this screwed-up game?"

Tex gave a halfhearted laugh, and Shane realized the man reeked of exhaustion. Bone weary, from the dark circles under his eyes to the wrinkles in his navy nylon jacket that looked as if he'd slept in it. This was Shane's first close-up of Tex since that day outside Cedar Key when he'd impersonated a sheriff's deputy. He'd aged ten years. Guess extortion and kidnapping weren't relaxing occupations.

"You're right about it being a game, but it isn't my game, remember?" Tex poked the rifle in Shane's chest. "Go on down."

Shane frowned, turned, and continued a half-dozen more steps, finally reaching a long rectangular room that appeared to be a combination galley and dining area. Being in the center of the boat, it probably offered stability in rough seas, but it was grim and windowless. Not like his beautiful boat, which was by now probably halfway to its final resting place.

He sat in a scarred wooden chair, pulling it up to the table for camouflage in case he got a chance to pull his knife and give Tex a little surprise.

Tex sat opposite him, keeping the rifle fixed on his target. If Shane could keep him talking long enough, he'd relax his hold. Even a trained soldier couldn't hold a weapon in firing position like that indefinitely, and right now Tex looked more like a tired, stressed-out civilian than a soldier.

"You keep calling this a game," Shane said. "So why'd you change the rules on us? Even if you don't think we can find the Templars' cross by the deadline, why try to kill us at this point? All you did was assure we'd fail—and we had a solid lead, by the way, before you blew my boat to hell."

Tex looked at him with an expression that chilled Shane to the soles of his neoprene boots. Cold hatred. He'd almost made the mistake of humanizing the guy, but the man behind that mask of loathing wouldn't think twice about killing any of them.

"As if you don't know." Tex leaned forward, lowering the gun slightly. "And if you hurt him, you won't be able to run far enough. You got that? It won't matter what my boss wants, or when. If that Canadian lunatic touches him, I will kill you all, beginning with your hippie pal and your new fuck-buddy Gillian Campbell."

Shane felt his own version of cold fury settle over him and welcomed it. Time to turn and confront, in the Burke way. He had no idea what Tex was talking about, except that it had to do with Chevy and . . . Shane smiled, aware that his own expression was probably as chilling as the one Tex had given him. That old son of a bitch Chevy had somehow gotten his hands on Son of Tex, and Tex didn't like it.

Shane's smile widened. "Doesn't feel too good, does it? Having someone out there who could blow you and your boss right out of the water like you did my boat?" Only Tex hadn't mentioned what his colleague might say; he'd been concerned about them hurting him. Maybe he *was* Tex's son or at least had some personal connection. "Doesn't feel too good knowing somebody you care about could be having his fingernails ripped out, does it?"

Yeah, okay, Chevy probably wasn't engaged in torture, but Tex didn't know that.

"He won't help you any." The muscles in the man's jaw twitched; Shane could practically hear teeth grinding. "You might hurt me and my . . . friend, but my employer still wants what he wants."

Shane leaned over the table, slipping his right hand to his waist and grasping the hilt of the knife. "Exactly. So how is your employer going to feel when he finds out you sank our dive boat just after I'd found the wreck of *The Marcus Aurelius*?"

"You're bluffing."

Shane smiled again. "Am I? You're going to take that risk? I have a photo back on the mainland of a plate I pulled off the wreckage, ready for you to share with your boss."

The plate was the one he'd pulled from the concretions on that first exploratory dive. Chevy had dated it to a nineteenth-century wreck, but Tex didn't know that. They'd shot pictures of it, still covered in marine matter, just in case they needed to show Tex and his boss some tangible progress in order to buy more time.

Shane smiled again. "Guess if you kill me, that won't happen. How will your employer like it that you were the one who cost him the Templars' cross—all because you couldn't control your temper?"

He almost asked how Secretary of State Flynn would feel about it, but caught himself. No point in playing that card yet, if it were even true.

Tex recovered quickly, but not so quickly that Shane hadn't seen the flash of fear in his eyes like a streak of lightning. He was afraid of his boss.

"If I kill you all, he'll never know the difference." Tex raised the rifle, a semiautomatic with a pistol grip, and put his finger on the trigger. Shane figured even if Tex were a lousy shot, it would be hard to keep from getting his head blown off at this range. Talking time was done.

He shoved the heavy table toward Tex, and barely registered the surprised expression and the falling rifle before he lunged across the table with the knife, burying its serrated steel blade in Tex's upper arm. Serrated blades were great for divers because they'd cut through anything. Except, apparently, the stretchy threads of cheap nylon jackets. In the time it took Shane to dislodge his blade, extracting a chunk of bloody flesh and a triangle of ripped blue fabric as well, Tex had regained control of the rifle.

Both of them froze for a few heartbeats. Long enough for both to register that Tex had grabbed the barrel end of the rifle instead of the stock. Then chaos and movement returned. Shane's vision blurred when a sharp pain lanced across his left temple and he lost his balance. He landed facedown and had a quick view of dirty industrial-green carpet before he grasped his knife from where it had fallen next to him, rolled to his back, and froze again. This time, Tex stood over him with the rifle in firing position.

Without thinking, he reached out and jerked Tex's right foot from beneath him, rolling to keep the older man from landing on top of him. Tex managed to shoot on his way down, the blast digging into the floor next to Shane's left ear, before the rifle clattered out of Tex's hands again. They both looked for the weapon and saw it at the same time.

"You're one dead son of a bitch." Tex made a grab for the rifle at the same time as Shane. His long arms—his wingspan, Charlie called it—had shamed Shane as a kid, but they came in handy now. He extended his hand and knocked the rifle out of reach.

Tex was still grasping at it when Shane balled his right fist and plowed into Tex's jaw with a fierce uppercut, then another, and then a hard punch in the gut for good measure. The last blow sent Tex reeling.

Shane was breathing hard, but Tex no longer tried to fight back. He'd curled around his midsection with his eyes closed. Too bad the son of a bitch wasn't dead.

Shane reached past him for the rifle and tapped him on the temple with the barrel. "Get up, Tex. This particular part of the game is over."

Tex didn't speak, just climbed to his feet slowly, holding his belly, and didn't make eye contact.

"Up to the deck." Shane followed him, rifle in a relaxed carry that would be easy to transition to firing position. The higher they climbed from the bowels of *The Breton*, the more the ship's pitch and roll threatened their balance. Ahead of him, Shane saw Tex reach out several times to brace his hands on the walls.

Finally, they got to the pilothouse, and Shane had to decide what he was going to do. He'd boarded the boat with the plan to kill Tex, but now he realized he couldn't do it. If they'd been in a fight where he had to defend himself, sure. If the rifle had gone off while they were scrambling for it, fine. But killing the man while he stood here like a beaten puppy? Shane didn't have it in him. If he killed Tex now, it made him no better than them.

Fuck. Of all the inconvenient times to develop a conscience.

He reached into a compartment over the pilothouse exit, pulled down an orange life vest, and shoved it at Tex. "Put it on."

Tex took it, frowning as if he didn't know what it was. Then understanding dawned and he shook his head. "No, you can't put me out in this weather. I'll drown. Just shoot me if you want to."

"Look, I'm giving you a fighting chance, which is more than you've given us. Put it on." They weren't far offshore from Scatarie Island. Tex could swim that distance, or let the waves carry him in. Chevy had told them there were unoccupied summer homes on the island, so he could find shelter if he looked. "Only first . . ."

Despite what the movies showed, discharging a rifle one-handed wasn't an easy task, and Shane hadn't done it since his Marine days. Hopefully, Tex didn't know that. Shane shifted the weapon into his right hand with the stock tucked under his arm and used his left hand to pat down Tex's jacket. In a pocket, he found what he was looking for—a cell phone.

Before he could pull it out, Tex leaned over and charged headfirst into Shane's rib cage. The air left his lungs with a burning whoosh, and they both hit the floor.

The rifle's discharge sounded like hell itself had come to *The Breton.*

29

The ocean between the Zodiac and *The Breton* churned and swelled in endless, mindless chaos. Gillian strained to see through the fog, praying for a sign of Shane. But she could barely make out the shrouded silhouette of *The Breton*, much less identify what bubbles on the surface came from waves and which ones might indicate a diver.

Shane's only been gone a couple of minutes and he knows what he's doing, idiot. Take care of Jagger.

She turned back to her navigator, who, to her alarm, struggled to stay upright next to the small orange steering platform. Damn it, he was weaving—and so was the Zodiac.

"Let me take over." She crawled toward him, reached out, and snagged her compass from his hand. If he dropped it in the water, they'd never find their way to the harbor in this strong current and fog.

To give Jagger credit, as soon as Gillian reached for the wheel, he crawled off the piloting seat and collapsed on the floor of the inflatable boat. He looked awful. Gillian didn't think she'd ever seen anyone so pale—at least not one that didn't qualify as an anatomy-class cadaver. The wind whipped his jacket away from his shoulder, revealing a bloody red stain blooming through the fibers of his white sweater. Damn it, he'd reopened the gunshot wound.

"You ever steer one of these?" Jagger asked—or at least that's what Gillian thought he asked. His voice wasn't strong, and the wind was.

She shook her head but held up the compass. In her mind, Main-à-Dieu Bay was due west, and then they'd curve north to reach the village and harbor . . . at some point. She couldn't even see the shoreline from here, but maybe when they got closer. "We stay hard to the west, correct?"

When Jagger didn't answer, she glanced back at him. Asleep—or, more likely, unconscious, which might be a blessing because this was not going to be a fun ride. She was on her own.

It took a couple of minutes to get a feel for the Zodiac, but she found it not unlike steering the outboard-powered boats on her parents' gator farm, only with a steering wheel instead of a shaft. The challenge was gauging how to ride the waves and maintain a westward direction. After each swell, she'd be knocked southward and have to compensate. It made for slowgoing.

Finally, she spotted an outcropping of rock in the distance. Moque Head, with any luck. Squinting through the fog, she made out a dim twinkle above it. Chevy's lighthouse.

It took another hour of fighting the current and praying her visual memory of the coastline was accurate, but Gillian finally saw a few lights in the distance to her north—lights that meant civilization and help. Her pulse rate, galloping since they'd watched *The Evangeline* explode, began to slow. As it did, fatigue rolled over her like one of the big swells threatening to topple the Zodiac on its side, and her brain began a nagging litany.

Why had Tex suddenly gone on the attack? If Shane was able to overtake him, would he kill him? And if Tex died, was there any hope for Holly? For Vivian? Harley? Any of them?

Especially if the man for whom Tex worked was, indeed, Weston Flynn.

Flynn's biggest vulnerability was his career and his public image. Exposure would ruin him, and threat of exposure might be enough to control him. They needed proof, though. They had only a hunch to go on right now. If she went to the media, a good reporter was more likely to write her off as a lunatic than investigate her claims.

Shit! Gillian's hand had grown slack on the steering wheel, and she didn't compensate for a large swell that threw the Zodiac back to the position of a half hour earlier. Damn it. She had to keep her mind on getting them to harbor. Figuring out what to do with Weston Flynn had to wait. If she got them lost at sea, crashed on the rocks, or killed—or all of the above—Flynn could start his stupid game again with a new set of puppets. But they'd still be dead.

Gillian gritted her teeth and blinked against the wind beating in her face. She turned the Zodiac north toward the source of the lights, occasionally glancing back at Jagger. Sometimes his eyes were open, sometimes not. She missed his silly songs and innocent, playful sense of humor. It was almost like steering a ghost ship, and she couldn't help but wonder if part of him had died forever. When she first met him, he'd seemed to always look for the best in people. But some people's best, they'd learned, was nothing but evil.

Gillian leaned forward, her eyes scanning the gray horizon against the gray water, trying to find the breakwaters that protected Main-à-Dieu harbor. If she cut north too soon, she'd end up on the rocks east of the harbor; too late, and she'd go ashore so far south of the village she'd never find help.

There! She spotted a dark horizontal line directly ahead and steered farther west to make the cut into the harbor. Once she'd cleared the first breakwater, she fought the diverted current and narrowly missed the second. Only when she'd cleared the second breakwater did she take a deep breath. They'd made it.

She looked back at Jagger and he mouthed what she thought was "good job." She'd take the praise.

A quick glance through the fog told her *The Breton* was not in the harbor. A part of her had hoped Shane had gotten control of Tex and his boat and had passed them somehow, reaching port first.

Instead, as she got to the nearest dock, she saw a man waiting at the end closest to land. Gillian recognized him—the same white-haired guy who'd been working in the harbormaster's office the day they first sailed into Main-à-Dieu—Ricky something-or-other. He waved as she killed the Zodiac engine and tied it to the pier; then he waited some more while she helped Jagger to his feet. Jag was wobbly but upright, so conditions were improving.

"Where's your real boat?" Ricky held out a hand and pulled Jagger to the dock, then helped Gillian out. He might look on the far side of seventy and have a nasty-sounding cough, but the man's grip was strong and steady. "Can't believe you made it across the passage in that raft."

"We ran into some trouble." Gillian gave Jagger a warning look. No point in volunteering anything. Chances were good that everybody in Main-à-Dieu had heard the explosion when *The Evangeline*'s fuel tanks blew. But because of the fog, chances also were good that no one realized what had happened. "Our friend stayed to take care of it, so he'll be in later." At least she prayed that was true.

The man took off his baseball cap and scratched at the tuft of white hair that danced in the stiff wind like the tentacles of a geriatric medusa. "Old Chevy asked me to take you guys up to the lighthouse. Don't much like goin' up there—'specially after dark. Guess we better go inside and wait a while for your friend, so I don't have to do it twice."

As much as she wanted to wait for Shane, Jagger needed Cleo and her nursing skills. "Thanks, but we really need to—"

"Won't have to wait after all. That looks like him coming in . . ." The man stuck his cap back on his head and frowned. "No, that's old Bill McCulloch's boat, *The Breton*. He leased her out through the end of the month to a couple of folks came in 'bout the same time as you."

Gillian's heart thumped as she watched *The Breton* make its way past the second breakwater and head toward them, her focus honed on the pilothouse to see who was in charge—Tex or Shane. Its progress seemed impossibly slow, and the fog settled into an inconvenient line right over the window in front of the pilot.

Oh, thank God. Gillian closed her eyes and would've sunk to her knees with relief if she'd thought herself capable of getting back up. She couldn't see Shane's face, but she was pretty sure she recognized his silhouette. He'd pushed back his dive hood, but the guy piloting the boat sure looked to be wearing a drysuit. Neoprene wasn't Tex's style.

"Now, how did your friend get his hands on *The Breton*?" Rick mused. "Are those other guys friends of yours?"

Gillian shrugged. "Something like that." Something like enemies. "Guess Shane had to leave *The Evangeline* out there." Where it had probably finished sinking by now, joining the layers of other lost dreams at the bottom of the Atlantic.

As tired as she was, Gillian wanted nothing more than to run down the dock to meet Shane, to throw her arms around him, to kiss him until she was breathless. Instead, she crossed her arms and walked out to meet him with plans for a calm greeting and a quick explanation of the pending ride up to the lighthouse.

As soon as her gaze met his, though, she recognized pain and worry and something else, something that made him look away. Something that caused him to clench his jaw and tighten his fists. The same look he used to get before he'd finally told her about the diving accident that had almost destroyed him with guilt.

"Whatever it is, it doesn't matter." She stepped into him and slipped her arms around his waist. "Later, you'll tell me what it is, and I'll say it again. It doesn't matter. As long as you're safe." Her one-sided hug stretched on for several seconds before she finally felt him relax and pull her against him. He smelled of the ocean. And blood.

"You're hurt." Gillian stepped back and noticed for the first time the darkening bruise next to his left eye, and the telltale red trickle down the side of his face.

"Not there. Here." Shane held up his left arm and let out a hiss of pain. "I think Cleo has another bullet to dig out."

Gillian's breath caught. Not just a bullet. The whole underside of his arm was a mess of bloody flesh and shredded drysuit. She wasn't sure even Cleo could handle that, but Gillian had learned not to underestimate their hostess.

"Cleo's gonna be a busy woman." She kept her voice light. "Come on. Mr. Ricky, the guy from the harbormaster's office, is going to drive us to the lighthouse."

"That should be interesting." Shane held his left arm tight against him and walked beside her to the harbor-office parking lot. Ricky and Jagger had gone ahead and stopped next to a silver sedan, and Gillian was relieved to see it was a four-door. She didn't think anyone besides herself—and she was iffy—could climb into a backseat.

"Interesting how? The lighthouse is going to be interesting?" Gillian looked over at him, concerned that he was going into shock. No telling how much blood he'd lost.

"We'll talk about it when we get there." He focused on the ground and didn't seem inclined to talk more, but Gillian had one more question that needed answering.

"Is Tex dead?"

Shane sighed. "I don't have a fucking clue."

Both Shane and Jagger remained silent on the drive to the lighthouse, which took more than a half hour, partly because Ricky drove like a snail and partly because of the fog. Gillian suspected their progress sans fog wouldn't have gone any faster.

"So you've known Chevy and Cleo a long time?" Gillian tried to keep a semblance of conversation going from the backseat. Jagger sat up front, and Shane had slumped down next to her, his long legs pressing into the back of the passenger seat.

She saw Ricky glance at her in the rearview mirror. "Most of my life. Main-à-Dieu's a small town. We like it that way." He pronounced the town *manadoo*, and she understood why he liked it. Same reason she loved Levy County.

"Cleo and my wife, Keitha, are cousins," he said. "We were more surprised than if a nor'easter had blown through in June when she married Chevy McKnight, the ornery old bastard." The last words, he delivered with a great deal of affection. "'Course those two, well, they march to their own drummer, eh?"

"You have no idea," Shane mumbled.

Gillian frowned at him before turning back to Ricky. "They're a little eccentric, but I like them."

And she did. It was ironic how Tex and his psychotic boss, who might or might not be the secretary of state, had brought together this disparate group of strangers who'd otherwise never have met, and yet, somehow, they'd become friends. If they made it through this, Gillian knew the friendships would last. They might be forged out of fear or coercion, but they were real. And some of them were more than friendships. What she felt for Shane was real, too.

The sedan slowed and then stopped at the path that led to the lighthouse. "Chevy told me not to drive through the gate. He also said you should wait on this side for Cleo to let you in." Ricky shook his head. "I don't even want to know what he's up to, but I'd do what he says."

"No worries about that." Shane opened his car door and slid out. Gillian watched him a couple of seconds before opening her own door. If he had an issue with Chevy and Cleo McKnight, she hoped he kept it to himself. They needed the couple, eccentric or not.

As soon as Jagger's door slammed shut and they were all out of his path, Ricky floored the sedan and drove away, his taillights disappearing quickly on the foggy mountain road.

"There you are; we were getting worried. Hold on a minute." Cleo walked up the path toward them, jingling a set of keys. She wore dark jeans that were a few inches too short but somehow worked with her sturdy boots, and a bib apron was tied over her red sweater. "Glad you got up here before full dark set in."

She unlocked a metal box attached to the inside of the gate and flipped a switch. "I'm turning off the electricity to the gate so you won't get zapped when you come through. But . . ." She pointed to a spot about a foot off the ground.

Leaning over, Gillian finally saw a thin silver wire. "Is that a booby trap?"

"A tripwire," Cleo said. "Goes all the way around the property. So make sure you step over it and don't set it off."

Jagger and Shane had also leaned over to look. "What happens if we set it off?" Jagger asked.

Cleo didn't answer at first. "Well, some lights will flash on," she finally said. "An alarm will go off. The lighthouse beacon will start turning. And Chevy will barrel out shooting first and asking questions as an afterthought."

Holy cow. "Is this because of our situation?" Gillian hoped so, because this truly went beyond eccentric and into paranoid-delusional territory. Then again, the man did believe in aliens.

Cleo laughed. "Oh, no, the security system is always set up. We just don't always turn it on."

Tex had been right when he called this place a fortified lighthouse. Once they'd all passed the tripwire test and made it to the lighthouse's single entrance, they found a steel security door Gillian didn't remember seeing before. So Chevy had done some extra fortification.

Once inside, Cleo locked the security door and the main door. "Can't be too careful. Let's go upstairs now. Chevy has a surprise . . ." She got a good look at Shane and Jagger for the first time, her sharp eyes resting on Jagger's face, then his shoulder, then Shane's head, then his arm. "Before the surprise, looks like I need to put on my nurse's hat. Second floor, boys. You know the way."

Jagger gave Cleo a one-armed hug as he passed her, but Shane simply treated her to a hard look. What was up with him? Gillian hugged Cleo and mouthed a "thank you" before following them up the spiral stairs. It was a long climb, because neither man was moving very fast.

"Gillie, why don't you go up to the third level and get these gentlemen some dry clothes?" Walking into what Cleo called her first-aid room, the older woman pointed Jagger to an armchair and steered Shane to a long wooden table. Last time Gillian had seen that table, Jagger had been laid out on it, getting a bullet removed.

A shard of guilt sliced through her. So many people had been hurt because of her, and yet she'd gone unscathed, at least physically. If she could've taken Shane's place, she'd be there.

Speaking of whom, he had halted inside the door and leaned against the doorjamb, still giving Cleo the stink eye. "Hop up here, Shane," Cleo said. "You're going first." She pulled out a pair of scissors and turned to look at Gillian. "Clothes?"

Gillian reluctantly edged past Shane to go back into the round central hallway where the spiral staircase led upward. She gave him a "play nice" look, but he ignored her. So she took her time going up the stairs, pausing halfway up to listen.

"I know you've got a few things to say, but you don't know the whole story," Cleo said. "So get your ass on the table and I'll tell it to you."

There was a pause, and then Cleo stuck her head out the door and raised her eyebrows at Gillian.

Right. Clothes.

Gillian climbed to the third floor and hung a right into the small bedroom she'd been sharing with Shane. Fatigue threatened to overwhelm her again. It seemed like a week since she and Shane had done the deepwater dive, not less than twelve hours. And what the heck was going on with Shane?

After retrieving running pants and a loose-fitting sweatshirt for him, the only thing she thought might go over his injured arm without hurting, she walked across the landing to Jagger's room. He was as messy as Shane was neat; a virtual tsunami of clothes covered every surface except the floor—probably protected only because Jagger had limited space in his hiking pack.

She picked out the least-wrinkled pants and long-sleeved tee and grabbed his iPod on the way out. His phone, like hers and Shane's, had been on *The Evangeline*. It probably lay in a bazillion pieces at the bottom of the Atlantic, waiting for some far-future diver to find it and wonder at its cultural significance.

Gillian returned to the stairs but heard voices coming from the lantern room above them. She'd assumed Chevy wasn't home since Cleo had met them at the gate, but she definitely heard his voice—and another one, vaguely familiar, that she couldn't place.

Climbing the stairs, she'd only planned to go far enough to eavesdrop, which seemed to have become her new hobby. She obviously wasn't as quiet as she thought, though, because halfway up, Chevy's voice rang out. "Might as well come on up instead'a standing there and breathing heavy."

"I was not breathing . . . heavy." Gillian stopped breathing at all when she rounded the top step and walked into the softly lit lantern room ringed by its wall of windows. Tonight, they showed only the black night sky. The scenery lay in the center of the room, duct-taped to a wooden chair. Son of Tex had a bruised face, a bloody smudge on his forehead, one eye swollen almost shut, and the other glaring at her as if she'd been the one beating on him.

Next to him stood Chevy, his deeply lined face grim and angry.

"Hi there, Gillie."

Speechless, Gillian spun to see who'd spoke to her from behind the staircase. In the shadows, on the cushioned armchair that Cleo had described as her favorite, sat Harley.

30

Shane kicked a chair out of his way en route to Cleo's "exam table." He wasn't really mad at her so much as he was mad, period. They'd finally gotten somewhere with this dive and Chevy had screwed everything up playing cowboy. Jagger looked like death warmed over. Harley was missing. And his fucking arm hurt.

"Sit up here and stop acting like a brat." Cleo patted the table, and Shane used his right arm to leverage himself up. That left arm wasn't going anywhere. He'd held it stiff against his side for so long, he wasn't sure he *could* move it.

After taking a look at his temple and declaring he'd live, Cleo took out a pair of scissors and cut the sleeve out of his drysuit—make that his fucking expensive drysuit—at the elbow. The neoprene splashed reddish-brown droplets of blood when it hit the white tile.

"I'm gonna cut this away at the shoulder and across the top," she said as she worked the scissors. "Keep your arm still until I'm ready to pull your sleeve away from the bottom. Then we'll see what we're dealing with, eh?"

"We're dealing with a guy who's just undone everything we've accomplished in the last month," he snapped. "That's what we're dealing with."

She seemed impassive as she cut away the fabric of his suit's upper sleeve, then sliced across the top so that only the fabric remaining was clamped to his side by his injured arm. She set the scissors on the edge of the table and picked up a stack of white bandages, probably for him to bleed all over.

When she looked up, her eyes were hard and angry. "And just what do you think you've accomplished in the last month, Shane Burke? You've still ended up at our door with your troubles, all because Chevy wouldn't say no to his old friend Charlie. Without us, you'd have had no idea where to dive. No safe place to stay. And your friend Harley would probably end up dead."

Harley? Shane frowned at her, trying to remember if they'd even mentioned Harley's name when they were filling them in on the situation.

She nodded. "That's right. Chevy saw the guy you call Tex leave *The Breton* this morning after you went out, so he went aboard to do some snooping around on your behalf." She waved a pair of tongs an inch from his nose. "You hear that? On your behalf. When he found that Garrison man hitting your friend Harley, well, what would you want him to do? Sit down for tea? Have a little talk?"

She turned and pointed the tongs at Jagger, who'd risen and gotten halfway to the door. "Your friend will still be upstairs when you get rebandaged, so plant your ass back in that chair, *Calvin*."

Shane exchanged a shocked look with Jagger. If Cleo knew to call him Calvin, that definitely meant Harley was nearby.

"Will he be okay?" Shane swallowed down a lump of crow. "And I'm sorry. He did the right thing." Garrison must be Son of Tex.

"Um-hm. Hold out your left arm and get ready to scream."

Holy fucking son of a bitch. Despite clamping his jaw shut, Shane couldn't stop a deep moan from escaping when Cleo ripped off the blood-soaked sleeve of neoprene. Its waterproof lining, despite being shredded by the bullet, had held in a surprising amount of blood, at least if the flood of crimson dripping off his arm was any indication.

The room swam in a film of gray so heavy it looked like the fog had spread inside the lighthouse.

"Whoa, now," Cleo said from a distance. "Lie back before you faint on me."

Faint was such an undignified word. *Pass out* or *lose consciousness* was much more manly. Shane let Cleo lower him onto his back on the table and only let a few tears slip out when she held his left arm aloft.

"This isn't too bad." She poured what felt like pure rubbing alcohol on the wound, and Shane gritted his teeth, fixing his gaze on a ceiling tile, determined not to make another pitiful whining sound. "Bullet just shaved off the bottom layer of subcutaneous fat."

Shane narrowed his eyes and hazarded a look at her. He did not have subcutaneous fat. Much. Apparently he had a lot less of it now on his left arm. "How do you know it didn't hit an artery—there are arteries in there."

Cleo shook her head. "What babies men are. Good Lord, I always told Chevy if men had to give birth, the world's population problem would clear up just like that." Apparently finished torturing the wound with alcohol, she brought out a thick pack and some tape and began bandaging. "If that bullet had hit an inch higher and nicked the brachial artery, you'd have bled to death about"—she paused in her wrapping and looked at the ceiling, counting under her breath—"fifteen seconds after being hit."

Well, that was comforting.

"Think you can sit up without fainting?"

"Real men don't faint." He struggled up with her help and waited while she made quick work of bandaging his head.

Jagger's wounds didn't need to be restitched, she decided, and after another bandaging job, she finally declared them fit to leave. "Gillian was supposed to bring clothes for you. You're both still half-soaked, but she must've found the others and forgot. They're in the lantern room."

It took a shameful amount of time for both of them to walk upstairs, and they arrived at the top puffing as if they'd done a marathon instead of a slow crawl up two flights of a spiral staircase.

Cleo followed them, armed with the painkillers Shane had refused to take. He couldn't afford to be dopey and drugged.

He stopped inside the door, letting Jagger go around him and straight to Harley. A white bandage circled Harley's head, and a garden of bruises bloomed across his arms—and probably other places Shane couldn't see. Between the three of them and their bandages, the room looked like a hospital ward.

Harley stood with Gillian's help and wrapped Jagger in a bear hug. Gillian and Shane shared a smile. Harley was, in a lot of ways, as much a father to Jagger as Charlie was to him, and Shane was grateful enough to offer Chevy a handshake. "Thanks for that." He nodded at Jag and Harley.

"And for that." He looked at Son of Tex, who definitely had seen better days. He struggled against his prison of brown duct tape and mumbled against the gag, which looked suspiciously like it had been woven out of Cleo's bandages.

"What do we know about him?" Shane sat in the chair Chevy nudged toward him with his heavy work boot. Son of Tex had fallen silent and now watched with dull brown eyes.

Jagger and Harley deserved to have some time, but Shane motioned Gillian to join them, and she pulled up a chair next to Shane's.

Chevy leaned over and handed Shane a wallet and a cell phone. He kept his voice low. "That's all we found of use. They rented that boat from a local guy looking for a little off-season income. He isn't in on it; I've known him for years."

Shane flipped open the wallet to reveal a Texas driver's license. "Garland Garrison III." He looked up at Son of Tex. "Well, that's a mouthful."

"He goes by Trey," Chevy said. "Trey here got downright chatty about hour five of his capture."

The guy was in his twenties, with an address in a Dallas suburb. That was about all Shane could glean from the license. The wallet had a dozen credit cards—way more than the number carried by the average bear—and more than a thousand dollars in good old Ben Franklins. A bunch of folded receipts might prove useful, but he'd look at those later.

Handing Gillian the wallet, he examined the cell phone, nodding when he saw that most of the calls made and received had been to and from "Dad." He hit the call button and waited a few seconds. From inside the dry inner lining of his dive suit came a buzzing noise and a baritone country singer crooning about cowboys.

At the sound, Trey's eyes widened, and he began twisting and trying to talk again.

"Yeah, I have Daddy's phone. How 'bout that?" Shane leaned back in his chair and unzipped the front of his suit enough to pull out the smartphone in its sleek silver case. An expensive case.

"Wait." Gillian leaned forward. "You mean Son of Tex really *is* the son of Tex?"

"Yep." Shane hadn't taken his eyes off Trey. "Do a web search for Garland Garrison Jr., aka Tex. Let's see what turns up."

She took Trey's phone and walked around the room. Once she'd found a signal, she sat down and began pressing keys.

Shane reached over and pulled down Trey's gag.

His voice was dry and raspy. "Where's my father?"

In his peripheral vision, Shane saw Gillian look up, waiting for the answer. "Someplace very cold and very dark, if he's lucky." He turned to Chevy. "Can a middle-aged man who's been drenched in seawater survive alone overnight on Scatarie this time of year?"

Chevy bellowed with laughter, creases forming in his cheeks that changed his look from demented alien-hunter to jolly grandpa. "You have style, Mr. Burke, just like old Charlie. I expected you to say you shot the son of a bitch, but you at least gave him a chance."

Yeah, well, Shane hadn't been willing to cross the line from self-defense to murder. He sought out Gillian and felt a weight lift when she smiled at him and nodded. He'd worried that she would think him weak if he'd let Tex live or careless if he'd killed the guy without knowing their loved ones were safe.

When had her approval become so important to him?

That question he couldn't answer, so he turned his attention back to Trey, who was sputtering threats. "Wait, wait, wait." Shane mimicked a zipper across his mouth, and Trey fell silent. "Whether or not we send anyone to save your father depends on what you tell us," he said. "For example, I'd like to hear about Garland Garrison's relationship with Secretary of State Weston Flynn."

Trey froze. Only for a second, but a second was long enough for Shane to see what he needed. They'd been right. That was the good news. It was also the bad news—how the hell did they call out someone like Flynn? They still needed proof, and he hoped Tex's phone had it. Between navigating one-armed and trying to maneuver through the fog with a blood-gushing wound, he hadn't had time to take more than a cursory glance at it.

Gillian rejoined them, her cheeks flushed pink. "Listen to this." She held the phone toward the light so that she could better read the screen. "'Garland Garrison, known to his friends as Gar, is a third-generation Dallas-area cattle rancher whose claim to fame is the fellow deer-hunting enthusiast who joins him at his ranch for a week each fall: his childhood friend Weston Flynn.'

"We were right." She looked up, and her smile faded. Shane gauged that she'd just gone through his own series of thoughts and come to the same conclusion.

We have his name. We have the tie between Flynn and Tex.

But how do we prove it? And how do we keep ourselves safe?

31

Gillian closed her eyes and let the mild ocean breeze caress her cheeks, the soft sunlight warming her even though sunrise had been only two hours earlier. The Zodiac zipped along at a good clip, leaving Chevy's workboat, *The Klaatu*, anchored off Ragged Rocks Cove. This time, they knew where they were diving, and Cleo steered them between the two massive sunkers, as close as she deemed safe.

Jagger had remained at the lighthouse with Harley, guarding Trey and under threat from Cleo that if he reopened his wound again, he'd have to endure more stitches. When they'd driven away from the lighthouse this morning, after Chevy had disabled his security and loaded everyone into his pickup, the sounds of Mick Jagger singing "Sympathy for the Devil" had been echoing down the cliffs of Moque Head. Gillian suspected Trey would be well and truly *stoned* before the morning was done unless Harley put an end to it.

They'd tried to convince Shane not to dive, but he'd refused to consider sitting it out. Gillian would do her best to keep an eye on his injured arm, but she was glad not to be doing her first deepwater dive alone, and into a cavern, at that. Talk about a recipe for a disaster.

She and Shane had talked all night, lying in the narrow bed at the lighthouse. Not all talk, of course. Their lovemaking was gentle and slow and lingering, every move made to bring them as close together as possible, for as long as possible. Today, the thirtieth day since Gillian had gotten her first call from Tex, this part of their lives would end. They'd either succeed in the plans they made between kisses, or they'd fail. Failure was permanent. So many things could go wrong, Gillian had lost count. But at least they felt more in control of their future than anytime in the last month. They'd allowed themselves a one-tank dive before setting their plan in motion.

When the sun began to turn the eastern horizon pink, they dressed in the gear they'd managed to save plus what Chevy had managed to get for them in Sydney last night, including Shane's new drysuit. He'd grumbled because it was red, then grumbled some more when Cleo had bandaged his arm so thickly he compared himself to the Michelin Man.

Now they were here, and Gillian couldn't help the excitement that stirred in her gut as she pulled on her mask and fins and checked her BC and weight belt—a little heavier this morning thanks to a small, sharp pickax. Another late-night shopping find from Chevy.

"Okay, kids. This is as far as I can take you in. I'm dropping anchor." Cleo pressed the windlass on the back of the Zodiac, and as the heavy iron anchor dropped, Gillian looked at Shane.

He smiled at her, green eyes crinkling behind his mask. "You ready?"

She better be. "I'm ready."

As soon as the anchor hit bottom, Gillian wedged her regulator into her mouth, clamped one hand over the front to hold it in place and the other on the strap underneath her hood, and thrust her knees toward her chest. It was a perfect roll in. She hit the water flat on her back, with her tank absorbing most of the pressure. Kicking for the surface, she cleared her snorkel and gave the "okay" sign to Shane and Cleo, moving away to give Shane room to enter.

As soon as he'd entered, surfaced, and given Cleo his okay, they adjusted their buoyancy and followed the line down, side by side. Gillian hadn't done much diving since the car wreck; it was just one of many things she'd closed off in her compartmentalization of life before Ethan died and life after. She'd thought a lot about Ethan recently, remembering his sunny grin, with her dark eyes and Sam's auburn hair, with Gillian's tenacious curiosity and Sam's ability to find joy in simple things without questioning them. He'd truly been the best of both of them.

She'd done a lot of thinking about Sam, too, and Shane's observation that when she talked about the accident, Ethan was the one whose loss she mentioned. She had been angry at Sam, but just as angry at herself. They'd simply married too early, realized they wanted different things, and grown apart. Only instead of the usual progression to divorce and new lives, he'd died and she'd martyred herself to guilt.

If nothing else, this experience with Tex and Weston Flynn had taught her that life was precious and not something one should give up lightly.

Shane knocked on her tank to get her attention and motioned for her to follow him with lights on. She flicked on the light attached to her mask and checked her dive calculator. They were near a hundred feet and the rocky bottom was in sight.

This part of the ocean floor was trickier than the area she'd dived last time, darker and colder even through the drysuit. She stayed behind Shane and to his right, thankful the currents weren't as big a factor at this depth. He was guiding himself mostly with his right arm and his legs, protecting the left arm. That had been his plan, and so far it seemed to be working.

He held out his arm with a "stay" motion, and they slowed down. Soon, Gillian saw why: a massive wall of dark rock loomed ahead of them. She couldn't even see the top of it, much less how they'd get through it to reach Shane's cavern.

He pointed to the right, motioned her to go slowly, and swam toward what looked like a vertical crack in the rock wall. Only when they got within a few feet of it and their lights bounced off it together did Gillian realize it was the narrow opening Shane had described. They had found it!

Shane squeezed through first, then motioned her to come in behind him. Once they cleared the zigzagged opening, Gillian had to remember to breathe as their lights cast a blue glow onto a sight she'd never even dreamed. The ocean floor here was sandier than that outside the cavern, almost smooth in some places and dotted with small rocks in others. The ever-present kelp hadn't reached its leathery tentacles here, maybe because it couldn't get what it needed for sustenance, so the walls were bare but for the cracks and crevices in the rock itself. Overhead, rocky stalactites hung like chandeliers.

She gasped, releasing a slew of air bubbles, when Shane knocked on her tank again. He grinned; she hated that he'd caught her rubber-necking. On the other hand, it was worth gawking at.

They'd planned their strategy, going over the pros and cons of splitting up to examine the cavern versus staying together. The need to cover more ground won out, though, and Shane had told her what to look for in the concretions at the base of the rock walls and in the deeper crevices. At least in this confined space, they didn't have to worry about getting separated.

Gillian swam to the left of the opening, Shane to the right. She checked her dive computer. They had an hour maximum before heading up, giving them time for decompression stops. As agreed, she looked for places where Shane had already dislodged pieces of metal, pulling out her small pickax and digging out coins. She slipped each one into the liner of her BC, then dug a bit deeper to see if anything more could be gathered quickly. The coins would be their proof, if they needed it, that they'd found the wreckage of *The Marcus Aurelius*.

Once she'd gotten in a rhythm, she was able to go fast, not bothering to look at the coins but stuffing them away and moving on. She'd collected at least a dozen when she came upon a coin that wouldn't dislodge. She moved on—they had plenty, and that one hadn't looked like gold. But something about the shape of it stuck with her. It had been flatter than the other coins she'd pulled out.

Circling back, she scanned her light along the wall until she found the concretion again. It was only about knee-high, so she crouched on the ocean floor and worked at it with the pickax. When she finally uncovered the edge, her building excitement deflated. The flat edge was bigger than a coin; in fact, it looked like a plate.

Plates wouldn't be of much value, but they were often inscribed with a maker or date, so even more than the coins it could prove that this was—or wasn't—treasure from *The Marcus Aurelius*. She looked around to see how far Shane had gotten. She was holding her own in terms of progress around the cavern, so a few minutes to dig out a plate might be worthwhile. Proving this was the ship on which Duncan Campbell had died could assure their plan of success.

Gillian adjusted her light and began to methodically pick at the concretions around the plate, trying not to hit the plate itself. Who knew how fragile this stuff was after so long underwater? Which, of course, was why marine archaeologists were so adamant that treasure not be removed from its watery preservation, especially in deep wrecks where the cold helped protect it.

So, yeah, she felt guilty as each tap of her pickax pulled away a little bit of history. But not guilty enough to stop. They'd come too far, and there was too much at stake.

She'd cleared off a good half of the plate when she saw something else wedged against the top of the plate and raised her ax to try and remove it.

Then she stopped, waving away the water and looking more closely. Two metal objects, not one, touched the plate at different points, and she couldn't figure out what it might be. She began working around the objects, picking at one solid bit of concretion between them that seemed to be holding this whole part of the structure together.

Finally, with a series of jerks that caused her breathing rate to rise and probably used up an extra five minutes of gas, she pulled it loose. Her momentum carried her off her feet in a cloud of shell and sand, and she got up slowly, giving it time to settle.

She waved the drifting particles from in front of her find and stared not at the three-quarters of the plate now exposed, but at the cross that sat on top of it, two of its points resting downward. It was about the length of her hand, and she could see evidence of elaborate metalwork, even after four hundred years of saltwater damage.

Gillian closed her eyes and forced herself to breathe slowly, to stay calm. They couldn't waste gas. She spun around to look for Shane, banging her pickax against her tank. He turned, frowned, swam to her, eyebrows raised. She pointed at the wall.

He swam closer, and she could tell when he saw it. He adjusted his light, then began working at it with his glove, but not with his pickax. Gillian swam up beside him to see what he was doing—and committed the cardinal sin of divers. She held her breath.

But they'd found it. With both their lights trained on the cross, his rubbing exposed a stone that held a hint of deep, brilliant red. Ruby or garnet—it didn't matter which. They'd found it.

Shane pulled back, staring at their own holy grail, and Gillian found herself mesmerized by it too. A Campbell had likely been the last one to see this thing more than four centuries ago, and now another Campbell, his ancestor, was the first to see it again. But instead of representing the hope of a new life, this cross had caused only pain and fear. Greed for it had driven Duncan Campbell to his grave, and greed for it had threatened to destroy everyone Gillian loved.

She looked up and found Shane watching her. The question in his eyes was obvious, and they'd talked around its answer all night. It would be her call; he'd been adamant about that.

"If you find the cross, will you take it?" he'd asked. "And if you take it, will you give it to Weston Flynn?"

Until now, she hadn't had an answer.

* * *

Back at the lighthouse, Shane and Gillian sat in the lantern room alone. Harley had prepared platefuls of sandwiches that were waiting for them when they returned from the dive, but she'd been too nervous to do more than nibble around the edges. Finding the cross hadn't given her the feeling she expected. Oh, the initial elation had been there, but they still had the hardest part of the plan to carry out, and she felt the weight of it.

Finally, Shane had suggested they go to the lantern room and get it done.

Noon had come and gone a few minutes ago, and the autumn sun shone high overhead. The fog was absent, and for the first time in two weeks, Gillian looked down the cliff at brilliant green water moving with restless energy beneath a clear blue sky. When they'd returned to Main-à-Dieu after their dive, the waterfront had been abuzz with talk of a man's body that had washed ashore at Scatarie and been found by an early-morning kayaker. The guy had no identification on him. He'd been wearing a life jacket but had hit his head on the rocks, or so the rumors said. And it was one of the guys who'd rented *The Breton*. The other guy, unaccounted for, had apparently returned the boat to the Main-à-Dieu harbor.

Mr. Ricky had relayed this information to them with a straight face, and Gillian knew if anyone found out that Shane had brought *The Breton* into port last night, they wouldn't learn it from their friendly harbormaster.

Shane felt guilty about Tex, but Gillian didn't. Shane hadn't heard the man's cold voice describing Holly's kitty-cat dress, threatening to hurt a three-year-old to carry out the whims of a rich, power-mad politician.

No, she didn't feel guilty about the death of Garland Garrison Jr., and she'd do her best to keep Shane from feeling it. What they'd do with Trey was a subject no one had an answer to. For now, he was on an extended visit with the McKnights, something Chevy, in his own perverse way, seemed to be enjoying.

Shane stood beside her and took her hand. "You sure you don't want me to make the call?"

God, yes, she wanted him to make the call. But she needed to do it. "No, I have to be the Burke man today."

He smiled and kissed the tip of her nose. "Turn and face the dragon?"

Exactly. She took a deep breath, sat in Cleo McKnight's favorite armchair, and pulled Tex's cell phone from her jeans pocket. She and Shane had been through Tex's list of calls sent and received, first eliminating the calls to themselves, then the ones to and from Trey.

That left one number which appeared on an almost daily basis, to and from a contact listed only as "Irish."

Weston Flynn wasn't any more an Irishman than Gillian was a Scotswoman; their families were too far removed and diluted. But she had no doubt "Irish" referred to their illustrious secretary of state.

She fixed Holly's picture in her mind, hit the call button, and put the phone on speaker. A momentary panic—*what if no one answered?*—disappeared when a voice came on the line. A voice that was deep, polished, and angry. "Gar, where the hell have you been? I'm due in fucking Turkey in forty-eight hours and we need this wrapped up. Might as well tell me that useless bitch and her diver are out of time, and I'm out thirty million dollars."

So that was the price of a life. Several lives. Thirty pieces of silver had changed the fate of humankind two millennia ago. Thirty million was today's going price for the lives of everyone she cared about.

"Sorry to disappoint you, Mr. Secretary, but you're dealing with the useless bitch now." Gillian could practically hear the wheels spinning in Flynn's brain as he tried to recover from this little surprise.

"Don't even think about hanging up," she added. "I've recorded your little outburst and I'm sure the recording, plus Garland Garrison Jr.'s testimony, would be enough to hang you for good. Just take one wrong step and it's done."

Being a stone-cold bitch was easier than Gillian expected. In fact, turning the screws was downright pleasurable.

Speaking of stone cold, Flynn's voice could freeze lava. "Trey would never talk. Where's Gar?"

"He's dead." Gillian glanced up at Shane, who was listening with his back turned to her, staring out to sea. "He met with an unfortunate accident while swimming. I'll save you the trouble of asking about Trey. He's staying with us, working through his grief—you know, talking about things always makes people feel better."

Flynn's voice dropped lower, and Gillian couldn't help but think how different he sounded from the glib politician giving sound bytes as he came and went at exotic airports and seats of international power. "What do you want?"

Shane took the seat next to Gillian, and nodded his encouragement. "I want you to cancel your plans for Turkey and make reservations for Quebec," she said. "Then schedule a puddle jumper to Sydney, Nova Scotia. You see, Mr. Flynn, we've found the Templars' cross and thought you might want to see it."

The audible intake of breath on the other end of the call told Gillian that Flynn's greed hadn't abated, even after hearing of the death of his childhood friend and chief flunky. Nice.

"You really found it?"

"Check your e-mail." Gillian sent a photo file to the phone number. Shane had taken it with his underwater camera, but the cross attached to its plate was clearly recognizable. A second photo showed it after Shane had rubbed off some of the muck, with their lights shining on it. A glint of red told the story.

"My God." Flynn's voice sounded muffled as he muttered to himself, probably while looking at the pictures. "My God. You found it. You have no idea . . . Ms. Campbell, I offered you a million dollars originally. If you turn over the cross without causing a ripple and release Trey, I'll triple it. For you and Mr. Burke as well."

She looked at Shane and smiled. If it had been only about money, they'd want a lot more than that. If it could be preserved outside cold storage, the cross was likely worth billions. But it had never been about money, not even for Shane. "We'll work out the details when you get here, Mr. Flynn, because I'll only turn the cross over to you personally."

"Well, that might not be possib—"

Oh yes, it would be possible, all right. "That's not negotiable. Expect another call soon, Mr. Secretary."

32

Weston Flynn gripped the armrests of his perch in the front of the fifty-two-seat plane as it made a noisy, bumpy descent over water toward the runway at McCurdy Airport in Sydney. In the hours between the takeoff in Quebec and the captain's "Welcome to Beautiful Cape Breton, Nova Scotia," he'd endured a whining toddler kicking his seat back, an octogenarian snoring across the aisle, and a tide of people jostling back and forth to the restroom located directly in front of his seat. And the plane didn't carry food, not even a fucking bag of peanuts.

West looked out the window, unsure what awaited him below. He regularly met with heads of state, observing complex protocols and hammering out sensitive negotiations of global importance. None in recent memory made him as nervous as this meeting with Gillian Campbell.

He had to give the woman credit. She and her motley crew of underachievers had turned the tables on him—the first time since he and his fellow collectors had started C7. She could ruin him, as she'd once again reminded him when she'd called late the night before with his travel instructions.

But she'd have to ruin him without the help of Trey Garrison, who should be joining his father in the heavenly realms by the end of the day. Gar's replacement, Eldon Maddox, had worked for West off and on the past decade, most recently shadowing the Campbell woman's young niece. He sat in the back of the plane, ready to carry out three assignments: first, to watch West's back while he was in Nova Scotia; second, once West was on his way back to the States, to take out Trey Garrison; and third, if West gave him the signal, to kill Gillian Campbell and Shane Burke. The others had simply been collateral and he had no interest in them.

With those two, it had become personal because of Gar. But only if the risk to himself was minimal. He truly mourned for Gar, who'd been a trusted confidante since they'd suffered through Boy Scouts together in Texas. Trey, on the other hand, had screwed up everything he'd done in his miserable life, from getting two girls pregnant before high school graduation to flunking out of the only college that had low-enough standards to admit him. The world wouldn't miss him.

So far, he'd let Gillian Campbell have her way, with one exception. He'd postponed his trip to Ankara, scheduled this flight with only Maddox for protection, and agreed to meet with her and Shane Burke in person. But only here at the Sydney airport. He'd drawn the line at driving to bumfuck rural Canada; that would be Maddox's job once West was finished with his business and it was time to tie up the loose end that was Trey Garrison.

But the ruby cross of the Knights Templars would be his. It was worth the cost, even the thirty million he'd be coughing up to be split among his fellow C7 members as a penalty for using the full month to procure his prize. Thirty million was nothing compared to such a treasure. He'd even taken the teasing phone call from that dot-com upstart Brent Sullivan with grace.

The plane bounced twice on the runway and taxied to a stop beside the small, well-kept terminal. To his surprise, Campbell and Burke had agreed to meet him here, offering to set up a room where they could speak privately. West unfolded the navy suit coat he'd taken off when he boarded, unwedged himself from his seat, and walked off the plane. He stepped to the side in the jetport, allowing other passengers to move ahead of him while he slipped into his coat.

He nodded at Maddox when he appeared in the doorway. His new private assistant was armed, although West didn't know how he'd managed security. Probably a bribe. Whether it was a gun or a grenade or a Taser, West felt confident he'd be protected if things went south.

Gillian Campbell looked prettier in person than she had on the TV show or in the photos Gar had sent him via phone. Could be the clothes. She wore a black tailored skirt and jacket with a deep blue blouse. Behind her, looking as comfortable as a monkey in a penguin suit, stood an equally well-dressed Shane Burke.

West was thankful no one had recognized him. Maybe he could get in and out of Sydney without anyone knowing he was here. His flight back to Quebec left in two hours. He'd spend the night there, celebrating the acquisition of the Templars' cross with a bottle of champagne, and fly directly to Ankara tomorrow.

Let's get this over with.

"Ms. Campbell, Mr. Burke." Flynn stopped in front of them, wondering why he'd been nervous at meeting with them. They might as well have *ordinary* stamped on their foreheads. "Shall we get this business done?"

Gillian smiled and pointed down the concourse. "We have a room set up about halfway down, on the left."

He looked at her purse, a leather messenger bag worn crossbody style. "Do you have it?"

Her smile grew wider. "It's ready to meet its new owner—as long as we agree to terms, of course."

Damn mercenary. "Of course."

She started to walk away but stopped when Shane stepped between them. "Your goon can stand outside." He jerked his head at Maddox, who was pretending to read the overhead monitors filled with lists of departures and arrivals. "But he can't come in the room with us."

West gave Shane his most intimidating glare, the ones his White House staff probably had nightmares about, but the man didn't flinch or look away. "Fine." They weren't going to try anything in the middle of an airport.

Shane nodded, and they walked past four Air Canada gates before Gillian stopped outside a door with a nameplate that read "Authorized Personnel Only."

"Ladies first." West wouldn't be the first one through the door into a space that had no doubt been rented with his money.

Gillian nodded and opened the door, which led into a large conference room set up with rows of chairs and a podium in front. "We're off to the side here," she said. A second door led to a small room with a table and four chairs in the center and a couple of upholstered chairs and conversation tables at the side. Some type of lounge, maybe.

"Let's start talking. I have a flight out in two hours. Unlike Mr. Burke here, I actually have a job."

He'd hoped to stir the pot a bit to gauge the emotional temperature of Gillian's companion since she had proven herself an ice queen. Burke didn't take the bait. He simply gave West an arrogant smirk, pulled out a chair, and sat at the table. "Gillian, let's not keep Mr. Secretary waiting; he has a plane to catch."

"Certainly." Gillian put the messenger bag on the table, opened it, and pulled out some papers. West looked for a glimpse of the cross while the bag was open, but she closed it before he saw more than a wallet and cell phone.

He might as well sit down and let them say their piece, trusting Maddox would be outside the door if he called.

As soon as he pulled the industrial gray office chair up to the table, Gillian slid a paper in front of him. "Here is a copy of the records pulled off Garland Garrison's cell phone, as well as those of his son

Trey." She picked up a second sheet, placing it atop the first. "Here is a transcript not only of our conversations last night, but also of two recorded messages retrieved from Trey Garrison's phone, wherein his father mentions you by name, in association with the kidnapping of Harley Dugan and the shooting of Calvin Mackie Jr."

A cold, alien feeling slid up West's spine. It was fear, something he hadn't felt often in his fifty-plus years. He'd underestimated Gillian Campbell. Badly.

She pulled out a small digital recorder and slid that toward him as well. "Here's the recording itself—one of several copies, I should add. You might be particularly interested in the part where Tex—Gar, as you call him—mentions that his old friend Weston Flynn would like him to make sure Harley Dugan was dead by the time day thirty had arrived. Let's see, I think that would be today. Too bad Harley escaped."

They paused at the sound of voices outside the door. "Is someone else meeting in the big room next door?" West felt an absurd desire to crawl under the table.

"Nothing for you to worry about." Gillian reached in her bag and pulled out one final sheet of paper. "Here's my favorite thing. This came from Gar's wallet."

Willing his hands to stop the infernal shaking that had begun at the appearance of the recorder, West reached for the paper and held it up in front of him. It was a photocopy of a receipt with a handwritten note beside it, in Gar's writing. The original receipt looked like it had been folded many times; all the creases showed up as black lines in the copy.

It detailed the rental of a workboat called *The Breton* for the month of September in Main-à-Dieu, Nova Scotia, for a sum of $10,000. The attached note read: *Charge to WF private account, #4624047972, SuisseBnc.*

"It proves nothing." West slapped the paper back on the table and shoved the pile back toward Gillian. "Absolutely nothing."

Shane, who'd been silently watching the proceedings, leaned forward. "It might not be enough to convict you in a courtroom, Mr. Secretary." He laced that title with sarcasm. If West had a gun with him right now, he'd shoot the bastard just to wipe the little smile off his face. "But it's enough to cast reasonable doubt about a man's suitability for public office. It's way more than enough to sink a presidential bid."

"Oh," Gillian said. "And just so you know? It might sound like a bad movie cliché, but clichés become that for a reason. There are copies of the papers and recordings, along with a full written account of the past thirty days from myself and Shane, left with everyone we know. If anything happens to us, our friends and family go public. As long as we're left alone, the documents stay sealed."

"We have a little extra insurance," Shane added. "Anything happens to us—or our families—we have extras in a safe deposit box that get sent to the *Washington Post, New York Times* . . . where else?" He looked at Gillian.

"Everywhere," she said.

West closed his eyes. They could be bluffing. Probably were bluffing. But he couldn't risk it. Everything he'd worked for would be gone. "What do you want?"

* * *

An hour later, West pushed his chair back from the table. His mood through the negotiations had spun from relief to anger to self-pity and back again, round and round and round.

He only had their word they wouldn't expose him; they had only his word he wouldn't have them killed. It was a draw.

In the past sixty minutes, he'd authorized sizable money transfers to both Gillian and Shane, transferred the remaining balance due on Shane's boat to a small bank in Florida, even set up a fucking trust fund for Gillian Campbell's niece.

One piece of business remained.

"I've done everything you demanded. Now, what about the Templars' cross?"

Gillian smiled, and patted her messenger bag. "Well, we considered leaving it alone and realized that wouldn't work—you'd just wait a while and ruin some other poor peoples' lives trying to get it. So we came up with a win-win situation for everybody." She stood up. "You asked about the people we've been hearing next door? It's time to see what they're up to."

West's emotions swerved back into the red zone, red for anger. "What the fuck are you playing at? You got what you wanted."

"And in return, I'm about to make you a hero, Mr. Flynn." She picked up her bag and nodded at Shane, who opened the door.

The murmur of voices reached them, and leaning back, West saw people filling all the seats visible from his vantage point. Maddox stuck his head in the door with an exasperated expression, moving back to let Gillian and Shane pass. "What do you want me to do?" he whispered when West finally got up and approached the door, fearful of what he'd see.

"Get down the coast and take care of Trey." He spoke softly. "Wait until the old guy in the lighthouse lets him go—it'll happen eventually. Make sure there's nothing left of him to find. Then get the hell back to Texas until you hear from me again. This job is over."

He didn't like it, but the game now had switched to *Salvage the Career*.

West stepped out of the doorway and froze as applause rang out. The people filling the seats craned their necks to look at him, then gave him a standing ovation. Cameras flashed in his face. *What the hell?*

At the front of the room, Gillian and Shane stood next to a small herd of men and women in business suits.

Shane stepped up to the podium and raised his hands for quiet. West stood there, frozen. His heart pounded, and he stuck his hands in his pockets to keep the goddamned cameras from catching him in the act of wiping clammy sweat off his palms.

"Thank you everyone." Shane spoke into the microphone. "I have to admit we've staged a surprise for US Secretary of State Weston Flynn today, which is why he's looking so confused. Come on up here, West."

Laughter and more applause. No walk to the gallows could ever have seemed longer or more ominous than his walk to the front of the room.

Shane clapped him on the shoulder a little hard to be good-natured, and West gritted his teeth, trying to make it look like a grin.

"My name is Shane Burke, and I'm a technical diver based in Florida." The room settled into silence, and West felt like he'd fallen into a bad surreal film. Shane went through a whole, exciting story about Duncan Campbell's theft of the Templars' cross, his voyage to Canada, and the wreck of *The Marcus Aurelius.* "My friend Gillian Campbell, a descendant of Duncan's, came to me with the story, but before we got anyone excited about it, we wanted to take a look around and see if we could find it. It's an important piece of history."

Shane blithered on about how expensive the scouting expedition had been. "Secretary Flynn here, who has a keen interest in history and the Templars, funded our expedition out of his own pocket, without any desire for publicity for himself," Shane said, giving West a sly, sidelong look. "And today, I'm pleased to announce that not only have we located and verified the wreckage of *The Marcus Aurelius,* but we have photographic evidence of the presence of the Knights Templars' cross. I can't tell you how much that's worth in today's money, but"—Shane shrugged his shoulders in an "aw-shucks" gesture—"it's a lot."

The rest of the "ceremony" went by in a blur. They had found the cross and left it, something West should've realized when they only had underwater photos of it. Then they'd reported the find, including a few gold coins, to the receiver of wrecks in Nova Scotia.

Now, "thanks to the generosity of Secretary Weston Flynn," Canada owned it, cross and all.

A fresh stick of gum couldn't erase the sour taste in West's mouth as he left the press conference with airport security, headed for his departure gate. His stomach rumbled with hunger, his right hand ached from a solid half hour of hearty handshaking, and he had an overwhelming urge to either cry or shoot something.

But what the hell. He'd be the goddamned financial savior of eastern Canada by the time it was all said and done.

EPILOGUE

"You seen this?"

Shane cracked open one eye and groaned at the sight of Gillian, sitting up in bed, naked except for the red-framed glasses she wore when her contact lenses were out. Which would be perfect for a game of *Sexy Librarian* . . . except for the laptop claiming all her attention.

He was going to throw the damned thing overboard. Before they'd moved onto *The Evangeline II*, he'd had no idea the extent of her Internet addiction.

"You really are obsessed, you know that? You need therapy." And he knew just the therapy she needed. He burrowed closer and slipped a hand under the sheet, sending his fingers on a little exploratory mission.

"Ahh . . . oh." Her voice was appropriately breathy, but her fingers continued to tap on the damned keyboard. He was beginning to hate that sound. "Wait, wait, wait. I need to read this."

He pulled his arm from beneath the sheet, balled up his pillow, and settled back with an apology to his unhappy morning hard-on. Clearly, he'd shacked up with a geek. They'd even discussed the *M* word, which neither of them had quite been able to say, but it had hovered around them like gnats during several recent conversations.

They'd spent Christmas at the Campbell gator farm in Louisiana, which had made the *M* word gnats buzz louder. He liked the Campbell clan. Gretchen and Holly had been there, and Gillian's parents had seemed suitably intrigued that he owned a diving school and lived on a pimped-out workboat. Not being conventional themselves, they didn't expect it of their daughter, the geek. Never mind that his diving school wouldn't really open until spring and had been financed with very dirty money. That, they'd never know.

Before this relationship progressed further, though, Shane had to rearrange Gillian's priorities. "We need to set some house rules. Number one: no reading of e-mail in bed, especially when there's uneaten chocolate within reach." He still daydreamed of chocolate-covered cherries.

She made a *pffft* sound. "We've been living together a month, Shane. The statute of limitations for rule making has passed."

"There's a special dispensation for people who live on boats."

"Well, okay. But you realize that house rule would force me to get out of bed earlier." She gave him a sexy sidelong glance. "You never know when I'll get tired of the computer and turn my mind to other things. Be a pity if I were dressed."

She had a point.

Finally, he sighed and gave in to the inevitable, consigned to the fact that he was destined to become one of those henpecked husb . . . men. "What are you reading, anyway?"

"A story from the newspaper in Cape Breton." She opened the lid of the laptop wider, which allowed Shane to see a familiar face on the screen.

He sat up and leaned over her shoulder. "Is that who I think it is?" The headline read "Body of Missing Texan Found."

She nodded. "Here's the lead: 'A decomposed body believed to be that of Garland Garrison III, missing since September 30, was discovered on the northern shore of Scatarie Island on Tuesday after being spotted by crew members of a passing freighter.' It goes on to talk about how he and his father had rented a boat in Main-à-Dieu back in September." She scrolled down the screen, reading. "Listen to this: 'Authorities attribute Garrison's death to natural causes and say they have no reason to suspect foul play.'"

Shane couldn't avoid a stab of pity for Trey Garrison, the classic rich-kid screwup who'd gotten in way over his head. "Flynn had it done. I'd bet the dive school on it. Probably three months ago, right after we left the lighthouse. Chevy had planned to let him go, so Flynn probably had somebody waiting for him."

Gillian closed the laptop, set it on the floor, and snuggled against Shane. "I talked to Cleo last night, and everything was fine with her and Chevy." She paused. "Do you think he'll ever come after us?"

He kissed Gillian's forehead and slipped an arm around her. He'd asked himself that question a lot in the past three months. "I don't think so. Flynn came out of this whole mess looking like a choirboy, and he wants the presidency."

If Weston Flynn got elected president, they'd have another moral dilemma to face. Talk about unfit to lead. "As long as we don't stir the pot, I don't think he will either. He has too much at risk."

Gillian didn't say anything, but Shane could guess her thoughts. There were no guarantees. Some part of them would probably always be looking over one shoulder, but so would Flynn.

In the meantime, though, it was New Year's Eve and they had the whole day to kill before the countdown-to-midnight party at Jagger's. His friend had taken to running his new bar and restaurant like a natural, although having co-owner Harley in the kitchen helped.

"So what's on tap for today?" She kissed him, soft and sweet.

He sneaked an arm over to the nightstand, slipped open the drawer, and pulled out the first thing he came to: a rich chocolate square oozing with caramel filling. "I think we should have breakfast."

"I like the way you think." Gillian unwrapped the candy and broke it apart, holding it up so a drip of caramel landed on her tongue. She licked her lips with that wicked little smile that made him very grateful she and her computer had stayed under the sheets.

She turned the other half of the chocolate square sideways, letting a slow drizzle of caramel trail down his chest, headed south.

Shane closed his eyes and smiled. *Damn, now we're talk—*

A thump sounded outside the door, and Gillian paused mid-caramel. "You expecting anybody?"

Charlie had moved into Gillian's trailer, but surely the old man hadn't driven his handicap-modified car down to Cedar Key this early.

"Boy, where the hell are you?"

He groaned. It was Charlie, all right, and he sounded annoyingly cheerful.

"Don't answer," Shane whispered. "He'll leave and go to Jagger's if he thinks we're not here." Charlie needed a hobby, but Shane didn't want to *be* that hobby.

Gillian swiped her tongue down his chest, licking and kissing away his caramel dreams. He wanted to cry.

The thumping sound of Charlie's crutch had passed the master suite and gone toward the salon—twice as big as the one on the original *Evangeline*—but now grew louder again.

"Shane Burke, I know you're here. I've got a great idea for your dive school. You should try . . ." The door burst open. "Why, howdy, Gillian."

Gillian shrieked and ducked under the covers. Shane caught a glimpse of his grinning uncle before a black freight train plowed him off the bed and onto the hard floor. He looked up into the large, white teeth of a snarling minion of Satan with peanut-butter breath.

Tank.

ACKNOWLEDGMENTS

Many thanks to the usual suspects: Marlene Stringer, who encouraged me to venture beyond the borders of the paranormal world; editor JoVon Sotak, who took a chance on a romantic thriller series built around the bad guys; and my awesome army of first readers: Miki, Roger, Katy, Liz, Elizabeth, and Sandy.

ABOUT THE AUTHOR

Susannah Sandlin is a native of Winfield, Alabama, and has worked as a writer and editor in educational publishing in Alabama, Illinois, Texas, California, and Louisiana. She currently lives in Auburn, Alabama, with two rescue dogs named after professional wrestlers (it was a phase). She has a no-longer-secret passion for Cajun and French-Canadian music and reality TV, and is on the hunt for a long-haul ice road trucker who also saves nuisance gators. Susannah is also the author of the award-winning Penton Legacy paranormal romance series: *Redemption, Absolution, Omega,* and *Allegiance*; the spinoff paranormal romance, *Storm Force*; and the Collectors series, beginning with *Lovely, Dark, and Deep.* As Suzanne Johnson, she writes the Sentinels of New Orleans urban fantasy series.